NO THOROUGHFARE
& Other Stories

CHARLES DICKENS AND WILKIE COLLINS

NO THOROUGHFARE
& Other Stories

ALAN SUTTON

First published in this edition in the United Kingdom in 1990 by
Alan Sutton Publishing Limited · Phoenix Mill · Far Thrupp
Stroud · Gloucestershire

Copyright © in this edition
Alan Sutton Publishing Limited 1990

British Library Cataloguing in Publication Data

Dickens, Charles *1812–1870*
    No thoroughfare : and other stories.
    1. Short stories in English, 1990 – Anthologies
    I. Title   II. Collins, Wilkie *1824–1889*
    823.0108 [FS]

    ISBN 0-86299-836-0

Cover picture: detail from Quai des Bergues in 1845 *by Dickenman*
(photograph: Nicolas Bouvier)

Typeset in 9/10 Bembo.
Typesetting and origination by
Alan Sutton Publishing Limited.
Printed in Great Britain by
The Guernsey Press Company Limited.
Guernsey, Channel Islands.

CONTENTS

BIOGRAPHICAL NOTES

CHARLES DICKENS (1812–70). A man of singular imagination, novelist, editor, journalist, theatrical producer, actor and a supporter of radical reform, Charles Dickens was one of the great Victorians. He was born in Portsmouth on 7 February 1812, the second child of John, a clerk in the Navy Pay Office, and Elizabeth, who were extroverts and continually living beyond their sufficient but modest means, apparently more interested in themselves than in their children. He spent a happy early childhood in Portsmouth, London and Chatham, entertained by the macabre stories of his nursemaid, and later by his own wide reading, and developing imagination. In 1822 John Dickens was reposted to London, and his financial situation, already perilous, quickly went from bad to worse. Charles was unable to attend school, and two years later was sent to work in a boot-blacking factory, where he met with some of the rougher elements of London life. Meanwhile his father was declared bankrupt, and escorted with his family to the Marshalsea, while Charles had lodgings near his work, and visited the prison frequently. Fortunately, this sad state of affairs lasted only a few months, and later in the year, at the age of twelve, Charles was sent back to school to complete his education. He left school at fifteen, and by the age of twenty-three had established himself as a journalist and man of the theatre.

Four years later he was a first ranking man of letters, a husband and a father. He had written the first of the *Sketches by Boz* in 1833, and, in 1836, *The Pickwick Papers* started to appear in serial form, to be followed by *Oliver Twist* (1838) and *Nicholas Nickleby* (1839). Dickens had become editor of *Bentley's Miscellany*, in which the first parts of *The Mudfog Papers* were published in 1837, and was receiving a steady income. He had married Catherine Hogarth in 1836, and had been devastated by the death, one year later, of Mary, his sister-in-law, whom he

loved dearly. By 1839 he was able to move his impecunious
parents to Devon, and buy a family house in London. His
writings were based on his own experiences and concerns:
childhood problems and poverty pervade *Oliver Twist*; ideas of
education and the theatre appear in *Nicholas Nickleby*; while in
The Old Curiosity Shop (1841) he invokes memories of the
beloved Mary, and *Barnaby Rudge* (also 1841) reflects Dickens's
visits to Newgate Prison, his intimate knowledge of the
London underworld and his political sympathies.

Dickens's experiences were broadened in 1842, when he
made a triumphant visit to America. Although he was warmly
welcomed, he did not like America, and was profoundly
affected by his encounters with slavery and a visit to a penal
institute practising solitary confinement. His criticism of
American society was lightly veiled in the ensuing *American
Notes* (1842), and continued in *Martin Chuzzlewit* (1844),
another study of a disturbed childhood, which included a
journey to the States. Dickens's support for radical reformers
in England developed with his reputation, and he was frequently a public speaker for charitable institutions. He was
particularly concerned with the plight of children, and was
inspired to write *A Christmas Carol* (1843) by a visit to Miss
Angela Burdett Coutts's Ragged School for Deprived
Cockney Children, in order 'to present the poor in a favourable light to the rich'.

In 1844, after ten years of intensive work, Dickens took his
family to Italy for a year's break. The family included five
children and Georgina, Catherine's younger sister, who had
lived with the family since 1842. Not unnaturally for a man of
his temperament, Dickens missed London and his many
friends, but was stimulated by an experiment in mesmerism
with Madame de la Rue, an attractive English woman who
suffered from hallucinations. This relationship and the foreign
environment exacerbated the relationship between Dickens and
his wife, and marked the beginning of their final estrangement.

The next six years (1845–51) were busy ones. Besides spending
nine months travelling and writing in Switzerland and Paris,
Dickens was working as actor-manager of an amateur dramatic
group, performing in London and touring the provinces. He
was involved in an abortive attempt to establish a radical

newspaper, but finally, in 1850, achieved his dream of producing his own journal, *Household Words*, which was an instant success, and employed many of Dickens's friends, his father and his father-in-law. Its purpose was to generate social awareness and press for social reform. Two years earlier Dickens had opened Urania Cottage, a home for reclaimed prostitutes, under the patronage of Angela Coutts, and he retained responsibility for it as an unpaid superintendent. During these years he worked on *Dombey and Son* (1848), a study in selfishness, and *David Copperfield* (1850), a semi-autobiographical novel, which explored once more Dickens's own unsatisfactory childhood. In 1851 a series of misfortunes afflicted the Dickens household. After the birth of their ninth child Catherine suffered a nervous breakdown and was taken to Malvern for treatment. While she was away, first Charles's father and then his last child died. Restlessness and concern for Catherine's well-being induced Dickens to move the family to a new home in Tavistock Square, while ideas of a new book whirled through his mind.

Bleak House (1853) was completed when Dickens was forty-one, and the end of that year saw Dickens give the first of his famous public readings of his own work. But the years of frenzied activity had taken their toll, and during that same year Dickens had been forced to take holidays in Europe, to avoid a nervous breakdown. Although he escaped a breakdown, Dickens continued to be possessed by a restlessness and feverish energy which he never lost, in spite of taking regular working holidays in Folkestone and France. *Bleak House* is a vast rambling criticism of the British legal system, and, like it, his two subsequent novels were satirical comments on Victorian 'systems'. *Hard Times* (1854) comments on the effects of mechanization on society and education, while in *Little Dorrit* (1857) Dickens explores the way in which people are imprisoned in their social milieu. Little Dorrit herself was modelled on Georgina Hogarth, who had lived with the family for the last fourteen years, a companion to Catherine, nanny to the ten children and beloved 'sister' of Charles. In 1857 Dickens, still involved in theatricals, took a production of his friend Wilkie Collins's melodrama *The Frozen Deep* to Manchester, and invited the actress Mrs Ternan and two of her daughters to take the female parts.

Ellen Ternan, the younger daughter, was an attractive eighteen-year-old. Dickens fell in love with her, and within the year, in spite of criticism from his friends, colleagues and readers, he had separated from Catherine, who moved out of Tavistock House. Since he now had three households to maintain, Tavistock House, Gad's Hill, which he had purchased as a country residence in 1857, and Mrs Dickens's new home in Gloucester Cresent, as well as the Ternans to support, Dickens needed to supplement his income, and this he did by making extensive tours to give public readings in England, Scotland and Ireland. At the same time he continued his work as editor and journalist for *Household Words* until, through ill feeling, he changed publishers, and started producing a new journal called *All the Year Round*. The publication of the new magazine stimulated the writing of the next two serial novels: *A Tale of Two Cities* (1859), to establish a wide readership, and *Great Expectations* (1861), to maintain it. The first explored themes of death and resurrection against the violence of the French Revolution, while the second returned to thoughts of childhood and adolescent love in a plot involving mistaken identity. The journal also contained many shorter stories including 'The Signalman' (1866).

In 1860 Dickens sold Tavistock House, and the next few years were spent at Gad's Hill, or in London or Paris, giving regular readings and writing *Our Mutual Friend* (1865), a study of material greed and mistaken identity. He also paid regular visits to Ellen, who was now living in Slough. The years were beginning to tell, and although he was now a wealthy man, he continued to press himself beyond the limit. In 1865 he suffered the first of regular bouts of trouble with his feet, as well as being badly shaken in a rail accident. However, in 1867, at the age of fifty-five, he set out for a victorious five-month reading tour of the States, returning to a hero's welcome. But his final tour of the English provinces was not completed because of ill health, and in January 1870, he gave his last readings in London. He died on 9 June 1870 of a cerebral haemorrhage, leaving his final novel, *Edwin Drood*, unfinished. He was buried in Poet's Corner, Westminster Abbey.

WILLIAM WILKIE COLLINS was born on 8 January 1824, in New Cavendish Street, London, the elder son of William Collins, a fashionable and successful painter of the early nineteenth century, who counted among his friends Wordsworth and Coleridge. William Collins was a religious man, and in his strict observances may have been a repressive influence on his son, who appears to have inherited his mother Harriet Geddes's attractive and friendly personality. Wilkie was named after his godfather, Sir David Wilkie, RA, a bachelor and close friend of the family.

Little is known of Wilkie's early life. His brother, Charles, was born in 1828, and the family lived comfortably, first in Hampstead, then in Bayswater, where Wilkie attended Maida Hill Academy. The following year the whole family left for Italy, where they spent two years, visiting the major art collections and learning Italian. On their return, Wilkie attended a private boarding school in Highbury, where his storytelling talent was recognized and exploited by a senior prefect who demanded, with the threat of physical violence, to be entertained. 'Thus,' wrote Collins, 'I learnt to be amusing on a short notice and have derived benefit from those early lessons.'

When he left school in 1840, he showed no inclination to enter the Church, as his father wished, and chose, without enthusiasm, the world of commerce, accepting a post with Antrobus & Co., tea importers. He was totally unsuited to the regularity of business life, preferring to escape to the vibrant atmosphere of Paris. He started to write articles and short stories, which were accepted for publication, albeit anonymously, and in 1846 his father agreed that he should leave commerce and take up law, which would, in theory, provide him with a regular income. He studied at Lincoln's Inn Fields, and was finally called to the bar, but his legal knowledge was to be applied creatively in his novels, rather than practically in the law courts.

In his early twenties Collins was painting as well as writing. He had many friends who were artists, and he supported the new Pre-Raphaelite movement. In 1848 he had a picture exhibited in the Royal Academy. In the same year his first book was published: the memoirs of his father, who had died the previous year. These were diligently researched and provided a training ground for the emerging writer, developing his thorough methodical approach to compilation and exercising his descriptive ability. His first novel, *Antonia*, was published by Bentley two years later. Although of no great literary merit, it was written in the then popular mode of historical romance, and so enjoyed instant success. The following year Bentley published *Rambles Beyond Railways*, an account of a holiday in Cornwall, which reflected Collins's life-long love of wild and remote places.

It was in the same year, 1851, that Wilkie Collins first met Charles Dickens, an introduction effected by their mutual friend, the artist, Augustus Egg. The meeting was significant for both, leading to a close friendship and working partnership from which both benefited. Dickens had found a friend of more stable temperament than himself, affable and tolerant, responsive to his restless demanding nature. From Collins he acquired the skill of economic and taut plotting, as evidenced in *A Tale of Two Cities* (which may be interestingly compared with Collins's story of the French Revolution, *Sister Rose*, published in 1855), and in his later novels. Collins was welcomed by the Dickens family, and spent many holidays with them in England and France. He was encouraged and guided in his writing by Dickens, and he must have been stimulated by the latter's enthusiasm and vitality. The two authors worked together on Dickens's magazines, *Household Words*, and *All the Year Round*. Collins was employed as an editor, and many of his works appeared first in these publications, while both writers collaborated on several short stories.

'A Terribly Strange Bed' – Collins's first work in the macabre genre – was the first of his short stories to appear in *Household Words*, in 1852. The following year the magazine saw the publication of 'Gabriel's Marriage', a story of a Breton fishing community. In the interim, Dickens had turned down 'Mad Monkton', a study of inherited insanity, as unsuitable subject matter, and this was later published by *Fraser's Magazine* in 1855. These two, along with 'Sister Rose', 'The Yellow Mask', and 'A Stolen Letter', were originally published in *Household Words*, and reprinted in *After Dark* (1855), for which anthology Collins wrote the successfully economic and melo-dramatic 'Lady of Glenwith Grange' (an inspiration for Miss Haversham?). *A Rogue's Life*, Collins's venture into the pica-resque, was serialized in 1856. This was followed in 1857 by *The Dead Secret*, a full length novel, which in its complexity suggests the author's technical potential. 'The Biter Bit', which was published in 1858 and is commonly held to be the first humorous detective story, shows Collins's development of the epistolary form. Both of his two greatest novels, *The Woman in White* and *The Moonstone*, appeared first as serial-izations in *All the Year Round* – as did the less well known *No Name*. This unconventional study of illegitimacy was published in its full form in 1862, two years after the masterpiece of suspense and drama, *The Woman in White*, and six years before his original detective story, *The Moonstone*, appeared as complete books.

Another interest shared by Collins and Dickens was a love of the theatre. *The Frozen Deep* (1857) written by Collins and starring Dickens, was inspired by an interest in the Arctic exploration of the time. It was followed by a series of minor productions, the stage version of 'No Thoroughfare' (with combined authorship), enjoying a record run of two hundred nights in 1867.

Anyone meeting Collins in those days would have seen:

A neat figure of a cheerful plumpness, very small feet and hands, a full brown beard, a high and rounded forehead, a small nose not naturally intended to support a pair of large spectacles behind which his eyes shone with humour and friendship.

R.C. Lehmann, *Memories of Half a Century*

But how many would have glimpsed, as did the young artist, Rudolf Lehmann, the strange far-off look in his eyes, which gave the impression of investing 'almost everything with an air of mystery and romance'? It was suggestive of a depth of personality not accessible to many, but demonstrated by the author's expressed unconventional views of the class and social *mores* of the day; which were further borne out by what is known of his personal life. During the 1860s, Collins met and fell in love with Caroline Graves, who had a daughter by a previous marriage. He never married her, but lived with mother and daughter for most of the remainder of his life. In 1868 Caroline mysteriously married another, and Collins entered into a relationship with Martha Judd, by whom he had three children. However, by the early 1870s, he was once more living with Caroline, who was still known as Mrs Graves. It has been suggested that Martha Judd may have been employed originally by Collins as an amanuensis. Over the years Collins's health had been deteriorating. He was a victim of gout, which attacked his whole body, including his eyes. He suffered a particularly severe attack in 1868, when his mother died, and he was working on *The Moonstone*. A dedicated woman, capable of disregarding his suffering and attending only to his words, was employed, to whom Collins dictated the rest of the work, but she has never been named.

In 1870 Charles Dickens died. During the previous ten years Collins had produced his best work: the three novels serialized in *All the Year Round*; *Armadale* (1866) in the *Cornhill Magazine*, and *Man and Wife* (1870) in *Cassell's Magazine*. But with Dickens's death, something in Collins seemed to die too, although his popularity remained undiminished. His novels, produced regularly until his death, were widely read, and his was some of the first fiction to appear in cheap editions. In the 1870s he enjoyed some success with the stage versions of his novels, which were produced both in London and the provinces. Not only was Collins's work popular in England; his novels and plays were translated and produced in most European countries, including Russia, and were widely available in America. In 1873 Collins was invited to give readings in the eastern United States and Canada. Although his reading lacked the vitality of Dickens, the Americans were charmed by him.

Of course, it was not only Dickens's death which adversely affected Collins's work. His gout was becoming persistent, and he relied increasingly on laudanum to relieve the pain. However, he never lost his mental clarity, taking care to be properly informed about medicine, drugs and chemistry, as is clearly shown in *Heart and Science* (1883) and the detailed notes he left for his last novel, *Blind Love* (1890) – completed, posthumously, at his request, by Walter Besant. During his later years his social life was restricted by poor health, but he did not become a recluse as has been suggested. He maintained close friendships with Charles Reade, Holman Hunt, the Beard and the Lehmann families, and theatrical people, including Ada Cavendish and Mary Anderson. In 1889, after being involved in a cab accident, Collins's health rapidly declined, and he died while suffering from bronchitis on 23 September. He was buried at Kensal Green Cemetery.

SHEILA MICHELL

INTRODUCTION

This collection of short stories demonstrates Dickens's mastery of the genre. Starting with *The Pickwick Papers*, he wrote his books in serial form, thus starting a publishing phenomenon that dominated the literary scene during the nineteenth century. His shorter fiction is less well known than his novels, but deserves greater attention, not least because of the autobiographical nature of much of it.

Two of the stories – 'No Thoroughfare' and 'The Lazy Tour of Two Idle Apprentices' – were jointly written with his friend, Wilkie Collins. Collins's reputation has increased in recent years, and the centenary of his death was the focus of considerable attention – not least because of his extraordinary private life, revealed in William Clarke's masterly biography, *The Secret Life of Wilkie Collins* (Allison and Busby).

'The Lazy Tour' was first published in instalments in *Household Words* during October 1857, only a month after the trip undertaken by Dickens and Collins had taken place. The speed with which the piece was written and published is remarkable, but even more so is its autobiographical nature – indeed, it is something of a confession on Dickens's part.

In August 1857 Dickens had staged Collins's play, *The Frozen Deep*, at the Free Trade Hall, Manchester. Earlier that year the play had appeared in London, performed by amateurs, but the size of the Manchester venue neccessitated the hire of professional actresses, among them Ellen Ternan. His marriage already in a precarious state, Dickens fell in love with Ellen and found it difficult to hide his feelings. Indeed, barely two weeks after his return from the tour with Collins, he made alterations in his London home which meant that henceforth he and his wife Catharine would sleep in separate rooms.

In 'The Lazy Tour' Dickens dubs Collins and himself with the names of Hogarth's idle apprentices (there was a set of

Hogarth's prints on the walls of his home, Gad's Hill): he becomes Francis Goodchild, while Collins is designated Thomas Idle. The two characters discuss love after Idle has sung 'Annie Laurie' while resting in a meadow. Goodchild (Dickens) says that he would not 'Lay me doon and dee' but would 'get me oop and peetch into somebody'. Idle (Collins), by contrast, takes a languid view of the matter, announcing that 'It's trouble enough' to fall out of love, so he keeps out of it altogether. Far from doing so in real life, Collins maintained two households, though he did resolutely refrain from getting married!

'The Lazy Tour' records the accident on Carrick Fell when Collins badly sprained his ankle, and traces the tour from Carlisle to Doncaster. Dickens's excuse for going to Doncaster was to witness the race week there. His real reason was that it afforded him the chance to see Ellen Ternan again, as she was due to appear at the Doncaster Theatre. Although there is no direct evidence of his having attended on the night she was playing, he certainly attended on the previous night, when he was dismayed by the audience, who at once recognized and acclaimed him. It seems likely, however, that he did also go and see the play when Ellen was appearing, since his outburst at the behaviour of the audience would seem to have been triggered by seeing her insulted:

> A most odious tendency . . . to put vile constructions on sufficiently innocent phrases in the play, and then applaud them in a Satyr-like manner . . . remarks are so horrible, that Mr Goodchild, for the moment, even doubts whether that *is* a wholesome Art, which sets women apart on a high floor before such a thing as this. . . .

That Ellen Ternan was much on his mind during the Doncaster race week is clear from the following and other references to Mr Goodchild's state of mind: 'He is suspected by Mr Idle of having fallen into a dreadful state concerning a pair of little lilac gloves and a little bonnet.'

Dickens went on a number of continental jaunts with Collins, and Europe is the setting for the denouement of 'No Thoroughfare', published in the double Christmas number of

Dickens's journal, *All The Year Round*, in 1867. Unfortunately, Dickens destroyed Collins's letters, but Collins preserved those from Dickens, and these give us a glimpse into the mechanics of their literary collaboration. Here Dickens is writing from Gad's Hill on 23 August 1867:

> My dear Wilkie,
> I have done the overture, but I don't write to make *that* feeble report. I have a general idea which I hope will supply the kind of interest we want. Let us arrange to culminate in a wintry flight and pursuit across the Alps, under lonely circumstances, and against warnings. Let us get into all the horrors and dangers of such an adventure under the most terrific circumstances. . . . If you will keep this in your mind as I will in mine, urging the story toward it as we go along, we shall get a very avalanche of power out of it, and thunder it down on the readers' heads. . . .

From the office of *All The Year Round*, 9 October 1867:

> My dear Wilkie,
> Will you notice in the chapter 'Vendale Writes a Letter' that we are in some danger of making him foolish or contemptible in the eyes of the readers by being so blind. . . . A very slight alteration or two will remove the objection. I suggest that it should not then be quite so plain, even to the reader, that . . . is the man. . . . I am racking my brains for a good death to that respectable gentleman. . . .

'Hunted Down' was suggested by the crimes of Thomas Griffith Wainwright, forger and poisoner, on whom Dickens based the character of Julius Slinkton. He was clearly fascinated by Wainwright, and when he wrote *Little Dorrit* he borrowed some of Wainwright's attributes for the character of Rigaud. Although Wainwright had enjoyed the acquaintance of many of Dickens's early friends, he had vanished from literary society before Dickens's rise to fame with *The Pickwick Papers*. The two men did meet, however. While *Oliver Twist* was appearing Dickens asked to visit Newgate Prison with a party of friends, including Forster (later to be his

biographer) and Macready, the actor. Forster describes the
scene:

> In coming to the prisoners under remand, we were startled
> by a sudden tragic cry of 'My God! There's Wainwright!'
> In the shabby-genteel creature, with sandy disordered hair
> and dirty moustache, who had turned quickly round with a
> defiant stare at our entrance, looking at once mean and
> fierce, and quite capable of the cowardly murders he had
> committed, Macready had been horrified to recognize a
> man familiarly known to him in former years, and at
> whose table he had dined.

J. Cuming Walters wrote: 'By chance, which seems wholly
caprice, Dickens cast the scene of a sombre little story at
Hoghton, "George Silverman's Explanation", the morbid
study of a misunderstood nature, perhaps the least read and
least liked of his minor writings.' Modern critics, however, do
not agree, and Dickens himself, in the course of writing it,
remarked: 'Upon myself, it has made the strangest impression
of reality and originality!! And I feel as if I had read something
(by somebody else) which I should never get out of my head!'
  In the story Silverman finds himself constantly misjudged.
His pure motives are always wrongly interpreted. Yet he
himself has the feeling that, despite knowing he is being
wrongly judged, he is indeed guilty. Critics have seen hints in
this story of Dickens's own feelings of guilt, and strong
indications of his complicated state of mind during his association with Ellen Ternan.
  The series of chapters on 'Couples' is a little-known product
of Dickens's pen that combines a marvellous evocation of
Victorian family life with characterization that is timeless – we
have all met modern equivalents of the people described here.
In this respect they are very similar to the chapters in
Thackeray's *Book of Snobs* (1848; reprinted by Alan Sutton,
1989), which ruthlessly satirized the pretensions of Victorian
society.
  'The Bloomsbury Christening', the fourth piece of fiction
that Dickens published, originally formed a part of *Sketches by
Boz*. It describes a cross-grained old bachelor who 'was never

happy but when he was miserable'. He is invited by his nephew to be godfather to the nephew's child. After various mishaps in getting to church, he utterly ruins the festive atmosphere that the ceremony should have generated by making a speech full of dire forebodings and the most gloomy prognostications, sending the poor child's young mother running from the room in floods of tears!

These stories thus range from high drama to mordant wit, and remind us of the extraordinary breadth of talent that Dickens possessed, as well as adding to the available legacy of his work that we can enjoy.

ALAN S. WATTS

NO THOROUGHFARE
& Other Stories

NO THOROUGHFARE

by Charles Dickens and Wilkie Collins

The Overture

Day of the month and year, November the thirtieth one thousand eight hundred and thirty-five. London Time by the great clock of Saint Paul's, ten at night. All the lesser London churches strain their metallic throats. Some, flippantly begin before the heavy bell of the great cathedral; some, tardily begin three, four, half a dozen, strokes behind it; all are in sufficiently near accord, to leave a resonance in the air, as if the winged father who devours his children, had made a sounding sweep with his gigantic scythe in flying over the city.

What is this clock lower than most of the rest, and nearer to the ear, that lags so far behind to-night as to strike into the vibration alone? This is the clock of the Hospital for Foundling Children. Time was, when the Foundlings were received without question in a cradle at the gate. Time is, when inquiries are made respecting them, and they are taken as by favour from the mothers who relinquish all natural knowledge of them and claim to them for evermore.

The moon is at the full, and the night is fair with light clouds. The day has been otherwise than fair, for slush and mud, thickened with the droppings of heavy fog, lie black in the streets. The veiled lady who flutters up and down near the postern-gate of the Hospital for Foundling Children has need to be well shod to-night.

She flutters to and fro, avoiding the stand of hackney-coaches, and often pausing in the shadow of the western end of the great quadrangle wall, with her face turned towards the gate. As above her there is the purity of the moonlit sky, and below her there are the defilements of the pavement, so may

1

she, haply, be divided in her mind between two vistas of reflection or experience? As her footprints crossing and recrossing one another have made a labyrinth in the mire, so may her track in life have involved itself in an intricate and unravellable tangle?

The postern–gate of the Hospital for Foundling Children opens, and a young woman comes out. The lady stands aside, observes closely, sees that the gate is quietly closed again from within, and follows the young woman.

Two or three streets have been traversed in silence before she, following close behind the object of her attention, stretches out her hand and touches her. Then the young woman stops and looks round, startled.

'You touched me last night, and, when I turned my head, you would not speak. Why do you follow me like a silent ghost?'

'It was not,' returned the lady, in a low voice, 'that I would not speak, but that I could not when I tried.'

'What do you want of me? I have never done you any harm?'

'Never.'

'Do I know you?'

'No.'

'Then what can you want of me?'

'Here are two guineas in this paper. Take my poor little present, and I will tell you.'

Into the young woman's face, which is honest and comely, comes a flush as she replies: 'There is neither grown person nor child in all the large establishment that I belong to, who hasn't a good word for Sally. I am Sally. Could I be so well thought of, if I was to be bought?'

'I do not mean to buy you; I mean only to reward you very slightly.'

Sally firmly, but not ungently, closes and puts back the offering hand. 'If there is anything I can do for you, ma'am, that I will not do for its own sake, you are much mistaken in me if you think that I will do it for money. What is it you want?'

'You are one of the nurses or attendants at the Hospital, I saw you leave to–night and last night.'

'Yes, I am. I am Sally.'

'There is a pleasant patience in your face which makes me believe that very young children would take readily to you.'

'God bless 'em! So they do.'

The lady lifts her veil, and shows a face no older than the nurse's. A face far more refined and capable than hers, but wild and worn with sorrow.

'I am the miserable mother of a baby lately received under your care. I have a prayer to make to you.'

Instinctively respecting the confidence which has drawn aside the veil, Sally – whose ways are all ways of simplicity and spontaneity – replaces it, and begins to cry.

'You will listen to my prayer?' the lady urges. 'You will not be deaf to the agonised entreaty of such a broken suppliant as I am?'

'Oh dear, dear, dear!' cries Sally. 'What shall I say, or can I say! Don't talk of prayers. Prayers are to be put up to the Good Father of All, and not to nurses and such. And there! I am only to hold my place for half a year longer, till another young woman can be trained up to it. I am going to be married. I shouldn't have been out last night, and I shouldn't have been out to-night, but that my Dick (he is the young man I am going to be married to) lies ill, and I help his mother and sister to watch him. Don't take on so, don't take on so!'

'O good Sally, dear Sally,' moans the lady, catching at her dress entreatingly. 'As you are hopeful and I am hopeless; as a fair way in life is before you, which can never, never, be before me; as you can aspire to become a respected wife, and as you can aspire to become a proud mother; as you are a living loving woman, and must die; for GOD'S sake hear my distracted petition1'

'Deary, deary, deary ME!' cried Sally, her desperation culminating in the pronoun, 'what am I ever to do? And there! See how you turn my own words back upon me. I tell you I am going to be married, on purpose to make it clearer to you that I am going to leave, and therefore couldn't help you if I would, Poor Thing, and you make it seem to my own self as if I was cruel in going to be married and *not* helping you. It ain't kind. Now, is it kind, Poor Thing?'

'Sally! Hear me, my dear. My entreaty is for no help in the

future. It applies to what is past. It is only to be told in two words.'

'There! This is worse and worse,' cries Sally, 'supposing that I understand what two words you mean.'

'You do understand. What are the names they have give my poor baby? I ask no more than that. I have read of the customs of the place. He has been christened in the chapel, and registered by some surname in the book. He was received last Monday evening. What have they called him?'

Down upon her knees in the foul mud of the by-way into which they have strayed – an empty street without a thorough-fare, giving on the dark gardens of the Hospital – the lady would drop in her passionate entreaty, but that Sally prevents her.

'Don't! Don't! You make me feel as if I was setting myself up to be good. Let me look in your pretty face again. Put your two hands in mine. Now, promise. You will never ask me anything more than the two words?'

'Never! Never!'

'You will never put them to a bad use, if I say them?'

'Never! Never!'

'Walter Wilding.'

The lady lays her face upon the nurse's breast, draws her close in her embrace with both arms, murmurs a blessing and the words, 'Kiss him for me!' and is gone.

Day of the month and year, the first Sunday in October, one thousand eight hundred and forty-seven. London time by the great clock of Saint Paul's half-past one in the afternoon. The clock of the Hospital for Foundling Children is well up with the Cathedral to-day. Service in the chapel is over, and the Foundling children are at dinner.

There are numerous lookers-on at the dinner, as the custom is. There are two or three governors, whole families from the congregation, smaller groups of both sexes, individual strag-glers of various degrees. The bright autumnal sun strikes freshly into the wards; and the heavy-framed windows through which it shines, and the panelled walls on which it strikes, are such windows and such walls as pervade Hogarth's pictures. The girls' refectory (including that of the younger children) is the principal attraction. Neat attendants silently glide about the orderly and silent tables; the lookers-on move or stop as the fancy takes them; comments in whispers on face such a number from such a window are not unfrequent; many of the faces are of a character to fix attention. Some of the visitors from the outside public are accustomed visitors. They have established a speaking acquaintance with the occupants of particular seats at the tables, and halt at those points to bend down and say a word or two. It is no disparagement to their kindness that those points are generally points where personal attractions are. The monotony of the long spacious rooms and the double lines of faces, is agreeably relieved by those incidents, although so slight.

A veiled lady, who has no companion, goes among the company. It would seem that curiosity and opportunity have never brought her there before. She has the air of being a little troubled by the sight, and, as she goes the length of the tables, it is with a hesitating step and an uneasy manner. At length she comes to the refectory of the boys. They are so much less popular than the girls that it is bare of visitors when she looks in at the doorway.

But just within the doorway, chances to stand, inspecting, an elderly female attendant: some order of matron or housekeeper. To whom the lady addresses natural questions: As, how many boys? At what age are they usually put out in life? Do they often take a fancy to the sea? So, lower and lower in tone until the lady puts the question: 'Which is Walter Wilding?'

Attendant's head shaken. Against the rules.

'You know which is Walter Wilding?'

So keenly does the attendant feel the closeness with which the lady's eyes examine her face, that she keeps her own eyes fast upon the floor, lest by wandering in the right direction they should betray her.

'I know which is Walter Wilding, but it is not my place, ma'am, to tell names to visitors.'

'But you can show me without telling me.'

The lady's hand moves quietly to the attendant's hand. Pause and silence.

'I am going to pass round the tables,' says the lady's interlocutor, without seeming to address her. 'Follow me with your eyes. The boy that I stop at and speak to, will not matter to you. But the boy that I touch, will be Walter Wilding. Say nothing more to me, and move a little away.'

Quickly acting on the hint, the lady passes on into the room, and looks about her. After a few moments, the attendant, in a staid official way, walks down outside the line of tables commencing on her left hand. She goes the whole length of the line, turns, and comes back on the inside. Very slightly glancing in the lady's direction, she stops, bends forward, and speaks. The boy whom she addresses, lifts his head and replies. Good humouredly and easily, as she listens to what he says, she lays her hand upon the shoulder of the next boy on his right. That the action may be well noted, she keeps her hand on the shoulder while speaking in return, and pats it twice or thrice before moving away. She completes her tour of the tables, touching no one else, and passes out by a door at the opposite end of the long room.

Dinner is done, and the lady, too, walks down outside the line of tables commencing on her left hand, goes the whole length of the line, turns, and comes back on the inside. Other people have strolled in, fortunately for her, and stand sprinkled about. She lifts her veil, and stopping at the touched boy, asks how old he is?

'I am twelve, ma'am,' he answers, with his bright eyes fixed on hers.

'Are you well and happy?'

'Yes, ma'am.'

'May you take these sweetmeats from my hand?'

'If you please to give them to me.'

In stooping low for the purpose, the lady touches the boy's face with her forehead and with her hair. Then, lowering her veil again, she passes on, and passes out without looking back.

Act I

The Curtain Rises

In a court-yard in the City of London, which was No Thoroughfare either for vehicles or foot-passengers; a court-yard diverging from a steep, a slippery, and a winding street connecting Tower-street with the Middlesex shore of the Thames; stood the place of business of Wilding and Co. Wine Merchants. Probably, as a jocose acknowledgement of the obstructive character of this main approach, the point nearest to its base at which one could take the river (if so inodorously minded) bore the appellation Break-Neck-Stairs. The court-yard itself had likewise been descriptively entitled in old time, Cripple Corner.

Years before the year one thousand eight hundred and sixty-one, people had left off taking boat at Break-Neck-Stairs, and watermen had ceased to ply there. The slimy little causeway had dropped into the river by a slow process of suicide, and two or three stumps of piles and a rusty iron mooring-ring were all that remained of the departed Break-Neck glories. Sometimes, indeed, a laden coal barge would bump itself into the place, and certain laborious heavers, seemingly mud-engendered, would arise, deliver the cargo in the neighbourhood, shove off, and vanish; but at most times the only commerce of Break-Neck-Stairs arose out of the conveyance of casks and bottles, both full and empty, both to and from the cellars of Wilding and Co. Wine Merchants. Even that commerce was but occasional, and through three-fourths of its rising tides and dirty indecorous drab of a river would come solitarily oozing and lapping at the rusty ring, as if it had heard of the Doge and the Adriatic, and wanted to be married to the great conserver of its filthiness, the right Honourable the Lord Mayor.

Some two hundred and fifty yards on the right, up the opposite hill (approaching it from the low ground of Break-

Neck-Stairs) was Cripple Corner. There was a pump in Cripple Corner, there was a tree in Cripple Corner. All Cripple Corner belonged to Wilding and Co. Wine Merchants. Their cellars burrowed under it, their mansion towered over it. It really had been a mansion in the days when merchants inhabited the City, and had a ceremonious shelter to the doorway without visible support, like the sounding- board over an old pulpit. It had also a number of long narrow strips of window, so disposed in its grave brick front as to render it symmetrically ugly. It had also on its roof, a cupola with a bell in it.

'When a man at five-and-twenty can put his hat on, and can say "this hat covers the owner of this property and of the business which is transacted *on* this property," I consider, Mr Bintrey, that, without being boastful, he may be allowed to be deeply thankful. I don't know how it may appear to you, but so it appears to me.'

Thus Mr Walter Wilding to his man of law, in his own counting-house; taking his hat down from its peg to suit the action to the word, and hanging it up again when he had done so, not to overstep the modesty of nature.

An innocent, open-speaking, unused-looking man, Mr Walter Wilding, with a remarkably pink and white complexion, and a figure much too bulky for so young a man, though of a good stature. With crispy curling brown hair, and amiable bright blue eyes. An extremely communicative man; a man with whom loquacity was the irrestrainable outpouring of contentment and gratitude. Mr Blintrey, on the other hand, a cautious man with twinkling beads of eyes in a large over-hanging bald head, who inwardly but intensely enjoyed the comicality of openness of speech, or hand, or heart.

'Yes,' said Mr Bintrey. 'Yes. Ha, ha!'

A decanter, two wine-glasses, and a plate of biscuits, stood on the desk.

'You like this forty-five year old port wine?' said Mr Wilding.

'Like it?' repeated Mr Bintrey. 'Rather, sir!'

'It's from the best corner of our best forty-five year old bin' said Mr Wilding.

'Thank you, sir,' said Mr Bintrey. 'It's most excellent.'

He laughed again, as he held up his glass and ogled it, at the highly ludicrous idea of giving away such wine.

'And now,' said Wilding, with a childish enjoyment in the discussion of affairs, 'I think we have got everything straight, Mr Bintrey.'

'Everything straight,' said Bintrey.

'A partner secured—'

'Partner secured,' said Bintrey.

'A housekeeper advertised for—'

'Housekeeper advertised for,' said Bintrey, '"apply personally at Cripple Corner, Great Tower-street, from ten to twelve" – to-morrow, by-the-by.'

'My late dear mother's affairs wound up—'

'Wound up,' said Bintrey.

'And all charges paid.'

'And all charges paid,' said Bintrey, with a chuckle: probably occasioned by the droll circumstance that they had been paid without a haggle.

'The mention of my late dear mother,' Mr Wilding continued, his eyes filling with tears and his pocket-handkerchief drying them, 'unmans me still, Mr Bintrey. You know how I loved her; you (her lawyer) know how she loved me. The utmost love of mother and child was cherished between us, and we never experienced one moment's division or unhappiness from the time when she took me under her care. Thirteen years in all! Thirteen years under my late dear mother's care, Mr Bintrey, and eight of them her confidentially acknowledged son! You know the story, Mr Bintrey, who but you sir!' Mr Wilding sobbed and dried his eyes, without attempt at concealment, during these remarks.

Mr Bintrey enjoyed his comical port, and said, after rolling it in his mouth: 'I know the story.'

'My late dear mother, Mr Bintrey,' pursued the wine-merchant, 'had been deeply deceived, and had cruelly suffered. But on that subject my late dear mother's lips were for ever sealed. By whom deceived, or under what circumstances, Heaven only knows. My late dear mother never betrayed her betrayer.'

'She had made up her mind,' said Mr Bintrey, again turning his wine on his palate,' and she could hold her peace.' An amused twinkle in his eyes pretty plainly added— 'A devilish deal better than *you* ever will!'

'"Honour", said Mr Wilding, sobbing as he quoted from the Commandments, '"thy father and thy mother, that thy days may be long in the land". When I was in the Foundling, Mr Bintrey, I was at such a loss how to do it, that I apprehended my days would be short in the land. But afterwards I came to honour my mother deeply, profoundly. And I honour and revere her memory. For seven happy years, Mr Bintrey,' pursued Wilding, still with the same innocent catching in his breath, and the same unabashed tears, 'did my excellent mother article me to my predecessors in this business, Pebbleson Nephew. Her affectionate forethought likewise apprenticed me to the Vintners' Company, and made me in time a Free vintner, and – and – everything else that the best of mothers could desire. When I came of age, she bestowed her inherited share in this business upon me; it was her money that afterwards bought out Pebbleson Nephew, and painted in Wilding and Co.; it was she who left me everything she possessed, but the mourning ring you wear. And yet, Mr Bintrey,' with a fresh burst of honest affection, 'she is no more. It is little over half a year since she came into the Corner to read on that door-post with her own eyes WILDING AND CO. WINE MERCHANTS. And yet she is no more!'

'Sad. But the common lot, Mr Wilding,' observed Bintrey. 'At some time or other we must all be no more.' He placed the forty-five year old port wine in the universal condition, with a relishing sigh.

'So now, Mr Bintrey,' pursued Wilding, putting away his pocket-handkerchief, and smoothing his eyelids with his fingers, 'now that I can no longer show my love and honour for the dear parent to whom my heart was mysteriously turned by Nature when she first spoke to me, a strange lady, I sitting at our Sunday dinner-table in the Foundling, I can at least show that I am not ashamed of having been a Foundling, and that I, who never knew a father of my own, wish to be a father to all in my employment. Therefore,' continued Wilding, becoming enthusiastic in his loquacity, 'therefore, I want a thoroughly good housekeeper to undertake this dwelling-house of Wilding and Co. Wine Merchants, Cripple Corner, so that I may restore in it some of the old relations betwixt employer and employed! So that I may live in it on the spot where my money is made! So that I may daily sit at the head of the table at which the people in my employment eat together, and may eat of the same roast and boiled, and drink of the same beer! So that the people in my employment may lodge under the same roof with me! So that we may one and all – I beg your pardon, Mr Bintrey, but that old singing in my head has suddenly come on, and I shall feel obliged if you will lead me to the pump.'

Alarmed by the excessive pinkness of his client, Mr Bintrey lost not a moment in leading him forth into the court-yard. It was easily done, for the counting-house in which they talked together opened on to it, at one side of the dwelling-house. There, the attorney pumped with a will, obedient to a sign from the client, and the client laved his head and face with both hands, and took a hearty drink. After these remedies, he declared himself much better.

'Don't let your good feelings excite you,' said Bintrey, as they returned to the counting-house, and Mr Wilding dried himself on a jack-towel behind an inner door.

'No, no. I won't,' he returned, looking out of the towel. 'I won't. I have not been confused, have I?'

'Not at all. Perfectly clear.'

'Where did I leave off, Mr Bintrey?'

'Well, you left off – but I wouldn't excite myself, if I was you, by taking it up again just yet.'

'I'll take care. I'll take care. The singing in my head came on at where, Mr Bintrey?'

'At roast, and boiled, and beer,' answered the lawyer, prompting – 'lodging under the same roof – and one and all—'

'Ah! And one and all singing in the head together—'

'Do you know I really *would not* let my good feelings excite me, if I was you,' hinted the lawyer again, anxiously. 'Try some more pump.'

'No occasion, no occasion. All right, Mr Bintrey. And one and all forming a kind of family! You see, Mr Bintrey, I was not used in my childhood to that sort of individual existence which most individuals have led, more or less, in their childhood. After that time I became absorbed in my late dear mother. Having lost her, I find that I am more fit for being one of a body than one by myself one. To be that, and at the same time to do my duty to those dependent on me, and attach them to me, has a patriarchal and pleasant air about it. I don't know how it may appear to you, Mr Bintrey, but so it appears to me.'

'It is not I who am all-important in the case, but you,' returned Bintrey. 'Consequently, how it may appear to me, is of very small importance.'

'It appears to *me*,' said Mr Wilding, in a glow, 'hopeful, useful, de-lightful!'

'Do you know,' hinted the lawyer again, 'I really would not ex—'

'I am not going to. Then there's Handel.'

'There's who?' asked Bintrey.

'Handel, Mozart, Haydn, Kent, Purcell, Doctor Arne, Greene, Mendelssohn. I know the choruses to those anthems by heart. Foundling Chapel Collection. Why shouldn't we learn them together!'

'Who learn them together?' asked the lawyer, rather shortly.

'Employer and employed.'

'Aye, aye!' returned Bintrey, mollified; as if he had half expected the answer to be, Lawyer and client. 'That's another thing.'

'Not another thing, Mr Bintrey! The same thing. A part of the bond among us. We will form a Choir in some quiet church near the Corner here, and, having sung together of a Sunday with a relish, we will come home and take an early dinner together with a relish. The object that I have at heart now, is to get this system well in action without delay, so that my new partner may find it founded when he enters on his partnership.'

'All good be with it!' exclaimed Bintrey, rising. 'May it prosper! is Joey Ladle to take a share in Handel, Mozart, Haydn, Kent, Purcel, Doctor Arne, Greene, and Mendels-sohn?'

'I hope so.'

'I wish them all well out of it,' returned Bintrey, with much heartiness. 'Good-bye, sir.'

They shook hands and parted. Then (first knocking with his knuckles for leave) entered to Mr Wilding, from a door of communication between his private counting-house and that in which his clerks sat, the Head Cellarman of the cellars of Wilding and Co. Wine Merchants, and erst Head Cellarman of the cellars of Pebbleson Nephew. The Joey Ladle in question. A slow and ponderous man, of the drayman order of human architecture, dressed in a corrugated suit and bibbed apron, apparently a composite of door-mat and rhinoceros-hide.

'Respecting this same boarding and lodging, Young Master Wilding,' said he.

'Yes, Joey?'

'Speaking for myself, Young Master Wilding – and I never did speak and I never do speak for no one else – *I* don't want no boarding nor yet no lodging. But if you wish to board me and to lodge me, take me. I can peck as well as most men. Where I peck, ain't so high a object with me as What I peck. Nor even so high a object with me as How Much I peck. Is all to live in the house, Young Master Wilding? The two other cellarmen, the three porters, the two 'prentices, and the odd men?'

'Yes. I hope we shall all be an united family, Joey.'

'Ah!' said Joey. 'I hope they may be.'

'They? Rather say we, Joey.'

Joey Ladle shook his head. 'Don't look to me to make we on it, Young Master Wilding, not at my time of life and under the circumstances which has formed my disposition. I have said to Pebbleson Nephew many a time, when they have said to me, "Put a livelier face upon it, Joey" – I have said to them, "Gentlemen, it is all very well for you that has been accustomed to take your wine into your systems by the conwivial channel of your throttles, to put a lively face upon it; but," I says "I have been accustomed to take *my* wine in at the pores of the skin, and, took that way, it acts different. It acts depressing. It's one thing, gentlemen," I says to Pebbleson Nephew, "to charge your glasses in a dining-room with a Hip Hurrah and a Jolly Companions Every One, and it's another thing to be charged yourself, through the pores, in a low dark cellar and a mouldy atmosphere. It makes all the difference betwixt bubbles and wapours," I tells Pebbleson Nephew. And so it do. I've been a cellarman my life through with my mind fully given to the business. What's the consequence? I'm as muddled a man as lives – you won't find a muddleder man than me – nor yet you won't find my equal in molloncolly. Sing of Filling the bumper fair, Every drop you sprinkle, O'er the brow of care, Smooths away a wrinkle? Yes. P'raps so. But try filling yourself through the pores, underground, when you don't want to it!'

'I am sorry to hear this, Joey. I had even thought that you might join a singing-class in the house.'

'Me sir? No, no, Young Master Wilding, you won't catch Joey Ladle muddling the Armony. A pecking-machine, sir, is all that I am capable of proving myself, out of my cellars; but that you're welcome to, if you think it's worth your while to keep such a thing on your premises.'

'I do, Joey.'

'Say no more, sir. The Business's word is my law. And you're a going to take Young Master George Vendale partner into the old Business?'

'I am Joey.'

'More changes, you see! But don't change the name of the Firm again. Don't do it Young Master Wilding. It was bad luck enough to make it Yourself and Co. Better by far have left it Pebbleson Nephew that good luck always stuck to. You should never change luck when it's good, sir.'

'At all events, I have no intention of changing the name of the House again, Joey.'

'Glad to hear it, and wish you good day, Young Master Wilding. But you had better by half,' muttered Joey Ladle, inaudibly, as he closed the door and shook his head, 'have let the name alone from the first. You had better by half have followed the luck instead of crossing it.'

Enter the Housekeeper

The wine-merchant sat in his dining-room next morning, to receive the personal applicants for the vacant post in his establishment. It was an old-fashioned wainscoted room; the panels ornamented with festons of flowers carved in wood; with an oaken floor, a well-worn Turkey carpet, and dark mahogany furniture, all of which had seen service and polish under Pebbleson Nephew. The great sideboard had assisted at many business-dinners given by Pebbleson Nephew to their connexion, on the principle of throwing sprats overboard to catch whales; and Pebbleson Newphew's comprehensive three-sided plate-warmer, made to fit the whole front of the large fireplace, kept watch beneath it over a sarcophagus-shaped cellaret that had in its time held many a dozen of Pebbleson Nephew's wine. But the little rubicund old bachelor with a pigtail whose portrait was over the sideboard (and who could easily be identified as decidedly Pebbleson and decidedly not Nephew), had retired into another sarcophagus, and the plate-warmer had grown as cold as he. So, the golden and black griffins that supported the candelabra, with black balls in their mouths at the end of gilded chains, looked as if in their old age they had lost all heart for playing at ball, and were dolefully exhibiting their chains in the Missionary line of inquiry, whether they had not earned emancipation by this time, and were not griffins and brothers?

Such a Columbus of a morning was the summer morning, that it discovered Cripple Corner. The light and warmth pierced in at the open windows, and irradiated the picture of a lady hanging over the chimney-piece, the only other decoration of the walls.

'My mother at five-and-twenty,' said Mr Wilding to himself, as his eyes enthusiastically followed the light to the portrait's face, 'I hang up here, in order that visitors may admire my mother in the bloom of her youth and beauty. My mother at fifty I hang in the seclusion of my own chamber, as a remembrance sacred to me. Oh! It's you Jarvis!'

These latter words he addressed to a clerk who had tapped at the door, and now looked in.

'Yes sir. I merely wished to mention that it's gone ten, sir, and that there are several females in the Counting-House,'

'Dear me!' said the wine-merchant, deepening in the pink of his complexion and whitening in the white, 'are there several? So many as several? I had better begin before there are more. I'll see them one by one, Jarvis, in the order of their arrival.'

Hastily entrenching himself in his easy-chair at the table behind a great inkstand, having first placed a chair on the other side of the table opposite his own seat, Mr Wilding entered on his task with considerable trepidation.

He ran the gauntlet that must be run on any such occasion. There were the usual species of profoundly unsympathetic women, and the usual species of much too sympathetic women. There were buccaneering widows who came to seize him, and who griped umbrellas under their arms, as if each umbrella were he, and each griper had got him. There were towering maiden ladies who had seen better days, and who came armed with clerical testimonials to their theology, as if he were Saint Peter with his keys. There were gentle maiden ladies who came to marry him. There were professional housekeepers, like non-commissioned officers, who put him through his domestic exercise, instead of submitting themselves to catechism. There were languid invalids to whom salary was not so much an object as the comforts of a private hospital. There were sensitive creatures who burst into tears on being addressed, and had to be restored with glasses of cold water. There were some respondents who came two together, a highly promising one and a wholly unpromising one: of whom the promising one answered all questions charmingly, until it would at last appear that she was not a candidate at all, but only the friend of the unpromising one, who had glowered in absolute silence and apparent injury.

At last, when the good wine-merchant's simple heart was failing him, there entered an applicant quite different from all the rest. A woman, perhaps fifty, but looking younger, with a face remarkable for placid cheerfulness, and a manner no less remarkable for its quiet expression of equability of temper. Nothing in her dress could have been changed to her advantage. Nothing in the noiseless self-possession of her manner could have been changed to her advantage. Nothing could have been in better unison with both, than her voice when she answered the question: 'What name shall I have the pleasure of noting down?' with the words, 'My name is Sarah Goldstraw. Mrs Goldstraw. My husband has been dead many years, and we had no family.'

Half a dozen questions had scarcely extracted as much to the purpose from any one else. The voice dwelt so agreeably on Mr Wilding's ear as he made his note, that he was rather long about it. When he looked up again, Mrs Goldstraw's glance had naturally gone round the room, and now returned to him from the chimney-piece. Its expression was one of frank readiness to be questioned, and to answer straight.

'You will excuse my asking you a few questions?' said the modest wine-merchant.

'Oh, surely, sir. Or I should have no business here.'

'Have you filled the station of housekeeper before?'

'Only once. I have lived with the same widow lady for twelve years. Ever since I lost my husband. She was an invalid, and is lately dead: which is the occasion of my now wearing black.'

'I do not doubt that she has left you the best credentials?' said Mr Wilding.

'I hope I may say, the very best. I thought it would save trouble, sir, if I wrote down the name and address of her representatives, and brought it with me.' Laying a card on the table.

'You singularly remind me, Mrs Goldstraw,' said Wilding, taking the card beside him, 'of a manner and tone of voice that I was once acquainted with. Not of an individual – I feel sure of that, though I cannot recall what it is I have in my mind – but of a general bearing. I ought to add, it was a kind and pleasant one.'

She smiled, as she rejoined: 'At least, I am very glad of that, sir.'

'Yes,' said the wine-merchant, thoughtfully repeating his last phrase, with a momentary glance at his future house-keeper, 'it was a kind and pleasant one. But that is the most I can make of it. Memory is sometimes like a half-forgotten dream. I don't know how it may appear to you, Mrs Goldstraw, but so it appears to me.'

Probably it appeared to Mrs Goldstraw in a similar light for she quietly assented to the proposition. Mr Wilding then offered to put himself at once in communication with the gentlemen named upon the card: a firm of proctors in Doctors' Commons. To this, Mrs Goldstraw thankfully assented. Doctors' Commons not being far off, Mr Wilding suggested the feasibility of Mrs Goldstraw's looking in again, say in three hours' time. Mrs Goldstraw readily undertook to do so. In fine, the result of Mr Wilding's inquiries being eminently satisfactory, Mrs Goldstraw was that afternoon engaged (on her own perfectly fair terms) to come to-morow and set up her rest as housekeeper in Cripple Corner.

The Housekeeper Speaks

On the next day Mrs Goldstraw arrived, to enter on her domestic duties.

Having settled herself in her own room, without troubling the servants, and without wasting time, the new housekeeper announced herself as waiting to be favoured with any instructions which her master might wish to give her. The wine-merchant received Mrs Goldstraw in the dining-room, in which he had seen her on the previous day; and, the usual preliminary civilities having passed on either side, the two sat down to take counsel together on the affairs of the house.

'About the meals sir?' said Mrs Goldstraw. 'Have I a large, or a small, number to provide for?'

'If I can carry out a certain old-fashioned plan of mine,' replied Mr Wilding, 'you will have a large number to provide for. I am a lonely single man, Mrs Goldstraw; and I hope to live with all the persons in my employment as if they were members of my family. Until that time comes, you will only have me, and the new partner whom I expect immediately, to provide for. What my partner's habits may be, I cannot yet say. But I may describe myself as a man of regular hours, with an invariable appetite that you may depend upon to an ounce.'

'About breakfast, sir?' asked Mrs Goldstraw. 'Is there anything particular—?'

She hesitated, and left the sentence unfinished. Her eyes turned slowly away from her master, and looked towards the chimney-piece. If she had been a less excellent and experienced housekeeper, Mr Wilding might have fancied that her attention was beginning to wander at the very outset of the interview.

'Eight o'clock is my breakfast-hour,' he resumed. 'It is one of my virtues to be never tired of broiled bacon, and it is one of my vices to be habitually suspicious of the freshness of eggs.' Mrs Goldstraw looked back at him, still a little divided between her master's chimney-piece and her master. 'I take tea,' Mr Wilding went on; 'and I am perhaps rather nervous and fidgety about drinking it, within a certain time after it is made. If my tea stands too long—'

He hesitated, on his side, and left the sentence unfinished. If he had not been engaged in discussing a subject of such paramount interest to himself as his breakfast, Mrs Goldstraw might have fancied that *his* attention was beginning to wander at the very outset of the interview.

'If your tea stands too long sir—?' said the housekeeper, politely taking up her master's lost thread.

'If my tea stands too long,' repeated the wine-merchant, mechanically, his mind getting further and further away from his breakfast, and his eyes fixing themselves more and more inquiringly on his housekeeper's face. 'If my tea— Dear, dear me, Mrs Goldstraw! what *is* the manner and tone of voice that you remind me of? It strikes me even more strongly to-day, than it did when I saw you yesterday. What can it be?'

'What can it be?' repeated Mrs Goldstraw.

She said the words, evidently thinking while she spoke them of something else. The wine-merchant, still looking at her inquiringly, observed that her eyes wandered towards the chimney-piece once more. They fixed on the portrait of his mother, which hung there, and looked at it with the slight contraction of the brow which accompanies a scarcely conscious effort of memory. Mr Wilding remarked:

'My late dear mother, when she was five-and-twenty.'

Mrs Goldstraw thanked him with a movement of the head for being at the pains to explain the picture, and said, with a cleared brow, that it was the portrait of a very beautiful lady.

Mr Wilding, falling back into his former perplexity, tried once more to recover that lost recollection, associated so closely, and yet so undiscoverably, with his new housekeeper's voice and manner.

'Excuse my asking you a question which has nothing to do with me or my breakfast,' he said. 'May I inquire if you have ever occupied any other situation than the situation of housekeeper?'

'Oh yes, sir. I began life as one of the nurses at the Foundling.'

'Why, that's it!' cried the wine-merchant, pushing back his

chair. 'By Heaven! Their manner is the manner you remind me of!'

In an astonished look at him, Mrs Goldstraw changed colour, checked herself, turned her eyes upon the ground, and sat still and silent.

'What is the matter?' asked Mr Wilding.

'Do I understand that you were in the Foundling, sir?'

'Certainly. I am not ashamed to own it.'

'Under the name you now bear?'

'Under the name of Walter Wilding.'

'And the lady—?' Mrs Goldstraw stopped short, with a look at the portrait which was now unmistakably a look of alarm.

'You mean my mother,' interrupted Mr Wilding.

'Your – mother,' repeated the housekeeper, a little constrainedly, 'removed you from the Foundling? At what age, sir?'

'At between eleven and twelve years old. It's quite a romantic adventure, Mrs Goldstraw.'

He told the story of the lady having spoken to him, while he sat at dinner with the other boys in the Foundling, and of all that had followed, in his innocently communicative way. 'My poor mother could never have discovered me,' he added, 'if she had not met with one of the matrons who pitied her. the matron consented to touch the boy whose name was "Walter Wilding" as she went round the dinner-tables – and so my mother discovered me again, after having parted from me as an infant at the Foundling doors.'

At those words Mrs Goldstraw's hand, resting on the table, dropped helplessly into her lap. She sat, looking at her new master, with a face that had turned deadly pale, and with eyes that expressed an unutterable dismay.

'What does this mean?' asked the wine-merchant. 'Stop!' he cried. 'Is there something else in the past time which I ought to associate with you? I remember my mother telling me of another person at the Foundling, to whose kindness she owed a debt of gratitude. When she first parted with me, as an infant, one of the nurses informed her of the name that had been given to me in the institution. You were that nurse?'

'God forgive me, sir – I was that nurse!'

'God forgive you?'

'We had better get back, sir (if I may make so bold as to say so), to my duties in the house,' said Mrs Goldstraw. 'Your breakfast-hour is eight. Do you lunch, or dine, in the middle of the day?'

The excessive pinkness which Mr Bintrey had noticed in his client's face began to appear there once more. Mr Wilding put his hand to his head, and mastered some momentary confusion in that quarter, before he spoke again.

'Mrs Goldstraw,' he said, 'you are concealing something from me!'

The housekeeper obstinately repeated, 'Please to favour me, sir, by saying whether you lunch, or dine, in the middle of the day?'

'I don't know what I do the middle of the day. I can't enter into my household affairs, Mrs Goldstraw, till I know why you regret an act of kindness to my mother, which she always spoke of gratefully to the end of her life. You are not doing me a service by your silence. You are agitating me, you are alarming me, you are bringing on the singing in my head.'

His hand went up to his head again, and the pink in his face deepened by a shade or two.

'It's hard, sir, on just entering your service,' said the housekeeper, 'to say what may cost me the loss of your good will. Please to remember, end how it may, that I only speak because you have insisted on my speaking, and because I see that I am alarming you by my silence. When I told the poor lady, whose portrait you have got there, the name by which her infant was christened in the Foundling, I allowed myself to forget my duty, and dreadful consequences, I am afraid, have followed from it. I'll tell you the truth, as plainly as I can. A few months from the time when I had informed the lady of her baby's name, there came to our institution in the country another lady (a stranger), whose object was to adopt one of our children. She brought the needful permission with her, and after looking at a great many of the children, without being able to make up her mind, she took a sudden fancy to one of the babies – a boy – under my care. Try, pray try, to compose yourself sir! It's no use disguising it any longer. The child the stranger took away was the child of that lady whose portrait hangs there!'

Mr Wilding started to his feet. 'Impossible!' he cried out, vehemently. 'What are you talking about? What absurd story are you telling me now? There's her portrait! Haven't I told you so already? The portrait of my mother!'

'When that unhappy lady removed you from the Foundling in after years,' said Mrs Goldstraw, gently, 'she was the victim, and you were the victim, sir, of a dreadful mistake.'

He dropped back into his chair. 'The room goes round with me,' he said. 'My head! My head!' The housekeeper rose in alarm, and opened the windows. Before she could get to the door to call for help, a sudden burst of tears relieved the oppression which had at first almost appeared to threaten his life. He signed entreatingly to Mrs Goldstraw not to leave him. She waited until the paroxysm of weeping had worn itself out. He raised his head as he recovered himself, and looked at her with angry unreasoning suspicion of a weak man.

'Mistake?' he said, wildly repeating her last word. 'How do I know you are not mistaken yourself?'

'There is no hope that I am mistaken, sir. I will tell you why, when you are better fit to hear it.'

'Now! Now!'

The tone in which he spoke warned Mrs Goldstraw that it would be cruel kindness to let him comfort himself a moment longer with the vain hope that she might be wrong. A few words would end it – and those few words she determined to speak.

'I have told you,' she said, 'that the child of the lady whose portrait hangs there, was adopted in its infancy, and taken away by a stranger. I am as certain of what I say as that I am now sitting here, obliged to distress you, sir, sorely against my will. Please to carry your mind on, now, to about three months after that time. I was then at the Foundling, in London, waiting to take some children to our institution in the country. There was a question that day about naming an infant – a boy – who had just been received. We generally named them out of the Directory. On this occasion, one of the gentlemen who managed the Hospital happened to be looking over the Register. He noticed that the name of the baby who had been adopted ("Walter Wilding") was scratched out – for the reason, of course that the child had been removed for good from our care. "Here's a name to let," he said. "Give it to the new foundling who has been received to-day." The name was given and the child was christened. You sir, were that child.'

The wine-merchant's head dropped on his breast. 'I was that child!' he said to himself, trying helplessly to fix the idea in his mind. 'I was that child!'

'Not very long after you had been received into the Institution sir,' pursued Mrs Goldstraw, 'I left my situation there to be married. If you will remember that, and if you can give your mind to it, you will see for yourself how the mistake happened. Between eleven and twelve years passed before the lady, whom you have believed to be your mother, returned to the Foundling, to find her son, and to remove him to her own home. The lady only knew that her infant had been called "Walter Wilding". The matron who took pity on her, could but point out the only "Walter Wilding" known in the Institution. I, who might have set the matter right, was far away from the Foundling and all that belonged to it. There was nothing – there was really nothing that could prevent this terrible mistake from taking place. I feel for you – I do indeed, sir! You must think – and with reason – that it was an evil hour that I came here (innocently enough, I'm sure), to apply for your housekeeper's place. I feel as if I was to blame – I feel as if I ought to have had more self-command. If I had only been able to keep my face from showing you what that portrait and what your own words put into my mind – you need never, to your dying day, have known what you know now.'

Mr Wilding looked up suddenly. The inbred honesty of the man rose in protest against the housekeeper's last words. His mind seemed to steady itself, for the moment, under the shock that had fallen on it.

'Do you mean to say that you would have concealed this from me if you could?' he exclaimed.

'I hope I should always tell the truth, sir, if I was asked,' said Mrs Goldstraw. 'And I know it is better for *me* that I should not have a secret of this sort weighing on my mind. But is it better for *you*? What use can it serve now—?'

'What use? Why, good Lord! If your story is true—'

'Should I have told it, sir, as I am now situated, if it had not been true?'

'I beg your pardon,' said the wine-merchant. 'You must make allowance for me. This dreadful discovery is something I can't realise even yet. We loved each other so dearly – I felt so fondly that I was her son. She died, Mrs Goldstraw, in my arms – she died blessing me as only a mother *could* have blessed me. And now, after all these years, to be told she was *not* my mother! O me, O me! I don't know what I am saying!' he cried, as the impulse of self-control under which he had spoken a moment since, flickered, and died out. 'It was not this dreadful grief – it was something else that I had it in my mind to speak of. Yes, yes. You surprised me – you wounded me just now. You talked as if you would have hidden this from me, if you could. Don't talk in that way again. It would have been a crime to have hidden it. You mean well, I know. I don't want to distress you – you are a kind-hearted woman. But you don't remember what my position is. She left me all that I possess, in the firm persuasion that I was her son. I am not her son. I have taken the place, I have innocently got the inheritance of another man. He must be found! How do I know he is not at this moment in misery, without bread to eat? He must be found! My only hope of bearing up against the shock that has fallen on me, is the hope of doing something which *she* would have approved. You must know more, Mrs Goldstraw, than you have told me yet. Who was the stranger who adopted the child? You must have heard the lady's name?'

'I never heard it, sir. I have never seen her, or heard of her, since.'

'Did she say nothing when she took the child away? Search your memory. She must have said something.'

'Only one thing, sir, that I can remember. It was a miserably bad season, that year; and many of the children were suffering from it. When she took the baby away, the lady said to me, laughing, "Don't be alarmed about his health. He will be brought up in a better climate than this – I am going to take him to Switzerland."'

'To Switzerland? What part of Switzerland?'

'She didn't say, sir.'

'Only that faint clue!' said Mr Wilding. 'And a quarter of a century has passed since the child was taken away! What am I to do?'

'I hope you won't take offence at my freedom, sir,' said Mrs Goldstraw; 'but why should you distress yourself about what is to be done? He may not be alive now, for anything you know. And, if he is alive, it's not likely he can be in any distress. The lady who adopted him was a bred and born lady – it was easy to see that. And she must have satisfied them at the Foundling that she could provide for the child, or they would never have let her take him away. If I was in your place, sir – please to excuse my saying so – I should comfort myself with remembering that I had loved that poor lady whose portrait you have got there – truly loved her as my mother, and that she had truly loved me as her son. All she gave to you, she gave for the sake of that love. It never altered while she lived; and it won't alter, I'm sure, as long as *you* live. How can you have a better right, sir, to keep what you have got than that?'

Mr Wilding's immovable honesty saw the fallacy in his housekeeper's point of view at a glance.

'You don't understand me,' he said. 'It's *because* I loved her that I feel it a duty – a sacred duty – to do justice to her son. If he is a living man, I must find him: for my own sake, as well as for his. I shall break down under this dreadful trial, unless I employ myself – actively, instantly employ myself – in doing what my conscience tells me ought to be done. I must speak to my lawyer; I must set my lawyer at work before I sleep to-night.' He approached a tube in the wall of the room, and called down through it to the office below. 'Leave me for a little Mrs Goldstraw,' he resumed; 'I shall be more composed, I shall be better able to speak to you later in the day. We shall get on well – I hope we shall get on well together – in spite of what has happened. It isn't your fault; I know it isn't your fault. There! There! Shake hands; and – and do the best you can in the house – I can't talk about it now.'

The door opened as Mrs Goldstraw advanced towards it; and Mr Jarvis appeared.

'Send for Mr Bintrey,' said the wine-merchant. 'Say I want to see him directly.'

The clerk unconsciously suspended the execution of the order, by announcing 'Mr Vendale,' and showing in the new partner in the firm of Wilding and Co.

'Pray excuse me for one moment, George Vendale,' said Wilding. 'I have a word to say to Jarvis. Send for Mr Bintrey,' he repeated – 'send at once.'

Mr Jarvis laid a letter on the table before he left the room. 'From our correspondents at Neuchâtel, I think, sir. The letter has got the Swiss postmark.'

The New Characters on the Scene

The words, 'The Swiss Postmark', following so soon upon the housekeeper's reference to Switzerland, wrought Mr Wilding's agitation to such a remarkable height, that his new partner could not decently make a pretence of letting it pass unnoticed.

'Wilding,' he asked hurriedly, and yet stopping short and glancing around as if for some visible cause of his state of mind: 'what is the matter?'

'My good George Vendale,' returned the wine-merchant, giving his hand with an appealing look, rather as if he wanted help to get over some obstacle, than as if he gave it in welcome or salutation: 'My good George Vendale, so much is the matter, that I shall never be myself again. It is impossible that I can ever be myself again. For, in fact, I am not myself.'

The new partner a brown-cheeked handsome fellow, of about his own age, with a quick determined eye and an impulsive manner, retorted with natural astonishment: 'Not yourself?'

'Not what I supposed myself to be,' said Wilding.

'What, in the name of wonder, *did* you suppose yourself to be that you are not?' was the rejoinder, delivered with a cheerful frankness, inviting confidence from a more reticent man. 'I may ask without impertinence, now that we are partners.'

'There again!' cried Wilding, leaning back in his chair, with a lost look at the other. 'Partners! I had not right to come into this business. It was never meant for me. My mother never meant it should be mine. I mean, his mother meant it should be his – if I mean anything – or if I am anybody.'

'Come, come,' urged his partner, after a moment's pause, and taking possession of him with the calm confidence which inspires a strong nature when it honestly desires to aid a weak one. 'Whatever has gone wrong, has gone wrong through no fault of yours, I am very sure. I was not in this counting-house with you under the old *régime*, for three years, to doubt you, Wilding. We were not younger men than we are, together, for that. Let me begin our partnership by being a serviceable partner, and setting right whatever is wrong. Has that letter anything to do with it?'

'Hah!' said Wilding, with his hand to his temple. 'There again! My head! I was forgetting the coincidence. The Swiss postmark.'

'At a second glance I see that the letter is unopened, so it is not very likely to have much to do with the matter,' said Vendale, with comforting composure. 'Is it for you, or for us?'

'For us,' said Wilding.

'Suppose I open it and read it aloud, to get it out of our way?'

'Thank you, thank you.'

'The letter is only from our champagne-making friends, the House at Neuchâtel. "Dear Sir. We are in receipt of yours of the 28th ult., informing us that you have taken your Mr Vendale into partnership, whereon we beg you to receive the assurance of our felicitations. Permit us to embrace the occasion of specially commending to you, M. Jules Oben-reizer." Impossible!'

Wilding looked up in quick apprehension, and cried, 'Eh?'

'Impossible sort of name,' returned his partner, slightly – 'Obenreizer. "– Of specially commending to you M. Jules Obenreizer, of Soho-square, London (north side), henceforth fully accredited as our agent, and who has already had the honour of making the acquaintance of your Mr Vendale, in his (said M. Obenreizer's) native country, Switzerland." To be sure: pooh pooh, what have I been thinking of ! I remember now; "when travelling with his niece."'

'With his—?' Vendale had so slurred the last word, that Wilding had not heard it.

'When travelling with his Niece. Obenreizer's Niece,' said Vendale, in a somewhat superfluously lucid manner. 'Niece of Obenreizer. (I met them in my first Swiss tour, travelled a little with them, and lost them for two years; met them again, my Swiss tour before last, and have lost them ever since.) Obenreizer. Niece of Obenreizer. To be sure! Possible sort of name, after all! "M. Obenreizer is in possession of our absolute confidence, and we do not doubt you will esteem his merits." Duly signed by the house, "Defresnier et Cie". Very well. I undertake to see M. Obenreizer presently, and clear him out of the way. That clears the Swiss postmark out of the way. So now, my dear Wilding, tell me what I can clear out of *your* way, and I'll find a way to clear it.'

More than ready and grateful to be thus taken charge of, the honest wine-merchant wrung his partner's hand, and, beginning his tale by pathetically declaring himself an Impostor, told it.

'It was on this matter, no doubt, that you were sending for Bintrey when I came in?' said his partner, after reflecting.

'It was.'

'He has experience and a shrewd head; I shall be anxious to know his opinion. It is bold and hazardous in me to give you mine before I know his, but I am not good at holding back. Plainly, then, I do not see these circumstances as you see them. I do not see your position as you see it. As to your being an Impostor, my dear Wilding, that is simply absurd, because no man can be that without being a consenting party to an imposition. Clearly you never were so. As to your enrichment by the lady who believed you to be her son, and whom you were forced to believe, on her own showing, to be your mother, consider whether that did not arise out of the personal relations between you. You gradually became much attached to her; she gradually became much attached to you. It was on you, personally you, as I see the case, that she conferred these worldly advantages; it was from her personally her, that you took them.'

'She supposed me,' object Wilding, shaking his head, 'to have a natural claim upon her, which I had not.'

'I must admit that,' replied his partner, 'to be true. But if she had made the discovery that you have made, six months before she died, do you think it would have cancelled the years you were together, and the tenderness that each of you had conceived for the other, each on increasing knowledge of the other?'

'What I think,' said Wilding, simply but stoutly holding to the bare fact, 'can no more change the truth than it can bring down the sky. The truth is that I stand possessed of what was meant for another man.'

'He may be dead,' said Vendale.

'He may be alive,' said Wilding. 'And if he is alive, have I not – innocently, I grant you innocently – robbed him of enough? Have I not robbed him of all the happy time that I enjoyed in his stead? Have I not robbed him of the exquisite delight that filled my soul when that dear lady,' stretching his hand towards the picture, 'told me she was my mother? Have I not robbed him of all the care she lavished on me? Have I not even robbed him of all the devotion and duty that I so proudly gave to her? Therefore it is that I ask myself. George Vendale, and I ask you, where is he? What has become of him?'

'Who can tell!'

'I must try to find out who can tell. I must institute inquiries. I must never desist from prosecuting inquiries. I will live upon the interest of my share – I ought to say his share – in this business, and will lay up the rest for him. When I find him, I may perhaps throw myself upon his generosity; but I will yield up all to him. I will, I swear. As I loved and honoured her,' said Wilding, reverently kising his hand towards the picture, and then covering his eyes, with it. 'As I loved and honoured her, and have a world of reasons to be grateful to her!' And so broke down again.

His partner rose from the chair he had occupied, and stood beside him with a hand softly laid upon his shoulder. 'Walter, I knew you before to-day to be an upright man, with a pure conscience and a fine heart. It is very fortunate for me that I have the privilege to travel on in life so near to so trustworthy a man. I am thankful for it. Use me as your right hand, and rely upon me to the death. Don't think the worse of me if I protest to you that my uppermost feeling at present is a confused, you may call it an unreasonable, one. I feel far more pity for the lady and for you, because you did not stand in your supposed relations, than I can feel for the unknown man (if he ever became a man), because he was unconsciously displaced. You have done well in sending for Mr Bintrey. What I think will be a part of his advice, I know is the whole of mine. Do not move a step in this serious matter precipitately. The secret must be kept among us with great strictness, for to part with it lightly would be to invite fraudulent claims, to encourage a host of knaves, to let loose a flood of perjury and plotting. I have no more to say now, Walter, than to remind you that you sold me a share in your business, expressly to save yourself from more work than your present health is fit for, and that I bought it expressly to do work, and mean to do it.'

With these words, and a parting grip of his partner's shoulder that gave them the best emphasis they could have had, George Vendale betook himself presently to the counting-house, and presently afterwards to the address of M. Jules Obenreizer.

As he turned into Soho-square, and directed his steps towards its north side, a deepened colour shot across his sun-browned face, which Wilding, if he had been a better observer, or had been less occupied with his own trouble, might have noticed when his partner read aloud a certain passage in their Swiss correspondent's letter, which he had not read so distinctly as the rest.

A curious colony of mountaineers has long been enclosed within that small flat London district of Soho. Swiss watchmakers, Swiss silver-chasers, Swiss jewellers, Swiss importers of Swiss musical boxes and Swiss toys of various kinds, draw close together there. Swiss professors of music, painting, and languages; Swiss artificers in steady work; Swiss couriers, and other Swiss servants chronically out of place; industrious Swiss laundresses and clear-starchers; mysteriously existing Swiss of both sexes; Swiss, creditable and Swiss discreditable; Swiss to be trusted by all means, and Swiss to be trusted by no means; these diverse Swiss particles are attracted to a centre in the district of Soho. Shabby Swiss eating-houses, coffee-houses, and lodging-houses, Swiss drinks and dishes, Swiss service for Sundays, and Swiss schools for week-days, are all to be found there. Even the native-born English taverns drive a sort of broken-English trade; announcing in their windows Swiss whets and drams, and sheltering in their bars Swiss skirmishes of love and animosity on most nights in the year.

When the new partner in Wilding and Co. rang the bell of the door bearing the blunt inscription OBENREIZER on a brass plate – the inner door of a substantial house, whose ground story was devoted to the sale of Swiss clocks – he passed at once into domestic Switzerland. A white-tiled stove for winter-time filled the fireplace of the room into which he was shown, the room's bare floor was laid together in a neat pattern of several ordinary woods, the room had a prevalent air of surface bareness and much scrubbing; and the little square of flowery carpet by the sofa, and the velvet chimney-board with its capacious clock and vases of artificial flowers, contended with that tone, as if, in bringing out the whole effect, a Parisian had adapted a dairy to domestic purposes.

Mimic water was dropping off a mill-wheel under the clock. The visitor had not stood before it, following it with his eyes, a minute, when M. Obenreizer, at his elbow, startled him by saying, in very good English, very slightly clipped: 'How do you do? So glad!'

'I beg your pardon. I didn't hear you come in.'

'Not at all! Sit please.'

Releasing his visitor's two arms, which he had lightly pinioned at the elbows by way of embrace, M. Obenreizer also sat, remarking, with a smile: 'You are well? So glad!' and touching his elbows atain.

'I don't know,' said Vendale, after exchange of salutations, 'whether you may yet have heard of me from your House at Neuchâtel?'

'Ah, yes!'

'In connexion with Wilding and Co.?'

'Ah surely!'

'Is it not odd that I should come to you, in London here, as one of the Firm of Wilding and Co., to pay the Firm's respects?'

'Not at all! What did I always observe when we were on the mountains? We call them vast; but the world is so little. So little is the world, that one cannot keep away from persons. There are so few persons in the world, that they continually cross and re-cross. So very little is the world, that one cannot get rid of a person. Not', touching his elbows again, with an ingratiatory smile, 'that one would desire to get rid of you.'

'I hope not, M. Obenreizer.'

'Please call me, in your country, Mr. I call myself so, for I love your country. If I *could* be English! But I am born. And you? Though descended from so fine a family, you have had the condescension to come into trade? Stop though. Wines? Is it trade in England or profession? Not fine art?'

'Mr Obenreizer,' returned Vendale, somewhat out of countenance, 'I was but a silly young fellow, just of age, when I first had the pleasure of travelling with you, and when you and I and Mademoiselle your niece – who is well?'

'Thank you. Who is well.'

'—Shared some slight glacier dangers together. If, with a boy's vanity, I rather vaunted my family, I hope I did so as a kind of introduction of myself. It was very weak, and in very bad taste; but perhaps you know our English proverb, "Live and learn."'

'You make too much of it,' returned the Swiss. 'And what the devil! After all, yours *was* a fine family,'

George Vendale's laugh betrayed a little vexation as he rejoined: 'Well! I was strongly attached to my parents, and when we first travelled together, Mr Obenreizer, I was in the first flush of coming into what my father and mother left me. So I hope it may have been, after all, more youthful openness of speech and heart than boastfulness.'

'All openness of speech and heart! No boastfulness!' cried Obenreizer. 'You tax yourself too heavily. You tax yourself, my faith! As if you was your Government taxing you! Besides, it commenced with me. I remember, that evening in the boat upon the lake, floating among the reflections of the mountains and valleys, the crags and pine woods, which were my earliest remembrance, I drew a word-picture of my sordid childhood. Of our poor hut, by the waterfall which my mother showed to the travellers; of the cow-shed where I slept with the cow; of my idiot half-brother always sitting at the door, or limping down the Pass to beg; of my half-sister always spinning, and resting her enormous goitre on a great stone; of my being a famished naked little wretch of two or three years, when they were men and women with hard hands to beat me, I, the only child of my father's second marriage – if it even was a marriage. What more natural than for you to compare notes with me, and say, "We are as one by age; at that same time I sat upon my mother's lap in my father's carriage, rolling through the rich English streets, all luxury surrounding me, all squalid poverty kept far from me. such is *my* earliest remembrance as apposed to yours!"'

Mr Obenreizer was a black-haired young man of a dark complexion, through whose swarthy skin no red glow ever shone. When colour would have come into another cheek, a hardly discernible beat would come into his, as if the machinery for bringing up the ardent blood were there, but the machinery were dry. He was robustly made, well proportioned, and had handsome features. Many would have perceived that some surface change in him would have set them more at their ease with him, without being able to define what change. If his lips could have been made much thicker, and his neck much thinner, they would have found their want supplied.

But the great Obenreizer peculiarity was, that a certain nameless film would come over his eyes – apparently by the action of his own will – which would impenetrably veil, not only from those tellers of tales, but from his face at large, every expression save one of attention. It by no means followed that his attention should be wholly given to the person with whom he spoke, or even wholly bestowed on present sounds and objects. Rather, it was a comprehensive watchfulness of everything he had in his own mind, and everything that he knew to be, or suspected to be, in the minds of other men.

At this stage of the conversation, Mr Obenreizer's film came over him.

'The object of my present visit,' said Vendale, 'is, I need hardly say, to assure you of the friendliness of Wilding and Co., and of the goodness of your credit with us, and of our desire to be of service to you. We hope shortly to offer you our hospitality. Things are not quite in train with us yet, for my partner, Mr Wilding, is reorganising the domestic part of our establishment, and is interrupted by some private affairs. You don't know Mr Wilding, I believe?'

Mr Obenreizer did not.

'You must come together soon. He will be glad to have made your acquaintance, and I think I may predict that you will be glad to have made his. You have not been long-established in London, I suppose, Mr Obenreizer?'

'It is only now that I have undertaken this agency.'

'Mademoiselle your niece – is – not married?'

'Not married.'

George Vendale glanced about him, as if for any tokens of her.

'She had been in London?'

'She *is* in London.'

'When, and where, might I have the honour of recalling myself to her remembrance?'

Mr Obenreizer, discarding his film and touching his visitor's elbows as before, said lightly: 'Come up-stairs.'

Fluttered enough by the suddenness with which the interview he had sought was coming upon him after all, George Vendale followed upstairs. In a room over the chamber he had just quitted – a room also Swiss-appointed – a young lady sat near one of the three windows, working at an embroidery-frame; and an older lady sat with her face turned close to another white-tiled stove (though it was summer, and the stove was not lighted), cleaning gloves. The young lady wore an unusual quantity of fair bright hair, very prettily braided about a rather rounder white forehead than the average English type, and so her face might have been a shade – or say a light – rounder than the average English face, and her figure slightly rounder than the figure of the average English girl at nineteen. A remarkable indication of freedom and grace of limb, in her quiet attitude, and a wonderful purity and freshness of colour in her dimpled face and bright grey eyes, seemed fraught with mountain air. Switzerland too, though the general fashion of her dress was English, peeped out of the fanciful bodice she wore, and lurked in the curious clocked red stocking, and its little silver-buckled shoe. As to the elder lady, sitting with her feet apart upon the lower brass ledge of the stove, supporting a lap-full of gloves while she cleaned one stretched on her left hand, she was a true Swiss impersonation of another kind; from the breadth of her cushion-like back, and the ponderosity of her respectable legs (if the word be admissible), to the black velvet band tied tightly round her throat for the repression of a rising tendency to *goitre;* or, higher still, to her great copper-coloured gold ear-rings; or, higher still, to her head-dress of black gauze stretched on wire.

'Miss Marguerite,' said Obenreizer to the young lady, 'do you recollect this gentleman?'

'I think,' she answered, rising from her seat, surprised and a little confused: 'it is Mr Vendale?'

'I think it is,' said Obenreizer dryly. 'Permit me, Mr Vendale. Madame Dor.'

The elder lady by the stove, with the glove stretched on her left hand, like a glover's sign, half got up, half looked over her broad shoulder, and wholly plumped down again and rubbed away.

'Madame Dor,' said Obenreizer, smiling, 'is so kind as to keep me from the stain or tear. Madame Dor humours my weakness for being always neat, and devotes her time to removing every one of my specks and spots.'

Madame Dor, with the stretched glove in the air, and her eyes closely scrutinising its palm, discovered a tough spot in Mr Obenreizer at that instant, and rubbed hard at him. George Vendale took his seat by the embroidery-frame (having first taken the fair right hand that his entrance had checked), and glanced at the gold cross that dipped into the bodice, with something of the devotion of a pilgrim who had reached his shrine at last. Obenreizer stood in the middle of the room with his thumbs in his waistcoat-pockets, and became filmy.

'He was saying down-stairs, Miss Obenreizer,' observed Vendale, 'that the world is so small a place, that people cannot escape one another. I have found it much too large for me since I saw you last.'

'Have you travelled so far, then?' she inquired.

'Not so far, for I have only gone back to Switzerland each year; but I could have wished – and indeed I have wished very often – that the little world did not afford such opportunities for long escapes as it does. If it had been less, I might have found my fellow-travellers sooner, you know.'

The pretty Marguerite coloured, and very slightly glanced in the direction of Madame Dor.

'You find us at length, Mr Vendale. Perhaps you may lose us again.'

'I trust not. The curious coincidence that has enabled me to find you, encourages me to hope not.'

'What is that coincidence, sir, if you please?' A dainty little native touch in this turn of speech, and in its tone made it perfectly captivating, thought George Vendale, when again he noticed an instantaneous glance towards Madame Dor. A caution seemed to be conveyed in it, rapid flash though it was; so he quietly took heed of Madame Dor from that time forth.

'It is that I happen to have become a partner in a House of business in London, to which Mr Obenreizer happens this very day to be expressly recommended: and that, too, by another house of business in Switzerland, in which (as it turns out) we both have a commercial interest. He has not told you?'

'Ah!' cried Obenreizer, striking in, film-less. 'No. I had not told Miss Marguerite. The world is so small and so monotonous that a surprise is worth having in such a litle jog-trot place. It is as he tells you, Miss Marguerite. He, of so fine a family, and so proudly bred, has condescended to trade. To trade! Like us poor peasants who have risen from ditches!'

A cloud crept over the fair brow, and she cast down her eyes.

'Why, it is good for trade!' pursued Obenreizer, enthusiastically. 'It ennobles trade! It is the misfortune of trade, it is its vulgarity, that any low people – for example, we poor peasants – may take to it and climb by it. See you, my dear Vendale!' He spoke with great energy. 'The father of Miss Marguerite, my eldest half-brother, more than two times your age or mine, if living now, wandered without shoes, almost without rags, from that wretched Pass – wandered – wandered – got to be fed with the mules and dogs at an Inn in the main valley far away – got to be Boy there – got to be Ostler – got to be Waiter – got to be Cook – got to be Landlord. As Landlord, he took me (could he take the idiot beggar his brother, or the spinning monstrosity his sister?) to put as pupil to the famous watchmaker, his neighbour and friend. His wife dies when Miss Marguerite is born. What is his will, and what are his words, to me, when *he* dies, she being between girl and woman? "All for Marguerite, except so much by the year for you. You are young, but I make her your ward, for you were of the obscurest and the poorest peasantry, and so was I, and so was her mother; we were abject peasants all, and you will remember it." The thing is equally true of most of my countrymen, now in trade in this your London quarter of Soho. Peasants once; low-born drudging Swiss peasants. Then how good and great for trade:' here, from having been warm, he became playfully jubilant, and touched the young wine-merchant's elbows again with light embrace: 'to be exalted by gentlemen!'

'I do not think so,' said Marguerite, with a flushed cheek, and a look away from the visitor, that was almost defiant. 'I think it is as much exalted by us peasants.'

'Fie, fie, Miss Marguerite,' said Obenreizer. 'You speak in proud England.'

'I speak in proud earnest,' she answered, quietly resuming her work, 'and I am not English, but a Swiss peasant's daughter.'

There was a dismissal of the subject in her words, which Vendale could not contend against. He only said in an earnest manner, 'I most heartily agree with you, Miss Obenreizer, and I have already said so, as Mr Obenreizer will bear witness,' which he by no means did, 'in this house.'

Now, Vendale's eyes were quick eyes, and sharply watching Madame Dor by times, noted something in the broad back view of that lady. There was considerable panto-mimic expression in her glove-cleaning. It had been very softly done when he spoke with Marguerite, or it had altogether stopped, like the action of a listener. When Oben-reizer's peasant-speech came to an end, she rubbed most vigorously, as if applauding it. And once or twice as the glove (which she always held before her, a little above her face) turned in the air, or as this finger went down, or that went up, he even fancied that it made some telegraphic communication to Obenreizer: whose back was certainly never turned upon it, though he did not seem at all to heed it.

Vendale observed, to, that in Marguerite's dismissal of the subject twice forced upon him to his misrepresentation, there was an indignant treatment of her guardian which she tried to check: as though she would have flamed out against him, but for the influence of fear. He also observed – though this was not much – that he never advanced within the distance of her at which he first placed himself: as though there were limits fixed between them. Neither had be ever spoken of her without the prefix 'Miss', though whenever he uttered it, it was with the faintest trace of an air of mockery. And now it occurred to Vendale for the first time that something curious in the man which he had never before been able to define, was definable as a certain subtle essence of mockery that eluded touch or analysis. He felt convinced that Marguerite was in some sort of prisoner as to her free will – though she held her own against those two combined, by the force of her character, which was nevertheless inadequate to her release. To feel convinced of this, was not to feel less disposed to love her than he had always been. In a word, he was desperately in love with her, and thoroughly determined to pursue the opportunity which had opened at last.

For the present, he merely touched upon the pleasure that Wilding and Co. would soon have in entreating Miss Obenreizer to honour their establishemnt with her presence – a curious old place, though a bachelor house withal – and so did not protract his visit beyond such a visit's ordinary length. Going down stairs, conducted by his host, he found the Obenreizer counting-house at the back of the entrance-hall, and several shabby men in outlandish garments, hanging about, whom Obenreizer put aside that he might pass, with a few words in *patois*.

'Countrymen,' he explained, as he attended Vendale to the door. 'Poor compatriots. Grateful and attached like dogs! Good-bye. To meet again. So glad!'

Two more light touches on his elbows dismissed him into the street.

Sweet Marguerite at her frame and Madame Dor's broad back at her telegraph, floated before him to Cripple Corner. On his arrival there, Wilding was closeted with Bintrey. The cellar doors happening to be open, Vendale lighted a candle in a cleft stick, and went down for a cellarous stroll. Graceful Marguerite floated before him faithfully, but Madame Dor's broad back remained outside.

The vaults were very spacious, and very old. There had been a stone crypt down there, when bygones were not bygones; some said, part of a monkish refectory; some said, of a chapel; some said of a Pagan temple. It was all one now. Let who would, make what he liked of a crumbled pillar and a broken arch or so. Old Time had made what *he* liked of it, and was quite indifferent to contradiction.

The close air, the musty smell, and the thunderous rumbling in the streets above, as being out of the routine of ordinary life, went well enough with the picture of pretty Marguerite holding her own against those two. So Vendale went on until, at a turning in the vaults, he saw a light like the light he carried.

'Oh! You are here, are you, Joey?'

'Oughtn't it rather to go, "Oh! *You're* here, and you Master George?" For it's my business to be here. But it ain't yourn.'

'Don't grumble, Joey.'

'Oh *I* don't grumble,' returned the Cellarman. 'If anything grumbles, it's what I've took in through the pores; it ain't me. Have a care as something in *you* don't begin a-grumbling, Master George. Stop here long enough for the wapours to work, and they'll be at it.'

His present occupation consisted of poking his head into the bins, making measurements and mental calculations, and entering them in a rhinoceros-hide-looking note-book, like a piece of himself.

'They'll be at it,' he resumed, laying the wooden rod that he measured with, across two casks, entering his last calculation, and straightening his back, 'trust 'em! And so you've regularly come into the business, Master George?'

'Regularly. I hope you don't object, Joey?'

'*I* don't, bless you. But Wapours objects that you're too young. You're both on you too young.'

'We shall get over that objection day by day, Joey.'

'Aye, Master George; but I shall day by day get over the objection that I'm too old, and so I shan't be capable of seeing much improvement in you.'

The retort so tickled Joey Ladle that he grunted forth a laugh and delivered it again, grunting forth another laugh after the second edition of 'improvement in you'.

'But what's no laughing matter, Master George,' he resumed, straightening his back once more, 'is, that Young Master Wilding has gone and changed the luck. Mark my words. He has changed the luck, and he'll find it out. *I* ain't been down here all my life for nothing! *I* know by what I notices down here, when it's a-going to rain, when it's a-going to hold up, when it's a-going to blow, when it's a-going to be calm. *I* know, by what I notices down here, when the luck's changed, quite as well.'

'Has this growth on the roof anything to do with your divination?' asked Vendale, holding his light towards a gloomy ragged growth of dark fungus, pendent from the arches with a very disagreeable and repellent effect. 'We are famous for this growth in this vault, aren't we?'

'We are, Master George,' replied Joey Ladle, moving a step or two away, 'and if you'll be advised by me, you'll let it alone.'

Taking up the rod just now laid across the two casks, and faintly moving the languid fungus with it, Vendale asked, 'Aye, indeed? Why so?'

'Why, not so much because it rises from the casks of wine, and may leave you to judge what sort of stuff a Cellarman takes into himself when he walks in the same all the days of his life, nor yet so much because at a stage of its growth it's maggots, and you'll fetch 'em down upon you,' returned Joey Ladle, still keeping away, 'as for another reason, Master George.'

'What other reason?'

'(I wouldn't keep on touchin' it, if I was you, sir.) I'll tell you if you'll come out of the place. First, take a look at its colour, Master Goerge.'

'I am doing so.'

'Done, sir. Now, come out of the place.'

He moved away with his light, and Vendale followed with his. When Vendale came up with him, and they were going back together, Vendale, eyeing him as they walked through the arches, said: 'Well, Joey? The colour.'

'It is like clotted blood, Master George?'

'Like enough, perhaps.'

'More than enough, I think,' muttered Joey Ladle, shaking his head solemnly.

'Well, say it is like; say it is exactly like. What then.?'

'Master George, they do say—'

'Who?'

'How should I know who?' rejoined the Cellarman, apparently much exasperated by the unreasonable nature of the question. 'Them! Them as says pretty well everything, you know. How should I know who They are, if you don't?'

'True. Go on.'

'They do say that the man that gets by any accident a piecē of that dark growth right upon his breast, will, for sure and certain, die by Murder.'

As Vendale laughingly stopped to meet the Cellarman's eyes, which he had fastened on his light while dreamily saying those words, he suddenly became conscious of being struck upon his own breast by a heavy hand. Instantly following with his eyes the action of the hand that struck him – which was his companion's – he saw that it had beaten off his breast a web or clot of the fungus, even then floating to the ground.

For a moment he turned upon the cellarman almost as scared a look as the cellarman turned upon him. But in another moment they had reached the daylight at the foot of the cellar-steps, and before he cheerfully sprang up them, he blew out his candle and the superstition together.

Exit Wilding

On the morning of the next day, Wilding went out alone, after leaving a message with his clerk. 'If Mr Vendale should ask for me,' he said, 'or if Mr Bintrey should call, tell them I am gone to the Foundling.' All that his partner had said to him, all that his lawyer, following on the same side, could urge, had left him persisting unshaken in his own point of view. To find the lost man, whose place he had usurped, was now the para-mount interest of his life, and to inquire at the Foundling was plainly to take the first step in the direction of discovery. To the Foundling, accordingly, the wine-merchant now went.

The once-familiar aspect of the building was altered to him, as the look of the portrait over the chimney-piece was altered to him. His one dearest association with the place which had sheltered his childhood had been broken away from it for ever. A strange reluctance possessed him, when he stated his business at the door. His heart ached as he sat alone in the waiting-room while the Treasurer of the institution was being sent for to see him. When the interview began, it was only by a painful effort that he could compose himself sufficiently to mention the nature of his errand.

The Treasurer listened with a face which promised all needful attention, and promised nothing more.

'We are obliged to be cautious,' he said, when it came to his turn to speak, 'about all inquiries which are made by strangers.'

'You can hardly consider me a stranger,' answered Wilding, simply. 'I was one of your poor lost children here, in the bygone time.'

The Treasurer politely rejoined that this circumstance inspired him with a special interest in his visitor. But he pressed, nevertheless, for that visitor's motive in making his inquiry. Without further preface, Wilding told him his motive, suppressing nothing.

The Treasurer rose, and led the way into the room in which the registers of the institution were kept. 'All the information which our books can give is heartily at your service,' he said. 'After the time that has elapsed, I am afraid it is the only information we have to offer you.'

The books were consulted, and the entry was found, expressed as follows:

'3rd March 1836. Adopted, and removed from the Foundling Hospital, a male infant, named Walter Wilding. Name and condition of the person adopting the child – Mrs Jane Ann Miller, widow. Address – Lime-Tree Lodge, Groombridge Wells. References – the Reverend John Harker, Groombridge Wells; and Messrs. Giles, Jeremie, and Giles, bankers, Lombard-street.'

'Is that all?' asked the wine-merchant. 'Had you no after-communication with Mrs Miller?'

'None – or some reference to it must have appeared in this book.'

'May I take a copy of the entry?'

'Certainly! You are a little agitated. Let me make the copy for you.'

'My only chance, I suppose,' said Wilding, looking sadly at the copy, 'is to inquire at Mrs Miller's residence, and to try if her references can help me?'

'That is the only chance I see at present,' answered the

Treasurer. 'I heartily wish I could have been of some further assistance to you.'

With those farewell words to comfort him, Wilding set forth on the journey of investigation which began from the Foundling doors. The first stage to make for, was plainly the house of business of the bankers in Lombard-street. Two of the partners in the firm were inaccessible to chance-visitors when he asked for them. The third, after raising certain inevitable difficulties, consented to let a clerk examine the Ledger marked with the initial letter 'M.' The account of Mrs Miller, widow, of Groombridge Wells, was found. Two long lines, in faded ink, were drawn across it; and at the bottom of the page there appeared this note: 'Account closed, September 30th, 1837.'

So the first stage of the journey was reached – and so it ended in No Thoroughfare! After sending a note to Cripple Corner to inform his partner that his absence might be prolonged for some hours, Wilding took his place in the train, and stated for the second stage on the journey – Mrs Miller's residence at Groombridge Wells.

Mothers and children travelled with him; mothers and children met each other at the station; mothers and children were in the shops when he entered them to inquire for Lime-Tree Lodge. Everywhere the nearest and dearest of human relations showed itself happily in the happy light of day. Everywhere, he was reminded of the treasured delusion from which he had been awakened so cruelly – of the lost memory which had passed from him like a reflection from a glass.

Inquiring here, inquiring there, he could hear of no such place as Lime-Tree Lodge. Passing a house-agent's office, he went in wearily, and put the question for the last time. The house-agent pointed across the street to a dreary mansion of many windows, which might have been a manufactory, but which was an hotel. 'That's where Lime-Tree Lodge stood; sir,' said the man, 'ten years ago.'

The second stage reached, and No Thoroughfare again!

But one chance was left. The clerical reference, Mr Harker, still remained to be found. Customers coming in at the moment to occupy the house-agent's attention, Wilding went down the street, and, entering a bookseller's shop, asked if he could be informed of the Reverend John Harker's present address.

The bookseller looked unaffectedly shocked and astonished, and made no answer.

Wilding repeated his question.

The bookseller took up from his counter a prim little volume in a binding of sober grey. He handed it to his visitor, open at the title page. Wilding read:

'The martyrdom of the Reverend John Harker in New Zealand. Related by a former member of his flock.'

Wilding put the book down on the counter. 'I beg your pardon,' he said, thinking a little perhaps, of his own present martyrdom while he spoke. The silent bookseller acknowledged the apology by a bow. Wilding went out.

Third and last stage, and No Thoroughfare for the third and last time.

There was nothing more to be done; there was absolutely no choice but to go back to London, defeated at all points. From time to time on the return journey, the wine-merchant looked at his copy of the entry in the Foundling Register. There is one among the many forms of despair – perhaps the most pitiable of all – which persists in disguising itself as Hope. Wilding checked himself in the act of throwing the useless morsel of paper out of the carriage window. 'It may lead to something yet,' he thought. 'While I live, I won't part with it. When I die, my executors shall find it sealed up with my will.'

Now, the mention of his will set the good wine-merchant on a new track of thought, without diverting his mind from its engrossing subject. He must make his will immediately.

The application of the phrase No Thoroughfare to the case had originated with Mr Bintrey. In their first long conference following the discovery, that sagacious personage had a hundred times repeated, with an obstructive shake of the head, 'No Thoroughfare, Sir, No Thoroughfare. My belief is that there is no way out of this at this time of day, and my advice is, make yourself comfortable where you are.'

In the course of the protracted consultation, a magnum of the forty-five-year-old port wine had been produced for the

wetting of Mr Bintrey's legal whistle; but the more clearly he
saw his way through the wine, the more emphatically he did
not see his way through the case; repeating as often as he set
his glass down empty, 'Mr Wilding, No Thoroughfare. Rest
and be thankful.'

It is certain that the honest wine-merchant's anxiety to make
a will, originated in profound conscientiousness; though it is
possible (and quite consistent with his rectitude) that he may
unconsciously have derived some feeling of relief from the
prospect of delegating his own difficulty to two other men
who were to come after him. Be that as it may, he pursued his
new track of thought with great ardour, and lost no time in
begging George Vendale and Mr Bintrey to meet him in
Cripple Corner and share his confidence.

'Being all three assembled with closed doors,' said Mr
Bintrey, addressing the new partner on the occasion, 'I wish to
observe, before our friend (and my client) entrusts us with his
further views, that I have endorsed what I understand from
him to have been your advice, Mr Vendale, and what would
be the advice of every sensible man. I have told him that he
positively must keep his secret. I have spoken with Mrs
Goldstraw, both in his presence and in his absence; and if
anybody is to be trusted (which is a very large IF), I think she is
to be trusted to that extent. I have pointed out to our friend
(and my client), that to set on foot random inquiries would
not only be to raise the Devil, in the likeness of all the
swindlers in the Kingdom, but would also be to waste the
estate. Now you see, Mr Vendale, our friend (and my client)
does not desire to waste the estate, but on the contrary, desires
to husband it for what he considers – but I can't say I do – the
righful owner, if such rightful owner should ever be found. I
am very much mistaken if he ever will be, but never mind
that. Mr Wilding and I are, at least, agreed that the estate is not
to be wasted. Now, I have yielded to Mr Wilding's desire to
keep an advertisement at intervals flowing through the newspapers, cautiously inviting any person who may know anything about that adopted infant, taken from the Foundling
Hospital, to come to my office; and I have pledged myself that
such advertisement shall regularly appear. I have gathered
from our friend (and my client) that I meet you here today to

take his instructions, not to give him advice. I am prepared to
receive his instructions, and to respect his wishes; but you will
please observe that this does not imply my approval of either
as a matter of professional opinion.'

Thus Mr Bintrey; talking quite as much *at* Wilding as *to*
Vendale. And yet, in spite of his care for his client, he was so
amused by his client's Quixotic conduct, as to eye him from
time to time with twinkling eyes, in the light of a highly
comical curiosity.

'Nothing,' observed Wilding, 'can be clearer. I only wish
my head were as clear as yours, Mr Bintrey.'

'If you feel that singing in it, coming on,' hinted the lawyer,
with an alarmed glance, 'put it off. – I mean the interview.'

'Not at all, I thank you,' said Wilding. 'What was I going
to—'

'Don't excite yourself, Mr Wilding,' urged the lawyer.

'No; I *wasn't* going to,' said the wine-merchant. 'Mr
Bintrey and George Vendale, would you have any hesitation
or objection to become my joint trustees and executors, or can
you at once consent?'

'*I* consent,' replied George Vendale, readily.

'*I* consent,' said Bintrey, not so readily.

'Thank you both. Mr Bintrey, my instructions for my last
will and testament are short and plain. Perhaps you will now
have the goodness to take them down. I leave the whole of my
real and personal estate, without any exception or reservation
whatsoever, to you two, my joint trustees and executors, in
trust to pay over the whole to the true Walter Wilding, if he
shall be found and identified within two years of my death.
Failing that, in trust to you two to pay over the whole as a
benefaction and legacy to the Foundling Hospital.'

'Those are all your instructions, are they, Mr Wilding?'
demanded Bintrey, after a blank silence, during which nobody
had looked at anybody.

'The whole.'

'And as to those instructions, you have absolutely made up
your mind, Mr Wilding?'

'Absolutely, decidedly, finally.'

'It only remains,' said the lawyer, with one shrug of his
shoulders, 'to get them into technical and binding form, and

to execute and attest. Now does that press? Is there any hurry about it? You are not going to die yet, sir.'

'Mr Bintrey,' answered Wilding, gravely, 'when I am going to die is within other knowledge than yours or mine. I shall be glad to have this matter off my mind, if you please.'

'We are lawyer and client again,' rejoined Bintrey, who, for the nonce, had become almost sympathetic. 'If this day week – here, at the same hour – will suit Mr Vendale and yourself, I will enter in my Diary that I attend you accordingly.'

The appointment was made, and in due sequence kept. This will was formally signed, sealed, delivered, and witnessed, and was carried off by Mr Bintrey for safe storage among the papers of his clients, ranged in their respective iron boxes, with their respective owners' names outside, on iron tiers in his consulting-room, as if that legal sanctuary were a condensed Family Vault of Clients.

With more heart than he had lately had for former subjects of interest, Wilding then set about completing his patriarchal establishment, being much assisted not only by Mrs Goldstraw but by Vendale too: who, perhaps, had in his mind the giving of an Obenreizer dinner as soon as possible. Anyhow, the establishment being reported in sound working order, the Obenreizers, Guardian and Ward, were asked to dinner, and Madame Dor was included in the invitation. If Vendale had been over head and ears in love before – a phrase not to be taken as implying the faintest doubt about it – this dinner plunged him down in love ten thousand fathoms deep. Yet for the life of him, he could not get one word alone with charming Marguerite. So surely as a blessed moment seemed to come, Obenreizer, in his filmy state, would stand at Vendale's elbow, or the broad back of Madame Dor would appear before his eyes. That speechless matron was never seen in a front view, from the moment of her arrival to that of her departure – except at dinner. And from the instant of her retirement to the drawing-room, after a hearty participation in that meal, she turned her face to the wall again.

Yet, through four or five delightful though distracting hours, Marguerite was to be seen, Marguerite was to be heard. Marguerite was to be occasionally touched. When they made the round of the old dark cellars, Vendale led her by the hand;

when she sang to him in the lighted room at night, Vendale, standing by her, held her relinquished gloves, and would have bartered against them every drop of the forty-five year old, though it had been forty-five times forty-five years old, and its nett price forty-five times forty-five pounds per dozen. And still, when she was gone, and a great gap of an extinguisher was clapped on Cripple Corner, he tormented himself by wondering, did she think that he admired her! Did she think that he adored her! Did she suspect that she had won him, heart and soul! Did she care to think at all about it! And so, Did she and Didn't she, up and down the gamut, and above the line and below the line, dear, dear! Poor restless heart of humanity! To think that the men who were mummies thousands of years ago, did the same, and ever found the secret how to be quiet after it!

'What do you think, George,' Wilding asked him next day, 'of Mr Obenreizer? (I won't ask you what you think of Miss Obenreizer).'

'I don't know,' said Vendale, 'and I never did know, what to think of him.'

'He is well informed and clever,' said Wilding.

'Certainly clever.'

'A good musician.' (He had played very well, and sung very well, overnight.)

'Unquestionably a good musician.'

'And talks well.'

'Yes,' said George Vendale, ruminating, 'and talks well. Do you know, Wilding, it oddly occurs to me, as I think about him, that he doesn't keep silence well!'

'How do you mean? He is not obtrusively talkative.'

'No, and I don't mean that. But when he is silent, you can hardly help vaguely, though perhaps most unjustly, mistrusting him. Take people whom you know and like. Take any one you know and like.'

'Soon done, my good fellow,' said Wilding. 'I take you.'

'I didn't bargain for that, or foresee it,' returned Vendale, laughing. 'However, take me. Reflect for a moment. Is your approving knowledge of my interesting face, mainly founded (however various the momentary expressions it may include) on my face when I am silent?'

'I think it is,' said Wilding.

'I think so too. Now, you see, when Obenreizer speaks – in other words, when he is allowed to explain himself away – he comes out right enough; but when he has not the opportunity of explaining himself away, he comes out rather wrong. Therefore it is, that I say he does not keep silence well. And passing hastily in review such faces as I know, and don't trust, I am inclined to think, now I give my mind to it, that none of them keep silence well.'

This proposition in Physiognomy being new to Wilding, he was at first slow to admit it, until asking himself the question whether Mrs Goldstraw kept silence well, and remembering that her face in repose decidedly invited trustfulness, he was as glad as men usually are to believe what they desire to believe.

But, as he was very slow to regain his spirits or his health, his partner, as another means of setting him up – and perhaps also with contingent Obenreizer views – reminded him of those musical schemes of his in connexion with his family, and how a singing-class was to be formed in the house, and a choir in a neighbouring church. The class was established speedily, and, two or three of the people having already some musical knowledge, and singing tolerably, the Choir soon followed. The latter was led and chiefly taught, by Wilding himself: who had hopes of converting his dependents into so many Found-lings, in respect of their capacity to sing sacred choruses.

Now, the Obenreizers being skilled musicians it was easily brought to pass that they should be asked to join these musical unions. Guardian and Ward consenting, or Guardian consent-ing for both, it was necessarily brought to pass that Vendale's life became a life of absolute thraldom and enchantment. For, in the mouldy Christopher-Wren church on Sundays, with its dearly beloved brethren assembled and met together, five-and-twenty strong, was not that Her voice that shot like light into the darkest places, thrilling the walls and pillars as though they were pieces of his heart! What time, too Madame Dor in a corner of the high pew, turning her back upon everybody and everything, could not fail to be ritualistically right at some moment of the service; like the man whom the doctors recommended to get drunk once a month, and who, that he might not overlook it, got drunk every day.

But, even those seraphic Sundays were surpassed by the Wednesday concerts established for the patriarchal family. At those concerts she would sit down to the piano and sing them, in her own tongue, songs of her own land, songs calling from the mountain-tops to Vendale, 'Rise above the grovelling level country; come far away from the crowd; pursue me as I mount higher, higher, higher, melting into the azure distance; rise to my supremest height of all, and love me here!' Then would the pretty bodice, the clocked stocking, and the silver-buckled shoe be, like the broad forehead and the bright eyes, fraught with the spring of a very chamois, until the strain was over.

Not even over Vendale himself did these songs of hers cast a more potent spell than over Joey Ladle in his different way. Steadily refusing to muddle the harmony by taking any share in it, and evincing the supremest contempt for scales and such like rudiments of music – which, indeed, seldom captivate mere listeners – Joey did at first give up the whole business for a bad job, and the whole of the performers for a set of howling Dervishes. But, descrying traces of unmuddled harmony in a part-song one day, he gave his two under-cellarmen faint hopes of getting on towards something in course of time. An anthem of Handel's led to further encouragement from him: though he objected that that great musician must have been down in some of them foreign cellars pretty much, for to go and say the same thing so many times over; which, took it in how you might, he considered a certain sign of your having took it in somehow. On a third occasion, the public appearance of Mr Jarvis with a flute, and of an odd man with a violin, and the performance of a duet by the two, did so astonish him that, solely of his own impulse and motion, he became inspired with the words, 'Ann Koar!' repeatedly pronouncing them as if calling in a familiar manner for some lady who had distinguished herself in the orchestra. But this was his final testimony to the merits of his mates, for, the instrumental duet being performed at the first Wednesday concert, and being presently followed by the voice of Marguerite Obenreizer, he sat with his mouth wide open, entranced, until she had finished; when, rising in his place with much solemnity, and prefacing what he was about to say with a bow that specially included Mr Wilding in it, he delivered himself of the gratifying sentiment: 'Arter that, ye may all on ye get to bed!' And ever afterwards declined to render homage in any other words to the musical powers of the family.

Thus began a separate personal acquaintance between Marguerite Obenreizer and Joey Ladle. She laughed so heartily at his compliment, and yet so abashed by it, that Joey made bold to say to her, after the concert was over, he hoped he wasn't so muddled in his head as to have took a liberty? She made him a gracious reply, and Joey ducked in return.

'You'll change the luck time about, Miss,' said Joey, ducking again. 'It's such as you in the place that can bring round the luck of the place.'

'Can I? Round the luck?' she answered, in her pretty English, and with a pretty wonder. 'I fear I do not understand. I am so stupid.'

'Young Master Wilding, Miss,' Joey explained confidentially, though not much to her enlightenment, 'changed the luck, afore he took in young Master George. So I say, and so, they'll find. Lord! Only come into the place and sing over the luck a few times, Miss, and it won't be able to help itself!'

With this, and with a whole brood of ducks, Joey backed out of the presence. But Joey being a privileged person, and even an involuntary conquest being pleasant to youth and beauty, Marguerite merrily looked out for him next time.

'Where is my Mr Joey, please' she asked of Vendale.

So Joey was produced and shaken hands with, and that became an Institution.

Another Institution arose in this wise. Joey was a little hard of hearing. He himself said it was 'Wapours,' and perhaps it might have been; but whatever the cause of the effect, there the effect was, upon him. On this first occasion he had been seen to sidle along the wall, with his left hand to his left ear, until he had sidled himself into a seat pretty near the singer, in which place and position he had remained, until addressing to his friends the amateurs the compliment before mentioned. It was observed on the following Wednesday that Joey's action as a Pecking Machine was impaired at dinner, and it was rumoured about the table that this was explainable by his high-strung expectations of Miss Obenreizer's singing, and his fears of not getting a place where he could hear every note and syllable. The rumour reaching Wilding's ears, he in his good nature called Joey to the front at night before Marguerite began. Thus the Institution came into being that on succeeding nights, Marguerite, running her hands over the keys before singing, always said to Vendale, 'Where is my Mr Joey, please?' and that Vendale always brought him forth, and stationed him near by. That he should then, when all eyes were upon him, express in his face the utmost contempt for the exertions of his friends and confidence in Marguerite alone, whom he would stand contemplating, not unlike the rhinoceros out of the spelling-book, tamed and on his hind legs, was a part of the Institution. Also that when he remained after the singing in his most ecstatic state, some bold spirit from the back should say, 'What do you think of it, Joey?' and he should be goaded to reply, as having that instant conceived the retort, 'Arter that ye may all on ye get to bed!' These were other parts of the Institution.

But, the simple pleasures and small jests of Cripple Corner were not destined to have a long life. Underlying them from the first was a serious matter, which every member of the patriarchal family knew of, but which, by tacit agreement, all forbore to speak of. Mr Wilding's health was in a bad way.

He might have overcome the shock he had sustained in the one great affection of his life, or he might have overcome his consciousness of being in the enjoyment of another man's property; but the two together were too much for him. A man haunted by twin ghosts, he became deeply depressed. The inseparable spectres sat at the board with him, ate from his platter, drank from his cup, and stood by his bedside at night. When he recalled his supposed mother's love, he felt as though he had stolen it. When he rallied a litle under the respect and attachment of his dependents, he felt as though he were even fraudulent in making them happy, for that should have been the unknown man's duty and gratification.

Gradually, under the pressure of his brooding mind, his body stooped, his step lost its elasticity, his eyes were seldom lifted from the ground. He knew he could not help the deplorable mistake that had been made, but he knew he could not mend it; for the days and weeks went by, and no one claimed his name of his possessions. And now there began to creep over him, a cloudy consciousness of often-recurring confusion in his head. He would unaccountably lose, sometimes whole hours, sometimes a whole day and night. Once, his rembrance stopped as he sat at the head of the dinner-table, and was blank until daybreak. Another time, it stopped as he was beating time to their singing, and went on again when he and his partner were walking in the courtyard by the light of the moon, half the night later. He asked Vendale (always full of consideration, work, and help) how this was? Vendale only replied, 'You have not been quite well; that's all.' He looked for explanation into the faces of his people. But they would put if off with, 'Glad to see you looking so much better, sir;' or 'Hope you're doing nicely now, sir;' in which was no information at all.

At length, when the partnership was but five months old, Walter Wilding took to his bed, and his housekeeper became his nurse.

'Lying here, perhaps you will not mind my calling you Sally, Mrs Goldstraw?' said the poor wine-merchant.

'It sounds more natural to me, sir, than any other name, and I like it better.'

'Thank you, Sally. I think, Sally, I must of late have been subject to fits. Is that so, Sally? Don't mind telling me now.'

'It has happened, sir.'

'Ah! that is the explanation!' he quietly remarked. 'Mr Obenreizer, Sally, talks of the world being so small that it is not strange how often the same people come together, and come together, at various places, and in various stages of life. But it does seem strange, Sally, that I should, as I may say, come round to the Foundling to die.'

He extended his hand to her, and she gently took it.

'You are not going to die, dear Mr Wilding.'

'So Mr Bintrey said, but I think he was wrong. That old child-feeling is coming back upon me, Sally. The old hush and rest, as I used to fall asleep.'

After an interval he said, in a placid voice, 'Please kiss me, Nurse,' and, it was evident, believed himself to be lying in the old Dormitory.

As she had been used to bend over the fatherless and

motherless children, Sally bent over the fatherless and motherless man, and put her lips to his forehead, murmuring: 'God bless you!'

'God bless you!' he replied, in the same tone.

After another interval, he opened his eyes in his own character, and said. 'Don't move me, Sally, because of what I am going to say; I lie quite easily. I think my time is come. I don't know how it may appear to you, Sally, but—'

Insensibility fell upon him for a few minutes; he emerged from it once more.

'– I don't know how it may appear to you, Sally, but so it appears to me.'

When he had thus conscientiously finished his favourite sentence, his time came, and he died.

Act II

Vendale Makes Love

The summer and autumn had passed. Christmas and the New Year were at hand.

As executors honestly bent on performing their duty towards the dead, Vendale and Bintrey had held more than one anxious consultation on the subject of Wilding's will. The lawyer had declared, from the first, that it was simply impossible to take any useful action in the matter at all. The only obvious inquiries to make, in relation to the lost man, had been made already by Wilding himself; with this result, that time and death together had not left a trace of him discoverable. To advertise for the claimant to the property, it would be necessary to mention particulars – a course of proceeding which would invite half the impostors in England to present themselves in the character of the true Walter Wilding. 'If we find a chance of tracing the lost man, we will take it. If we don't, let us meet for another consultation on the first anniversary of Wilding's death.' So Bintrey advised. And so, with the most earnest desire to fulfil his dead friend's wishes, Vendale was fain to let the matter rest for the present.

Turning from his interest in the past to his interest in the future, Vendale still found himself confronting a doubtful prospect. Months on months had passed since his first visit to Soho-square – and through all that time, the one language in which he had told Marguerite that he loved her was the language of the eyes, assisted, at convenient opportunities, by the language of the hand.

What was the obstacle in his way? The one immovable obstacle which had been in his way from the first. No matter how fairly the opportunities looked, Vendale's efforts to speak with Marguerite alone, ended invariably in one and the same

55

result. Under the most accidental circumstances, in the most innocent manner possible, Obenreizer was always in the way.

With the last days of the old year came an unexpected chance of spending an evening with Marguerite, which Vendale resolved should be a chance of speaking privately to her as well. A cordial note from Obenreizer invited him, on New Year's Day, to a litle family dinner in Soho-square. 'We shall be only four,' the note said. 'We shall be only two,' Vendale determined, 'before the evening is out!'

New Year's Day, among the English, is associated with the giving and receiving of dinners, and with nothing more. New Year's Day, among the foreigners, is the grand opportunity of the year for the giving and receiving of presents. It is occasionally possible to acclimatise a foreign custom. In this instance Vendale felt no hesitation about making the attempt. His one difficulty was to decide what his New Year's gift to Marguerite should be. The defensive pride of the peasant's daughter – morbidly sensitive to the inequality between her social position and his – would be secretly roused against him if he ventured on a rich offering. A gift, which a poor man's purse might purchase, was the one gift that could be trusted to find its way to her heart, for the giver's sake. Stoutly resisting temptation, in the form of diamonds and rubies, Vendale bought a brooch of the filigree-work of Genoa – the simplest and most unpretending ornament that he could find in the jeweller's shop.

He slipped his gift into Marguerite's hand as she held it out to welcome him on the day of the dinner.

'This is your first New Year's Day in England,' he said. 'Will you let me help to make it like a New Year's Day at home?'

She thanked him, a little constrainedly, as she looked at the jeweller's box, uncertain what it might contain. Opening the box, and discovering the studiously simple form under which Vendale's little keepsake offered itself to her, she penetrated his motive on the spot. Her face turned on him brightly, with a look which said, 'I own you have pleased and flattered me.' never had she been so charming, in Vendale's eyes, as she was at that moment. Her winter dress – a petticoat of dark silk, with a bodice of black velvet rising to her neck, and enclosing it so softly in a little circle of swansdown – heightened, by all the force of contrast, the dazzling fairness of her hair and her complexion. It was only when she turned aside from him to the glass, and, taking out the brooch that she wore, put his New Year's gift in its place, that Vendale's attention wandered far enough away from her to discover the presence of other persons in the room. He now became conscious that the hands of Obenreizer were affectionately in possession of his elbows. He now heard the voice of Obenreizer thanking him for his attention to Marguerite with the faintest possible ring of mockery in its tone. ('Such a simple present, dear sir! and showing such nice tact!') He now discovered, for the first time, that there was one other guest, and but one, besides himself, whom Obenreizer presented as a compatriot and friend. The friend's face was mouldy, and the friend's figure was fat. His age was suggestive of the autumnal period of human life. In the course of the evening he developed extraordinary capacities. One was a capacity for silence; the other was a capacity for emptying bottles.

Madame Dor was not in the room. Neither was there any visible place reserved for her when they sat down to table. Obenreizer explained that it was 'the good Dor's simple habit to dine always in the middle of the day. She would make her excuses later in the evening.' Vendale wondered whether the good Dor had, on this occasion, varied her domestic employment from cleaning Obenreizer's gloves to cooking Obenreizer's dinner. This at least was certain – the dishes served were, one and all, as achievements in cookery, high above the reach of the rude elementary art of England. The dinner was unobtrusively perfect. As for the wine, the eyes of the speechless friend rolled over it, as in solemn ecstasy. Sometimes he said 'Good!' when a bottle came in full; and sometimes he said 'Ah!' when a bottle went out empty – and there his contributions to the gaiety of the evening ended.

Silence is occasionally infectious. Oppressed by private anxieties of their own, Marguerite and Vendale appeared to feel the influence of the speechless friend. The whole responsibility of keeping the talk going rested on Obenreizer's shoulders, and manfully did Obenreizer sustain it. He opened his heart in the character of an enlightened foreigner, and sang the praises of England. When other topics ran dry, he returned to this inexhaustible source, and always set the stream running again as copiously as ever. Obenreizer would have given an arm, an eye, or a leg to have been born an Englishman. Out of England there was no such institution as a home, no such thing as a fireside, no such object as a beautiful woman. His dear Miss Marguerite would excuse him, if he accounted for *her* attractions on the theory that English blood must have mixed at some former time with their obscure and unknown ancestry. Survey this English nation, and behold a tall, clean, plump, and solid people! Look at their cities! What magnificence in their public buildings! What admirable order and propriety in their streets! Admire their laws, combining the eternal principle of justice with the other eternal principle of pounds, shillings, and pence; and applying the product to all civil injuries, from an injury to a man's honour, to an injury to a man's nose! You have ruined my daughter – pounds, shillings, and pence! You have knocked me down with a blow in my face – pounds, shillings, and pence! Where was the material prosperity of such a country as *that* to stop? Obenreizer, projecting himself into the future, failed to see the end of it. Obenreizer's enthusiasm entreated permission to exhale itself, English fashion, in a toast. Here is our modest little dinner over, here is our frugal dessert on the table, and here is the admirer of England conforming to national customs, and making a speech! A toast to your white cliffs of Albion, Mr Vendale! To your national virtues, your charming climate, and your fascinating women! To your Hearths, to your Homes, to your Habeas Corpus, and to all your other institutions! In one word – to England! Heep–heep–heep! Hooray!

Obenreizer's voice had barely chanted the last of the English cheer, the speechless friend had barely drained the last drop out of his glass, when the festive proceedings were interrupted by a modest tap at the door. A woman-servant came in, and approached her master with a little note in her hand. Obenreizer opened the note with a frown; and, after reading it with an expression of genuine annoyance, passed it on to his compatriot and friend. Vendale's spirits rose as he watched these proceedings. Had he found an ally in the annoying little note? Was the long-looked-for chance actually coming at last?

'I am afraid there is no help for it?' said Obenreizer, addressing his fellow-countryman. 'I am afraid we must go.'

The speechless friend handed back the letter, shrugged this heavy shoulders, and poured himself out a last glass of wine. His fat fingers lingered fondly round the neck of the bottle. They pressed it with a little amatory squeeze at parting. His globular eyes looked dimly, as through an intervening haze, at Vendale and Marguerite. His heavy articulation laboured, and brought forth a whole sentence at a birth. 'I think,' he said, 'I should have liked a little more wine.' His breath failed him after that effort; he gasped, and walked to the door.

Obenreizer addressed himself to Vendale with an appearance of the deepest distress.

'I am so shocked, so confused, so distressed,' he began. 'A misfortune has happened to one of my compatriots. He is alone, he is ignorant of your language – I and my good friend, here, have no choice but to go and help him. What can I say in my excuse? How can I describe my affliction at depriving myself in this way of the honour of your company?'

He paused, evidently expecting to see Vendale take up his hat and retire. Discerning his opportunity at last, Vendale determined to do nothing of the kind. He met Obenreizer dexterously, with Obenreizer's own weapons.

'Pray don't distress yourself,' he said. 'I'll wait here with the greatest pleasure till you come back.'

Marguerite blushed deeply, and turned away to her embroidery-frame in a corner by the window. The film showed itself in Obenreizer's eyes, and the smile came something sourly to Obenreizer's lips. To have told Vendale that there was no reasonable prospect of his coming back in good time would have been to risk offending a man whose favourable opinion was of solid commercial importance to him. Accepting his defeat with the best possible grace, he declared himself to be equally honoured and delighted by Vendale's proposal. 'So frank, so friendly, so English!' he bustled about, apparently looking for something he wanted, disappeared for a moment through the folding-doors communicating with the next room, came back with his hat and coat, and protesting that he would return at the earliest possible moment, embraced Vendale's elbows, and vanished from the scene in company with the speechless friend.

Vendale turned to the corner by the window, in which Marguerite had placed herself with her work. There, as if she had dropped from the ceiling, or come up through the floor – there, in the old attitude, with her face to the stove – sat an Obstacle that had not been foreseen, in the person of Madame Dor! She half got up, half looked over her broad shoulders at Vendale, and plumped down again. Was she at work? Yes. Cleaning Obenreizer's gloves, as before? No; darning Obenreizer's stockings.

The case was now desperate. Two serious considerations presented themselves to Vendale. Was it possible to put Madame Dor into the stove? The stove wouldn't hold her. Was it possible to treat Madame Dor, not as a living woman, but as an article of furniture? Could the mind be brought to contemplate this respectable matron purely in the light of a chest of drawers, with a black gauze head-dress accidentally left on the top of it? Yes, the mind could be brought to do that. With a comparatively trifling effort, Vendale's mind did it. As he took his place on the old-fashioned window-seat, close by Marguerite and her embroidery, a slight movement appeared in the chest of drawers, but no remark issued from it. Let is be remembered that solid furniture is not easy to move, and that it has this advantage in consequence – there is no fear of upsetting it.

Unusually silent and unusually constrained – with the bright colour fast fading from her face, with a feverish energy possessing her fingers – the pretty Marguerite bent over her embroidery, and worked as if her life depended on it. Hardly less agitated himself, Vendale felt the importance of leading her very gently to the avowal which he was eager to make – to the other sweeter avowal still, which he was longing to hear. A woman's love is never to be taken by storm; it yields insensibly to a system of gradual approach. It ventures by the roundabout way, and listens to the low voice. Vendale led her memory back to their past meetings when they were travelling together in Switzerland. They revived the impressions, they recalled the events, of the happy bygone time. Little by little, Marguerite's constraint vanished. She smiled, she was interested, she looked at Vendale, she grew idle with her needle, she made false stitches in her work. Their voices sank

lower and lower; their faces bent nearer and nearer to each
other as they spoke. And Madame Dor? Madame Dor
behaved like an angel. She never looked round; she never said
a word; she went on with Obenreizer's stockings. Pulling each
stocking up tight over her left arm, and holding that arm aloft
from time to time, to catch the light on her work, there were
moments, delicate and indescribable moments, when Madame
Dor appeared to be sitting upside down, and contemplating
one of her own respectable legs elevated in the air. As the
minutes wore on, these elevations followed each other at
longer and longer intervals. Now and again, the black gauze
head-dress nodded, dropped forward, recovered itself. A little
heap of stockings slid softly from Madame Dor's lap, and
remained unnoticed on the floor. A prodigious ball of worsted
followed the stockings, and rolled lazily under the table. The
black gauze head-dress nodded, dropped forward, recovered
itself, nodded again, dropped forward again, and recovered
itself no more. A composite sound, partly as of the purring of
an immense cat, partly as of the planing of a soft board, rose
over the hushed voices of the lovers, and hummed at regular
intervals through the room. Nature and Madame Dor had
combined together in Vendale's interests. The best of women
was asleep.

Marguerite rose to stop – not the snoring – let us say, the
audible repose of Madame Dor. Vendale laid his hand on her
arm, and pressed her back gently into her chair.

'Don't disturb her,' he whispered. 'I have been waiting to
tell you a secret. Let me tell it now.'

Marguerite resumed her seat. She tried to resume her
needle. It was useless; her eyes failed her; her hand failed her;
she could find nothing.

'We have been talking,' said Vendale, 'of the happy time
when we first met, and first travelled together. I have a
confession to make. I have been concealing something. When
we spoke of my first visit to Switzerland, I told you of all the
impressions I had brought back with me to England – except
one. Can you guess what that one is?'

Her eyes looked steadfastly at the embroidery, and her face
turned a little away from him. Signs of disturbance began to
appear in her neat velvet bodice, round the region of the

brooch. She made no reply. Vendale pressed the question without mercy.

'Can you guess what the one Swiss impression is, which I have not told you yet?'

Her face turned back towards him, and a faint smile trembled on her lips.

'An impression of the mountains, perhaps?' she said, slily.

'No; a much more precious impression than that.'

'Of the lakes?'

'No. The lakes have not grown dearer and dearer in remembrance to me every day. The lakes are not associated with my happiness in the present, and my hopes in the future. Marguerite! All that makes life worth having hangs, for me, on a word from your lips. Marguerite! I love you!'

Her head drooped, as he took her hand. He drew her to him, and looked at her. The tears escaped from her downcast eyes, and fell slowly over her cheeks.

'Oh, Mr Vendale,' she said, sadly, 'it would have been kinder to have kept your secret. Have you forgotten the distance between us?

'Marguerite – a distance of your making. My love, my darling, there is no higher rank in goodness, there is no higher rank in beauty, than yours! Come! Whisper the one little word which tells me you will be my wife!'

She sighed bitterly. 'Think of your family,' she murmured; 'and think of mine!'

Vendale drew her a little nearer to him.

'If you dwell on such an obstacle as that,' he said, 'I shall think but one thought – I shall think I have offended you.'

She started, and looked up. 'Oh, no!' she exclaimed, innocently. The instant the words passed her lips, she saw the constructon that might be placed on them. Her confession had escaped her in spite of herself. A lovely flush of colour overspread her face. She made a momentary effort to disengage herself from her lover's embrace. She looked up at him entreatingly. She tried to speak. The words died on her lips in the kiss that Vendale pressed on them. 'Let me go, Mr Vendale!' she said, faintly.

'Call me George.'

She laid her head on his bosom. All her heart went out to

him at last. 'George!' she whispered.

'Say you love me!'

Her arms twined themselves gently round his neck. Her lips, timidly touching his cheek, murmured the delicious words – 'I love you!'

In the moment of silence that followed, the sound of the opening and closing of the house-door came clear to them through the wintry stillness of the street.

Marguerite started to her feet.

'Let me go!' she said. 'He has come back!'

She hurried from the room, and touched Madame Dor's shoulder in passing. Madame Dor woke up with a loud snort, looked first over one shoulder and then over the other, peered down into her lap, and discovered neither stockings, worsted, nor darning-needle in it. At the same moment, footsteps became audible ascending the stairs. 'Mon Dieu!' said Madame Dor, addressing herself to the stove, and trembling violently. Vendale picked up the stockings and the ball, and huddled them all back in a heap over her shoulder. 'Mon Dieu!' said Madame Dor, for the second time, as the avalanche of worsted poured into her capacious lap.

The door opened, and Obenreizer came in. His first glance round the room showed him that Marguerite was absent.

'What!' he exclaimed, 'my niece is away? My niece is not here to entertain you in my absence? This is unpardonable. I shall bring her back instantly.'

Vendale stopped him.

'I beg you will not disturb Miss Obenreizer,' he said. 'You have returned, I see, without your friend?'

'My friend remains, and consoles our afflicted compatriot. A heart-rending scene, Mr Vendale. The household gods at the pawnbroker's braced in silence. My admirable friend alone possessed his composure. He sent out, on the spot, for a bottle wine.'

'Can I say a word to you in private, Mr Obenreizer?'

'Assuredly.' He turned to Madame Dor. 'My good creature, you are sinking for want of repose. Mr Vendale will excuse you.'

Madame Dor rose, and set forth sideways on her journey from the stove to bed. She dropped a stocking. Vendale picked it up for her, and opened one of the folding-doors. She advanced a step, and dropped three more stockings. Vendale, stooping to recover them as before, Obenreizer interfered with profuse apologies, and with a warning look at Madame Dor. Madame Dor acknowledged the look by dropping the whole of the stockings in a heap, and then shuffling away panic-stricken from the scene of disaster. Obenreizer swept up the complete collection fiercely in both hands. 'Go!' he cried, giving his prodigious handful a preparatory swing in the air. Madame Dor said, 'Mon Dieu,' and vanished into the next room, pursued by a shower of stockings.

'What must you think, Mr Vendale,' said Obenreizer, closing the door, 'of this deplorable intrusion of domestic details? For myself, I blush at it. We are beginning the New Year as badly as possible; everything has gone wrong to-night. Be seated, pray – and say, what I may offer you? Shall we pay our best respects to another of your noble English institutions? It is my study to be, what you call, jolly. I propose a grog.'

Vendale declined the grog with all needful respect for that noble institution.

'I wish to speak to you on a subject in which I am deeply interested,' he said. 'You must have observed, Mr Obenreizer, that I have, from the first, felt no ordinary admiration for your charming niece?'

'You are very good. In my niece's name, I thank you.'

'Perhaps you have noticed, latterly, that my admiration for Miss Obenreizer has grown into a tenderer and deeper feeling— ?'

'Shall we say friendship, Mr Vendale?'

'Say love – and we shall be nearer to the truth.'

Obenreizer started out of his chair. The faintly discernible beat, which was his nearest approach to a change of colour, showed itself suddenly in his cheeks.

'You are Miss Obenreizer's guardian,' pursued Vendale. 'I ask you to confer upon me the greatest of all favours – I ask you to give me her hand in marriage.'

Obenreizer dropped back into his chair. 'Mr Vendale,' he said, 'you petrify me.'

'I will wait,' rejoined Vendale, 'until you have recovered yourself.'

'One word before I recover myself. You have said nothing about this to my niece?'

'I have opened my whole heart to your niece, and I have reason to hope—'

'What!' interposed Obenreizer. 'You have made a proposal to my niece, without first asking for my authority to pay your addresses to her?' He struck his hand on the table, and lost his hold over himself for the first time in Vendale's experience of him. 'Sir!' he exclaimed indignantly, 'what sort of conduct is this? As a man of honour, speaking to a man of honour, how can you justify it?'

'I can only justify it as one of our English institutions,' said Vendale quietly. 'You admire our English institutions. I can honestly tell you, Mr Obenreizer, that I regret what I have done. I can only assure you that I have not acted in the matter with any intentional disrespect towards yourself. This said, may I ask you to tell me plainly what objection you see to favouring my suit?'

'I see this immense objection,' answered Obenreizer, 'that my niece and you are not on a social equality together. My niece is the daughter of a poor peasant; and you are the son of a gentleman. You do us an honour,' he added, lowering himself again gradually to his customary polite level, 'which deserves, and has, our most grateful acknowledgements. But the inequality is too glaring; the sacrifice is too great. You English are a proud people, Mr Vendale. I have observed enough of this country to see that such a marriage as you propose would be a scandal here. Not a hand would be held out to your peasant-wife; and all your best friends would desert you.'

'One moment,' said Vendale, interposing on his side. 'I may claim, without any great arrogance, to know more of my country-people in general, and of my own friends in particular, than you do. In the estimation of everybody whose opinion is worth having, my wife herself would be the one sufficient justification of my marriage. If I did not feel certain – observe, I say certain – that I am offering her a position which she can accept without so much as the shadow of humiliation – I would never (cost me what it might) have asked her to be my wife. Is there any other obstacle that you see? Have you any personal objection to me?'

Obenreizer spread out both his hands in courteous protest. 'Personal objection!' he exclaimed. 'Dear sir, the bare question is painful to me.'

'We are both men of business,' pursued Vendale, 'and you naturally expect me to satisfy you that I have the means of supporting a wife. I can explain my pecuniary position in two words. I inherit from my parents a fortune of twenty-thousand pounds. In half of that sum I have only a life-interest, to which, if I die leaving a widow, my widow succeeds. If I die, leaving children, the money itself is divided among them, as they come of age. The other half of my fortune is at my own disposal, and is invested in the wine-business. As it stands at present, I cannot state my return from my capital embarked at more than twelve hundred a year, and the yearly value of my life-interest – and the total reached a present annual income of fifteen hundred pounds. I have the fairest prospect of soon making it more. In the mean time, do you object to me on pecuniary grounds?'

Driven back to his last entrenchment, Obenreizer rose, and took a turn backwards and forwards in the room. For the moment, he was plainly at a loss what to say or do next.

'Before I answer that last question,' he said, after a little close consideration with himself, 'I beg leave to revert for a moment to Miss Marguerite. You said something just now which seemed to imply that she returns the sentiment with which you are pleased to regard her?'

'I have the inestimable happiness,' said Vendale, 'of knowing that she loves me.'

Obenreizer stood silent for a moment, with the film over his eyes, and the faintly perceptible beat becoming visible again in his cheeks.

'If you will excuse me for a few minutes,' he said with ceremonious politeness, 'I should like to have the opportunity of speaking to my niece.' With those words, he bowed, and quitted the room.

Left by himself, Vendale's thoughts (as a necessary result of the interview, thus far) turned instinctively to the consideration of Obenreizer's motives. He had put obstacles in the way of the courtship; he was now putting obstacles in the way of the marriage – a marriage offering advantages which even his ingenuity could not dispute. On the face of it, his conduct was incomprehensible. What did it mean?

Seeking, under the surface, for the answer to that question – and remembering that Obenreizer was a man of about his own age; also, that Marguerite was, strictly speaking, his half-niece only – Vendale asked himself, with a lover's ready jealousy, whether he had a rival to fear, as well as a guardian to conciliate. The thought just crossed his mind, and no more. The sense of Marguerite's kiss still lingering on his cheek reminded him gently that even the jealousy of a moment was now a treason to *her*.

On reflection, it seemed most likely that a personal motive of another kind might suggest the true explanation of Obenreizer's conduct. Marguerite's grace and beauty were precious ornaments in that little household. They gave it a special social attraction and a special social importance. They armed Obenreizer with a certain influence in reserve, which he could always depend upon to make his house attractive, and which he might always bring more or less to bear on the forwarding of his own private ends. Was he the sort of man to resign such advantages as were here implied, without obtaining the fullest possible compensation for the loss? A connexion by marriage with Vendale offered him solid advantages, beyond all doubt. But there were hundreds of men in London with far greater power and far wider influence than Vendale possessed. Was it possible that this man's ambition secretly looked higher than the highest prospects that could be offered to him by the alliance now proposed for his niece? As the question passed through Vendale's mind, the man himself reappeared – to answer it, or not to answer it, as the event might prove.

A marked change was visible in Obenreizer when he resumed his place. His manner was less assured, and there were plain traces about his mouth of recent agitation which had not been sucessfully composed. Had he said something, referring either to Vendale or to himself, which had roused Marguerite's spirit, and which had placed him, for the first time, face to face with a resolute assertion of his niece's will? It might or might not be. This only was certain – he looked like a man who had met with a repulse.

'I have spoken to my niece,' he began. 'I find, Mr Vendale, that even your influence has not entirely blinded her to the social objections to your proposal.'

'May I ask,' returned Vendale, 'if that is the only result of your interview with Miss Obenreizer?'

A momentary flash leapt out through the Obenreizer film.

'You are the master of the situation,' he answered, in a tone of sardonic submission. 'If you insist on my admitting it, I do admit it in those words. My niece's will and mine used to be one, Mr Vendale. You have come between us, and her will is now yours. In my country, we know when we are beaten, and we submit with our best grace. I submit, with my best grace, on certain conditions. Let us revert to the statement of your pecuniary position. I have an objection to you, my dear sir – a most amazing, a most audacious objection, from a man in my position to a man in yours.'

'What is it?'

'You have honoured me by making a proposal for my niece's hand. For the present (with best thanks and respects), I beg to decline it.'

'Why?'

'Because you are not rich enough.'

The objection, as the speaker had foreseen, took Vendale completely by surprise. For the moment he was speechless.

'Your income is fifteen hundred a year,' pursued Obenreizer. 'In my miserable country I should fall on my knees before your income, and say, "What a princely fortune!" In wealthy England, I sit as I am, and say, "A modest independence, dear sir; nothing more. Enough, perhaps, for a wife in your own rank of life, who has no social prejudices to conquer. Not more than half enough for a wife who is a meanly born foreigner, and who has all your social prejudices against her." Sir! If my niece is ever to marry you, she will have what you call uphill work of it in taking her place at starting. Yes, yes; this is not your view, but it remains, immovably remains, my view for all that. For my niece's sake, I claim that this uphill work shall be made as smooth as possible. Whatever material advantages she can have to help her, ought, in common justice, to be hers. Now, tell me, Mr Vendale, on your fifteen hundred a year can your wife have a house in a fashionable quarter, a footman to open her door, a butler to wait at her table, and a carriage and horses to drive about in? I see the answer in your face – your face says, No. Very good. Tell me one more thing, and I have done. Take the mass of your educated, accomplished, and lovely countrywomen, is it, or is it not, the fact that a lady who has a house in a fashionable quarter, a footman to open her door, a butler to wait at her table, and a carriage and horses to drive about in, is a lady who has gained four steps in female estimation, at starting? Yes? or No?'

'Come to the point,' said Vendale. 'You view this question as a question of terms. What are your terms?'

'The lowest terms, dear sir, on which you can provide your wife with those four steps at starting. Double your present income – the most rigid economy cannot do it in England on less. You said just now that you expected greatly to increase the value of your business. To work – and increase it! I am a good devil after all! On the day when you satisfy me, by plain proofs, that your income has risen to three thousand a year, ask me for my niece's hand, and it is yours.'

'May I inquire if you have mentioned this arrangement to Miss Obenreizer?'

'Certainly. She has a last little morsel of regard still left for me, Mr Vendale, which is not yours yet; and she accepts my terms. In other words, she submits to be guided by her guardian's regard for her welfare, and by her guardian's superior knowledge of the world.' He threw himself back in his chair, in firm reliance on his position, and in full possession of his excellent temper.

Any open assertion of his own interests, in the situation in which Vendale was now placed, seemed to be (for the present at least) hopeless. He found himself literally left with no ground to stand on. Whether Obenreizer's objections were the genuine product of Obenreizer's own view of the case, or whether he was simply delaying the marriage in the hope of ultimately breaking it off altogether – in either of these events, any present resistance on Vendale's part would be equally useless. There was no help for it but to yield, making the best terms that he could on his own side.

'I protest against the conditions you impose on me,' he began.

'Naturally,' said Obenreizer; 'I dare say I should protest, myself, in your place.'

'Say, however,' pursued Vendale, 'that I accept your terms. In that case, I must be permitted to make two stipulations on my part. In the first place I shall expect to be allowed to see your niece.'

'Aha! To see my niece? And to make her in as great a hurry to be married as you are yourself? Suppose I say, no? You would see her perhaps without my permission?'

'Decidedly!'

'How delighfully frank! How exquisitely English! You shall see her, Mr Vendale, on certain days, which we will appoint together. What next?'

'Your object to my income,' proceeded Vendale, 'has taken me completely by surprise. I wish to be assured against any repetition of that surprise. Your present views of my qualification for marriage require me to have an income of three thousand a year. Can I be certain, in the future, as your experience of England enlarges, that your estimate will rise no higher?'

'In plain English,' said Obenreizer, 'you doubt my word?'

'Do you purpose to take *my* word for it when I inform you that I have doubled my income? asked Vendale. 'If my memory does not deceive me, you stipulated, a minute since, for plain proofs?'

'Well played, Mr Vendale! You combine the foreign quickness with the English solidity. Accept my best congratulations. Accept, also, my written guarantee.'

He rose; seated himself at a writing-desk at a side-table, wrote a few lines, and presented them to Vendale with a low bow. The engagement was perfectly explicit, and was signed and dated with scrupulous care.

'Are you satisfied with your guarantee?'

'I am satisfied.'

'Charmed to hear it, I am sure: We have had our little skirmish – we have really been wonderfully clever on both sides. For the present our affairs are settled. I bear no malice. You bear no malice. Come, Mr Vendale, a good English shake hands.'

Vendale gave his hand, a little bewildered by Obenreizer's sudden transitions from one humour to another.

'When may I expect to see Miss Obenreizer again?' he asked, as he rose to go.

'Honour me with a visit to-morrow,' said Obenreizer, 'and we will settle it then. Do have a grog before you go! No? Well! Well! We will reserve the grog till you have your three thousand a year, and are ready to be married. Aha! When will that be?'

'I made an estimate some months since, of the capacities of my business,' said Vendale. 'If that estimate is correct, I shall double my present income—'

'And be married!' added Obenreizer.

And be married,' repeated Vendale, 'within a year from this time. Good night.'

Vendale Makes Mischief

When Vendale entered his office the next morning, the dull commercial routine at Cripple Corner met him with a new face. Marguerite had an interest in it now! The whole machinery which Wilding's death had set in motion, to realise the value of the business – the balancing of ledgers, the estimating of debts, the taking of stock, and the rest of it – was now transformed into machinery which indicated the changes for and against a speedy marriage. After looking over results, as presented by his accountant, and checking additions and subtractions, as rendered by the clerks, Vendale turned his attention to the stock-taking department next, and sent a message to the cellars, desiring to see the report.

The Cellarman's appearance, the moment he put his head in at the door of his master's private room, suggested that something very extraordinary must have happened that morning. There was an approach to alacrity in Joey Ladle's movements! There was something which actually simulated cheerfulness in Joey Ladle's face!

'What's the matter?' asked Vendale. 'Anything wrong?'

'I should wish to mention one thing,' answered Joey. 'Young Mr Vendale, I have never set myself up for a prophet.'

'Who ever said you did?'

'No prophet, as far as I've heard tell of that profession,' proceeded Joey, 'ever lived principally underground. No prophet, whatever else he might take in at the pores, ever took in wine from morning to night, for a number of years together. When I said to young Master Wilding, respecting his changing the name of the firm, that one of these days he might find he'd changed the luck of the firm – did I put myself forward as a prophet? No I didn't. Has what I said to him come true? Yes, it has. In the time of Pebbleson Nephew, Young Mr Vendale, no such thing was ever known as a mistake made in a consignment delivered at these doors. There's a mistake been made now. Please to remark that it happened before Miss Margaret came here. For which reason it don't go against what I've said respecting Miss Margaret singing round the luck. Read that sir,' concluded Joey, pointing attention to a special passage in the report, with a forefinger which appeared to be in process of taking in through the pores nothing more remarkable than dirt. 'It's foreign to my nature to crow over the house I serve, but I feel it a kind of a solemn duty to ask you to read that.'

Vendale read as follows: – 'Note, respecting the Swiss champagne. An irregularity has been discovered in the last consignment received from the firm of Defresnier and Co.' Vendale stopped, and referred to a memorandum-book by his side. 'That was in Mr Wilding's time,' he said. 'The vintage was a particularly good one, and he took the whole of it. The Swiss champagne has done very well, hasn't it?'

'I don't say it's done badly,' answered the Cellarman. 'It may have got sick in our customers' bins, or it may have bust in our customer's hands. But I don't say it's done badly with *us*.'

Vendale resumed the reading of the note: 'We find the number of the cases to be quite correct by books. But six of them, which present a slight difference from the rest in the brand, have been opened, and have been found to contain a red wine instead of champagne. The similarity in the brands, we suppose, caused a mistake to be made in sending the consignment from Neuchâtel. The error has not been found to extend beyond six cases.'

'Is that all!' exclaimed Vendale, tossing the note away from him.

Joey Ladle's eye followed the flying morsel of paper drearily.

'I'm glad to see you take it easy, sir,' he said. 'Whatever happens, it will be always a comfort to you to remember that you took it easy at first. Sometimes one mistake leads to another. A man drops a bit of orange-peel on the pavement by mistake, and another man treads on it by mistake, and there's a job at the hospital, and a party crippled for life. I'm glad you take it easy, sir. In Pebbleson Nephew's time we shouldn't have taken it easy till we had seen the end of it. Without desiring to crow over the house, Young Mr Vendale, I wish you well through it. No offence, sir,' said the Cellarman, opening the door to go out, and looking in again ominously before he shut it. 'I'm muddled and molloncolly, I grant you. But I'm an old servant of Pebbleson Nephew, and I wish you well through them six cases of red wine.'

Left by himself, Vendale laughed, and took up his pen. 'I may as well send a line to Defresnier and Company,' he thought, 'before I forget it.' He wrote at once in these terms:

Dear Sirs. We are taking stock, and a trifling mistake has been discovered in the last consignment of champagne sent by your house to ours. Six of the cases contain red wine – which we hereby return to you. The matter can easily be set right, either by your sending us six cases of the champagne, if they can be produced, or, if not, by your crediting us with the value of six cases on the amount last paid (five hundred pounds) by our firm to yours. Your faithful servants.

WILDING AND CO.

This letter despatched to the post, the subject dropped at once out of Vendale's mind. He had other and far more interesting matters to think of. Later in the day he paid the visit to Obenreizer which had been agreed on between them. Certain evenings in the week were set apart which he was privileged to spend with Marguerite – always, however, in the presence of a third person. On this stipulation Obenreizer politely but positively insisted. The one concession he made was to give Vendale his choice of who the third person should be. Confiding in past experience, his choice fell unhesitatingly upon the excellent woman who mended Obenreizer's stockings. On hearing of the responsibility entrusted to her, Madame Dor's intellectual nature burst suddenly into a new stage of development. She waited till Obenreizer's eye was off her – and then she looked at Vendale, and dimly winked.

The time passed – the happy evenings with Marguerite came and went. It was the tenth morning since Vendale had written to the Swiss firm, when the answer appeared on his desk, with the other letters of the day:

Dear Sirs, We beg to offer our excuses for the little mistake which has happened. At the same time, we regret to add that the statement of our error, with which you have favoured us, has led to a very unexpected discovery. The affair is a most serious one for you and for us. The particulars are as follows:

Having no more champagne of the vintage last sent to you, we made arrangements to credit your firm with the value of the six cases, as suggested by yourself. On taking this step, certain forms observed in our mode of doing business necessitated a reference to our bankers' book, as well as to our ledger. The result is a moral certainty that no such remittance as you mention can have reached our house, and a literal certainty that no such remittance has been paid to our account at the bank.

It is needless, at this stage of the proceedings, to trouble you with details. The money has unquestionably been stolen in the course of its transit from you to us. Certain peculiarities which we observe, relating to the manner in which the fraud has been perpetrated, lead us to conclude that the thief may have calculated on being able to pay the missing sum to our bankers, before an inevitable discovery followed the annual striking of our balance. This would not have happened, in the usual course, for another three months. During that period, but for your letter, we might have remained perfectly unconscious of the robbery that has been committed.

We mention this last circumstance, as it may help to show you that we have to do, in this case, with no ordinary thief. Thus far we have not even a suspicion of who that thief is. But we believe you will assist us in making some advance towards discovery, by examining the receipt (forged, of course) which has no doubt purported to come to you from our house. Be pleased to look and see whether it is a receipt entirely in manuscript, or whether it is a numbered and printed form which merely requires the filling in of the amount. The settlement of this apparently trivial question is, we assure you, a matter of vital importance. Anxiously awaiting your reply, we remain, with high esteem and consideration.

DEFRESNIER & CIE.

Vendale laid the letter on his desk, and waited a moment to steady his mind under the shock that had fallen on it. At the time of all others when it was most important to him to increase the value of his business, that business was threatened with a loss of five hundred pounds. He thought of Marguerite, as he took the key from his pocket and opened the iron chamber in the wall in which the books and papers of the firm were kept.

He was still in the chamber, searching for the forged receipt, when he was startled by a voice speaking close behind him.

'A thousand pardons,' said the voice; 'I am afraid I disturb you.'

He turned, and found himself face to face with Marguerite's guardian.

'I have called,' pursued Obenreizer, 'to know if I can be of any use. Business of my own takes me away for some days to Manchester and Liverpool. Can I combine any business of yours with it? I am entirely at your disposal, in the character of commercial traveller for the firm of Wilding and Co.'

'Excuse me for one moment,' said Vendale; 'I will speak to you directly.' He turned round again, and continued his search among the papers. 'You come at a time when friendly offers are more than usually precious to me,' he resumed. 'I have had very bad news this morning from Neuchâtel.'

'Bad news!' exclaimed Obenreizer. 'From Defresnier and Company?'

'Yes. A remittance we sent to them has been stolen. I am threatened with a loss of five hundred pounds. What's that?'

Turning sharply, and looking into the room for the second time, Vendale discovered his envelope-case overthrown on the floor, and Obenreizer on his knees picking up the contents.

'All my awkwardness!' said Obenreizer. 'This dreadful news of yours startled me; I stepped back—' He became too deeply interested in collecting the scattered evelopes to finish the sentence.

'Don't trouble yourself,' said Vendale. 'The clerk will pick the things up.'

'This dreadful news!' repeated Obenreizer, persisting in collecting the envelopes. 'This dreadful news!'

'If you will read the letter,' said Vendale, 'you will find I have exaggerated nothing. There it is, open on my desk.'

He resumed his search, and in a moment more discovered the forged receipt. It was on the numbered and printed form, described by the Swiss firm. Vendale made a memorandum of the number and the date. Having replaced the receipt and locked up the iron chamber, he had leisure to notice Obenreizer, reading the letter in the recess of a window at the far end of the room.

'Come to the fire,' said Vendale. 'You look perished with the cold out there. I will ring for some more coals.'

Obenreizer rose, and came slowly back to the desk. 'Marguerite will be as sorry to hear of this as I am,' he said, kindly. 'What do you mean to do?'

'I am in the hands of Defresnier and Company,' answered Vendale. 'In my total ignorance of the circumstances, I can only do what they recommend. The receipt which I have just found, turns out to be the numbered and printed form. They seem to attach some special importance to its discovery. You have had experience, when you were in the Swiss house, of their way of doing business. Can you guess what object they have in view?'

Obenreizer offered a suggestion.

'Suppose I examine the receipt?' he said.

'Are you ill?' asked Vendale, startled by the change in his face, which now showed itself plainly for the first time. 'Pray go to the fire. You seem to be shivering – I hope you are not going to be ill?'

'Not I!' said Obenreizer. 'Perhaps I have caught cold. Your English climate might have spared an admirer of your English institutions. Let me look at the receipt.'

Vendale opened the iron chamber. Obenreizer took a chair, and drew it close to the fire. He held both hands over the flames.

'Let me look at the receipt,' he repeated, eagerly, as Vendale reappeared with the paper in his hand. At the same moment a porter entered the room with a fresh supply of coals. Vendale told him to make a good fire. The man obeyed the order with a disastrous alacrity. As he stepped forward and raised the scuttle, his foot caught in a fold of the rung, and he discharged his entire cargo of coals into the grate. The result was an instant smothering of the flame, and the production of a stream of yellow smoke, without a visible morsel of fire to account for it.

'Imbecile!' whispered Obenreizer to himself, with a look at the man which the man remembered for many a long day afterwards.

'Will you come into the clerks' room?' asked Vendale. 'They have a stove there.'

'No, no. No matter.'

Vendale handed him the receipt. Obenreizer's interest in examining it appeared to have been quenched as suddenly and as effectually as the fire itself. He just glanced over the document, and said, 'No; I don't understand it! I am sorry to be of no use.'

'I will write to Neuchâtel by to-night's post,' said Vendale, putting away the receipt for the second time. 'We must wait, and see what comes of it.'

'By to-night's post,' repeated Obenreizer. 'Let me see. You will get the answer in eight or nine days' time. I shall be back before that. If I can be of any service, as commercial traveller, perhaps you will let me know between this and then. You will send me written instructions? My best thanks. I shall be most anxious for your answer from Neuchâtel. Who knows? It may be a mistake, my dear friend, after all. Courage! Courage! Courage!' He had entered the room with no appearance of being pressed for time. He now snatched up his hat, and took his leave with the air of a man who had not another moment to lose.

Left by himself, Vendale took a turn thoughtfully in the room.

His previous impression of Obenreizer was shaken by what he had heard and seen at the interview which had just taken place. He was disposed, for the first time, to doubt whether, in this case, he had not been a little hasty and hard in his judgement on another man. Obenreizer's surprise and regret, on hearing the news from Neutchâtel, bore the plainest marks of being honestly felt – not politely assumed for the occasion. With troubles of his own to encounter, suffering, to all appearance, from the first insidious attack of a serious illness, he had looked and spoken like a man who really deplored the disaster that had fallen on his friend. Hitherto, Vendale had tried vainly to alter his first opinion of Marguerite's guardian, for Marguerite's sake. All the generous instincts in his nature now combined together and shook the evidence which had seemed unanswerable up to this time. 'Who knows?' he thought, 'I may have read that man's face wrongly, after all.'

The time passed – the happy evenings with Marguerite came and went. It was again the tenth morning since Vendale had written to the Swiss firm; and again the answer appeared on his desk with the other letters of the day:

Dear Sir. My senior partner, M. Defresnier, has been called away, by urgent business, to Milan. In his absence (and with his full concurrence and authority), I now write to you again on the subject of the missing five hundred pounds.

Your discovery that the forged receipt is executed upon one of our numbered and printed forms has caused inexpressible surprise and distress to my partner and to myself. At the time when your remittance was stolen, but three keys were in existence opening the strong box in which our receipt-forms are invariably kept. My partner had one key; I had the other. The third was in the possession of a gentleman who, at that period, occupied a position of trust in our house. We should as soon have thought of suspecting one of ourselves as of suspecting this person. Suspicion now points at him, nevertheless. I cannot prevail on myself to inform you who the person is, so long as there is the shadow of a chance that he may come innocently out of the inquiry which must now be instituted. Forgive my silence; the motive of it is good.

The form our investigation must now take is simple enough. The handwriting on your receipt must be compared, by competent persons whom we have at our disposal, with certain specimens of handwriting in our possession. I cannot send you the specimens, for business reasons, which, when you hear them, you are sure to approve. I must beg you to send me the receipt to Neuchâtel – and, in making this request, I must accompany it by a word of necessary warning.

If the person, at whom suspicion now points, really proves to be the person who has committed this forgery and theft, I have reason to fear that circumstances may have already put him on his guard. The only evidence against him is the evidence in your hands, and he will move heaven and earth to obtain and destroy it. I strongly urge you not to trust the receipt to the post. Send it to me, without loss of time, by a private hand, and choose nobody for your messenger but a person long established in your own employment, accustomed to travelling, capable of speaking French; a man of courage, a man of honesty, and, above all things, a man who can be trusted to let no stranger scrape acquaintance with him on the route. Tell no one – absolutely no one – but your messenger of the turn this matter has now taken. The safe transit of the receipt may depend on your interpreting *literally* the advice which I give you at the end of this letter.

I have only to add that every possible saving of time is now of the last importance. More than one of our receipt-forms is missing – and it is impossible to say what new frauds may not be committed, if we fail to lay our hands on the thief.

Your faithful servant.

ROLLAND
(Signing for Defresnier and C[IE]).

Who was the suspected man? In Vendale's position, it seemed useless to inquire.

Who was to be sent to Neuchâtel with the receipt? Men of courage and men of honesty were to be had at Cripple Corner for the asking. But where was the man who was accustomed to foreign travelling, who could speak the French language, and who could be really relied on to let no stranger scrape acquaintance with him on his route? There was but one man at hand who combined all those requisites in his own person, and that man was Vendale himself.

It was a sacrifice to leave his business; it was a greater sacrifice to leave Marguerite. But a matter of five hundred pounds was involved in the pending inquiry; and a literal interpretation of M. Rolland's advice was insisted on in terms which there was no trifling with. The more Vendale thought of it, the more plainly the necessity faced him, and said, 'Go!'

As he locked up the letter with the receipt, the association of ideas reminded him of Obenreizer. A guess at the identity of the suspected man looked more possible now. Obenreizer might know.

The thought had barely passed through his mind, when the door opened, and Obenreizer entered the room.

'They told me at Soho-square you were expected back last night,' said Vendale, greeting him. 'Have you done well in the country? Are you better?'

A thousand thanks. Obenreizer had done admirably well; Obenreizer was infinitely better. And now, what news? Any letter from Neuchâtel?

'A very strange letter,' answered Vendale. 'The matter has taken a new turn, and the letter insists – without excepting anybody – of my keeping our next proceedings a profound secret.'

'Without excepting anybody?' repeated Obenreizer. As he said the words, he walked away again, thoughtfully, to the window at the other end of room, looked out for a moment, and suddenly came back to Vendale. 'Surely they must have forgotten?' he resumed, 'or they would have excepted *me*?'

'It is Monsieur Rolland who writes,' said Vendale. 'And, as you say, he must certainly have forgotten. That view of the matter quite escaped me. I was just wishing I had you to consult, when you came into the room. And here I am tied by a formal prohibition, which cannot possibly have been intended to include you. How very annoying!'

Obenreizer's filmy eyes fixed on Vendale attentively.

'Perhaps it is more than annoying!' he said. 'I came this morning not only to hear the news, but to offer myself as messenger, negotiator – what you will. Would you believe it? I have letters which oblige me to go to Switzerland immediately.

Messages, documents, anything – I could have taken them all to Defresnier and Rolland for you.'

'You are the very man I wanted,' returned Vendale. 'I had decided, most unwillingly, on going to Neuchâtel myself, not five minutes since, because I could find no one here capable of taking my place. Let me look at the letter again.'

He opened the strong room to get at the letter. Obenreizer, after first glancing round him to make sure they were alone, followed a step or two and waited, measuring Vendale with his eye. Vendale was the tallest man, and unmistakably the strongest man also of the two. Obenreizer turned away, and warmed himself at the fire.

Meanwhile, Vendale read the last paragraph in the letter for the third time. There was the plain warning – there was the closing sentence, which insisted on a literal interpretation of it. The hand, which was leading Vendale in the dark, led him on that condition only. A large sum was at stake: a terrible suspicion remained to be verified. If he acted on his own responsibility, and if anything happened to defeat the object in view, who would be blamed? As a man of business, Vendale had but one course to follow. He locked the letter up again.

'It is most annoying,' he said to Obenreizer – 'it is a piece of forgetfulness on Monsieur Rolland's part which puts me to serious inconvenience, and places me in an absurdly false position towards you. What am I to do? I am acting in a very serious matter, and acting entirely in the dark. I have no choice but to be guided, not by the spirit, but by the letter of my instructions. You understand me, I am sure? You know, if I had not been fettered in this way, how gladly I should have accepted your services?'

'Say no more!' returned Obenreizer. 'In your place I should have done the same. My good friend, I take no offence. I thank you for your compliment. We shall be travelling companions, at any rate,' added Obenreizer. 'You go, as I go, at once?'

'At once. I must speak to Marguerite first, of course!'

'Surely! Surely! Speak to her this evening. Come, and pick me up on the way to the station. We go together by the mail train to-night?'

'By the mail train to-night.'

It was later than Vendale had anticipated when he drove up to the house in Soho-square. Business difficulties, occasioned by his sudden departure, had presented themselves by dozens. A cruelly large share of the time which he had hoped to devote to Marguerite had been claimed by duties at his office which it was impossible to neglect.

To his surprise and delight, she was alone in the drawing-room when he entered it.

'We have only a few minutes, George,' she said. 'But Madame Dor has been good to me – and we can have those few minutes alone.' She threw her arms round his neck, and whispered eagerly, 'Have you done anything to offend Mr Obenreizer?'

'I!' exclaimed Vendale, in amazement.

'Hush!' she said, 'I want to whisper it. You know the little photograph I have got of you. This afternoon it happened to be on the chimney-piece. He took it up and looked at it – and I saw his face in the glass. I know you have offended him! He is merciless; he is revengeful; he is as secret as the grave. Don't go with him, George – don't go with him!'

'My own love,' returned Vendale, 'you are letting your fancy frighten you! Obenreizer and I were never better friends than we are at this moment.'

Before a word more could be said, the sudden movement of some ponderous body shook the floor of the next room. The shock was followed by the appearance of Madame Dor. 'Obenreizer!' exclaimed this excellent person in a whisper, and plumped down instantly in her regular place by the stove.

Obenreizer came in with a courier's bag strapped over his shoulder.

'Are you ready?' he asked, addressing Vendale. 'Can I take anything for you? You have no travelling-bag. I have got one. Here is the compartment for papers, open at your service.'

'Thank you,' said Vendale. 'I have only one paper of importance with me; and that paper I am bound to take charge of myself. Here it is,' he added, touching the breast-pocket of his coat, 'and here it must remain till we get to Neuchâtel.'

As he said those words, Marguerite's hand caught his, and pressed it significantly. She was looking towards Obenreizer. Before Vendale could look, in his turn, Obenreizer had wheeled round, and was taking leave of Madame Dor.

'Adieu my charming niece!' he said, turning to Marguerite next. 'En route my friend, for Neuchâtel!' he tapped Vendale lightly over the breast-pocket of his coat, and led the way to the door.

Vendale's last look was for Marguerite. Marguerite's last words to him were, 'Don't go!'

Act III

In the Valley

It was about the middle of the month of February when Vendale and Obenreizer set forth on their expedition. The winter being a hard one, the time was bad for travellers. So bad was it that these two travellers, coming to Strasbourg, found its great inns almost empty. And even the few people they did encounter in that city, who had started from England or from Paris on business journeys towards the interior of Switzerland, were turning back.

Many of the railroads in Switzerland that tourists pass easily enough now, were almost or quite impracticable then. Some were not begun; more were not completed. On such as were open, there were still large gaps of old road where communication in the winter season was often stopped; on others, there were weak points where the new work was not safe, either under conditions of severe frost, or of rapid thaw. The running of trains on this last class was not to be counted on in the worst time of the year, was contingent upon weather, or was wholly abandoned through the months considered the most dangerous.

At Strasbourg there were more travellers' stories afloat, respecting the difficulties of the way further on, than there were travellers to relate them. Many of these tales were as wild as usual; but the more modestly marvellous did derive some colour from the circumstance that people were indisputably turning back. However, as the road to Basle was open, Vendale's resolution to push on was in no wise disturbed. Obenreizer's resolution was necessarily Vendale's, seeing that he stood at bay thus desperately – he must be ruined, or must destroy the evidence that Vendale carried about him, even if he destroyed Vendale with it.

The state of mind of each of these two fellow-travellers

towards the other was this. Obenreizer, encircled by impend-
ing ruin through Vendale's quickness of action, and seeing the
circle narrowed every hour by Vendale's energy, hated him
with the animosity of a fierce cunning lower animal. He had
always had instinctive movements in his breast against him;
perhaps, because of that old sore of gentleman and peasant;
perhaps, because of the openness of his nature; perhaps,
because of his better looks; perhaps, because of his success
with Marguerite; perhaps, on all those grounds, the two last
not the least. And now he saw in him besides, the hunter who
was tracking him down. Vendale, on the other hand, always
contending generously against his first vague mistrust, now
felt bound to contend against it more than ever: reminding
himself, 'He is Marguerite's guardian. We are on perfectly
friendly terms; he is my companion of his own proposal, and
can have no interested motive in sharing this undesirable
journey.' To which pleas in behalf of Obenreizer, chance
added one consideration more, when they came to Basle, after
a journey of more than twice the average duration.

They had had a late dinner, and were alone in an inn room
there, overhanging the Rhine: at that place rapid and deep,
swollen and loud. Vendale lounged upon a couch, and
Obenreizer walked to and fro: now, stopping at the window,
looking at the crooked reflections of the town lights in the
dark water (and peradventure thinking, 'If I could fling him
into it!'); now, resuming his walk with his eyes upon the floor.

'Where shall I rob him, if I can? Where shall I murder him, if
I must?' So, as he paced the room, ran the river, ran the river,
ran the river.

The burden seemed to him at last, to be growing so plain
that he stopped; thinking it as well to suggest another burden
to his companion.

'The Rhine sounds to-night,' he said with a smile, 'like the
old waterfall at home. That waterfall which my mother
showed to travellers (I told you of it once). The sound of it
changed with the weather, as does the sound of all falling
waters and flowing waters. When I was pupil of the
watchmaker, I remembered it as sometimes saying to me for
whole days, "Who are you, my little wretch? Who are you,
my little wretch?" I remembered it as saying, other times,

when its sound was hollow, and storm was coming up the Pass: "Boom, boom, boom. Beat him, beat him, beat him." Like my mother enraged – if she was my mother.'

'If she was?' said Vendale, gradually changing his attitude to a sitting one. 'If she was? Why do you say "if"?'

'What do I know?' replied the other negligently, throwing up his hands and letting them fall as they would. 'What would you have? I am so obscurely born, that how can I say? I was very young, and all the rest of the family were men and women, and my so-called parents were old. Anything is possible of a case like that.'

'Did you ever doubt—?'

'I told you once, I doubt the marriage of those two,' he replied, throwing up his hands again, as if he were throwing the unprofitable subject away. 'But here I am in Creation. *I* come of no fine family. What does it matter?'

'At least you are Swiss,' said Vendale, after following him with his eyes to and fro.

'How do I know?' he retorted abruptly, and stopping to look back over his shoulder. 'I say to you, at least you are English. How do you know?'

'By what I have been told from infancy.'

'Ah! I know of myself that way.'

'And,' cried Vendale, pursuing the thought that he could not drive back, 'by my earliest recollections.'

'I also. I know of myself that way – if that way satisfies.'

'Does it not satisfy you?'

'It must. There is nothing like "it must" in this little world. It must. Two short words those, but stronger than long proof or reasoning.'

'You and poor Wilding were born in the same year. You were nearly of an age,' said Vendale, again thoughtfully looking after him as he resumed his pacing up and down.

'Yes. Very nearly.'

Could Obenreizer be the missing man? In the unknown associations of things, was there a subtler meaning than he himself thought, in that theory so often on his lips about the smallness of the world? Had the Swiss letter presenting him, followed so close on Mrs Goldstraw's revelation concerning the infant who had been taken away to Switzerland, because he was that infant grown a man? In a world where so many depths lie unsounded, it might be. The chances, or the laws – call them either – that had wrought out the revival of Vendale's own acquaintance with Obenreizer, and had ripened it into intimacy, and had brought them here together this present winter night, were hardly less curious; while read by such a light, they were seen to cohere towards the furtherance of a continuous and an intelligible purpose.

Vendale's awakened thoughts ran high while his eyes musingly followed Obenreizer pacing up and down the room, the river ever running to the tune: 'Where shall I rob him, if I can? Where shall I murder him, if I must?' The secret of his dead friend was in no hazard from Vendale's lips; but just as his friend had died of its weight, so did he in his lighter succession feel the burden of the trust, and the obligation to follow any clue, however obscure. He rapidly asked himself, would he like this man to be the real Wilding? No. Argue down his mistrust as he might, he was unwilling to put such a substitute in the place of his late guileless, outspoken, childlike partner. He rapidly asked himself, would he like this man to be rich? No. He had more power than enough over Marguerite as it was, and wealth might invest him with more. Would he like this man to be Marguerite's Guardian, and yet proved to stand in no degree of relationship towards her, however disconnected and distant? No. But these were not considerations to come between him and fidelity to the dead. Let him see to it that they passed him with no other notice than the knowledge that they *had* passed him, and left him bent on the discharge of a solemn duty. And he did see to it, so soon that he followed his companion with ungrudging eyes, while he still paced the room; that companion, whom he supposed to be moodily reflecting on his own birth, and not on another man's – least of all what man's – violent Death.

The road in advance from Basle to Neuchâtel was better than had been represented. The latest weather had done it good. Drivers, both of horses and mules, had come in that evening after dark, and had reported nothing more difficult to be overcome than trials of patience, harness, wheels, axles, and whipcord. A bargain was soon struck for a carriage and horses, to take them on in the morning, and to start before daylight.

'Do you lock your door at night when travelling?' asked Obenreizer, standing warming his hands by the wood fire in Vendale's chamber, before going to his own.

'Not I. I sleep too soundly.'

'You are so sound a sleeper?' he retorted, with an admiring look. 'What a blessing!'

'Anything but a blessing to the rest of the house,' rejoined Vendale, 'if I had to be knocked up in the morning from the outside of my bedroom door.'

'I, too,' said Obenreizer, 'leave open my room. But let me advise you, as a Swiss who knows: always, when you travel in my country, put your papers – and, of course, your money – under your pillow. Always the same place.'

'You are not complimentary to your countrymen,' laughed Vendale.

'My countrymen,' said Obenreizer, with that light touch of his friend's elbows by way of Good Night and benediction, 'I suppose, are like the majority of men. And the majority of men will take what they can get. Adieu! At four in the morning.'

'Adieu! At four.'

Left to himself, Vendale raked the logs together, sprinkled over them the white woodashes lying on the hearth, and sat down to compose his thoughts. But they still ran high on their latest theme, and the running of the river tended to agitate rather than to quiet them. As he sat thinking, what little disposition he had had to sleep, departed. He felt it hopeless to lie down yet, and sat dressed by the fire. Marguerite, Wilding, Obenreizer, the business he was then upon, and a thousand hopes and doubts that had nothing to do with it, occupied his mind at once. Everything seemed to have power over him, but slumber. The departed disposition to sleep kept far away.

He had sat for a long time thinking, on the hearth, when his candle burned down, and its light went out. It was of little moment; there was light enough in the fire. He changed his attitude, and, leaning his arm on the chair-back, and his chin upon that hand, sat thinking still.

But he sat between the fire and the bed, and, as the fire flickered in the play of air from the fast-flowing river, his enlarged shadow fluttered on the white wall by the bedside.

His attitude gave it an air, half of mourning, and half of bending over the bed imploring. His eyes were observant of it, when he became troubled by the disagreeable fancy that it was like Wilding's shadow, and not his own.

A slight change of place would cause it to disappear. He made the change, and the apparition of his disturbed fancy vanished. He now sat in the shade of a little nook beside the fire, and the door of the room was before him.

It had a long cumbrous iron latch. He saw the latch slowly and softly rise. The door opened a very little, and came to again: as though only the air had moved it. But he saw that the latch was out of the hasp.

The door opened again very slowly, until it opened wide enought to admit some one. It afterwards remained still for a while, as though cautiously held open on the other side. The figure of a man then entered, and its face turned towards the bed, and stood quiet just within the door. Until it said, in a low half-whisper, at the same time taking one step forward: 'Vendale!'

'What now?' he answered, springing from his seat; 'who is it?'

It was Obenreizer, and he uttered a cry of surprise as Vendale came upon him from the unexpected direction. 'Not in bed?' he said, catching him by both shoulders with an instinctive tendency to a struggle, 'Then something *is* wrong!'

'What do you mean?' said Vendale, releasing himself.

'First tell me; you are not ill?'

'Ill? No.'

'I have had a bad dream about you. How is it that I see you up and dressed?'

'My good fellow, I may as well ask you how is it that I see *you* up and undressed.'

'I have told you why. I have had a bad dream about you. I tried to rest after it, but it was impossible. I could not make up my mind to stay where I was, without knowing you were safe; and yet I could not make up my mind to come in here. I have been minutes hesitating at the door. It is so easy to laugh at a dream that you have not dreamed. Where is your candle?'

'Burnt out,'

'I have a whole one in my room. Shall I fetch it?'

'Do so.'

His room was very near, and he was absent for but a few seconds. Coming back with the candle in his hand, he kneeled down on the hearth and lighted it. As he blew with his breath a charred billet into flame for the purpose, Vendale looking down at him, saw that his lips where white and not easy of control.

'Yes!' said Obenreizer, setting the lighted candle on the table, 'it was a bad dream. Only look at me!'

His feet were bare; his red-flannel shirt was thrown back at the throat, and its sleeves were rolled above the elbows; his only other garment, a pair of under pantaloons or drawers, reaching to the ankles, fitted him close and tight. A certain lithe and savage appearance was on his figure, and his eyes were very bright.

'If there had been a wrestle with a robber, as I dreamed,' said Obenreizer, 'you see, I was stripped for it.'

'And armed, too,' said Vendale, glancing at his girdle.

'A traveller's dagger, that I always carry on the road,' he answered carelessly, half drawing it from its sheath with his left hand, and putting it back again. 'Do you carry no such thing?'

'Nothing of the kind.'

'No pistols?' said Obenreizer, glancing at the table, and from it to the untouched pillow.

'Nothing of the sort.'

'You Englishmen are so confident! You wish to sleep?'

'I have wished to sleep this long time, but I can't do it.'

'I neither, after the bad dream. My fire has gone the way of your candle. May I come and sit by yours? Two o'clock! It will so soon be four, that it is not worth the trouble to go to bed again.'

'I shall not take the trouble to go to bed at all, now,' said Vendale; 'sit here and keep me company, and welcome.'

Going back to his room to arrange his dress, Obenreizer soon returned in a loose cloak and slippers, and they sat down on opposite sides of the hearth. In the interval, Vendale had replenished the fire from the wood basket in his room, and Obenreizer had put upon the table a flask and cup from his.

'Common cabaret brandy, I am afraid,' he said pouring out; 'bought upon the road, and not like yours from Cripple

Corner. But yours is exhausted; so much the worse. A cold night, a cold time of night, a cold country, and a cold house. This may be better than nothing; try it.'

Vendale took the cup, and did so.

'How do you find it?'

'It has a coarse after-flavour,' said Vendale, giving back the cup with a slight shudder, 'and I don't like it.'

'You are right,' said Obenreizer, tasting, and smacking his lips; 'it *has* a coarse after-flavour, and *I* don't like it. Booh! It burns, though!' He had flung what remained in the cup, upon the fire.

Each of them leaned an elbow on the table, reclined his head upon his hand, and sat looking at the flaring logs. Obenreizer remained watchful and still; but Vendale, after certain nervous twitches and starts, in one of which he rose to his feet and looked wildly about him, fell into the strangest confusion of dreams. He carried his papers in a leather case or pocket-book, in an inner breast-pocket of his buttoned travelling coat; and whatever he dreamed of, in the lethargy that got possession of him, something importunate in these papers called him out of that dream, though he could not wake from it. He was belated on the steppes of Russia (some shadowy person gave the name to the place) and Marguerite; and yet the sensation of a hand at his breast, softly feeling the outline of the pocket book as he lay asleep before the fire, was present to him. He was shipwrecked in an open boat at sea, and having lost his clothes, had no other covering than an old sail; and yet a creeping hand, tracing outside all the other pockets of the dress he actually wore, for papers, and finding none answer its touch, warned him to rouse himself. He was in the ancient vault at Cripple Corner, to which was transferred the very bed substantial and present in that very room at Basle; and Wilding (not dead, as he had supposed, and yet he did not wonder much) shook him, and whispered, 'Look at that man! Don't you see he has risen, and is turning the pillow? Why should he turn the pillow, if not to seek those papers that are in your breast? Awake!' And yet he slept, and wandered off into other dreams.

Watchful and still, with his elbow on the table and his head upon that hand, his companion at length said: 'Vendale! We are called. Past Four!' Then opening his eyes, he saw, turned sideways on him, the filmy face of Obenreizer.

'You have been in a heavy sleep,' he said. 'The fatigue of constant travelling and the cold!'

'I am broad awake now,' cried Vendale, springing up, but with an unsteady footing. 'haven't you slept at all?'

'I may have dozed, but I seem to have been patiently looking at the fire. Whether or no, we must wash, and breakfast, and turn out. Past four, Vendale; past four!'

It was said in a tone to rouse him, for already he was half asleep again. In his preparation for the day, too, and at his breakfast, he was often virtually asleep while in mechanical action. It was not until the cold dark day was closing in, that he had any distincter impressions of the ride than jingling bells, bitter weather, slipping horses, frowning hill-sides, bleak woods, and a stoppage at some wayside house of entertainment, where they had passed through a cowhouse to reach the travellers' room above. He had ben conscious of little more, except of Obenreizer sitting thoughtful at his side all day, and eyeing him much.

But when he shook off his stupor, Obenreizer was not at his side. The carriage was stopping to bait at another wayside house; and a line of long narrow carts, laden with casks of wine, and drawn by horses with a quantity of blue collar and head-gear, were baiting too. These came from the direction in which the travellers were going, and Obenreizer (not thoughtful now, but cheerful and alert) was talking with the foremost driver. As Vendale stretched his limbs, circulated his blood, and cleared off the lees of his lethargy, with a sharp run to and fro in the bracing air, the line of carts moved on: the drivers all saluting Obenreizer as they passed him.

'Who are those?' asked Vendale.

'They are our carriers – Defresnier and Company's,' replied Obenreizer. 'Those are our casks of wine.' He was singing to himself, and lighting a cigar.

'I have been drearily dull company today,' said Vendale. 'I don't know what has been the matter with me.'

'You had no sleep last night; and a kind of brain-congestion frequently comes, at first, of such cold,' said Obenreizer. 'I have seen it often. After all, we shall have our journey for nothing, it seems.'

'How for nothing?'

'The House is at Milan. You know, we are a Wine House at Neuchâtel, and a Silk House at Milan? Well, Silk happening to press of a sudden more than Wine, Defresnier was summoned to Milan. Rolland, the other partner, has been taken ill since his departure, and the doctors will allow him to see no one. A letter awaits you at Neuchâtel to tell you so. I have it from our chief carrier whom you saw me talking with. He was surprised to see me, and said he had that word for you if he met you. What do you do? Go back?'

'Go on,' said Vendale.

'On?'

'On? Yes. Across the Alps, and down to Milan.'

Obenreizer stopped in his smoking to look at Vendale, and then smoked heavily, looked up the road, looked down the road, looked down at the stones in the road at his feet.

'I have a very serious matter in charge,' said Vendale; 'more of these missing forms may be turned to as bad account, or worse; I am urged to lose no time in helping the house and take the thief; and nothing shall turn me back.'

'No?' cried Obenreizer, taking out his cigar to smile, and giving his hand to his fellow-traveller. 'Then nothing shall turn *me* back. Ho, driver! Despatch. Quick there! Let us push on!'

They travelled through the night. There had been snow, and there was a partial thaw, and they mostly travelled at a foot-pace, and always with many stoppages to breathe the splashed and floundering horses. After an hour's broad daylight, they drew rein at the inn-door at Neuchâtel, having been some eight-and-twenty hours in conquering some eighty English miles.

When they had hurriedly refreshed and changed, they went together to the house of business of Defresnier and Company. There they found the letter which the wine-carrier had described, enclosing the tests and comparisons of handwriting essential to the discovery of the Forger. Vendale's determination to press forward, without resting, being already taken, the only question to delay them was by what Pass could they cross the Alps? Respecting the state of the two Passes of the St Gotthard and Simplon, the guides and mule-drivers differed greatly; and both Passes were still far enough off, to prevent the travellers from having the benefit of any recent experience of either. Besides which, they well knew that a fall of snow might altogether change the described conditions in a single hour, even if they were correctly stated. But, on the whole, the Simplon appearing to be the hopefuller route, Vendale decided to take it. Obenreizer bore little or no part in the discussion, and scarcely spoke.

To Geneva, to Lausanne, along the level margin of the lake to Vevay, so into the winding valley between the spurs of the mountains, and into the valley of the Rhone. The sound of the carriage-wheels, as they rattled on, through the day, through the night, became as the wheels of a great clock, recording the hours. No change of weather varied the journey, after it had hardened into a sullen frost. In a sombre-yellow sky, they saw the Apline ranges; and they saw enough of snow on nearer and much lower hill-tops and hillsides, to sully, by contrast the purity of lake, torrent, and watefall, and make the villges look discoloured and dirty. But no snow fell, nor was there any snow-drift on the road. The stalking along the valley of more or less of white mist, changing on their hair and dress into icicles, was the only variety between them and the gloomy sky. And still by day, and still by night, the wheels. And still they rolled, in the hearing of one of them, to the burden, altered from the burden of the Rhine: 'The time is gone for robbing him alive, and I must murder him.'

They came, at length, to the poor litle town of Brieg, at the foot of the Simplon. They came there after dark, but yet could see how dwarfed men's works and men became with the immense mountains towering over them. Here they must lie for the night; and here was warmth of fire, and lamp, and dinner, and wine, and after-conference resounding, with guides and drivers. No human creature had come across the Pass for four days. The snow above the snow-line was too soft for wheeled carriage, and not hard enough for sledge. There was snow in the sky. There had been snow in the sky for days past, and the marvel was that it had not fallen, and the certainty was that it must fall. No vehicle could cross. The journey might be tried on mules, or it might be tried on foot; but the best guides must be paid danger-price in either case, and that, too, whether they succeeded in taking the two travellers across, or turned for safety and brought them back.

In this discussion, Obenreizer bore no part whatever. He sat silently smoking by the fire until the room was cleared and Vendale referred to him.

'Bah! I am weary of these poor devils and their trade,' he said, in reply. 'Always the same story. It is the story of their trade to-day, as it was the story of their trade when I was a ragged boy. What do you and I want? We want a knapsack each, and a mountain-staff each. We want no guide; we should guide him; he would not guide us. We have our portmanteaus here, and we cross together. We have been on the mountains together before now, and I am mountain-born, and I know this Pass – Pass! – rather High Road! – by heart. We will leave these poor devils, in pity, to trade with others; but they must not delay us to make a pretence of earning money. Which is all they mean.'

Vendale, glad to be quit of the dispute, and to cut the knot: active, adventurous, bent on getting forward, and therefore very susceptible to the last hint: readily assented. Within two hours, they had purchased what they wanted for the expedition, had packed their knapsacks, and lay down to sleep.

At break of day, they found half the town collected in the narrow street to see them depart. The people talked together in groups; the guides and drivers whispered apart, and looked up at the sky; no one wished them a good journey.

As they began the ascent, a gleam of sun shone from the otherwise unaltered sky, and for a moment turned the tin spires of the town to silver.

'A good omen!' said Vendale (though it died out while he spoke). 'Perhaps our example will open the Pass on this side.'

'No; we shall not be followed,' returned Obenreizer, looking up at the sky and back at the valley. 'We shall be alone up yonder.'

On the Mountain

The road was fair enough for stout walkers, and the air grew lighter and easier to breathe as the two ascended. But the settled gloom remained as it had remained for days back. Nature seemed to have come to a pause. The sense of hearing, no less than the sense of sight, was troubled by having to wait so long for the change, whatever it might be, that impended. The silence was as palpable and heavy as the lowering clouds – or rather cloud, for there seemed to be but one in all the sky, and that one covering the whole of it.

Although the light was thus dismally shrouded, the prospect was not obscured. Down in the valley of the Rhône behind them, the stream could be traced through all its many windings, oppressively sombre and solemn in its one leaden hue, a colourless waste. Far and high above them, glaciers and suspended avalanches overhung the spots where they must pass by-and-by; deep and dark below them on their right, were awful precipice and roaring torrent; tremendous mountains arose in every vista. The gigantic landscape, uncheered by a touch of changing light or a solitary ray of sun, was yet terribly distinct in its ferocity. The hearts of two lonely men might shrink a little, if they had to win their way for miles and hours among a legion of silent and motionless men – mere men like themselves – all looking at them with fixed and frowning front. But how much more, when the legion is of Nature's mightiest works, and the frown may turn to fury in an instant!

As they ascended, the road became gradually more rugged and difficult. But the spirits of Vendale rose as they mounted higher, leaving so much more of the road behind them conquered. Obenreizer spoke little, and held on with a determined purpose. Both, in respect of agility and endurance, were well qualified for the expedition. Whatever the born mountaineer read in the weather-tokens, that was illegible to the other, he kept to himself.

'Shall we get across to-day?' asked Vendale.

'No,' replied the other. 'You see how much deeper the snow lies here than it lay half a league lower. The higher we mount, the deeper the snow will lie. Walking is half wading even now. And the days are so short! If we get as high as the fifth Refuge, and lie tonight at the Hospice, we shall do well.'

'Is there no danger of the weather rising in the night,' asked Vendale, anxiously, 'and snowing us up?'

'There is danger enough about us,' said Obenreizer, with a cautious glance onward and upward, 'to render silence our best policy. You have heard of the Bridge of the Ganther?'
- 'I have crossed it once.'

'In the summer?'

'Yes; in the travelling season.'

'Yes; but it is another thing at this season,' with a sneer, as though he were out of temper. 'This is not a time of year, or a state of things, on an Alpine Pass, that you gentlemen holiday-travellers know much about.'

'You are my Guide,' said Vendale, good humouredly. 'I trust to you.'

'I am your Guide,' said Obenreizer, 'and I will guide you to your journey's end. There is the Bridge before us.'

They had made a turn into a desolate and dismal ravine, where the snow lay deep below them, deep about them, deep on every side. While speaking, Obenreizer stood pointing at the Bridge, and observing Vendale's face, with a very singular expression on his own.

'If I, as Guide, had sent you over there, in advance, and encouraged you to give a shout or two, you might have brought down upon yourself tons and tons and tons of snow, that would not only have struck you dead, but buried you deep, at a blow.'

'No doubt,' said Vendale.

'No doubt. But this is not what I have to do, as Guide. So pass silently. Or, going as we go our indiscretion might else crush and bury *me*. Let us get on!'

There was a great accumulation of snow on the Bridge; and such enormous accumulations of snow overhung them from projecting masses or rock, that they might have been making their way through a stormy sky of white clouds. Using his staff skilfully, sounding as he went, and looking upward, with bent shoulders, as it were to resist the mere idea of a fall from above, Obenreizer softly led. Vendale closely followed. They were yet in the midst of their dangerous way, when there came a mighty rush, followed by a sound as of thunder. Obenreizer clapped his hand on Vendale's mouth and pointed to the track behind them. Its aspect had been wholly changed in a moment. An avalanche had swept over it, and plunged into the torrent at the bottom of the gulf below.

Their appearance at the solitary Inn not far beyond this terrible Bridge, elicited many expressions of astonishment from the people shut up in the house. 'We stay but to rest,' said Obenreizer, shaking the snow from his dress at the fire. 'This gentleman has very pressing occasion to get across – tell them, Vendale.'

'Assuredly, I have very pressing occasion. I must cross.'

'You hear, all of you. My friend has very pressing occasion to get across, and we want no advice and no help. I am as good a guide, my fellow-countrymen, as any of you. Now, give us to eat and drink.'

In exactly the same way, and in nearly the same words, when it was coming on dark and they had struggled through the greatly increased difficulties of the road, and had at last reached their destination for the night, Obenreizer said to the astonished people of the Hospice, gathering about them at the fire, while they were yet in the act of getting their wet shoes off, and shaking the snow from their clothes:

'It is well to understand one another, friends all. This gentleman—'

– 'Has,' said Vendale, readily taking him up with a smile, 'very pressing occasion to get across. Must cross.'

'You hear? – has very pressing occasion to get across, must cross. We want no advice and no help. I am mountain-born, and act as guide. Do not worry us by talking about it, but let us have supper, and wine, and bed.'

All through the intense cold of the night, the same awful stillness. Again at sunrise, no sunny tinge to gild or redden the snow. The same interminable waste of deathly white; the same immovable air; the same monotonous gloom in the sky.

'Travellers!' a friendly voice called to them from the door, after they were afoot, knapsack on back and staff in hand, as yesterday: 'recollect! There are five places of shelter, near together, on the dangerous road before you; and there is the wooden cross, and there is the next Hospice. Do not stray from the track. If the *Tourmente* comes on, take shelter instantly!'

'The trade of these poor devils!' said Obenreizer to his friend, with a contemptuous backward wave of his hand towards the voice. 'How they stick to their trade! You

Englishmen say we Swiss are mercenary. Truly, it does look like it.'

They had divided between the two knapsacks, such refreshments as they had been able to obtain that morning, and as they deemed it prudent to take. Obenreizer carried the wine as his share of the burden; Vendale, the bread and meat and cheese, and the flask of brandy.

They had for some time laboured upward and onward through the snow – which was now above their knees in the track, and of unknown depth elsewhere – and they were still labouring upward and onward through the most frightful part of that tremendous desolation, when snow began to fall. At first, but a few flakes descended slowly and steadily. After a little while the fall grew much denser, and suddenly it began without apparent cause to whirl itself into spiral shapes. Instantly ensuing upon this last change, an icy blast came roaring at them, and every sound and force imprisoned until now was let loose.

One of the dismal galleries through which the road is carried at that perilous point, a cave eked out by arches of great strength, was near at hand. They struggled into it, and the storm raged wildly. The noise of the wind, the noise of the water, the thundering down of displaced masses of rock and snow, the awful voices with which not only that gorge but every gorge in the whole monstrous range seemed to be suddenly endowed, the darkness as of night, the violent revolving of the snow which beat and broke it into spray and blinded them, the madness of everything around insatiate for destruction, the rapid substitution of furious violence for unnatural calm, and hosts of appalling sounds for silence: these were things, on the edge of a deep abyss, to chill the blood, though the fierce wind, made actually solid by ice and snow, had failed to chill it.

Obenreizer, walking to and fro in the gallery without ceasing, signed to Vendale to help him unbuckle his knapsack. They could see each other, but could not have heard each other speak. Vendale complying, Obenreizer produced his bottle of wine, and poured some out, motioning Vendale to take that for warmth's sake, and not brandy. Vendale again complying, Obenreizer seemed to drink after him, and the two walked backwards and forwards side by side; both well knowing that to rest or sleep would be to die.

The snow came driving heavily into the gallery by the upper end at which they would pass out of it, if they ever passed out; for greater dangers lay on the road behind them than before. The snow soon began to choke the arch. An hour more, and it lay so high as to block out half of the returning daylight. But it froze hard now, as it fell, and could be clambered through or over. The violence of the mountain storm was gradually yielding to a steady snowfall. The wind still raged at intervals, but not incessantly; and when it paused, the snow fell in heavy flakes.

They might have been two hours in their frightful prison, when Obenreizer, now crunching into the mound, now creeping over it with his head bowed down and his body touching the top of the arch, made his way out. Vendale followed close upon him, but followed without clear motive or calculation. For the lethargy of Basle was creeping over him again, and mastering his senses.

How far he had followed out of the gallery, or with what obstacles he had since contended, he knew not. He became roused to the knowledge that Obenreizer had set upon him, and that they were struggling desperately in the snow. He became roused to the remembrance of what his assailant carried in a girdle. He felt for it, drew it, struck at him, struggled again, struck at him again, cast him off, and stood face to face with him.

'I promised to guide you, to your journey's end,' said Obenreizer, 'and I have kept my promise. The journey of your life ends here. Nothing can prolong it. You are sleeping as you stand.'

'You are a villain. What have you done to me?'

'You are a fool. I have drugged you. You are doubly a fool, for I drugged you once before upon the journey, to try you. You are trebly a fool, for I am the thief and forger, and in a few moments I shall take those proofs against the thief and forger from your insensible body.'

The entrapped man tried to throw off the lethargy, but its fatal hold upon him was so sure that, even while he heard those words, he stupidly wondered which of them had been wounded, and whose blood it was that he saw sprinkled on the snow.

'What have I done to you,' he asked, heavily and thickly, 'that you should be – so base – a murderer?'

'Done to me? You would have destroyed me, but that you have come to your journey's end. Your cursed activity interposed between me, and the time I had counted on in which I might have replaced the money. Done to me? You have come in my way – not once, not twice, but again and again and again. Did I try to shake you off in the beginning, or no? You were not to be shaken off. Therefore you die here.'

Vendale tried to think coherently, tried to speak coherently, tried to pick up the iron-shod staff he had let fall; failing to touch it, tried to stagger on without its aid. All in vain, all in vain! He stumbled, and fell heavily forward on the brink of the deep chasm.

Stupefied, dozing, unable to stand upon his feet, a veil before his eyes, his sense of hearing deadened, he made such a vigorous rally that, supporting himself on his hands, he saw his enemy standing calmly over him, and heard him speak.

'You call me murderer,' said Obenreizer, with a grim laugh. 'The name matters very little. But at least I have set my life against yours, for I am surrounded by dangers, and may never make my way out of this place. The *Tourmente* is rising again. The snow is on the whirl. I must have the papers now. Every moment has my life in it.'

'Stop!' cried Vendale, in a terrible voice, staggering up with a last flash of fire breaking out of him, and clutching the thievish hands at his breast, in both of his. 'Stop! Stand away from me! God bless my Marguerite! Happily she will never know how I died. Stand off from me, and let me look at your murderous face. Let it remind me – of something – left to say.'

The sight of him fighting so hard for his senses and the doubt whether he might not for the instant be possessed by the strength of a dozen men, kept his opponent still. Wildy glaring at him, Vendale faltered out the broken words:

'It shall not be – the trust – of the dead – betrayed by me – reputed parents – misinherited fortune – see to it!'

As his head dropped on his breast, and he stumbled on the brink of the chasm as before, the thievish hands went once more, quick and busy, to his breast. He made a convulsive attempt to cry 'No!' desperately rolled himself over into the gulf; and sank away from his enemy's touch, like a phantom in a dreadful dream.

The mountain storm raged again, and passed again. The awful mountain-voices died away, the moon rose, and the soft and silent snow fell.

Two men and two large dogs came out at the door of the Hospice. The men looked carefully around them, and up at the sky. The dogs rolled in the snow, and took it into their mouths, and cast it up with their paws.

One of the men said to the other: 'We may venture now. We may find them in one of the five Refuges.' Each fastened on his back, a basket; each took in his hand, a strong spiked pole; each girded under his arms, a looped end of a stout rope, so that they were tied together.

Suddenly the dogs desisted from their gambols in the snow, stood looking down the ascent, put their noses up, put their noses down, became greatly excited, and broke into a deep loud bay together.

The two men looked in the faces of the two dogs. The two dogs looked, with at least equal intelligence, in the faces of the two men.

'Au secours, then! Help! To the rescue!' cried the two men. The two dogs, with a glad, deep, generous bark, bounded away.

'Two more mad ones!' said the men, stricken motionless, and looking away into the moonlight. 'Is it possible in such weather! And one of them a woman!'

Each of the dogs had the corner of a woman's dress in its mouth, and drew her along. She fondled their heads as she came up, and she came up through the snow with an accustomed tread. Not so the large man with her, who was spent and winded.

'Dear guides, dear friends of travellers! I am of your country. We seek two gentlemen crossing the Pass, who should have reached the Hospice this evening.'

'They have reached it, ma'amselle.'

'Thank Heaven! O thank Heaven!'

'But, unhappily, they have gone on again. We are setting forth to seek them even now. We had to wait until the *Tourmente* passed. It has been fearful up here.'

'Dear guides, dear friends of travellers! Let me go with you. let me go with you, for the love of GOD! One of those gentlemen is to be my husband. I love him, oh, so dearly. O so dearly! You see I am not faint, you see I am not tired. I am born a peasant girl. I will show you that I know well how to fasten myself to your ropes. I will do it with my own hands. I will swear to be brave and good. But let me go with you, let me go with you! If any mischance should have befallen him, my love would find him, when nothing else could. On my knees, dear friends of travellers! By the love of your dear mothers had for your fathers!'

The good rough fellows were moved. 'After all,' they murmured to one another, 'she speaks but the truth. She knows the ways of the mountains. See how marvellously she has come here! But as to Monsieur there, ma'amselle?'

'Dear Mr Joey,' said Marguerite, addressing him in his own tongue, 'you will remain at the house, and wait for me; will you not?'

'If I know'd which o' you two recommended it,' growled Joey Ladle, eyeing the two men with great indignation. 'I'd fight you for sixpence, and give you half-a-crown towards your expenses. No, miss. I'll stick by you as long as there's any sticking left in me, and I'll die for you when I can't do better.'

The state of the moon rendering it highly important that no time should be lost, and the dogs showing signs of great uneasiness, the two men quickly took their resolution. The rope that yoked them together was exchanged for a longer one; the party were secured, Marguerite second, and the Cellarman last; and they set out for the Refuges. The actual distance of those places was nothing; the whole five and the next Hospice to boot, being within two miles; but the ghastly way was whitened out and sheeted over.

They made no miss in reaching the Gallery where the two had taken shelter. The second storm of wind and snow had so wildly swept over it since, that their tracks were gone. But the dogs went to and fro with their noses down, and, were confident. The party stopping, however, at the further arch, where the second storm had been especially furious, and where the drift was deep, the dogs became troubled, and went about and about, in quest of a lost purpose.

The great abyss being known to lie on the right, they wandered too much to the left, and had to regain the way with infinite labour through a deep field of snow. The leader of the line had stopped it, and was taking note of the landmarks, when one of the dogs fell to tearing up the snow a little before them. Advancing and stooping to look at it, thinking that some one might be overwhelmed there, they saw that it was stained, and that the stain was red.

The other dog was now seen to look over the brink of the gulf, with his fore legs straightened out, lest he should fall into it, and to tremble in every limb. Then the dog who had found the stained snow joined him, and then they ran to and fro, distressed and whining. Finally, they both stopped on the brink together, and setting up their heads, howled dolefully.

'There is some one lying below,' said Marguerite.

'I think so,' said the foremost man. 'Stand well inward, the two last, and let us look over.'

The last man kindled two torches from his basket, and handed them forward. The leader taking one, and Marguerite the other, they looked down: now shading the torches, now moving them to the right or left, now raising them, now depressing them, as moonlight far below contended with black shadows. A piercing cry from Marguerite broke a long silence.

'My God! On a projecting point, where a wall of ice stretches forward over the torrent, I see a human form!'

'Where, ma'amselle, where?'

'See, there! On the shelf of ice below the dogs!'

The leader, with a sickened aspect, drew inward, and they were all silent. But they were not all inactive, for Marguerite, with swift and skilful fingers, had detached both herself and him from the rope in a few seconds.

'Show me the baskets. These two are the only ropes?'

'The only ropes here, ma'amselle; but at the Hospice—'

'If he is alive – I know it is my lover – he will be dead before you can return. Dear Guides! Blessed friends of travellers!

Look at me. Watch my hands. If they falter or go wrong, make me your prisoner by force. If they are steady and go right, help me to save him!'

She girded herself with a cord under the breast and arms, she formed it into a kind of jacket, she drew it into knots, she laid its end side by side with the end of the other cord, she twisted and twined the two together, she knotted them together, she set her foot upon the knots, she strained them, she held them for the two men to strain at.

'She is inspired,' they said to one another.

'By the Almighty's mercy!' she exclaimed. 'You both know that I am by far the lightest here. Give me the brandy and the wine, and lower me down to him. Then go for assistance and a stronger rope. You see that when it is lowered to me – look at this about me now – I can make it fast and safe to his body. Alive or dead, I will bring him up, or die with him. I love him passionately. Can I say more?'

They turned to her companion, but he was lying senseless on the snow.

'Lower me down to him,' she said, taking two little kegs they had brought, and hanging them about her, 'or I will dash myself to pieces! I am a peasant, and I know no giddiness or fear; and this is nothing to me, and I passionately love him. Lower me down!'

'Ma'amselle, ma'amselle, he must be dying or dead.'

'Dying or dead, my husband's head shall lie upon my breast, or I will dash myself to pieces.'

They yielded, overborne. With such precautions as their skill and the circumstances admitted, they let her slip from the summit, guiding herself down the precipitous icy wall with her hand, and they lowered down, and lowered down, and lowered down, until the cry came up: 'Enough!'

'Is it really he, and is he dead?' they called down, looking over.

The cry came up: 'He is insensible; but his heart beats. It beats against mine.'

'How does he lie?'

The cry came up: 'Upon a ledge of ice. It has thawed beneath him, and it will thaw beneath me. Hasten. If we die, I am content.'

One of the two men hurried off with the dogs at such

topmost speed as he could make; the other set up the lighted torches in the snow, and applied himself to recovering the Englishman. Much snow-chafing and some brandy got him on his legs, but delirious and quite unconscious where he was.

The watch remained upon the brink, and his cry went down continually: 'Courage! They will soon he here. How goes it?' And the cry came up: 'His heart still beats against mine. I warm him in my arms. I have cast off the rope, for the ice melts under us, and the rope would separate me from him: but I am not afraid.'

The moon went down behind the mountain tops, and all the abyss lay in darkness. The cry went dow: 'How goes it?' The cry came up: 'We are sinking lower, but his heart still beats against mine.'

At length, the eager barking of the dogs, and a flare of light upon the snow, proclaimed that help was coming on. Twenty or thirty men, lamps, torches, litters, ropes, blankets, wood to kindle a great fire, restoratives and stimulants, came in fast. The dogs ran from one man to another, and from this thing to that, and ran to the edge of the abyss, dumbly entreating Speed, speed, speed!

The cry went down: 'Thanks to God, all is ready. How goes it?'

The cry came up: 'We are sinking still, and we are deadly cold. His heart no longer beats against mine. Let no one come down, to add to our weight. Lower the rope only.'

The fire was kindled high, a great glare of torches lighted the sides of the precipice, lamps were lowered, a strong rope was lowered. She could be seen passing it round him, and making it secure.

The cry came up into a deathly silence: 'Raise! Softly!' They could see her diminished figure shrink, as he was swung into the air.

They gave no shout when some of them laid him on a litter, and others lowered another strong rope. The cry again came up into a deathly silence: 'Raise! Softly!' But when they caught her at the brink, they shouted, then they wept, then they gave thanks to Heaven, then they kissed her feet, then they kissed her dress, then the dogs caressed her, licked her icy hands, and with their honest faces warmed her frozen bosom!

She broke from them all, and sank over him on his litter, with both her loving hands upon the heart that stood still.

Act IV

The Clock-Lock

The pleasant scene was Neuchâtel; the pleasant month was April; the pleasant place was a notary's office; the pleasant person in it was the notary: a rosy, hearty, handsome old man, chief notary of Neuchâtel, known far and wide in the canton as Maître Voigt. Professionally and personally, the notary was a popular citizen. His innumerable kindnesses and his innumerable oddities had for years made him one of the recognised public characters of the pleasant Swiss town. His long brown frockcoat and his black skull-cap were among the institutions of the place; and he carried a snuff-box which, in point of size, was popularly believed to be without a parallel in Europe.

There was another person in the notary's office, not so pleasant as the notary. This was Obenreizer.

An oddly pastoral kind of office it was, and one that would never have answered in England. It stood in a neat backyard, fenced off from a pretty flower-garden. Goats browsed in the doorway, and a cow was within half-a-dozen feet of keeping company with the clerk. Maître Voigt's room was a bright and varnished little room, with panelled walls, like a toy-chamber. According to the seasons of the year, roses, sun-flowers, hollyhocks, peeped in at the windows. Maître Voigt's bees hummed through the office all the summer, in at this window and out at that, taking it frequently in their day's work, as if honey were to be made from Maître Voigt's sweet disposition. A large musical box on the chimney-piece, often trilled away at the Overture to Fra Diavolo, or a Selection from William Tell, with a chirruping liveliness that had to be stopped by force on the entrance of a client, and irrepressibly broke out again the moment his back was turned.

'Courage, courage my good fellow!' said Maître Voigt, patting Obenreizer on the knee, in a fatherly and a comforting way. 'You will begin a new life to-morrow morning in my office here.'

Obenreizer – dressed in mourning, and subdued in manner – lifted his hand, with a white handkerchief in it, to the region of his heart. 'The gratitude is here,' he said. 'But the words to express it are not here.'

'Ta-ta-ta! Don't talk to me about gratitude!' said Maître Voigt. 'I hate to see a man oppressed. I see you oppressed, and I hold out my hand to you by instinct. Besides, I am not too old yet, to remember my young days. Your father sent me my first client. (It was on a queston of half an acre of vineyard that seldom bore any grapes.) Do I owe nothing to your father's son? I owe him a debt of friendly obligation, and I pay it to you. That's rather neatly expressed, I think,' added Maître Voigt, in high good humour with himself. 'Permit me to reward my own merit with a pinch of snuff!'

Obenreizer dropped his eyes to the ground, as though he were not even worthy to see the notary take snuff.

'Do me one last favour, sir,' he said, when he raised his eyes. 'Do not act on impulse. Thus far, you have only a general knowledge of my position. Hear the case for and against me, in its details, before you take me into your office. Let me claim on your benevolence be recognised by your sound reason as well as by your excellent heart. In *that* case, I may hold up my head against the bitterest of my enemies, and build myself a new reputation on the ruins of the character I have lost.'

'As you will,' said Maître Voigt. 'You speak well, my son. You will be a fine lawyer one of these days.'

'The details are not many,' pursued Obenreizer. 'My troubles begin with the accidental death of my late travelling companion, my lost dear friend, Mr Vendale.'

'Mr Vendale,' repeated the notary. 'Just so. I have heard and read of the name, several times within these two months. The name of the unfortunate English gentleman who was killed on the Simplon. When you got that scar upon your cheek and neck.'

'– From my own knife,' said Obenreizer, touching what must have been an ugly gash at the time of its infliction.

'From your own knife,' assented the notary, 'and in trying to save him. Good, good, good. That was very good. Vendale.

Yes. I have several times, lately, thought it droll that I should once have had a client of that name.'

'But the world, sir,' returned Obenreizer, 'is *so* small!' Nevertheless he made a mental note that the notary had once had a client of that name.

'As I was saying, sir, the death of that dear travelling comrade begins my troubles. What follows? I save myself. I go down to Milan. I am received with coldness by Defresnier and Company. Shortly afterwards, I am discharged by Defresnier and Company. Why? They give no reason why. I ask, do they assail my honour? No answer. I ask, what is the imputation against me? No answer. I ask where are their proofs against me? No answer. I ask, what am I to think? The reply is, 'M. Obenreizer is free to think what he will. What M. Obenreizer thinks is of no importance to Defresnier and Comapny.' And that is all.'

'Perfectly. That is all,' assented the notary, taking a large pinch of snuff.

'But is that enough, sir?'

'That is not enough,' said Maître Voigt. 'The House of Defresnier are my fellow-townsmen – much respected, most esteemed – but the House of Defresnier must not silently destroy a man's character. You can rebut assertion. But how can you rebut silence?'

'Your sense of justice my dear patron,' answered Obenreizer, 'states in a word the cruelty of the case. Does it stop there? No. For, what follows upon that?'

'True, my poor boy,' said the notary, with a comforting nod or two; 'your ward rebels upon that.'

'Rebels is too soft a word,' retorted Obenreizer. 'My ward revolts from me with horror. My ward defies me. My ward withdraws herself from my authority, and takes shelter (Madame Dor with her) in the house of that English lawyer, Mr Bintrey, who replies to your summons to her to submit herself to my authority, that she will not do so.'

'– And who afterwards writes,' said the notary, moving his large snuff-box to look among the papers underneath it for the letter, 'that he is coming to confer with me.'

'Indeed?' replied Obenreizer, rather checked. 'Well, sir. Have I no legal rights?'

'Assuredly, my poor boy,' returned the notary. 'All but felons have their legal rights.'

'And who calls me felon?' said Obenreizer, fiercely.

'No one. Be calm under your wrongs. If the House of Defresnier would call you felon, indeed, we should know how to deal with them.'

While saying these words, he had handed Bintrey's very short letter to Obenreizer, who now read it and gave it back.

'In saying,' observed Obenreizer with recovered composure, 'that he is coming to confer with you, this English lawyer means that he is coming to deny my authority over my ward.'

'You think so?'

'I am sure of it. I know him. He is obstinate and contentious. You will tell me, my dear sir, whether my authority is unassailable, until my ward is of age?'

'Absolutely unassailable.'

'I will enforce it. I will make her submit herself to it. For,' said Obenreizer, changing his angry tone to one of grateful submission, 'I owe it to you, sir; to you, who have so confidently taken an injured man under your protection, and into your employment.'

'Make your mind easy,' said Maître Voigt. 'No more of this now, and no thanks! Be here to-morrow morning, before the other clerk comes – between seven and eight. You will find me in this room; and I will myself initiate you in your work. Go away! Go away! I have letters to write. I won't hear a word more.'

Dismissed with this generous abruptness, and satisfied with the favourable impression he had left on the old man's mind, Obenreizer was at leisure to revert to the mental note he had made that Maître Voigt once had a client whose name was Vendale.

'I ought to know England well enough by this time;' so his meditations ran, as he sat on a bench in the yard; 'and it is not a name I ever encountered there, except –' he looked involuntarily over his shoulder – 'as *his* name. Is the world so small that I cannot get away from him, even now when he is dead? He confessed at the last that he had betrayed the trust of the dead, and misinherited a fortune. And I was to see to it.

And I was to stand off, that my face might remind him of it. Why *my* face, unless it concerned *me?* I am sure of his words, for they have been in my ears ever since. Can there be anything bearing on them, in the keeping of this old idiot? Anything to repair my fortunes, and blacken his memory? He dwelt upon my earliest remembrances, that night at Basle. Why, unless he had a purpose in it?'

Maître Voigt's two largest he-goats were butting at him to butt him out of the place, as if for that desrespectful mention of their master. So he got up and left the place. But he walked along for a long time on the border of the lake, with his head drooped in deep thought.

Between seven and eight next morning, he presented himself again at the office. He found the notary ready for him, at work on some papers which had come in on the previous evening. In a few clear words, Maître Voigt explained the routine of the office, and the duties Obenreizer would be expected to perform. It still wanted five minutes to eight, when the preliminary instructions were declared to be complete.

'I will show you over the house and the offices,' said Maître Voigt, 'but I must put away these papers first. They come from the municipal authorities, and they must be taken special care of.'

Obenreizer saw his chance, here, of finding out the repository in which his employer's private papers were kept.

'Can't I save you the trouble, sir?' he asked. 'Can't I put those documents away under your directions?'

Maître Voigt laughed softly to himself; closed the portfolio in which the papers had been sent to him; handed it to Obenreizer.

'Suppose you try,' he said. 'All my papers of importance are kept yonder.'

He pointed to a heavy oaken door thickly studded with nails, at the lower end of the room. Approaching the door, with the portfolio, Obenreizer discovered, to his astonishment, that there were no means whatever of opening it from the outside. There was no handle, no bolt, no key, and (climax of passive obstruction!) no keyhole.

'There is a second door to this room?' said Obenreizer, appealing to the notary.

'No,' said Maître Voigt. 'Guess again.'

'There is a window?'

'Nothing of the sort. The window has been bricked up. The only way in, is the way by that door. Do you give it up?' cried Maître Voigt, in high triumph. 'Listen, my good fellow, and tell me if you hear nothing inside?'

Obenreizer listend for a moment, and started back from the door.

'I know!' he exclaimed. 'I heard of this when I was apprenticed here at the watchmaker's. Perrin Brothers have finished their famous clock-lock at last – and you have got it.?'

'Bravo!' said Maître Voigt. 'The clock-lock it is! There, my son! There you have one more of what the good people in this town call, "Daddy Voight's follies." With all my heart! Let those laugh who win. No thief can steal *my* keys. No burglar can pick *my* lock. No power on earth, short of a battering-ram or a barrel of gunpowder, can move that door, till my little sentinel inside – my worthy friend who goes 'Tick, Tick,' as I tell him – says, 'Open!' The big door obeys the little Tick, Tick, and the little Tick, Tick, obeys *me*. That!' cried Daddy Voigt, snapping his fingers, 'for all the thieves in Christendom!'

'May I see it in action?' asked Obenreizer. 'Pardon my curiosity, dear sir! You know that I was once a tolerable worker in the clock trade.'

'Certainly you shall see it in action,' said Maître Voigt. 'What is the time now? One minute to eight. Watch, and in one minute you will see the door open of itself.'

In one minute, smoothly and slowly and silently, as if invisible hands had set it free, the heavy door opened inward, and disclosed a dark chamber beyond. On three sides, shelves filled the walls, from floor to ceiling. Arranged on the shelves, were rows upon rows of boxes made in the pretty inlaid woodwork of Switzerland, and bearing inscribed on their fronts (for the most part in fanciful coloured letters) the names of the notary's clients.

Maître Voigt lighted a taper, and led the way into the room.

'You shall see the clock,' he said, proudly. 'I possess the greatest curiosity in Europe. It is only a privileged few whose eyes can look at it. I give the privilege to your good father's son – you shall be one of the favoured few who enter the room with me. See! Here it is, on the right-hand wall at the side of the door.'

'An ordinary clock,' exclaimed Obenreizer. 'No! Not an ordinary clock. It has only one hand.'

'Aha!' said Maître Voigt. 'Not an ordinary clock, my friend. No, no. That one hand goes round the dial. As I put it, so it regulates the hour at which the door shall open. See! The hand points to eight. At eight the door opened, as you saw for yourself.

'Does it open more than once in four-and-twenty hours?' asked Obenreizer.

'More than once?' repeated the notary, with great scorn. 'You don't know my good friend, Tick Tick! He will open the door as often as I ask him. All he wants, is his directions, and he gets them here. Look below the dial. Here is a half-circle of steel let into the wall, and here is a hand (called the regulator) that travels round it, just as *my* hand chooses. Notice, if you please, that there are figures to guide me on the half-circle of steel. Figure I. means: Open once in the four-and-twenty hours. Figure II. means; Open twice; and so on to the end. I set the regulator every morning, after I have read my letters, and when I know what my day's work is to be. Would you like to see me set it now? What is to-day? Wednesday. Good! This is the day of our rifle-club; there is little business to do: I grant a half-holiday. No work here to-day, after three o'clock. Let us first put away this portfolio of municipal papers. There! No need to trouble Tick-Tick to open the door until eight to-morrow. Good! I leave the dial-hand at eight; I put back the regualtor to 'I'. I close the door; and closed the door remains, past all opening by anybody, till to-morrow morning at eight.'

Obenreizer's quickness instantly saw the means by which he might make the clock-lock betray its master's confidence, and place its master's papers at his disposal.

'Stop, sir!' he cried, at the moment when the notary was closing the door. 'Don't I see something moving among the boxes – on the floor there?'

(Maître Voigt turned his back for a moment to look. In that moment, Obenreizer's ready hand put the regulator on, from the figure 'I'. to the figure 'II'. Unless the notary looked again at the half-circle of steel, the door would open at eight that evening, as well as at eight next morning, and nobody but Obenreizer would know it.)

'There is nothing!' said Maître Voigt. 'Your troubles have shaken your nerves, my son. Some shadow thrown by my taper; or some poor little beetle, who lives among the old lawyer's secrets, running away from the light. Hark! I hear your fellow-clerk in the office. To work! To work! And build to-day the first step that leads to your new fortunes!'

He good humouredly pushed Obenreizer out before him; extinguished the taper, with a last fond glance at his clock which passed harmlessly over the regualtor beneath; and closed the oaken door.

At three, the office was shut up. The notary and everybody in the notary's employment, with one exception, went to see the rifle-shooting. Obenreizer had pleaded that he was not in spirits for a public festival. Nobody knew what had become of him. It was believed that he had slipped away for a solitary walk.

The house and offices had been closed but a few minutes, when the door of a shining wardrobe, in the notary's shining room, opened, and Obenreizer stepped out. He walked to a window, unclosed the shutters, satisfied himself that he could escape unseen by way of the garden, turned back into the room, and took his place in the notary's easy chair. He was locked up in the house, and there were five hours to wait before eight o'clock came.

He wore his way through five hours: some times reading the books and newspapers that lay on the table; sometimes thinking; sometimes walking to and fro. Sunset came on. He closed the window-shutters before he kindled a light. The candle lighted, and the time drawing nearer and nearer, he sat, watch in hand, with his eys on the oaken door.

At eight, smoothly and softly and silently the door oepned.

One after another, he read the names on the outer rows of boxes. No such name as Vendale! He removed the outer row, and looked at the row behind. These were older boxes, and shabbier boxes. The four first that he examined, were inscribed with French and German names. The fifth bore a name which was almost illegible. He brought it out into the room, and examined it closely. There, covered thickly with time-stains and dust, was the name: 'Vendale.'

The key hung to the box by a string. He unlocked the box, took out four loose papers that were in it, spread them open on the table, and began to read them. He had not so occupied a minute, when his face fell from its expression of eagerness and avidity, to one of haggard astonishment and disappointment. But after a little consideration, he copied the papers. He then replaced the papers, replaced the box, closed the door, extinguished the candle, and stole away.

As his murderous and thievish footfall passed out of the garden, the steps of the notary and some one accompanying him stopped at the front door of the house. The lamps were lighted in the little street, and the notary had his door-key in his hand.

'Pray do not pass my house, Mr Bintrey,' he said. 'do me the honour to come in. It is one of our town half-holidays – our Tir – but my people will be back directly. It is droll that you should ask your way to the Hotel of me. Let us eat and drink before you go there.'

'Thank you; not to-night,' said Bintrey. 'Shall I come to you at ten to-morrow?'

'I shall be enchanted, sir, to take so early an opportunity of redressing the wrongs of my injured client,' returned the good notary.

'Yes,' retorted Bintrey; 'your injured client is all very well – but – a word in your ear.'

He whispered to the notary, and walked off. When then notary's housekeeper came home, she found him standing at his door motionless, with the key still in his hand, and the door unopened.

Obenreizer's Victory

The scene shifts again – to the foot of the Simplon, on the Swiss side.

In one of the dreary rooms of the dreary little inn at Brieg, Mr Bintrey and Maître Voigt sat together at a professional council of two. Mr Bintrey was searching in his despatch-box. Maître Voigt was looking towards a closed door, painted brown to imitate mahogany, and communicating with an inner room.

'Isn't it time he was here?' asked the notary, shifting his position, and glancing at a second door at the other end of the room, painted yellow to imitate deal.

'He *is* here,' answered Bintrey, after listening for a moment.

The yellow door was opened by a waiter, and Obenreizer walked in.

After greeting Maître Voigt with a cordiality which appeared to cause the notary no little embarrassment, Obenreizer bowed with grace and distant politeness to Bintrey. 'For what reason have I been brought from Neuchâtel to the foot of the mountain?' he inquired, taking the seat which the English lawyer had indicated to him.

'You shall be quite satisfied on that head before our interview is over,' returned Bintrey. 'For the present, permit me to suggest proceeding at once to business. There has been a correspondence, Mr Obenreizer, between you and your niece. I am here to represent your niece.'

'In other words, you, a lawyer, are here to represent an infraction of the law.'

'Admirably put!' said Bintrey. 'If all the people I have to deal with were only like you, what an easy profession mine would be! I am here to represent an infraction of the law – that is your point of view. I am here to make a compromise between you and your niece – that is my point of view.'

'There must be two parties to a compromise,' rejoined Obenreizer. 'I decline, in this case, to be one of them. The law gives me authority to control my niece's actions, until she comes of age. She is not yet of age; and I claim my authority.'

At this point Maître Voigt attempted to speak. Bintrey silenced him with a compassionate indulgence of tone and manner, as if he was silencing a favourite child.

'No, my worthy friend, not a word. Don't excite yourself unnecessarily; leave it to me.' He turned, and addressed himself again to Obenreizer. 'I can think of nothing comparable to you, Mr Obenreizer, but granite – and even that wears out in course of time. In the interests of peace and quietness –

for the sake of your own dignity – relax a little. If you will only delegate your authority to another person whom I know of, that person may be trusted never to lose sight of your niece, night or day!'

'You are wasting your time and mine,' returned Obenreizer. 'If my niece is not rendered up to my authority within one week from this day, I invoke the law. If you resist the law, I take her by force.'

He rose to his feet as he said the last word. Maître Voigt looked round again towards the brown door which led into the inner room.

'Have some pity on the poor girl,' pleaded Bintrey. 'Remember how lately she lost her lover by a dreadful death! Will nothing move you?'

'Nothing.'

Bintrey, in his turn, rose to his feet, and looked at Maître Voigt. Maître Voigt's hand, resting on the table, began to tremble. Maître Voigt's eyes remained fixed, as if by irresistible fascination, on the brown door. Obenreizer, suspiciously observing him, looked that way too.

'There is somebody listening in there!' he exclaimed, with a sharp backward glance at Bintrey.

'There are two people listening,' answered Bintrey.

'Who are they?'

'You shall see.'

With that answer, he raised his voice and spoke the next words – the two common words which are on everybody's lips, at every hour of the day: 'Come in!'

The brown door opened. Supported on Marguerite's arm – his sunburnt colour gone, his right arm bandaged and slung over his breast – Vendale stood before the murderer, a man risen from the dead.

In the moment of silence that followed, the singing of a caged bird in the courtyard outside was the one sound stirring in the room. Maître Voigt touched Bintrey, and pointed to Obenreizer. 'Look at him!' said the notary, in a whisper.

The shock had paralysed every movement in the villain's body, but the movement of the blood. His face was like the face of a corpse. The one vestige of colour left in it was a livid purple streak which marked the course of the scar, where his victim had wounded him on the cheek and neck. Speechless, breathless, motionless alike in eye and limb, it seemed as if, at the sight of Vendale, the death to which he had doomed Vendale had struck him where he stood. ̄

'Somebody ought to speak to him,' said Maître Voigt. 'Shall I?'

Even at that moment, Bintrey persisted in silencing the notary, and in keeping the lead in the proceedings to himself. Checking Maître Voigt by a gesture, he dismissed Marguerite and Vendale in these words:– 'The object of your appearance here is answered,' he said. 'if you will withdraw for the present, it may help Mr Obenreizer to recover himself.'

It did help him. As the two passed through the door, and closed it behind them, he drew a deep breath of relief. He looked round him for the chair from which he had risen, and dropped into it.

'Give him time!' pleaded Maître Voigt.

'No,' said Bintrey. 'I don't know what use he may make of it, if I do.' He turned once more to Obenreizer, and went on. 'I owe it to myself,' he said – 'I don't admit, mind, that I owe it to *you* – to account for my appearance in these proceedings, and to state what has been done under my advice, and on my sole responsibility. Can you listen to me?'

'I can listen to you.'

'Recall the time when you started for Switzerland with Mr Vendale,' Bintrey began. 'You had not left England four-and-twenty hours, before your niece committed an act of imprudence which not even your penetration could foresee. She followed her promised husband on his journey, without asking anybody's advice or permission, and without any better companion to protect her than a Cellarman in Mr Vendale's employment.

'Why did she follow me on the journey? And how came the Cellarman to be the person who accompanied her?'

'She followed you on the journey,' answered Bintrey, 'because she suspected there had been some serious collision between you and Mr Vendale, which had been kept secret from her; and because she rightly believed you to be capable of serving your interests, or of satisfying your enmity, at the price of a crime. As for the Cellarman, he was one, among the

other people in Mr Vendale's establishment, to whom she had
applied (the moment your back was turned) to know if
anything had happened between their master and you. The
Cellarman alone had something to tell her. A senseless
superstition, and a common accident which had happened to
his master, in his master's cellar, had connected Mr Vendale in
this man's mind with the idea of danger by murder. Your
niece surprised him into a confession, which aggravated
tenfold the terrors that possessed her. Aroused to a sense of the
mischief he had done, the man, of his own accord, made the
one atonement in his power. 'If my master is in danger, miss,'
he said, 'it's my duty to take care of *you*.' The two set forth
together – and, for once, a superstition has had its use. It
decided your niece on taking the journey; and it led the way to
saving a man's life. Do you understand me, so far?'

'I understand you, so far.'

'My first knowledge of the crime that you had committed,'
pursued Bintrey, 'came to me in the form of a letter from your
niece. All you need know is that her love and her courage
recovered the body of your victim, and aided the after-efforts
which brought him back to life. While he lay helpless at Brieg,
under her care, she wrote to me to come out to him. Before
starting, I informed Madame Dor that I knew Miss
Obenreizer to be safe, and knew where she was. Madame Dor
informed me, in return, that a letter had come for your niece,
which she knew to be in your handwriting. I took possession
of it, and arranged for the forwarding of any other letter
which might follow. Arrived at Brieg, I found Mr Vendale
out of danger, and at once devoted myself of hastening the day
of reckoning with you. Defresnier and Company warned you
off on suspicion; acting on information privately supplied by
me. Having stripped you of your false character, the next
thing to do was to strip you of your authority over your niece.
To reach this end, I not only had no scruple in digging the
pitfall under your feet in the dark – I felt a certain professional
pleasure in fighting you with your own weapons. By my
advice, the truth has been carefully concealed from you, up to
this day. By my advice the trap into which you have walked
was set for you (you know why, now, as well as I do) in this
place. There was but one certain way of shaking the devilish

self-control which has hitherto made you a formidable man. That way has been tried, and (look at me as you may) that way has succeeded. The last thing that remains to be done,' concluded Bintrey, producing two little slips of manuscript from his despatch-box, 'is to set your niece free. You have attempted murder, and you have committed forgery and theft. We have the evidence ready against you in both cases. If you are convicted as a felon, you know as well as I do what becomes of your authority over your niece. Personally, I should have preferred taking that way out of it. But considerations are pressed on me which I am not able to resist, and this interview must end, as I have told you already, in a compromise. Sign those lines, resigning all authority over Miss Obenreizer, and pledging yourself never to be seen in England or in Switzerland again; and I will sign an idemnity which secures you against further proceedings on our part.'

Obenreizer took the pen, in silence, and signed his niece's release. On receiving the indemnity in return, he rose, but made no movement to leave the room. He stood looking at Maître Voigt with a strange smile gathering at his lips, and a strange light flashing in his filmy eyes.

'What are you waiting for?' asked Bintrey.

Obenreizer pointed to the brown door. 'Call them back,' he answered. 'I have something to say in their presence before I go.'

'Say it in my presence,' retorted Bintrey. 'I decline to call them back.'

Obenreizer turned to Maître Voigt. 'Do you remember telling me that you once had an English client named Vendale?' he asked.   'Well,' answered the notary. 'And what of that?'

'Maître Voigt, your clock-lock has betrayed you.'

'What do you mean?'

'I have read the letters and certificates in your client's box. I have taken copies of them. I have got the copies here. Is there, or is there not, a reason for calling them back?'

For a moment the notary looked to and fro, between Obenreizer and Bintrey, in helpless astonishment. Recovering himself, he drew his brother-lawyer aside, and hurriedly spoke a few words close at his ear. The face of Bintrey – after first faithfully reflecting the astonishment on the face of Maître Voigt – suddenly altered its expression. He sprang, with the activity of a young man, to the door of the inner room, entered it, remained inside for a minute, and returned followed by Marguerite and Vendale. 'Now, Mr Obenreizer,' said Bintrey, 'the last move in the game is yours. Play it.'

'Before I resign my position as that young lady's guardian,' said Obenreizer, 'I have a secret to reveal in which she is interested. In making my disclosure, I am not claiming her attention for a narrative which she, or any other person present, is expected to take on trust. I am possessed of written proofs, copies of originals, the authenticity of which Maître Voigt himself can attest. Bear that in mind, and permit me to refer you, at starting, to a date long past – the month of February, is the year one thousand eight hundred and thirty-six.'

'Mark the date, Mr Vendale,' said Bintrey.

'My first proof,' said Obenreizer, taking a paper from his pocket-book. 'Copy of a letter, written by an English lady (married) to her sister, a widow. The name of the person writing the letter I shall keep suppressed until I have done. The name of the person to whom the letter is written I am willing to reveal. It is addressed to 'Mrs Jane Anne Miller, of Groombridge-wells, England.'

Vendale started, and opened his lips to speak. Bintrey instantly stopped him, as he had stopped Maître Voigt. 'No,' said the pertinacious lawyer. 'Leave it to me.'

Obenreizer went on:

'It is needless to trouble you with the first half of the letter,' he said. 'I can give the substance of it in two words. The writer's position at the time is this. She has been long living in Switzerland with her husband – obliged to live there for the sake of her husband's health. They are about to move to a new residence on the Lake of Neuchâtel in a week, and they will be ready to receive Mrs Miller as visitor in a fortnight from that time. This said, the writer next enters into an important domestic detail. She has been childless for years – she and her husband have now no hope of children; they are lonely; they want an interest in life; they have decided on adopting a child. Here the important part of the letter begins; and here, therefore, I read it to you word for word.'

He folded back the first page of the letter and read as follows:

'. . . Will you help us, my dear sister, to realise our new project? As English people, we wish to adopt an English child. This may be done, I believe at the Foundling: my husband's lawyers in London will tell you how. I leave the choice to you, with only these conditions attached to it – that the child is to be an infant under a year old, and is to be a boy. Will you pardon the trouble I am giving you, for my sake; and will you bring our adopted child to us, with your own children, when you come to Neuchâtel?

'I must add a word as to my husband's wishes in this matter. He is resolved to spare the child whom we make our own, any future mortification and loss of self-respect which might be caused by the discovery of his true origin. He will bear my husband's name, and he will be brought up in the belief that he is really our son. His inheritance of what we have to leave will be secured to him – not only according to the laws of England in such cases, but according to the laws of Switzerland also; for we have lived so long in this country, that there is a doubt whether we may not be considered as 'domiciled' in Switzerland. The one precaution left to take is to prevent any after-discovery at the Foundling. Now, our name is a very uncommon one; and if we appear on the Register of the Institution as the persons adopting the child, there is just a chance that something might result from it. Your name, my dear, is the name of thousands of other people; and if *you* will consent to appear on the Register, there need by no fear of any discoveries in that quarter. We are moving, by the doctor's orders, to a part of Switzerland in which our circumstances are quite unknown; and you, as I understand, are about to engage a new nurse for the journey when you come to see us. Under these circumstances, the child may appear as my child, brought back to me under my sister's care. The only servant we take with us from our old home is my own maid, who can be safely trusted. As for the lawyers in England and in Switzerland, it is their profession to keep secrets – and we may feel quite easy in that direction. So there you have our

harmless little conspiracy! Write by return of post, my love,
and tell me you will join it.'. . . .

'Do you still conceal the name of the writer of that letter?'
asked Vendale.

'I keep the name of the writer till the last,' answered
Obenreizer, 'and I proceed to my second proof – a mere slip of
paper, this time, as you see. Memorandum given to the Swiss
lawyer, who drew the documents referred to in the letter I
have just read, expressed as follows:– "Adopted from the
Foundling Hospital of England, 3rd March, 1836, a male
infant, called, in the Institution, Walter Wilding. Person
appearing on the register, as adopting the child, Mrs Jane
Anne Miller, widow, acting in this matter for her married
sister, domiciled in Switzerland." Patience!' resumed
Obenreizer, as Vendale, breaking loose from Bintrey, started
to his feet. 'I shall not keep the name concealed much longer.
Two more little slips of paper, and I have done. Third proof!
Certificate of Doctor Ganz, still living in practice at
Neuchâtel, dated July, 1838. The doctor certifies (you shall
read it for yourselves directly), first, that he attended the
adopted child in its infant maladies; second, that, three months
before the date of the certificate, the gentleman adopting the
child as his son died; third, that *on* the date of the certificate,
his widow and her maid, taking the adopted child with them
left Neuchâtel on their return to England. One more link now
added to this, and my chain of evidence is complete. The maid
remained with her mistress till her mistress's death, only a few
years since. The maid can swear to the identity of the adopted
infant, from his childhood to his youth – from his youth to his
manhood, as he is now. There is her address in England – and
there, Mr Vendale, is the fourth, and final proof!'

'Why do you address yourself to *me*?' said Vendale, as
Obenreizer threw the written address on the table.

Obenreizer turned on him, in a sudden frenzy of triumph.

'*Because you are the man*! If my niece married you, she
marries a bastard, brought up by public charity. If my niece
marries you, she marries an impostor, without name or
lineage, disguised in the character of a gentleman of rank and
family.'

'Bravo!' cried Bintrey. 'Admirably put, Mr Obenreizer! It only wants one word more to complete it. She marries – thanks entirely to your exertions – a man who inherits a handsome fortune, and a man whose origin will make him prouder than ever of his peasant-wife. George Vendale, as brother-executors, let us congratulate each other! Our dear dead friend's last wish on earth is accomplished. We have found the lost Walter Wilding. As Mr Obenreizer said just now – you are the man!'

The words passed by Vendale unheeded. For the moment he was conscious of but one sensation; he heard but one voice. Marguerite's voice was whispering to him: 'I never loved you, George, as I love you now!'

The Curtain Falls

May-Day. There is merry-making in Cripple Corner, the chimneys smoke, the patriarchal dining-hall is hung with garlands, and Mrs Goldstraw, the respected housekeeper, is very busy. For, on this bright morning the young master of Cripple Corner is married to its young mistress, far away: to wit, in the little town of Brieg, in Switzerland, lying at the foot of the Simplon Pass where she saved his life.

The bells ring gaily in the little town of Brieg, and flags are stretched across the street, and rifle shots are heard, and sounding music from brass instruments. Streamer-decorated casks of wine have been rolled out under a gay awning in the public way before the Inn, and there will be free feasting and revelry. What with bells and banners, draperies hanging from windows, explosion of gunpowder, and reverberation of brass music, the little town of Brieg is all in a flutter, like the hearts of its simple people.

It was a stormy night last night, and the mountains are covered with snow. But the sun is bright to-day, the sweet air is fresh, the tin spires of the little town of Brieg are burnished silver, and the Alps are ranges of far-off white cloud in a deep blue sky.

The primitive people of the little town of Brieg have built a greenwood arch across the street, under which the newly married pair shall pass in triumph from the church. It is inscribed, on that side, 'HONOUR AND LOVE TO MARGUERITE VENDALE!' for the people are proud of her to enthusiasm. This greeting of the bride under her new name is affectionately meant as a surpirse, and therefore the arrangement has been made that she, unconscious why, shall be taken to the church by a tortuous back way. A scheme not difficult to carry into execution in the crooked little town of Brieg.

So, all things are in readiness, and they are to go and come on foot. Assembled in the Inn's best chamber, festively adorned, are the bride and bridgegroom, the Neuchâtel notary, the London lawyer, Madame Dor, and a certain large mysterious Englishman, popularly know as Monseiur Zhoé-Ladelle. And behold Madame Dor, arrayed in a spotless pair of gloves of her own, with no hand in the air, but both hands clasped round the neck of the bride; to embrace whom Madame Dor has turned her broad back on the company, consistent to the last.

'Forgive me, my beautiful,' pleads Madame Dor, 'for that I ever was his she-cat!'

'She-cat, Madame Dor?'

'Engaged to sit watching my so charming mouse,' are the explanatory words of Madame Dor, delivered with a penitential sob.

'Why, you were our best friend! George, dearest, tell Madame Dor. Was she not our best friend?'

'Undoubtedly, darling. What should we have done without her?'

'You are both so generous,' cries Madame Dor, accepting consolation, and immediately relapsing. 'But I commenced as a she-cat.'

'Ah! But like the cat in the fairy-story, good Madame Dor,' says Vendale, saluting her cheek, 'you were a true woman. And, being a true woman, the sympathy of your heart was with true love.'

'I don't wish to deprive Madame Dor of her share in the embraces that are going on,' Mr Bintrey puts in, watch in hand, 'and I don't presume to offer any obejction to your having got yourselves mixed together, in the corner there, like the three Graces. I merely remark that I think it's time we were moving. What are *your* sentiments on that subject, Mr Ladle?'

'Clear, sir,' replies Joey, with a gracious grin. 'I'm clearer altogether, sir, for having lived so many weeks upon the surface. I never was half so long upon the surface afore, and it's done me a power of good. At Cripple Corner, I was too much below it. Atop of the Simpleton, I was a deal too high above it. I've found the medium here, sir. And if ever I take it in convivial, in all the rest of my days, I mean to do it this day, to the toast of "Bless 'em both."'

'I, too!' says Bintrey. 'And now, Monsieur Voigt, let you and me be two men of Marseilles, and allons, marchons, arm-in-arm!'

They go down to the door, where others are waiting for them, and they go quietly to the church, and the happy marriage takes place. While the ceremony is yet in progress, the notary is called out. When it is finished, he has returned, is standing behind Vendale, and touches him on the shoulder.

'Go to the side door, one moment, Monsieur Vendale. Alone. Leave Madame to me.'

At the side door of the church, are the same two men from the Hospice. They are snow-stained and travel-worn. They wish him joy, and then each lays his broad hand upon Vendale's breast, and one says in a low voice, while the other steadfastly regards him:

'It is here, Monsieu. Your litter. The very same.'

'My litter is here? Why?'

'Hush! For the sake of Madame. Your companion of that day—'

'What of him?'

The man looks at his comrade, and his comrade takes him up. Each keeps his hand laid earnestly on Vendale's breast.

'He had been living at the first Refuge, monsieur, for some days. The weather was now good, now bad.'

'Yes?'

'He arrived at our Hospice the day before yesterday, and, having refreshed himself with sleep on the floor before the fire, wrapped in his cloak, was resolute to go on, before dark, to the next Hospice. He had a great fear of that part of the way, and thought it would be worse to-morrow.'

'Yes?'

'He went on alone. He had passed the gallery, when an avalanche – like that which fell behind you near the Bridge of Ganther—'

'Killed him?'

'We dug him out, suffocated and broken all to pieces! But, monsieur, as to Madame. We have brought him here on the litter, to be buried. We must ascend the street outside. Madame must not see. It would be an accursed thing to bring the litter through the arch across the street, until Madame has passed through. As you descend, we who accompany the litter will set it down on the stones of the street the second to the right, and will stand before it. But do not let Madame turn her head towards the street the second to the right. There is no time to lose. Madame will be alarmed by your absence. Adieu!'

Vendale returns to his bride, and draws her hand through his unmaimed arm. A pretty procession awaits them at the main door of the church. They take their station in it, and descend the street amidst the ringing of the bells, the firing of the guns, the waving of the flags, the playing of the music, the shouts, the smiles and tears, of the excited town. Heads are uncovered as she passes, hands are kissed to her, all the people bless her. 'Heaven's benediction on the dear girl! See where she goes in her youth and beauty; she who so nobly saved his life!'

Near the corner of the street the second to the right, he speaks to her, and calls her attention to the windows on the opposite side. The corner well passed, he says: 'Do not look round, my darling, for a reason that I have,' and turns his head. Then, looking back along the street, he sees the litter and its bearers passing up alone under the arch, as he and she and their marriage train go down towards the shining valley.

THE LAZY TOUR OF TWO IDLE APPRENTICES

by Charles Dickens and Wilkie Collins

Chapter I

In the autumn month of September, eighteen hundred and fifty-seven, wherein these presents bear date, two idle apprentices, exhausted by the long hot summer and the long hot work it had brought with it, ran away from their employer. They were bound to a highly meritorious lady (named Literature), of fair credit and repute, though, it must be acknowledged, not quite so highly esteemed in the City as she might be. This is the more remarkable, as there is nothing against the respectable lady in that quarter, but quite the contrary; her family having rendered eminent service to many famous citizens of London. It may be sufficient to name Sir William Walworth, Lord Mayor under King Richard the Second, at the time of Wat Tyler's insurrection, and Sir Richard Whittington: which latter distinguished man and magistrate was doubtless indebted to the lady's family for the gift of his celebrated cat. There is also strong reason to suppose that they rang the Highgate bells for him with their own hands.

The misguided young men who thus shirked their duty to the mistress from whom they have received many favours, were actuated by the low idea of making a perfectly idle trip, in any direction. They had no intention of going anywhere, in particular; they wanted to see nothing, they wanted to know nothing, they wanted to learn nothing, they wanted to do nothing. They wanted only to be idle. They took to themselves (after HOGARTH), the names of Mr Thomas Idle and Mr Francis Goodchild; but, there was not a moral pin to choose between them, and they were both idle in the last degree.

Between Francis and Thomas, however, there was this difference of character: Goodchild was laboriously idle, and would take upon himself any amount of pains and labour to assure himself that he was idle; in short, had no better idea of idleness than that it was useless industry. Thomas Idle, on the other hand, was an idler of the unmixed Irish or Neapolitan type; a passive idler, a born-and-bred idler, a consistent idler, who practised what he would have preached if he had not been too idle to preach; a one entire and perfect chrysolite of idleness.

The two idle apprentices found themselves, within a few hours of their escape, walking down into the North of England. That is to say, Thomas was lying in a meadow, looking at the railway trains as they passed over a distant viaduct – which was *his* idea of walking down into the North; while Francis was walking a mile due South against time – which was *his* idea of walking down into the North. In the meantime the day waned, and the milestones remained unconquered.

'Tom,' said Goodchild, 'the sun is getting low. Up, and let us go forward!'

'Nay,' quoth Thomas Idle, 'I have not done with Annie Laurie yet.' And he proceeded with that idle but popular ballad, to the effect that for the bonnie young person of that name he would 'lay him doon and dee,' – equivalent, in prose, to lay down and die.

'What an ass that fellow was!' cried Goodchild, with the bitter emphasis of contempt.

'Which fellow?' asked Thomas Idle.

'The fellow in your song. Lay him doon and dee! Finely he'd show off before the girl by doing *that*. A Sniveller! Why couldn't he get up, and punch somebody's head!'

'Whose?' asked Thomas Idle.

'Anybody's. Everybody's would be better than nobody's! If I fell into that state of mind about a girl, do you think I'd lay me doon and dee? No, sir,' proceeded Goodchild, with a disparaging assumption of the Scottish accent, 'I'd get me oop and peetch into somebody. Wouldn't you?'

'I wouldn't have anything to do with her,' yawned Thomas Idle. 'Why should I take the trouble?'

'It's no trouble Tom, to fall in love,' said Goodchild, shaking his head.

'It's trouble enough to fall out of it, once you're in it,' retorted Tom. 'So I keep out of it altogether. It would be better for you, if you did the same.

Mr Goodchild, who is always in love with somebody, and not unfrequently with several objects at once, made no reply. He heaved a sigh of the kind which is termed by the lower orders 'a bellowser,' and then, heaving Mr Idle on his feet (who was not half so heavy as the sigh), urged him northward.

These two had sent their personal baggage on by train: only retaining, each a knapsack. Idle now applied himself to constantly regretting the train, to tracking it through the intricacies of Bradshaw's Guide, and finding out where it was now – and where now – and where now – and to asking what was the use of walking, when you could ride at such a pace as that. Was it to see the country? If that was the object, look at it out of carriage-windows. There was a great deal more of it to be seen there, than here. besides, who wanted to see the country? Nobody. And, again, who ever did walk? Nobody. Fellows set off to walk, but they never did it. They came back and said they did, but they didn't. Then why should he walk? He wouldn't walk. He swore it by this milestone!

It was the fifth from London, so far had they penetrated into the North. Submitting to the powerful chain of argument, Goodchild proposed a return to the Metropolis, and a falling back upon Euston Square Terminus. Thomas assented with alacrity, and as they walked down into the North by the next morning's express, and carried their knapsacks in the luggage-van.

It was like all other expresses, as every express is and must be. It bore through the harvested country, a smell like a large washing-day, and a sharp issue of steam as from a huge brazen tea-urn. The greatest power in nature and art combined, it yet glided over dangerous heights in the sight of people looking up from fields and roads, as smoothly and unreally as a light miniature plaything. Now, the engine shrieked in hysterics of such intensity, that it seemed desirable that the men who had her in charge should hold her feet, slap her hands, and bring her to; now, burrowed into tunnels with a stubborn and undemonstrative energy so confusing that the train seemed to be flying back into leagues of darkness. Here, were station after station, swallowed up by the express without stopping; here, stations where it fired itself in like a volley of cannon-balls, swooped away four country-people with nosegays and three men of business with portmanteaus, and fired itself off again, bang, bang, bang! At long intervals were uncomfort-able refreshment rooms, made more uncomfortable by the scorn of Beauty towards Beast, the public (but to whom she never relented, as Beauty did in the story, towards the other Beast), and where sensitive stomachs were fed, with a con-temptuous sharpness occasioning indigestion. Here, again, were stations with nothing going but a bell, and wonderful wooden razors set aloft on great posts, shaving the air. In these fields, the horses, sheep, and cattle were well used to the thundering meteor, and didn't mind; in those, they were all set scampering together, and a herd of pigs scoured after them. The pastoral country darkened, became coaly, become smoky, became infernal, got better, got worse, improved again, grew rugged, turned romantic; was a wood, a stream, a chain of hills, a gorge, a moor, a cathedral town, a fortified place, a waste. Now, miserable black dwellings, a black canal, and sick black towers of chimneys; now, a trim garden, where the flowers were bright and fair; now, a wilderness of hideous altars all a-blaze; now, the water meadows with their fairy rings; now, the mangy patch of unlet building ground outside the stagnant town, with the larger ring where the circus was last week. The temperature changed, the dialect changed, the people changed, faces got sharper, manner got shorter, eyes got shrewder and harder; yet all so quickly, that the spruce guard in the London uniform and silver lace, had not yet rumpled his shirt-collar, delivered half the dispatches in his shining little pouch, or read his newspaper.

Carlisle! Idle and Goodchild had got to Carlisle. It looked congenially and delightfully idle. Something in the way of public amusement had happened last month, and something else was going to happen before Christmas; and, in the meantime there was a lecture on India for those who liked it – which Idle and Goodchild did not. Likewise, by those who

liked them, there were impressions to be bought of all the
vapid prints, going and gone, and of nearly all the vapid
books. For those who wanted to put anything in missionary
boxes, here were the boxes. For those who wanted the
Reverend Mr Podgers (artist's proofs, thirty shillings), here
was Mr Podgers to any amount. Not less gracious and
abundant, Mr Codgers, also of the vineyard, but opposed to
Mr Podgers, brotherly tooth and nail. Here were guide-books
to the neighbouring antiquities, and eke the Lake country, in
several dry and husky sorts; here, many physically and
morally impossible heads of both sexes, for young ladies to
copy, in the exercise of the art of drawing; here, further, a
large impression of MR SPURGEON, solid as to the flesh, not to
say even something gross. The working young men of
Carlisle were drawn up, with their hands in their pockets,
across the pavements, four and six abreast, and appeared
(much to the satisfaction of Mr Idle) to have nothing else to
do. The working and growing young women of Carlisle,
from the age of twelve upwards, promenaded the streets in the
cool of the evening, and rallied the said young men. Sometimes the young men rallied the young women, as in the case
of a group gathered round an accordion-player, from among
whom a young man advanced behind a young woman for
whom he appeared to have a tenderness, and hinted to her that
he was there and playful, by giving her (he wore clogs) a kick.

On market morning, Carlisle woke up amazingly, and
became (to the two Idle Apprentices disagreeably and
reproachfully busy. There were its cattle market, its sheep
market, and its pig market down by the river, with raw-boned
and shock-headed Rob Roys hiding their Lowland dresses
beneath heavy plaids, prowling in and out among the animals,
and flavouring the air with fumes of whiskey. There was its
corn market down the main street, with hum of chaffering
over open sacks. There was its general market in the street
too, with heather brooms on which the purple flower still
flourished, and heather baskets primitive and fresh to behold.
With women trying on clogs and caps at open stalls, and
'Bible stalls' adjoining. With 'Doctor Mantle's Dispensary for
the cure of all Human Maladies and no charge for advice,' and
with Doctor Mantle's 'Laboratory of Medical, Chemical, and

Botanical Sciences' – both healing institutions established on
one pair of trestles, one board, and one sun-blind. With the
renowned phrenologist from London, begging to be favoured
(at sixpence each) with the company of clients of both sexes,
to whom, on examination of their heads, he would make
revelations 'enabling him or her to know themselves.'
Through all these bargains and blessings, the recruiting-
serjeant watchfully elbowed his way, a thread of War in the
peaceful skein. Likewise on the walls were printed hints that
the Oxford Blues might not be indisposed to hear of a few fine
active young men; and that whereas the standard of that
distinguished corps is full six feet 'growing lads of five feet
eleven' need not absolutely despair of being accepted.

Scenting the morning air more pleasantly than the buried
majesty of Denmark did, Messrs Idle and Goodchild rode
away from Carlisle at eight o'clock one forenoon, bound for
the village of Heske, Newmarket, some fourteen miles distant. Goodchild (who had already begun to doubt whether he
was idle: as his way always is when he has nothing to do), had
read of a certain black old Cumberland hill or mountain, called
Carrock, or Carrock Fell; and had arrived at the conclusion
that it would be the culminating triumph of Idleness to ascend
the same. Thomas Idle, dwelling on the pains inseparable
from that achievement, had expressed the strongest doubts of
the expediency, and even of the sanity, of the enterprise; but
Goodchild had carried his point, and they rode away.

Up hill and down hill, and twisting to the right and twisting
to the left, and with old Skiddaw (who has vaunted himself a
great deal more than his merits deserve; but that is rather the
way of the Lake country), dodging the apprentices in a
picturesque and pleasant manner. Good, water-proof, warm,
peasant houses, well white-limed, scantily dotting the road.
Clean children coming out to look, carrying other clean
children as big as themselves. Harvest still lying out and much
rained upon; here and there, harvest still unreaped. Well
cultivated gardens attached to the cottages, with plenty of
produce forced out of their hard soil. Lonely nooks, and wild;
but people can be born, and married, and buried in such
nooks, and can live and love, and be loved, there as elsewhere
thank God! (Mr Goodchild's remark.) By-and-by, the village.

Black, coarse-stoned, rough-windowed houses; some with outer staircases, like Swiss houses; a sinuous and stony gutter winding up hill and round the corner, by way of street. All the children running out directly. Women pausing in washing, to peep from doorways and very little windows. Such were the observations of Messrs Idle and Goodchild, as their conveyance stopped at the village shoemaker's. Old Carrock gloomed down upon it all a very ill-tempered state; and rain was beginning.

The village shoemaker declined to have anything to do with Carrock. No visitors went up Carrock. No visitors came there at all. Aa' the world ganged awa' yon. The driver appealed to the Innkeeper. The Innkeeper had two men working in the fields, and one of them should be called in, to go up Carrock as guide. Messrs. Idle and Goodchild, highly approving, entered the Innkeeper's house, to drink whiskey and eat oatcake.

The Innkeeper was not idle enough – was not idle at all, which was a great fault in him – but was a fine specimen of a north-country man, or any kind of man. He had a ruddy cheek, a bright eye, a well-knit frame, an immense hand, as cheery outspeaking voice, and a straight, bright, broad look. He had a drawing-room, too, up-stairs, which was worth a visit to the Cumberland Fells. (This was Mr Francis Goodchild's opinion, in which Mr Thomas Idle did not concur.)

The ceiling of this drawing-room was so crossed and re-crossed by beams of unequal lenghts, radiating from a centre in a corner, that it looked like a broken star-fish. The room was comfortably and solidly furnished with good mahogany and horsehair. It had a snug fire-side, and a couple of well-curtained windows, looking out upon the wild country behind the house. What it most developed was, an unexpected taste for little ornaments and nick-nacks, of which it contained a most surprising number. They were not very various, consisting in great part of waxen babies with their limbs more or less mutilated, appealing on one leg to the parental affections from under little cupping-glasses; but, Uncle Tom was there, in crockery, receiving theological instructions from Miss Eva, who grew out of his side like a wen, in an exceedingly rough state of profile propagandism.

Engravings of Mr Hunt's country-boy, before and after his pie, were on the wall, divided by a highly-coloured nautical piece, the subject of which had all her colours (and more) flying, and was making great way through a sea of a regualr pattern, like a lady's collar. A benevolent elderly gentleman of the last century, with a powdered head, kept guard, in oil and varnish, over a most perplexing piece of furniture on a table; in appearance between a driving seat an an angular knife-box, but, when opened, a musical instrument of tinkling wire, exactly like David's harp packed for travelling. Everything became a nick-nack in this curious room. The copper tea-kettle burnished up to the highest point of glory, took his station on a stand of his own at the greatest possible distance from the fire-place, and said, 'By your leave, not a kittle, but a bijou.' The Staffordshire-ware butter-dish with the cover on, got upon a little round occasional table in a window, with a worked top, and announced itself to the two chairs accidentally placed there, as an aid to polite conversation, a graceful trifle in china to be chatted over by callers, as they airily trifled away the visiting moments of a butterfly exist-ence, in that rugged old village on the Cumberland Fells. The very footstool could not keep the floor, but got upon the sofa, and therefrom proclaimed itself, in high relief of white and liver-coloured wool, a favourite spaniel coiled up for repose. Though, truly, in spite of its bright glass eyes, the spaniel was the least successful assumption in the collection: being perfec-tly flat, and dismally suggestive of a recent mistake in sitting down, on the part of some corpulent member of the family.

There were books, too, in this room; books on the table, books on the chimney-piece, books in an open press in the coner. Fielding was there, and Smollet was there, and Steele and Addison were there, in dispersed volumes; and there were tales of those who go down to the sea in ships, for windy nights; and there was really a choice of good books for rainy days or fine. It was so very pleasant to see these things in such a lonesome by place – so very agreeable to find these evidences of a taste, however homely, that went beyond the beautiful cleanliness and trimness of the house – so fanciful to imagine what a wonder the room must be to the little children born in the gloomy village – what grand impressions of it those of them who became wanders over the earth would carry away; and how, at distant ends of the world, some old voyagers would die, cherisihing the belief that the finest apartment known to men was once in the Hesket-Newmarket Inn, in rare old Cumberland – it was such a charmingly lazy pursuit to entertain these rambling thoughts over the choice oat-cake and the genial whiskey, That Mr Idle and Mr Goodchild never asked themselves how it came to pass that the men in the fields were never heard of more, how the stalwart landlord replaced them without explanation, how his dog-cart came to be waiting at the door, and how everything was arranged without the least arrangement, for climbing to old Carrock's shoulders, and standing on his head.

Without a word in inquiry therefore, The Two Idle Apprentices drifted out resignedly into a fine, soft, close, drowsy, penetrating rain; got into the landlord's light dog-cart, and rattled off, through the village, for the foot of Carrock. The journey at the outset was not remarkable. The Cumberland road went up and down like other roads; the Cumberland curs burst out from backs of cottages and barked like other curs, and the Cumberland peasantry stared after the dog-cart amazedly, as long as it was in sight, like the rest of their race. The approach to the foot of the mountain resembled the approaches to the feet of most other mountains all over the world. The cultivation gradually ceased, the trees grew gradually rare, the road became gradually rougher, and the sides of the mountain looked gradually more and more lofty, and more and more difficult to get up. The dog-cart was left at a lonely farm-house. The landlord borrowed a large umbrella, and, assuming in an instant the character of the most cheerful and adventurous of guides, led the way to the ascent. Mr Goodchild looked eagerly at the top of the mountain, and, feeling apparently that he was now going to be very lazy indeed, shone all over wonderfully to the eye, under the influence of the contentment within and the moisture without. Only in the bosom of Mr Thomas Idle did Despondency now hold her gloomy state. He kept it a secret; but he would have given a very handsome sum, when the ascent began, to have been back again at the inn. The sides of Carrock looked fearfully steep, and the top of Carrock was hidden in mist.

The rain was falling faster and faster. The knees of Mr Idle – always weak on walking excursions – shivered and shook with fear and damp. The wet was already penetrating through the young man's outer coat to a brand new shooting-jacket, for which he had reluctantly paid the large sum of two guineas on leaving town; he had no stimulating refreshment about him but a small packet of clammy gingerbread nuts; he had nobody to give him an arm, nobody to push him gently behind, nobody to pull him up tenderly in front, nobody to speak to who really felt the difficulties of the ascent, the dampness of the rain, the denseness of the mist, and the unutterable folly of climbing, undriven, up any steep place in the world, when there is level ground within reach to walk on instead. Was it for this that Thomas had left London? London, where there are nice short walks in level public gardens, with benches of repose set up at convenient distances for weary travellers – London, where rugged stone is humanely pounded into little lumps for the road, and intelligently shaped into smooth slabs for the pavement! No! It was not for the laborious ascent of the crags of Carrock that Idle had left his native city and travelled to Cumberland. Never did he feel more disastrously convinced that he had committed a very grave error in judgement than when he found himself standing in the rain at the bottom of a steep mountain, and knew that the responsibility rested on his weak shoulders of actually getting to the top of it.

The honest landlord went first, the beaming Goodchild followed, the mournful Idle brought up the rear. From time to time, the two foremost members of the expedition changed places in the order of march; but the rearguard never altered his position. Up the mountain or down the mountain, in the water or out of it, over the rocks, through the bogs, skirting the heather, Mr Thomas Idle was always the last, and was always the man who had to be looked after and waited for. At first the ascent was delusively easy: the sides of the mountain sloped gradually, and the material of which they were composed was a soft spongy turf, very tender and pleasant to walk upon. After a hundred yards or so, however, the verdant scene and the easy slope disappeared, and the rocks began. Not noble, massive rocks, standing upright, keeping a certain regularity in their positions, and possessing, now and then, flat tops to sit upon, but little, irritating, comfortless rocks, littered about anyhow by Nature; treacherous, disheartening rocks of all sorts of small shapes and small sizes, bruisers of tender toes and trippers-up of wavering feet. When these impediments were passed, heather and slough followed. Here the steepness of the ascent was slightly mitigated; and here the exploring party of three turned round to look at the view below them. The scene of the moorland and the fields was like a feeble water-colour drawing half sponged out. The mist was darkening, the rain was thickening, the trees were dotted about like spots of faint shadow, the division-lines which mapped out the field were all getting blurred together, and the lonely farm-house where the dog-cart had been left, loomed spectral in the grey light like the last human dwelling at the end of the habitable world. Was this a sight worth climbing to see? Surely – surely not!

Up again – for the top of Carrock is not reached yet. The landlord, just as good-tempered and obliging as he was at the bottom of the mountain. Mr Goodchild brighter in the eyes and rosier in the face than ever; full of cheerful remarks and apt quotations; and walking with a springiness of step wonderful to behold. Mr Idle, farther and farther in the rear, with the water squeaking in the toes of his boots, with his two-guinea shooting-jacket clinging damply to his aching sides, with his over-coat so full of rain, and standing out so pyramidically stiff, in consequence, from his shoulders downwards, that he felt as if he was walking in a gigantic extinguisher – the despairing spirit within him representing but too aptly the candle that had just been put out. Up and up and up again, till a ridge is reached, and the outer edge of the mist on the summit of Carrock is darkly and drizzling near. Is this the top? No, nothing like the top. It is an aggravating peculiarity of all mountains, that, although they have only one top when they are seen (as they ought always to be seen) from below, they turn out to have a perfect erruption of false tops whenever the traveller is sufficiently ill-advised to go out of his way for the purpose of ascending them. Carrock is but a trumpery little mountain of fifteen hundred feet, and it presumes to have false tops, and even precipices, as if it was Mont Blanc. No matter;

Goodchild enjoys it, and will go on; and Idle, who is afraid of
being left behind by himself must follow. On entering the
edge of the mist, the landlord stops, and says he hopes that it
will not get any thicker. It is twenty years since he last
ascended Carrock, and it is barely possible, if the mist
increases, that the party may be lost on the mountain.
Goodchild hears this dreadful intimation, and is not in the least
impressed by it. He marches for the top that is never to be
found, as if he was the Wandering Jew, bound to go on for
ever, in defiance of everything. The landlord faithfully
accompanies him. The two, to the dim eye of Idle, far below,
look in the exaggerative mist, like a pair of friendly giants,
mounting the steps of some invisible castle together. Up and
up, and then down a little, and then up, and then along a strip
of level ground, and then up again. The wind, a wind
unknown in the happy valley, blows keen and strong; the
rain-mist gets impenetrable; a dreary little cairn of stones
appears. The landlord adds one to the heap, first walking all
round the cairn as if he were about to perform an incantation,
then dropping the stone on to the top of the heap with the
gesture of a magician adding an ingredient to a cauldron in full
bubble. Goodchild sits down by the cairn as if it was his
study-table at home; Idle, drenched and panting, stands up
with his back to the wind, ascertains distinctly that this is the
top at last, looks round with all the little curiosity that is left in
him, and gets, in return, a magnificent view of – Nothing!

The effect of this sublime spectacle on the minds of the
exploring party is a litle injured by the nature of the direct
conclusion to which the sight of it points – the said conclusion
being that the mountain mist has actually gathered round
them, as the landlord feared it would. It now becomes
imperatively necessary to settle the exact situation of the farm-
house in the valley at which the dog-cart has been left, before
the travellers attempt to descend. While the landlord is
endeavouring to make this discovery in his own way, Mr
Goodchild plunges his hand under his wet coat, draws out a
little red morocco-case, opens it, and displays to the view of
his companions a neat pocket-compass. The north is found,
the point at which the farm-house is situated is settled, and the
descent begins. After a little downward walking, Idle (behind

as usual) sees his fellow-travellers turn aside sharply – tries to follow them – loses them in the mist – is shouted after, waited for, recovered – and then find that a halt has been ordered, partly on his account, partly for the purpose of again consulting the compass.

The point in debate is settled as before between Goodchild and the landlord, and the expedition moves on, not down the mountain, but marching straight forward round the slope of it. The difficulty of following this new route is acutely felt by Thomas Idle. He finds the hardship of walking at all, greatly increased by the fatigue of moving his feet straight forward along the side of a slope, when their natural tendency, at every step, is to turn off at a right angle, and go straight down the declivity. Let the reader imagine himself to be walking along the roof of a barn, instead of up or down it, and he will have an exact idea of the pedestrian difficulty in which the travellers had now involved themselves. In ten minutes more Idle was lost in the distance again, was shouted for, waited for, recovered as before; found Goodchild repeating his observation of the compass, and remonstrated warmly against the sideway route that his companions persisted in following. It appeared to be the uninstructed mind of Thomas that when three men want to get to the bottom of a mountain, their business is to walk down it; and he put this view of the case, not only with emphasis, but even with some irritability. He was answered from the scientific eminence of the compass on which his companions were mounted, that there was a frightful chasm somewhere near the foot of Carrock, called the Black Arches, into which the travellers were sure to march in the mist, if they risked continuing the descent from the place where they had now halted. Idle received this answer with the silent respect which was due to the commanders of the expedition, and followed along the roof of the barn, or rather the side of the mountain, reflecting upon the assurance which he received on starting again, that the object of the party was only to gain 'a certain point'; and, this haven attained, to continue the descent afterwards until the foot of Carrock was reached. Though quite unexceptionable as an abstract form of expression, the phrase 'a certain point' has the disadvantage of sounding rather vaguely when it is pronounced on unknown ground, under a canopy of mist much thicker than a London fog. Nevertheless, after the compass, this phrase was all the clue the party had to hold by, and Idle clung to the extreme end of it as hopefully as he could.

More sideway walking, thicker and thicker mist, all sorts of points reached except the 'certain point'; third loss of Idle, third shouts for him, third recovery of him, third consultation of compass. Mr Goodchild draws it tenderly from his pocket, and prepares to adjust it on a stone. Something falls on the turf – it is the glass. Something else drops immediately after – it is the needle. The compass is broken, and the exploring party is lost!

It is the practice of the English portion of the human race to receive all great disasters in dead silence. Mr Goodchild restored the useless compass to his pocket without saying a word, Mr Idle looked at the landlord, and the landlord looked at Mr Idle. There was nothing for it now but to go on blindfold, and trust to the chapter of chances. Accordingly, the lost travellers moved forward, still walking round the slope of the mountain, still desperately resolved to avoid the Black Arches, and to succeed in reaching the 'certain point'.

A quarter of an hour brought them to the brink of a ravine, at the bottom of which there flowed a muddy little stream. Here another halt was called, and another consultation took place. The landlord, still clinging pertinaciously to the idea of reaching the 'point,' voted for crossing the ravine and going on round the slope of the mountain. Mr Goodchild, to the great relief of his fellow-traveller, took another view of the case, and backed Mr Idle's proposal to descend Carrock at once, at any hazard – the rather as the running stream was a sure guide to follow from the mountain to the valley. Accordingly, the party descended to the rugged and stony banks of the stream; and here again. Thomas lost ground sadly, and fell far behind his travelling companions. Not much more than six weeks had elapsed since he had sprained one of his ankles, and he began to feel this same ankle getting rather weak when he found himself among the stones that were strewn about the running water. Goodchild and the landlord were getting father and farther ahead of him. He saw them cross the stream and disappear round a projection on its banks.

He heard them shout the moment after as a signal that they had halted and were waiting for him. Answering the shout, he mended his pace, crossed the stream where they had crossed it, and was within one step of the opposite bank, when his foot slipped on a wet stone, his weak ankle gave a twist outwards, a hot, rending, tearing pain ran through it at the same moment, and down fell the idlest of the Two Idle Apprentices, crippled in an instant.

The situation was now, in plain terms, one of absolute danger. There lay Mr Idle writhing with pain, there was the mist as thick as ever, there was the landlord as completely lost as the strangers whom he was conducting, and there was the compass broken in Goodchild's pocket. To leave the wretched Thomas on unknown ground was plainly impossible and to get him to walk with a badly sprained ankle seemed equally out of the question. However, Goodchild (brought back by his cry for help) bandaged the ankle with a pocket-handkerchief, and assisted by the landlord, raised the crippled Apprentice to his legs, offered him a shoulder to lean on, and exhorted him for the sake of the whole party to try if he could walk. Thomas, assisted by the shoulder on one side, and a stick on the other, did try, with what pain and difficulty those only can imagine who have sprained an ankle and have had to tread on it afterwards. At a pace adapted to the feeble hobbling of a newly-lamed man, the lost party moved on, perfectly ignorant whether they were on the right side of the mountain or the wrong, and equally uncertain how long Idle would be able to contend with the pain in his ankle, before he gave in altogether and fell down again, unable to stir another step.

Slowly and more slowly, as the clog of crippled Thomas weighed heavily and more heavily on the march of the expedition, the lost travellers followed the windings of the stream, till they came to a faintly-marked cart-track, branching off nearly at right angles, to the left. after a little consultation it was resolved to follow this dim vestige of a road in the hope that it might lead to some farm or cottage, at which Idle could be left in safety. It was now getting on towards the afternoon, and it was fast becoming more than doubtful whether the party, delayed in the progress as they now were, might not be overtaken by the darkness before the right route was found, and be condemned to pass the night on the mountain, without bit or drop to comfort them, in their wet clothes.

The cart-track grew fainter and fainter, until it was washed out altogether by another little stream, dark, turbulent, and rapid. The landlord suggested, judging by the colour of the water, that it must be flowing from one of the lead mines in the neighbourhood of Carrock; and the travellers accordingly kept by the stream for a little while, in the hope of possibly wandering towards help in that way. After walking forward about two hundred yards, they came upon a mine indeed, but a mine, exhausted and abandoned; a dismal, ruinous place, with nothing but the wreck of its works and buildings left to speak for it. Here, there were a few sheep feeding. The landlord looked at them earnestly, thought he recognised the marks on them – then thought he did not – finally gave up the sheep in despair – and walked on, just as ignorant of the whereabouts of the party as ever.

The march in the dark, literally as well as metaphorically in the dark, had now been continued for three-quarters of an hour from the time when the crippled Apprentice had met with his accident. Mr Idle, with all the will to conquer the pain in his ankle, and to hobble on, found the power-rapidly failing him, and felt that another ten minues at most would find him at the end of his last physical resources. He had just made up his mind on this point, and was about to communicate the dismal result of his reflections, to his companions, when the mist suddenly brightened, and began to lift straight ahead. In another minute, the landlord, who was in advance, proclaimed that he saw a tree. Before long, other trees appeared – then a cottage – then a house beyond the cottage, and a familiar line of road rising behind it. Last of all, Carrock itself loomed darkly into view, far away to the right hand. The party had not only got down the mountain without knowing how, but had wandered away from it in the mist, without knowing why – away, far down on the very moor by which they had approached the base of Carrock that morning.

The happy lifting of the mist, and the still happier discovery that the travellers had groped their way, though by a very round-about direction, to within a mile or so of the part of the valley in which farm-house was situated, restored Mr Idle's sinking spirits and reanimated his failing strength. While the landlord ran off to get the dog-cart, Thomas was assisted by Goodchild to the cottage which had been the first building seen when the darkness brightened, and was propped up against the garden-wall, like an artist's lay-figure waiting to be forwarded, until the dog-cart should arrive from the farm-house below. In due time – and a very long time it seemed to Mr Idle – the rattle of wheels was heard, and the crippled Apprentice was lifted into his seat. As the dog-cart was driven back to the inn, the landlord related an anecdote which he had just heard at the farm-house, of an unhappy man who had been lost, like his two guests and himself, on Carrock; who had passed the night there alone; who had been found the next morning, 'scared and starved'; and who never went out afterwards, except on his way to the grave. Mr Idle heard this sad story, and derived at least one useful impression from it. Bad as the pain in his ankle was, he contrived to bear it patiently, for he felt grateful that a worse accident had not befallen him in the wilds of Carrock.

Chapter II

The dog-cart, with Mr Thomas Idle and his ankle on the hanging seat behind, Mr Francis Goodchild and the Innkeeper in front, and the rain in spouts and splashes everywhere, made the best of its way back to the little Inn; the broken moor country looking like miles upon miles of Pre-Adamite sop, or the ruins of some enormous jorum of antedeluvian toast-and-water. The trees dripped; the eaves of the scattered cottages dripped; the barren stone-walls dividing the land, dripped; the yelping dogs dripped; carts and waggons under ill-roofed penthouses, dripped; melancholy cocks and hens perching on the shafts, or seeking shelter underneath them, dripped, Mr Goodchild dripped, Thomas Idle dripped, the Innkeeper dripped; the mare dripped; the vast curtains of mist and cloud that passed before the shadowy forms of the hills, streamed water as they were drawn across the landscape. Down such steep pitches that the mare seemed to be trotting on her head;

and up such steep pitches that she seemed to have a supplementary leg in her tail, the dog-cart jolted and tilted back to the
village. It was too wet for the women to look out, it was too
wet even for the children to look out; all the doors and
windows were closed, and the only sign of life or motion was
in the rain-punctured puddles.

Whisky and oil to Thomas Idle's ankle, and whisky without
oil to Francis Goodchild's stomach, produced an agreeable
change in the systems of both: soothing Mr Idle's pain, which
was sharp before, and sweetening Mr Goodchild's temper,
which was sweet before. Portmanteaus being then opened and
clothes changed, Mr Goodchild, through having no change of
outer garments but broadcloth and velvet, suddenly became a
magnificent portent in the innkeeper's house, a shining frontis-
piece to the Fashions for the month, and a frightful anomaly in
the Cumberland village.

Greatly ashamed of his splendid appearance, the conscious
Goodchild quenched it as much as possible, in the shadow of
Thomas Idle's ankle, and in the corner of the little covered
carriage that started with them for Wigton – a most desirable
carriage for any country, except for its having a flat roof and no
sides; which caused the plumps of rain accumulating on the
roof to play vigorous games of bagatelle into the interior all the
way, and to score immensely. It was comforable to see how the
people coming back in open carts from Wigton market made
no more of the rain than if it were sunshine; how the Wigton
policeman taking a country walk of half-a-dozen miles
(apparently for pleasure), in resplendent uniform, accepted
saturation as his normal state; how clerks and schoolmasters in
black loitered along the road without umbrellas, getting
varnished at every step; how the Cumberland girls, coming out
to look after the Cumberland cows, shook the rain from their
eyelashes and laughed it away; and how the rain continued to
fall upon all, as it only does fall in hill countries.

Wigton market was over, and its bare booths were smoking
with rain all down the street. Mr Thomas Idle, melo-
dramatically carried to the Inn's first floor, and laid upon three
chairs (he should have had the sofa, if there had been one), Mr
Goodchild went to the window to take an observation of
Wigton, and report what he saw to his disabled companion.

'Brother Francis, brother Francis,' cried Thomas Idle. 'What do you see from the turret?'

'I see,' said Brother Francis, 'what I hope and believe to be one of the most dismal places ever seen by eyes. I see the houses with their roofs of dull black, their stained fronts, and their dark-rimmed windows, looking as if they were all in mourning. As every little puff of wind comes down the street, I see a perfect train of rain let off along the wooden stalls in the market-place and exploded against me. I see a very big gas-lamp in the centre which I know, by a secret instinct, will not be lighted to-night. I see a pump, with a trivet underneath its spout whereon to stand the vessels that are brought to be filled with water. I see a man come to pump, and he pumps very hard, but no water follows, and he strolls empty away.'

'Brother Francis, brother Francis,' cried Thomas Idle, 'what more do you see from the turret, besides the man and the pump, and the trivet and the houses all in mourning and the rain?'

'I see,' said Brother Francis, 'one, two, three, four, five, linen-drapers' shops in front of me. I see a linen-draper's shop next door to the right – and there are five more linen-drapers' shops down the corner to the left. Eleven homicidal linen-drapers' shops within a short stone's throw, each with its hands at the throats of all the rest! Over the small first-floor of one of these linen-drapers' shops apears the wonderful inscription, BANK.'

'Brother Francis, brother Francis,' cried Thomas Idle, 'what more do you see from the turret, besides the eleven homicidal linen-drapers' shops, and the wonderful inscription "Bank" on the small first-floor, and the man and the pump and the trivet and the houses all in mourning and the rain?'

'I see, said Brother Francis, 'the depository for Christian Knowledge, and through the dark vapour I think I again make out Mr Spurgeon looming heavily. Her Majesty the Queen, God bless her, printed in colours, I am sure I see. I see the Ilustrated London News of several weeks ago, and I see a sweetmeat shop – which the proprietor calls a "Salt Warehouse" – with one small female child in a cotton bonnet looking in on tip-toe, oblivious of rain. And I see a watchmaker's, with only three great pale watches of a dull metal hanging in his window, each in a separate pane.'

'Brother Francis, brother Francis,' cried Thomas Idle, 'what more do you see of Wigton, besides these objects, and the man and the pump and the trivet and the houses all in mourning and the rain?'

'I see nothing more,' said Brother Francis, 'and there is nothing more to see, except the curlpaper bill of the theatre, which was opened and shut last week (the manager's family played all the parts), and the short, square, chinky omnibus that goes to the railway, and leads too rattling a life over the stones to hold together long. O yes! Now, I see two men with their hands in their pockets and their backs towards me.'

'Brother Francis, brother Francis,' cried Thomas Idle, 'what do you make out from the turret, of the expression of the two men with their hands in their pockets and their backs towards you?'

'They are mysterious men,' said brother Francis, 'with inscrutable backs. They keep their backs towards me with persistency. If one turns an inch in any direction, the other turns an inch in the same direction, and no more. They turn very stiffly, on a very little pivot, in the middle of the market-place. Their appearance is partly of a mining, partly of a ploughing, partly of a stable, character. They are looking at nothing – very hard. Their backs are slouched, and their legs are curved with much standing about. Their pockets are loose and dog's-eared, on account of their hands being always in them. They stand to be rained upon, without any movement of impatience or dissatisfaction, and they keep so close together that an elbow of each jostles an elbow of the other, but they never speak. They spit at times, but speak not. I see it growing darker and darker, and still I see them, sole visible population of the place, standing to be rained upon with their backs towards me, and looking at nothing very hard.'

'Brother Francis, brother Francis,' cried Thomas Idle, 'before you draw down the blind of the turret and come in to have your head scorched by the hot gas, see if you can, and impart to me, something of the expression of those two amazing men.'

'The murky shadows,' said Francis Goodchild, 'are gathering fast; and the wings of evening, and the wings of coal, are folding over Wigton. Still, they look at nothing very hard, with their backs towards me. Ah! Now, they turn, and I see—'

'Brother Francis, brother Francis,' cried Thomas Idle, 'tell me quickly what you see of the two men of Wigton!'

'I see,' said Francis Goodchild, 'that they have no expression at all. And now the town goes to sleep, undazzled by the large unlighted lamp in the market-place; and let no man wake it.'

At the close of the next day's journey, Thomas Idle's ankle became much swollen and inflamed. There are reasons which will presently explain themselves for not publicly indicating the exact direction in which that journey lay, or the place in which it ended. It was a long day's shaking of Thomas Idle over the rough roads, and a long day's getting out and going on before the horses, and fagging up hills, and scouring down hills, on the part of Mr Goodchild, who in the fatigues of such labours congratulated himself on attaining a high point of idleness. It was at a little town, still in Cumberland, that they halted for the night – a very little town, with the purple and brown moor close upon its one street; a curious little ancient market-cross set up in the midst of it; and the town itself looking, much as if it were a collection of great stones piled on end by the Druids long ago, which a few recluse people had once hollowed out for habitations.

'Is there a doctor here?' asked Mr Goodchild, on his knee, of the motherly landlady of the little Inn: stopping in his examination of Mr Idle's ankle, with the aid of a candle.

'Ey, my word!' said the landlady, glancing doubtfully at the ankle for herself; 'there's Doctor Speddie.'

'Is he a good Doctor?'

'Ey!' said the landlady, 'I ca' him so. A' cooms efther nae doctor that I ken. Mair nor which a's just *the* doctor heer.'

'Do you think he is at home!'

Her reply was, 'Gang awa', Jock, and bring him.'

Jock, a white-headed boy, who, under pretence of stirring up some bay salt in a basin of water for the laving of this unfortunate ankle, had greatly enjoyed himself for the last ten minutes in splashing the carpet, set off promptly. A very few minutes had elapsed when he showed the doctor in, by tumbling against the door before him and bursting it open with his head.

'Gently, Jock, gently,' said the doctor as he advanced with a quiet step. 'Gentlemen, a good evening. I am sorry that my presence is required here. A slight accident, I hope? A slip and a fall? Yes, yes, yes, Carrock indeed? Hah! Does that pain you, sir? No doubt, it does. It is the great connecting ligament here, you see, that has been badly strained. Time and rest, sir! They are often the recipe in greater cases,' with a slight sigh, 'and often the recipe in small. I can send a lotion to relieve you, but we must leave the cure to timer and rest.'

This he said, holding Idle's foot on his knee between his two hands, as he sat over against him. He had touched it tenderly and skilfully in explanation of what he said, and, when his careful examination was completed, softly returned it to its former horizontal position on a chair.

He spoke with a little irresolution whenever he began, but afterwards fluently. He was a tall, thin, large-boned, old gentleman, with an appearance at first sight of being hard-featured; but, at a second glance, the mild expression of his face and some particular touches of sweetness and patience about his mouth, corrected this impression and assigned his long professional rides, by day and night, in the bleak hill-weather, as the true cause of that appearance. He stooped very little, though past seventy and very grey. His dress was more like that of a clergyman than a country doctor, being a plain black suit, and a plain white neck-kerchief tied behind like a band. His black was the worse for wear, and there were darns in his coat, and his linen was a little frayed at the hems and edges. He might have been poor – it was likely enough in that out-of-the-way spot – or he might have been a little self-forgetful and eccentric. Anyone could have seen directly, that he had neither wife nor child at home. He had a scholarly air with him, and that kind of considerate humanity towards others which claimed a gentle consideration for himself. Mr Goodchild made this study of him while he was examining the limb, and as he laid it down. Mr Goodchild wishes to add that he considers it a very good likeness.

It came out in the course of a little conversation, that Doctor Speddie was acquainted with some friends of Thomas Idle's and had, when a young man, passed some years in Thomas Idle's birthplace on the other side of England. Certain idle labours, the fruit of Mr Goodchild's apprenticeship, also happened to be well known to him. The lazy travellers were thus placed on a more intimate footing with the Doctor than the casual circumstances of the meeting would of themselves have established; and when Doctor Speddie rose to go home, remarking that he would send his assistant with the lotion, Francis Goodchild said that was unnecessary, for by the Doctor's leave, he would accompany him, and bring it back. (Having done nothing to fatigue himself for a full quarter of an hour, Francis began to fear that he was not in a state of idleness.)

Doctor Speddie politely assented to the proposition of Francis Goodchild, 'as it would give him the pleasure of enjoying a few more minutes of Mr Goodchild's society than he could otherwise have hoped for,' and they went out together into the village street. The rain had nearly ceased, the clouds had broken before a cool wind from the north-east, and stars were shining from the peaceful heights beyond them.

Doctor Speddie's house was the last house in the place. Beyond it, lay the moor, all dark and lonesome. The wind moaned in a low, dull, shivering manner round the little garden, like a houseless creature that knew the winter was coming. It was exceedingly wild and solitary. 'Roses,' said the Doctor, when Goodchild touched some wet leaves overhanging the stone porch; 'but they get cut to peices.'

The Doctor opened the door with a key he carried, and led the way into a low but pretty ample hall with rooms on either side. The door of one of these stood open, and the Doctor entered it, with a word of welcome to his guest. It, to, was a low room, half surgery and half parlour, with shelves of books and bottles against the walls, which were of a very dark hue. There was a fire in the grate, the night being damp and chill. Leaning against the chimney-piece looking down into it, stood the Doctor's Assistant.

A man of a most remarkable appearance. Much older than Mr Goodchild had expected, for he was at least two-and-fifty; but, that was nothing. What was startling in him was his remarkable paleness. His large black eyes, his sunken cheeks, his long and heavy iron-grey hair, his wasted hands, and even the attenuation of his figure, were at first forgotten in his extraordinary pallor. There was no vestige of colour in the man. When he turned his face, Francis Goodchild started as if a stone figure had looked round at him.

'Mr Lorn,' said the Doctor. 'Mr Goodchild.'

The Assistant, in a distraught way – as if he had forgotten something – as if he had forgotten everything, even to his own name and himself – acknowledged the visitor's presence, and stepped further back into the shadow of the wall behind him. But, he was so pale that his face stood out in relief against the dark wall, and really could not be hidden so.

'Mr Goodchild's friend has met with an accident, Lorn,' said Doctor Speddie. 'We want the lotion for a bad sprain.'

A pause.

'My dear fellow, you are more than usually absent to-night. The lotion for a bad sprain.'

'Ah! Yes! Directly.'

He was evidently relieved to turn away, and to take his white face and his wild eyes to a table in a recess among the bottles. But, though he stood there, compounding the lotion with his back towards them, Goodchild could not, for many moments, withdraw his gaze from the man. When he at length did so, he found the doctor observing him, with some trouble in his face. 'He is absent,' explained the Doctor, in a low voice. 'Always absent. Very absent.'

'Is he ill?'

'No, not ill.'

'Unhappy?'

'I have my suspicions that he was,' assented the Doctor, 'once.'

Francis Goodchild could not but observe that the Doctor accompanied these words with a benignant and protecting glance at their subject, in which there was much of the expression with which an attached father might have looked at a heavily afflicted son. Yet, that they were not father and son must have been plain to most eyes. The Assistant, on the other hand, turning presently to ask the Doctor some question, looked at him with a wan smile as if he were his whole reliance and sustainment in life.

It was in vain for the Doctor in his easy chair, to try to lead the mind of Mr Goodchild in the opposite easy chair, away from what was before him. Let Mr Goodchild do what he would to follow the Doctor, his eyes and thoughts reverted to the assistant. The Doctor soon perceived it, and, after falling silent, and musing in a little perplexity, said:

'Lorn!'

'My dear Doctor.'

'Would you go to the Inn, and apply that lotion? You will show the best way of applying it, far better than Mr Goodchild can.'

'With pleasure.'

The Assistant took his hat, and passed like a shadow to the door.

'Lorn!' said the doctor, calling after him.

He returned.

'Mr Goodchild will keep me company till you come home. Don't hurry. Excuse my calling you back.'

'It is not,' said the Assistant, with his former smile, 'the first time you have called me back, dear Doctor.' With those words he went away.

'Mr Goodchild,' said Doctor Speddie, in a low voice, and with his former troubled expression of face, 'I have seen that your attention has been concentrated on my friend.'

'He fascinates me. I must apologise to you, but he had quite bewildered and mastered me.'

'I find that a lonely existence and a long secret,' said the Doctor, drawing his chair a little nearer to Mr Goodchild's, 'become in the course of time very heavy. I will tell you something. You may make what use you will of it, under fictitious names. I know I may trust you. I am the more inclined to confidence to-night, through having been unexpectedly led back, by the current of our conversation at the Inn, to scenes in my early life. Will you please to draw a little nearer?'

Mr Goodchild drew a little nearer, and the Doctor went on thus: speaking, for the most part, in so cautious a voice, that the wind, though it was far from high, occasionally got the better of him.

When this present nineteenth century was younger by a good many years than it is now, a certain friend of mine, named Arthur Holliday, happened to arrive in the town of Doncaster, exactly in the middle of the race-week, or in other words, in the middle of the month of September. He was one of those reckless rattle-pated, open-hearted, and open-mouthed young gentlemen, who possess the gift of familiarity in its highest perfection, and who scramble carelessly along the journey of life making friends, as the phrase is, wherever they go. His father was a rich manufacturer, and had bought landed property enough in one of the midland counties to make all the born squires in his neighbourhood thoroughly envious of him. Arthur was his only son, possessor in prospect of the great estate and the great business after his father's death; well supplied with money, and not too rigidly looked after, during his father's lifetime. Report, or scandal, whichever you please, said that the old gentleman had been rather wild in his youthful days, and that, unlike most parents, he was not disposed to be violently indignant when he found that his son took after him. This may be true or not. I myself only knew the elder Mr Holliday when he was getting on in years; and then he was as quiet and as respectable a gentleman as ever I met with.

Well, one September, as I told you, young Arthur comes to Doncaster, having decided all of a sudden, in his hare-brained way, that he would go to the races. He did not reach the town till towards the close of the evening, and he went at once to see about his dinner and bed at the principal hotel. Dinner they were ready enough to give him; but as for a bed, they laughed when he mentioned it. In the race-week at Doncaster, it is no uncommon thing for visitors who have not bespoken apartments, to pass the night in their carriages at the inn doors. As for the lower sort of strangers, I myself have often seen them, at that full time, sleeping out on the doorsteps for want of a covered place to creep under. Rich as he was, Arthur's chance of getting a night's lodging (seeing that he had not written beforehand to secure one) was more than doubtful. He tried the second hotel, and the third hotel, and two of the inferior inns after that; and was met everywhere by the same form of answer. No accommodation for the night of any sort was left. All the bright golden sovereigns in his pocket would not buy him a bed at Doncaster in the race-week.

To a young fellow of Arthur's temperament, the novelty of being turned away into the street, like a penniless vagabond, at every house where he asked for a lodging, presented itself in the light of a new and highly amusing piece of experience. He went on, with his carpet-bag in his hand, applying for a bed at every place of entertainment for travellers that he could find in Doncaster, until he wandered into the outskirts of the town. By this time, the last glimmer of twilight had faded out, the moon was rising dimly in a mist, the wind was getting cold, the clouds were gathering heavily, and there was every prospect that it was soon going to rain.

The look of the night had rather a lowering effect on young Holliday's good spirits. He began to contemplate the house-less situation in which he was placed, from the serious rather than the humorous point of view; and he looked about him, for another public-house to enquire at, with something very like downright anxiety in his mind on the subject of a lodging for the night. The suburban part of the town towards which he had now strayed was hardly lighted at all, and he could see nothing of the houses as he passed them, except that they got progressivley smaller and dirtier, the farther he went. Down the winding road before him shone the dull gleam of an oil lamp, the one faint, lonely light that struggled ineffectually with the foggy darkness all round him. He resolved to go on as far as this lamp, and then, if it showed him nothing in the shape of an Inn, to return to the central part of the town and to try if he could not at least secure a chair to sit down on, through the night, at one of the principal Hotels.

As he got near the lamp, he heard voices; and, walking close under it, found that it lighted the entrance to a narrow court, on the wall of which was painted a long hand in faded flesh-colour, pointing, with a lean fore-finger, to this inscrip-tion: THE TWO ROBINS.

Arthur turned into the court without hesitation, to see what The Two Robins could do for him. Four or five men were standing together round the door of the house which was at the bottom of the court, facing the entrance from the street. The men were all listening to one other man, better dressed than the rest, who was telling his audience something, in a low voice, in which they were apparently very much interested.

On entering the passage, Arthur was passed by a stranger with a knapsack in his hand, who was evidently leaving the house.

'No,' said the traveller with the knap-sack, turning round and addressing himself cheerfully to a fat, sly-looking, bald-headed man, with a dirty white apron on, who had followed him down the passage. 'No, Mr Landlord, I am not easily scared by trifles; but, I don't mind confessing that I can't quite stand *that*.'

It occurred to young Holliday, the moment he heard these words, that the stranger had been asked an exorbitant price for a bed at The Two Robins; and that he was unable or unwilling to pay it. The moment his back was turned, Arthur, comfortably conscious of his own well-filled pockets, addressed himself in a great hurry, for fear any other benighted traveller should slip in and forestall him, to the sly-looking landlord with the dirty apron and the bald head.

'If you have got a bed to let,' he said, 'and if that gentleman who has just gone out won't pay you your price for it, I will.'

The sly landlord looked hard at Arthur.

'Will you sir?' he asked, in a meditative, doubtful way.

'Name your price,' said young Holliday, thinking that the landlord's hesitation sprang from some boorish distrust of him. 'Name your price, and I'll give you the money at once, if you like?'

Arthur nearly laughed in the man's face; but thinking it prudent to control himself, offered the five shillings as seriously as he could. The sly landlord held out his hand, then suddenly drew it back again.

'You're acting all fair and above-board by me,' he said: 'and, before I take your money, I'll do the same by you. Look here, this is how it stands. You can have a bed all to yourself for five shillings; but you can't have more than a half-share of the room it stands in. Do you see what I mean, young gentleman?'

'Of course I do,' returned Arthur, a little irritably. 'You mean that it is a double-bedded room, and that one of the beds is occupied?'

The landlord nodded his head, and rubbed his double chin harder than ever. Arthur hesitated, and mechanically moved back a step or two towards the door. The idea of sleeping in the same room with a total stanger, did not present an attractive prospect to him. He felt more than half-inclined to drop his five shillings into his pocket, and to go out into the street once more.

'Is it yes, or no?' asked the landlord. 'Settle it as quick as you can, because there's lots of people wanting a bed at Doncaster tonight, besides you.'

Arthur looked towards the court, and heard the rain falling heavily in the street outside. He thought he would ask a question or two before he rashly decided on leaving the shelter of The Two Robins.

'What sort of man is it who has got the other bed?' he inquired. 'Is he a gentleman? I mean, is he a quiet, well-behaved person.?'

'The quietest man I ever came across,' said the landlord, rubbing his fat hands stealthily one over the other. 'As sober as a judge, and as regular as clock-work in his habits. It hasn't struck nine, not ten minutes ago, and he's in his bed already. I don't know whether that comes up to your notion of a quiet man: it goes a long way ahead of mine, I can tell you.'

'Is he asleep, do you think?' asked Arthur.

'I know he's asleep,' returned the landlord. 'And what's more, he's gone off so fast, that I'll warrant you don't wake him. This way, sir,' said the landlord, speaking over young Holliday's shoulder, as if he was addressing some new guest who was approaching the house.

'Here you are,' said Arthur, determined to be before-hand with the stranger, whoever he might be. 'I'll take the bed.' And he handed the five shillings to the landlord, who nodded, dropped the money carelessly into his waistcoat-pocket, and lighted a candle.

'Come up and see the room,' said the host of The Two Robins, leading the way to the staircase quite briskly, considering how fat he was.

They mounted to the second-floor of the house. The landlord half opened a door, fronting the landing, then stopped, and turned round to Arthur.

'It's a fair bargain, mind, on my side as well as on yours,' he said. 'You give me five shillings, I give you in return a clean, comfortable bed; and I warrant, beforehand, that you won't be interfered with, or annoyed in any way, by the man who sleeps in the same room with you.' Saying those words, he looked hard, for a moment, in young Holliday's face, and then led the way into the room.

It was larger and cleaner than Arhtur had expected it would be. The two beds stood parallel with each other – a space of about six feet intervening between them. They were both of the same medium size, and both had the same plain white curtains, made to draw, if necessary, all round them. The occupied bed was the bed nearest the window. The curtains were all drawn round this, except the half curtain at the bottom, on the side of the bed farthest from the window. Arthur saw the feet of the sleeping man raising the scanty clothes into a sharp little eminence, as if he was lying flat on his back. He took the candle, and advanced softly to draw the curtain – stopped half way, and listened for a moment – then turned to the landlord.

'He is a very quiet sleeper,' said Arthur.

'Yes,' said the landlord, 'very quiet.'

Young Holliday advanced with the candle, and looked in at the man cautiously.

'How pale he is!' said Arthur.

'Yes,' returned the landlord, 'pale enough, isn't he?'

Arthur looked closer at the man. The bed-clothes were drawn up to his chin, and they lay perfectly still over the region of his chest. Surprised and vaguely startled, as he noticed this, Arthur stooped down closer over the stranger; looked at his ashy, parted lips; listened breathlessly for an instant; looked again at the strangely still face, and the motionless lips and chest; and turned round suddenly on the landlord, with his own cheeks as pale for the moment as the hollow cheeks of the man on the bed.

'Come here,' he whispered, under his breath. 'Come here, for God's sake! The man's not asleep – he is dead!'

'You have found that out sooner than I thought you would,' said the landlord composedly. 'Yes, he's dead, sure enough. He died at five o'clock to-day.'

'How did he die? Who is he?' asked Arthur, staggered, for the moment, by the audacious coolness of the answer.

'As to who is he,' rejoined the landlord, 'I know no more about him than you do. There are his books and letters and things, all sealed up in that brown paper parcel, for the

Coroner's inquest to open to-morrow or next day. He's been here a week, paying his way fairly enough and stopping in-doors, for the most part, as if he was ailing. My girl brought him up his tea at five to-day; and as he was pouring of it out, he fell down in a faint, or a fit, or a compound of both, for anything I know. We could not bring him to – and I said he was dead. And the doctor couldn't bring him to – and the doctor said he was dead. And there he is. And the Coroner's inquest's coming as soon as it can. And that's as much as I know about it.'

Arthur held the candle close to the man's lips. The flame still burnt straight up, as steadily as ever. There was a moment of silence; and the rain pattered drearily through it against the panes of the window.

'If you haven't got nothing more to say to me,' continued the landlord, 'I suppose I may go. You don't expect your five shillings back do you? There's the bed I promised you, clean and comfortable. There's the man I warranted not to disturb you, quiet in this world for ever. If you're frightened to stop alone with him, that's not my look out. I've kept my part of the bargain, and I mean to keep the money. I'm not Yorkshire, myself, young gentleman; but I've lived long enough in these parts to have my wits sharpened; and I shouldn't wonder if you found out the way to brighten up yours, next time you come among us.' With these words, the landlord turned towards the door, and laughed to himself softly, in high satisfaction at his own sharpness.

Startled and shocked as he was, Arthur had by this time sufficiently recovered himself to feel indignant at the trick that had been played on him, and at the insolent manner in which the landlord exulted in it.

'Don't laugh,' he said sharply, 'till you are quite sure you have got the laugh against me. You shan't have the five shillings for nothing, my man. I'll keep the bed.'

'Will you?' said the landlord. 'Then I wish you a good night's rest.' With that brief farewell, he went out, and shut the door after him.

A good night's rest! The words had hardly been spoken, the door had hardly been closed, before Arthur half-repented the hasty words that had just escaped him. Though not naturally over-sensitive, and not wanting in courage of the moral as well as the physical sort, the presence of the dead man had an instantaneously chilling effect on his mind when he found himself alone in the room – alone, and bound by his own rash words to stay there till the next morning. An older man would have thought nothing of those words, and would have acted, without reference to them, as his calmer sense suggested. But Arthur was too young to treat the ridicule, even of his inferiors, with contempt – too young not to fear the momentary humiliation of falsifying his own foolish boast, more than he feared the trial of watching out the long night in the same chamber with the dead.

'It is but a few hours,' he thought to himself, 'and I can get away the first thing in the morning.'

He was looking towards the occupied bed as that idea passed through his mind, and the sharp angular eminence made in the clothes by the dead man's upturned feet again caught his eye. He advanced and drew the curtains, purposely abstaining, as he did so, from looking at the face of the corpse, lest he might unnerve himself at the outset by fastening some ghastly impression of it on his mind. He drew the curtain very gently, and sighed involuntarily as he closed it. 'Poor fellow,' he said, almost as sadly as if he had known the man. 'Ah, poor fellow!'

He went next to the window. The night was black, and he could see nothing from it. The rain still pattered heavily against the glass. He inferred, from hearing it, that the window was at the back of the house; remembering that the front was sheltered from the weather by the court and the buildings over it.

While he was still standing at the window – for even the dreary rain was a relief, because of the sound it made; a relief, also because it moved, and had some faint suggestion, in consequence, of life and companionship in it – while he was standing at the window, and looking vacantly into the black darkness outside, he heard a distant church-clock strike ten. Only ten! How was he to pass the time till the house was astir the next morning?

Under any other circumstances, he would have gone down to the public-house parlour, would have called for his grog,

and would have laughed and talked with the company assembled as familiarly as if he had known them all his life. But the
very thought of whiling away the time in this manner was
now distasteful to him. The new situation in which he was
placed seemed to have altered him to himself already. Thus
far, his life had been the common, trifling, prosaic, surface-life
of a prosperous young man, with no troubles to conquer, and
no trials to face. He had lost no relation whom he loved, no
friend whom he treasured. Till this night, what share he had of
the immortal inheritance that is divided amongst us all, had
lain dormant within him. Till this night, death and he had not
once met, even in thought.

He took a few turns up and down the room – then stopped.
the noise made by his boots on the poorly carpeted floor,
jarred on his ear. He hesitated a little, and ended by taking the
boots off, and walking backwards and forwards noiselessly.
all desire to sleep or to rest had left him. The bare thought of
lying down on the unoccupied bed instantly drew the picture
on his mind of a dreadful mimicry of the position of the dead
man. Who was he? What was the story of his past life? Poor he
must have been, or he would not have stopped at such a place
as The Two Robins Inn – and weakened, probably, by long
illness, or he could hardly have died in the manner which the
landlord had described. Poor, ill, lonely, – dead in a strange
place; dead with nobody but a stranger to pity him. A sad
story: truly, on the mere face of it, a very sad story.

While these thoughts were passing through his mind, he
had stopped insensibly at the window, close to which stood
the foot of the bed with the closed curtains. At first he looked
at it absently; then he became conscious that his eyes were
fixed on it; and then, a perverse desire took possession of him
to do the very thing which he had resolved not to do up to this
time – to look at the dead man.

He stretched out his hand towards the curtains; but checked
himself in the very act of undrawing them, turned his back
sharply on the bed, and walked towards the chimney-piece, to
see what things were placed on it, and to try if he could keep
the dead man out of his mind in that way.

There was a pewter inkstand on the chimney-piece, with
some mildewed remains of ink in the bottle. There were two

coarse china ornaments of the commonest kind; and there was a square of embossed card, dirty and fly-blown, with a collection of wretched riddles printed on it, in all sorts of ziz-zag directions, and in variously coloured inks. He took the card, and went away, to read it, to the table on which the candle was placed; sitting down, with his back resolutely turned to the curtained bed.

He read the first riddle, the second, the third, all in one corner of the card – then turned it round impatiently to look at another. Before he could begin reading the riddles printed here, the sound of the church-clock stopped him. Eleven. He had got through an hour of the time, in the room with the dead man.

Once more he looked at the card. It was not easy to make out the letters printed on it, in consequence of the dimness of the light which the landlord had left him – a common tallow candle, furnished with a pair of heavy old-fashioned steel snuffers. Up to this time, his mind had been too much occupied to think of the light. He had left the wick of the candle unsnuffed, till it had risen higher than the flame, and had burnt into an odd pent-house shape at the top, from which morsels of the charred cotton fell off, from time to time, in little flakes. He took up the snuffers now, and trimmed the wick. The light brightened directly, and the room became less dismal.

Again he turned to the riddles; reading them doggedly and resolutely, now in one corner of the card, now in another. All his efforts, however, could not fix his attention on them. He pursued his occupation mechanically, deriving no sort of impression from what he was reading. It was as if a shadow from the curtained bed had got between his mind and the gaily printed letters – a shadow that nothing could dispel. At last, he gave up the struggle, and threw the card from him impatiently, and took to walking softly up and down the room again.

The dead man, the dead man, the *hidden* dead man on the bed! There was the one persistent idea still haunting him. Hidden! Was it only the body being there, or was it the body being there, concealed, that was preying on his mind? He stopped at the window, with that doubt in him; once more listening to the pattering rain, once more looking out into the black darkness.

Still the dead man! The darkness forced his mind back upon itself, and set his memory at work, reviving, with a painfully-vivid distinctness the momentary impression it had received from his first sight of the corpse. Before long the face seemed to be hovering out in the middle of the darkness, confronting him through the window, with the paleness whiter, with the dreadful dull line of light between the imperfectly-closed eyelids broader than he had seen it – with the parted lips slowly dropping farther and farther away from each other – with the features growing larger and moving closer, till they seemed to fill the window and to silence the rain, and to shut out the night.

The sound of a voice, shouting below stairs, woke him suddenly from the dream of his own distempered fancy. He recognised it as the voice of the landlord. 'Shut up at twelve, Ben,' he heard it say. 'I'm off to bed.'

He wiped away the damp that had gathered on his forehead, reasoned with himself for a little while and resolved to shake his mind free of the ghastly counterfeit which still clung to it, by forcing himself to confront, if it was only for a moment, the solemn reality. Without allowing himself an instant to hesitate, he parted the curtains at the foot of the bed, and looked through.

There was the sad, peaceful, white face, with the awful mystery of stillness on it, laid back upon the pillow. No stir, no change there! He only looked at it for a moment before he closed the curtains again – but that moment steadied him, calmed him, restored him – mind and body – to himself.

He returned to his old occupation of walking up and down the room; persevering in it, this time, till the clock struck again. Twelve.

As the sound of the clock-bell died away, it was succeeded by the confused noise, down stairs, of the drinkers in the tap-room leaving the house. The next sound, after an interval of silence, was caused by the barring of the door, and the closing of the shutters, at the back of the Inn. Then the silence followed again, and was disturbed no more.

He was alone now – absolutely, utterly, alone with the dead man, till the next morning.

The wick of the candle wanted trimming again. He took up the snuffers – but paused suddenly on the very point of using them, and looked attentively at the candle – then back, over his shoulder, at the curtained bed – then again at the candle. It had been lighted, for the first time, to show him the way up-stairs, and three parts of it, at least, were already consumed. In another hour it would be burnt out. In another hour – unless he called at once to the man who had shut up the Inn, for a fresh candle – he would be left in the dark.

Strongly as his mind had been affected since he had entered the room, his unreasonable dread of encountering ridicule, and of exposing his courage to suspicion, had not altogether lost its influence over him, even yet. He lingered irresolutely by the table, waiting till he could prevail on himself to open the door, and call, from the landing to the man who had shut up the Inn. In his present hesitating frame of mind, it was a kind of relief to gain a few moments only by engaging in the trifling occupation of snuffing the candle. His hand trembled a little, and the snuffers were heavy and awkward to use. When he closed them on the wick, he closed them a hair's breadth too low. In an instant the candle was out, and the room was plunged in pitch darkness.

The one impression which the absence of light immediatley produced on his mind, was distrust of the curtained bed – distrust which shaped itself into no distinct idea, but which was powerful enough, in its very vagueness, to bind him down to his chair, to make his heart beat fast, and to set him listening intently. No sound stirred in the room but the familiar sound of the rain against the window, louder and sharper now than he had heard it yet.

Still the vague distrust, the inexpressible dread possessed him, and kept him in his chair. He had put his carpet-bag on the table when he first entered the room; and he now took the key from his pocket, reached out his hand softly, opened the bag, and groped in it for his travelling writing-case, in which he knew that there was a small store of matches. When he had got one of the matches, he waited before he struck it on the coarse wooden table, and listened intently again, without knowing why. Still there was no sound in the room but the steady, ceaseless, rattling sound of the rain.

He lighted the candle again, without another moment of delay; and, on the instant of its burning up, the first object in the room that his eyes sought for was the curtained bed.

Just before the light had been put out, he had looked in that direction, and had seen no change, no disarrangement of any sort, in the folds of the closely-drawn curtains.

When he looked at the bed, now, he saw, hanging over the side of it, a long white hand.

It lay perfectly motionelss, midway on the side of the bed, where the curtain at the head and the curtain at the foot met. Nothing more was visible. The clinging curtains hid everything but the long white hand.

He stood looking at it unable to stir, unable to call out; feeling nothing, knowing nothing; every faculty he possessed gathered up and lost in the one seeing faculty. How long that first panic held him he never could tell afterwards. It might have been only for a moment; it might have been for many minutes together. How he got to the bed – whether he ran to it headlong, or whether he approached it slowly – how he wrought himself up to unclose the curtains and look in, he never has remembered, and never will remember to his dying day. It is enough that he did go to the bed, and that he did look inside the curtains.

The man had moved. One of his arms was outside the clothes; his face was turned a little on the pillow; his eyelids were wide open. Changed as to position, and as to one of the features, the face was otherwise, fearfully and wonderfully unaltered. The dead paleness and the dead quiet were on it still.

One glance showed Arthur this – one glance, before he flew breathlessly to the door, and alarmed the house.

The man whom the landlord called 'Ben' was the first to appear on the stairs. In three words, Arthur told him what had happened, and sent him for the nearest doctor.

I, who tell you this story, was then staying with a medical friend of mine, in practice at Doncaster, taking care of his patients for him, during his absence in London; and I, for the time being, was the nearest doctor. They had sent for me from the Inn, when the stranger was taken ill in the afternoon; but I was not at home, and medical assistance was sought for elsewhere. When the man from The Two Robins rang the night-bell, I was just thinking of going to bed. Naturally enough, I did not believe a word of his story about 'a dead man who had come to life again.' However, I put on my hat, armed myself with one or two bottles of restorative medicine, and ran to the Inn, expecting to find nothing more remarkable, when I got there, than a patient in a fit.

My surprise at finding that the man had spoken the literal truth was almost, if not quite, equalled by my astonishment at finding myself face to face with Arthur Holliday as soon as I entered the bedroom. It was no time then for giving or seeking explanations. We just shook hands amazedly; and then I ordered everybody but Arthur out of the room, and hurried to the man on the bed.

The kitchen fire had not been long out. There was plenty of hot water in the boiler, and plenty of flannel to be had. With these and my medicines, and with such help as Arthur could render under my direction, I dragged the man, literally, out of the jaws of death. In less than an hour from the time when I had been called in, he was alive and talking in the bed on which he had been laid out to wait for the coroner's inquest.

You will naturally ask me, what had been the matter with him; and I might treat you, in reply, to a long theory, plentifully sprinkled with, what the children call, hard words. I prefer telling you that, in this case, cause and effect could not be satisfactorily joined together by any theory whatever. There are mysteries in life, and the conditions of it, which human science has not fathomed yet; and I candidly confess to you, that, in bringing that man back to existence, I was, morally speaking, groping hap-hazard in the dark. I know (from the testimony of the doctor who attended him in the afternoon) that the vital machinery, so far as its action is appreciable by our senses, had, in this case, unquestionably stopped; and I am equally certain (seeing that I recovered him) that the vital principle was not extinct. When I add, that he had suffered from a long and complicated illness, and that his whole nervous system was utterly deranged, I have told you all I really know of the physical conditon of my dead-alive patient at the Two Robins Inn.

When he 'came to,' as the phrase goes, he was a startling object to look at, with his colourless face, his sunken cheeks, his wild black eyes, and his long black hair. The first question he asked me about himself when he could speak, made me suspect that I had been called in to a man in my own profession. I mentioned to him my surmise; and he told me that I was right.

He said he had come last from Paris, where he had been attached to a hospital. That he had lately returned to England, on his way to Edinburgh, to continue his studies; that he had been taken ill on the journey; and that he had stopped to rest and recover himself at Doncaster. He did not add a word about his name, or who he was: and, of course, I did not question him on the subject. All I inquired when he ceased speaking, was what branch of the profession he intended to follow.

'Any branch,' he said bitterly, 'which will put bread into the mouth of a poor man.'

At this, Arthur, who had been hitherto watching him in silent curiosity, burst out impetuously in his usual good-humoured way:–

'My dear fellow!' (everybody was 'my dear fellow' with Arthur) 'now you have come to life again, don't begin by being down-hearted about your prospects. I'll answer for it, I can help you to some capital thing in the medical line – or, if I can't, I know my father can.'

The medical student looked at him steadily.

'Thank you,' he said coldly. Then added, 'May I ask who your father is?'

'He's well enough known all about this part of the country,' replied Arthur. 'He is a great manufacturer, and his name is Holliday,'

My hand was on the man's wrist during this brief conversation. The instant the name of Holliday was pronounced I felt the pulse under my fingers flutter, stop, go on suddenly with a bound, and beat afterwards, for a mintue or two, at the fever rate.

'How did you come here?' asked the stranger, quickly, excitably, passionately almost.

Arthur related briefly what had happened from the time of his first taking the bed at the inn.

'I am indebted to Mr Holliday's son then for the help that has saved my life,' said the medical student, speaking to himself, with a singular sarcasm in his voice. 'Come here!'

He held out, as he spoke, his long, white, bony right hand.

'With all my heart,' said Arthur taking the hand cordially. 'I may confess it now,' he continued, laughing, 'upon my honour, you almost frightened me out of my wits.'

The stranger did not seem to listen. His wild black eyes were fixed with a look of eager interest on Arthur's face, and his long bony fingers kept tight hold of Arthur's hand. Young Holliday, on his side, returned the gaze, amazed and puzzled by the medical student's odd language and manners. The two faces were close together; I looked at them; and, to my amazement, I was suddenly impressed by the sense of a likeness between them – not in features, or complexion, but solely in expression. It must have been a strong likeness, or I should certainly not have found it out, for I am naturally slow at detecting resemblances between faces.

'You have saved my life,' said the strange man, still looking hard in Arthur's face, still holding tightly by his hand. 'If you had been my own brother, you could not have done more for me than that.'

He laid a singularly strong emphasis on those three words 'my own brother,' and a change passed over his face as he pronounced them, – a change that no language of mine is competent to describe.

'I hope I have not done being of service to you yet,' said Arthur. 'I'll speak to my father, as soon as I get home.'

'You seem to be fond and proud of your father,' said the medical student. 'I suppose, in return, he is fond and proud of you?'

'Of course, he is!' answered Arthur, laughing. 'Is there anything wonderful in that? Isn't *your* father fond—'

The stranger suddenly dropped young Holliday's hand, and turned his face away.

'I beg your pardon,' said Arthur. 'I hope I have not unintentionally pained you. I hope you have not lost your father?'

'I can't well lose what I have never had,' retorted the medical student, with a harsh mocking laugh.

'What you have never had!'

The strange man suddenly caught Arthur's hand again, suddenly looked once more hard in his face.

'Yes,' he said, with a repetition of the bitter laugh. 'You have brought a poor devil back into the world, who has no business there. Do I astonish you? Well! I have a fancy of my own for telling you what men in my situation generally keep a secret. I have no name and no father. The merciful law of Society tells me I am Nobody's Son! Ask your father if he will be my father too, and help me on in life with the family name.'

Arthur looked at me, more puzzled than ever. I signed to him to say nothing, and then laid my fingers again on the man's wrist. No! In spite of the extraordinary speech that he had just made, he was not, as I had been disposed to suspect, beginning to get light-headed. His pulse, by this time, had fallen back to a quiet, slow beat, and his skin was moist and cool. Not a symptom of fever or agitation about him.

Finding that neither of us answered him, he turned to me, and began talking of the extraordinary nature of his case, and asking my advice about the future course of medical treatment to which he ought to subject himself. I said the matter required careful thinking over, and suggested that I should submit certain prescriptions to him the next morning. He told me to write them at once, as he would, most likely, be leaving Doncaster, in the morning, before I was up. It was quite useless to represent to him the folly and danger of such a proceeding as this. He heard me politely and patiently, but held to his resolution, without offering any reasons or any explanations, and repeated to me, that if I wished to give him a chance of seeing my prescription, I must write it at once. Hearing this, Arthur volunteered the loan of a travelling writing-case, which, he said, he had with him; and, bringing it to the bed, shook the notepaper out of the pocket of the case forthwith in his usual careless way. With the paper, there fell out on the counterpane of the bed a small packet of sticking-plaster, and a little water-colour drawing of a landscape.

The medical student took up the drawing and looked at it. His eye fell on some initials neatly written, in cypher, in one corner. He started, and trembled; his pale face grew whiter than ever; his wild black eyes turned on Arthur, and looked through and through him.

'A pretty drawing,' he said, in a remarkably quiet tone of voice.

'Ah! And done by such a pretty girl,' said Arthur. 'Oh, such a pretty girl! I wish it was not a landscape – I wish it was a portrait of her!'

'You admire her very much?'

Arthur, half in jest, half in earnest, kissed his hand for answer.

'Love at first sight!' he said, putting the drawing away again. 'But the course of it doesn't run smooth. It's the old story. She's monopolised as usual. Trammelled by a rash engagement to some poor man who is never likely to get money enough to marry her. It was lucky I heard of it in time, or I should certainly have risked a declaration when she gave me that drawing. Here, doctor! Here is pen, ink, and paper all ready for you.'

'When she gave you that drawing? Gave it. Gave it.' He repeated the words slowly to himself, and suddenly closed his eyes. A momentary distortion passed across his face, and I saw one of his hands clutch up the bedclothes and squeeze them hard. I thought he was going to be ill again, and begged that there might be no more talking. He opened his eyes when I spoke, fixed them once more searchingly on Arthur, and said, slowly and distinctly, 'You like her, and she likes you. The poor man may die out of your way. Who can tell that she may not give you herself as well as her drawing, after all?'

Before young Holliday could answer, he turned to me, and said in a whisper, 'Now for the prescription.' From that time, though he spoke to Arthur again, he never looked at him more.

When I had written the prescription, he examined it, approved of it, and then astonished us both by abruptly wishing us good night. I offered to sit up with him, and he shook his head. Arthur offered to sit up with him, and he said, shortly, with his face turned away, 'No.' I insisted on having somebody left to watch him. He gave way when he found I was determined, and said he would accept the services of the waiter at the inn.

'Thank you, both,' he said, as we rose to go. 'I have one last favour to ask – not of you, doctor, for I leave you to exercise your professional discretion – but of Mr Holliday.' His eyes, while he spoke, still rested steadily on me, and never once turned towards Arthur. 'I beg that Mr Holliday will not mention to any one – least of all to his father – the events that have occurred, and the words that have passed, in this room. I entreat him to bury me in his memory, as, but for him, I might have been buried in my grave. I cannot give my reasons for making this strange request. I can only implore him to grant it.'

His voice faltered for the first time, and he hid his face on the pillow. Arthur, completely bewildered, gave the required pledge. I took young Holliday away with me, immediately afterwards, to the house of my friend; determining to go back to the inn, and to see the medical student again before he had left in the morning.

I returned to the inn at eight o'clock, purposely abstaining from waking Arthur, who was sleeping off the past night's excitement on one of my friend's sofas. A suspicion had occurred to me, as soon as I was alone in my bedroom, which made me resolve that Holliday and the stranger whose life he had saved should not meet again, if I could prevent it. I have already alluded to certain reports, or scandals, which I knew of, relating to the early life of Arthur's father. While I was thinking, in my bed, of what had passed at the Inn – of the change in the student's pulse when he heard the name of Holliday; of the resemblance of expression that I had discovered between his face and Arthur's; of the emphasis he had laid on those three words, 'my own brother'; and of his incomprehensible acknowledgement of his own illegitimacy – while I was thinking of these things, the reports I have mentioned suddenly flew into my mind, and linked themselves fast to the chain of my previous reflections. Something within me whispered, 'It is best that those two young men should not meet again.' I felt it before I slept; I felt it when I woke; and I went, as I told you, alone to the Inn the next morning.

I had missed my only opportunity of seeing my nameless patient again. He had been gone nearly an hour when I inquired for him.

I have now told you everything that I know for certain, in relation to the man whom I brought back to life in the double-bedded room of the Inn at Doncaster. What I have next to add is matter for inference and surmise, and is not, strictly speaking, matter of fact.

I have to tell you, first, that the medical student turned out to be strangely and unaccountably right in assuming it as more than probable that Arthur Holliday would marry the young lady who had given him the water-colour drawing of the landscape. That marriage took place a little more than a year after the events occurred which I have just been relating. The young couple came to live in the neighbourhood in which I was then established in practice. I was present at the wedding, and was rather surprised to find that Arthur was singularly reserved with me, both before and after his marriage, on the subject of the young lady's prior engagement. He only referred to it once, when we were alone, merely telling me, on that occasion, that his wife had done all that honour and duty required of her in the matter, and that the engagement had been broken off with the full approval of her parents. I never heard more from him than this. For three years he and his wife live together happily. At the expiration of that time, the symptoms of a serious illness first declared themselves in Mrs Arthur Holliday. It turned out to be a long, lingering, hopeless malady. I attended her throughout. We had been great friends when she was well, and we became more attached to each other than ever when she was ill. I had many long and interesting conversations with her in the intervals when she suffered least. The result of one of those conversations I may briefly relate, leaving you to draw any inferences from it that you please.

The interview to which I refer, occurred shortly before her death. I called one evening, as usual, and found her alone, with a look in her eyes which told me that she had been crying. She only informed me at first, that she had been depressed in spirits; but, by little and little, she became more communicative, and confessed to me that she had been looking over some old letters, which had been addressed to her, before she had seen Arthur, by a man to whom she had been engaged to be married. I asked her how the engagement came to be broken off. She replied that it had not been broken off, but that it had died out in a very mysterious way. The person to whom she was engaged – her first love, she called him – was very poor, and there was no immediate prospect of their being married. He followed my profession, and went abroad to study. They had corresponded regularly, until the time when, as she believed, he had returned to England. From that period she heard no more of him. He was of a fretful, sensitive temperament; and she feared that she might have inadvertently done or said something that offended him. However that might be, he had never written to her again; and, after waiting a year, she had married Arthur. I asked when the first estrangement had begun, and found that the time at which she ceased to hear anything of her first lover exactly corresponded with the time at which I had been called in to my mysterious patient at The Two Robins Inn.

A fortnight after that conversation, she died. In course of time, Arthur married again. Of late years, he has lived principally in London, and I have seen little or nothing of him.

I have many years to pass over before I can approach to anything like a conclusion of this fragmentary narrative. And even when that later period is reached, the little that I have to say will not occupy your attention for more than a few minutes. Between six and seven years ago, the gentleman to whom I introduced you in this room, came to me, with good professional recommendations, to fill the position of my assistant. We met, not like strangers, but like friends – the only difference between us being, that I was very much surprised to see him, and that he did not appear to be at all surprised to see me. If he was my son, or my brother I believe he could not be fonder of me than he is; but he has never volunteered any confidence since he has been here, on the subject of his past life. I saw something that was familiar to me in his face when we first met; and yet it was also something that suggested the idea of change. I had a notion once that my patient at the Inn might be a natural son of Mr Holliday's; I had another idea that he might also have been the man who was engaged to Arthur's first wife; and I have a third idea, still clinging to me, that Mr Lorn is the only man in England who could really enlighten me, if he chose, on both those doubtful points. His hair is not black, now, and his eyes are dimmer than the piercing eyes that I remember, but, for all that, he is very like the nameless medical student of my younger days – very like him. And, sometimes, when I come home late at night, and find him asleep, and wake him, he looks, in coming to, wonderfully like the stranger at Doncaster, as he raised himself in the bed on that memorable night!

The doctor paused. Mr Goodchild who had been following every word that fell from his lips, up to this time, leaned forward eagerly to ask a question. Before he could say a word, the latch of the door was raised, without any warning sound of footsteps in the passage outside. A long, white, bony hand appeared through the opening, gently pushing the door, which was prevented from working freely on its hinges by a fold in the carpet under it.

'That hand! Look at that hand, Doctor!' said Mr Goodchild, touching him.

At the same moment, the doctor looked at Mr Goodchild, and whispered to him, significantly: 'Hush! he has come back.'

Chapter III

The Cumberland Doctor's mention of Doncaster Races, inspired Mr Francis Goodchild with the idea of going down to Doncaster to see the races. Doncaster being a good way off, and quite out of the way of the Idle Apprentices (if anything could be out of their way, who had no way), it necessarily followed that Francis perceived Doncaster in the race-week to be, of all possible idlenesses, the particular idleness that would completely satisfy him.

Thomas, wtih an enforced idleness grafted on the natural and voluntary power of his disposition, was not of this mind; objecting that a man compelled to lie on his back on a floor, a sofa, a table, a line of chairs, or anything he could get to lie upon, was not in racing condition, and that he desired nothing better than to lie where he was, enjoying himself in looking at the flies on the ceiling. But, Francis Goodchild, who had been walking round his companion in a circuit of twelve miles for two days, and had begun to doubt whether it was reserved for him ever to be idle in his life, not only overpowered this objection, but even converted Thomas Idle to a scheme he formed (another idle inspiration), of conveying the said Thomas to the sea-coast, and putting his injured leg under a stream of salt-water.

Plunging into this happy conception head-foremost, Mr Goodchild immediately referred to the country-map, and ardently discovered that the most delicious piece of sea-coast to be found within the limits of England, and the Channel Islands, all summed up together, was Allonby on the coast of Cumberland. There was the coast of Scotland opposite to Allonby, said Mr Goodchild with enthusiasm; there was a fine Scottish mountain on that Scottish coast; there were Scottish lights to be seen shining across the glorious Channel, and at Allonby itself there was every idle luxury (no doubt), that a watering-place could offer to the heart of idle man. Moreover, said Mr Goodchild, with his finger on the map, this exquisite retreat was approached by a coach-road, from a railway station called Aspatria – a name, in a manner, suggestive of the departed glories of Greece, associated with one of the most engaging and most famous of Greek women. On this point, Mr Goodchild continued at intervals to breathe a vein of classic fancy and eloquence exceedingly irksome to Mr Idle, until it appeared that the honest English pronunciation of that Cumberland country shortened Aspatria into 'Spatter.' After this supplementary discovery, Mr Goodchild said no more about it.

By way of Spatter, the crippled Idle was carried, hoisted, pushed, poked, and packed into and out of tavern resting-places, until he was brought at length within sniff of the sea. And now, behold the apprentices gallantly riding into Allonby in a one-horse fly, bent upon staying in that peaceful marine valley until the turbulent Doncaster time shall come round upon the wheel, in its turn among what are in sporting registers called the 'Fixtures' for the mouth.

'Do you see Allonby?' asked Thomas Idle.

'I don't see it yet,' said Francis, looking out of the window.

'It must be there,' said Thomas Idle.

'I don't see it,' returned Francis.

'It must be there,' repeated Thomas Idle, fretfully.

'Lord bless me!' exclaimed Francis, drawing in his head, 'I suppose this is it!'

'A watering-place,' retorted Thomas Idle, with the pardonable sharpness of an invalid, 'can't be five gentlemen in straw-hats, on a form on one side of a door, and four ladies in hats and falls, on a form on another side of a door, and three geese in a dirty little brook before them, and a boy's legs hanging over a bridge (with a boy's body I suppose on the other side of the parapet), and a donkey running away. What are you talking about?'

'Allonby, gentlemen,' said the most comfortable of land-ladies, as she opened one door of the carriage; 'Allonby, gentlemen,' said the most attentive of landlords, as he opened the other.

Thomas Idle yielded his arm to the ready Goodchild, and descended from the vehicle. Thomas, now just able to grope his way along, in a doubled-up condition, with the aid of two thick sticks, was no bad embodiment of Commodore Trunnion, or of one of those many gallant Admirals of the stage, who have all ample fortunes, gout, thick-sticks, tempers, wards, and nephews. With this distinguished naval appearance upon him, Thomas made a crab-like progress into a clean little bulk-headed room, where he slowly deposited himself on a sofa, with a stick on either hand of him, looking exceedingly grim.

'Francis,' said Thomas Idle, 'what do you think of this place?'

'I think,' returned Mr Goodchild, in a glowing way, 'it is everything we expected.'

'Hah!' said Thomas Idle.

'There is the sea,' cried Mr Goodchild, pointing out of the window; 'and here,' pointing to the lunch on the table, 'are shrimps. Let us—' here Mr Goodchild looked out of the window, as if in search of something, and looked in again, – 'let us eat 'em.'

The shrimps eaten and the dinner ordered, Mr Goodchild went out to survey the watering-place. As Chorus of the Drama, without whom Thomas could make nothing of the scenery, he by-and-bye returned, to have the following report screwed out of him.

In brief, it was the most delightful place ever seen.

'But,' Thomas Idle asked, 'where is it?'

'It's what you may call generally up and down the beach, here and there,' said Mr Goodchild, with a twist of his hand.

'Proceed,' said Thomas Idle.

It was, Mr Goodchild went on to say, in cross-examination, what you might call a primitive place. Large? No, it was not large. Who ever expected it to be large? Shape? What a question to ask! No shape. What sort of a street? Why, no street. Shops? Yes, of course (quite indignant). How many? Who ever went into a place to count the shops? Ever so many. Six? Perhaps. A library? Why, of course! (indignant again). Good collection of books? Most likely – couldn't say – had seen nothing in it but a pair of scales. Any reading-room? Of course, there was a reading-room. Where? Where! Why, over there. Where was over there? Why, *there!* Let Mr Idle carry his eye to that bit of waste-ground above high water-mark, where the rank grass and loose stones were most in a litter; and he would see a sort of a long ruinous brick loft, next door to a ruinous brick outhouse, which loft had a ladder outside, to get up by. That was the reading-room, and if Mr Idle didn't like the idea of a weaver's shuttle throbbing under a reading-room, that was his look out. *He* was not to dictate, Mr Goodchild supposed (indignant again), to the company.

'By-the-bye,' Thomas Idle observed; 'the company?'

Well! (Mr Goodchild went on to report) very nice company. Where were they? Why, there they were. Mr Idle could see the tops of their hats, he supposed. What? Those nine straw hats again, five gentlemen's and four ladies'? Yes, to be sure. Mr Goodchild hoped the company were not to be expected to wear helmets, to please Mr Idle.

Beginning to recover his temper at about this point, Mr Goodchild voluntarily reported that if you wanted to be primitive, you could be primitive here, and that if you wanted to be idle, you could be idle here. In the course of some days, he added, that there were three fishing-boats, but no rigging, and that there were plenty of fishermen who never fished. That they got their living entirely by looking at the ocean. What nourishment they looked out of it to support their strength, he couldn't say; but, he supposed it was some sort of Iodine. The place was full of their children, who were always upside down on the public buildings (two small bridges over the brook), and always hurting themselves or one another, so that their wailings made more continual noise in the air than could have been got in a busy place. The houses people lodged in, were nowhere in particular, and were in capital accordance with the beach; being all more or less cracked and damaged as its shells were, and all empty – as its shells were. Among them, was an edifice of destitute appearance, with a number of wall-eyed windows in it, looking desperately out to Scotland as if for help, which said it was a Bazaar (and it ought to know), and where you might buy anything you wanted – supposing what you wanted, was a little camp-stool or a child's wheelbarrow. The brook crawled or stopped between the houses and the sea, and the donkey was always running away, and when he got into the brook he was pelted out with stones, which never hit him, and which always hit some of the children who were upside down on the public buildings, and made their lamentations louder. This donkey was the public excitement of Allonby, and was probably supported at the public expense.

The foregoing descriptions, delivered in separate items, on separate days of adventurous discovery, Mr Goodchild severally wound up, by looking out of window, looking in again, and saying, 'But there is the sea, and here are the shrimps – let us eat 'em.'

There were fine sunsets at Allonby when the low flat beach, with its pools of water and its dry patches, changed into long bars of silver and gold in various states of burnishing, and there were fine views – on fine days – of the Scottish coast. But, when it rained at Allonby, Allonby thrown back upon its ragged self, became a kind of place which the donkey seemed to have found out, and to have his highly sagacious reasons for wishing to bolt from. Thomas Idle observed, too, that Mr Goodchild, with a noble show of disinterestedness, became every day more ready to walk to Maryport and back, for letters; and suspicions began to harbour in the mind of Thomas, that his friend deceived him, and that Maryport was a preferable place.

Therefore, Thomas said to Francis on a day when they had looked at the sea and eaten the shrimps, 'My mind misgives me, Goodchild, that you go to Maryport, like the boy in the story-book, to ask *it* to be idle with you.'

'Judge, then,' returned Francis, adopting the style of the story-book, 'with what success. I go to a region which is a bit of water-side Bristol, with a slice of Wapping, a seasoning of Wolverhampton, and a garnish of Portsmouth, and I say,

"Will *you* come and be idle with me?" And it answers, "No; for I am a great deal too vaporous, and a great deal too rusty, and a great deal too muddy, and a great deal too dirty altogether; and I have ships to load, and pitch and tar to boil, and iron to hammer, and steam to get up, and smoke to make, and stone to quarry, and fifty other disagreeable things to do, and I can't be idle with you." Then I go into jagged up-hill and down-hill streets, where I am in the pastrycook's shop at one moment, and next moment in savage fastnesses of moor and morass, beyond the confines of civilisation, and I say to those murky and black dusky streets, "Will *you* come and be idle with me?" To which they reply, "No, we can't, indeed, for we haven't the spirits, and we are startled by the echo of your feet on the sharp pavement, and we have so many goods in our shop-windows which nobody wants, and we have so much to do for a limited public which never comes to us to be done for, that we are altogether out of sorts and can't enjoy ourselves with any one." So I go to the Post-office, and knock at the shutter, and I say to the Post-master, "Will *you* come and be idle with me?" To which he rejoins, "No, I really can't, for I live, as you may see, in such a very little Post-office, and pass my life behind such a very little shutter, that my hand, when I put it out, is as the hand of a giant crammed through the window of a dwarf's house at a fair, and I am a mere Post-office anchorite in a cell much too small for him, and I can't get out, and I can't get in, and I have no space to be idle in, even if I would." So, the boy,' said Mr Goodchild, concluding the tale, 'comes back with the letters after all, and lives happy never afterwards.'

But it may, not unreasonably, be asked – while Francis Goodchild was wandering hither and thither, storing his mind with perpetual observation of men and things, and sincerely believing himself to be the laziest creature in existence all the time – how did Thomas Idle, crippled and confined to the house, contrive to get through the hours of the day?

Prone on the sofa, Thomas made no attempt to get through the hours, but passively allowed the hours to get through *him*. Where other men in his situation would have read books and improved their minds, Thomas slept and rested his body. Where other men would have pondered anxiously over their future prospects, Thomas dreamed lazily of his past life. The one solitary thing he did, which most other people would have done in his place, was to resolve on making certain alterations and improvements in his mode of existence, as soon as the effects of the misfortune that had overtaken him had all passed away. Remembering that the current of his life had hitherto oozed along in one smooth stream of laziness, occasionally troubled on the surface by a slight passing ripple of industry, his present ideas on the subject of self-reform, inclined him – not as the reader may be disposed to imagine, to project schemes for a new existence of enterprise and exertion – but, on the contrary, to resolve that he would never, if he could possibly help it, be active or industrious again, throughout the whole of his future career.

It is due to Mr Idle to relate that his mind sauntered towards this peculiar conclusion on distinct and logically-producible grounds. After reviewing, quite at his ease, and with many needful intervals of repose, the generally-placid spectacle of his past existence, he arrived at the discovery that all the great disasters which had tried his patience and equanimity in early life, had been caused by his having allowed himself to be deluded into imitating some pernicious example of activity and industry that had been set him by others. The trials to which he here alludes were three in number, and may be thus reckoned up: First, the disaster of being an unpopular and a thrashed boy at school; secondly, the disaster of falling seriously ill; thirdly, the disaster of becoming acquainted with a great bore.

The first disaster occurred after Thomas had been an idle and a popular boy at school, for some happy years. One Christmas-time, he was stimulated by the evil example, of a companion, whom he had always trusted and liked, to be untrue to himself, and to try for a prize at the ensuing half-yearly examination. He did try, and he got a prize – how, he did not distinctly know at the moment, and cannot remember now. No sooner, however, had the book – Moral Hints to the Young on the Value of Time – been placed in his hands, than the first troubles of his life began. The idle boys deserted him, as a traitor to their cause. The industrious boys avoided him, as a dangerous interloper; one of their number, who had always won the prize on previous occasions, expressing just resentment at the invasion of his privileges by calling Thomas into the play-ground, and then and there administering to him the first sound and genuine thrashing that he had received in his life. Unpopular from that moment, as a beaten boy, who belonged to no side and was rejected by all parties, young Idle soon lost caste with his masters, as he had previously lost caste with his school-fellows. He had forfeited the comfortable reputation of being the one lazy member of the youthful community whom it was quite hopeless to punish. Never again did he hear the head-master say reproachfully to an industrious boy who had committed a fault, 'I might have expected this in Thomas Idle, but it is inexcusable, sir, in you, who know better.' Never more, after winning that fatal prize, did he escape the retributive imposition, or the avenging birch. From that time, the masters made him work, and the boys would not let him play. From that time his social position steadily declined, and his life at school became a perpetual burden to him.

So, again, with the second disaster. While Thomas was lazy, he was a model of health. His first attempt at active exertion and his first suffering from severe illness are connected together by the intimate relations of cause and effect. Shortly after leaving school, he accompanied a party of friends to a cricket-field, in his natural and appropriate character of spectator only. On the ground it was discovered that the players fell short of the required number, and facile Thomas was persuaded to assist in making up the complement. At a certain appointed time, he was roused from peaceful slumber in a dry ditch, and placed before three wickets with a bat in his hand. Opposite to him, behind three more wickets, stood one of his bosom friends, filling the situation (as he was informed) of bowler. No words can describe Mr Idle's horror and amazement, when he saw this young man – on ordinary occasions, the meekest and mildest of human beings – suddenly contract his eyebrows, compress his lips, assume the aspect of an infuriated savage, run back a few steps, then run forward, and, without the slightest previous provocation, hurl a detestably hard ball with all his might straight at Thomas's legs. Stimulated to preternatural activity of body and sharp-

ness of eye by the instinct of self-preservation, Mr Idle
contrived, by jumping deftly aside at the right moment, and
by using his bat (ridiculously narrow as it was for the purpose)
as a shield, to preserve his life and limbs from the dastardly
attack that had been made on both, to leave the full force of the
deadly missile to strike his wicket instead of his leg; and to end
the innings, so far as his side was concerned, by being
immediately bowled out. Grateful for his escape he was about
to return to the dry ditch, when he was peremptorily stopped,
and told that the other side was 'going in,' and that he was
expected to 'field.' His conception of the whole art and
mystery of 'fielding,' may be summed up in the three words
of serious advice which he privately administered to himself
on that trying occasion – avoid the ball. Fortified by this sound
and salutory principle, he took his own course, impervious
alike to ridicule and abuse. Whenever the ball came near him,
he thought of his shins, and got out of the way immediately.
'Catch it!' 'Stop it!' 'Pitch it up!' were cries that he regarded
not. He ducked under it, he jumped over it, he whisked
himself away from it on either side. Never once, throughout
the whole innings did he and the ball come together on
anything approaching to intimate terms. The unnatural
activity of body which was necessarily called forth for the
accomplishment of this result threw Thomas Idle, for the first
time in his life, into a perspiration. The perspiration, in
consequence of his want of practice in the management of that
particular result of bodily activity, was suddenly checked; the
inevitable chill succeeded; and that, in its turn, was followed
by a fever. For the first time since his birth, Mr Idle found
himself confined to his bed for many weeks together, wasted
and worn by a long illness, of which his own disastrous
muscular exertion had been the sole first cause.

The third occasion on which Thomas found reason to
reproach himself bitterly for the mistake of having attempted
to be industrious, was connected with his choice of a calling in
life. Having no interest in the Church, he appropriately
selected the next best profession for a lazy man in England –
the Bar. Although the Benchers of the Inns of Court have
lately abandoned their students to make some show of
studying, in Mr Idle's time no such innovation as this existed.

Young men who aspired to the honourable title of barrister were, very properly, not asked to learn anything of the law, but were merely required to eat a certain number of dinners at the table of their Hall, and to pay a certain sum of money; and were called to the Bar as soon as they could prove that they had sufficiently complied with these extremely sensible regulations. Never did Thomas move more harmoniously in concert with his elders and betters than when he was qualifying himself for admission among the barristers of his native country. Never did he feel more deeply what real laziness was in all the serene majesty of its nature, than on the memorable day when he was called to the bar, after having carefully abstained from opening his law-books during his period of probation, except to fall asleep over them. How he could ever again have become industrious, even for the shortest period, after that great reward conferred upon his idleness, quite passes his comprehension. The kind benchers did everything they could to show him the folly of exerting himself. They wrote out his probationary exercise for him, and never expected him even to take the trouble of reading it through when it was written. They invited him, with seven other choice spirits as lazy as himself, to come and be called to the bar, while they were sitting over their wine and fruit after dinner. They put his oaths of allegiance, and his dreadful official denunciations of the Pope and the Pretender so gently into his mouth, that he hardly knew how the words got there. They wheeled all their chairs softly round from the table, and sat surveying the young barristers with their backs to their bottles, rather than stand up, or adjourn to hear the exercises read. And when Mr Idle and the seven unlabouring neophytes, ranged in order, as a class, with their backs considerately placed against a screen, had begun, in rotation, to read the exercises which they had not written, even then, each Bencher, true to the great lazy principle of the whole proceeding, stopped each neophyte before he had stammered through his first line, and bowed to him, and told him politely that he was a barrister from that moment. This was all the ceremony. It was followed by a social supper, and by the presentation, in accordance with ancient custom, of a pound of sweetmeats and a bottle of Madeira, offered in the way of needful refreshment, by each grateful neophyte to each beneficent Bencher. It may seem inconceivable that Thomas should ever have forgotten the great do-nothing principle instilled by such a ceremony as this; but it is, nevertheless, true, that certain designing students of industrious habits found him out, took advantage of his easy humour, persuaded him that it was discreditable to be a barrister and to know nothing whatever about the law, and lured him, by the force of their own evil example, into a conveyancer's chambers, to make up for lost time, and to qualify himself for practice at the Bar. After a fortnight of self-delusion, the curtain fell from his eyes; he resumed his natural character, and shut up his books. But the retribution which had hitherto always followed his little casual errors of industry followed them still. He could get away from the conveyancer's chambers, but he could not get away from one of the pupils, who had taken a fancy to him, – a tall, serious, raw-boned, hard-working, disputatious pupil, with ideas of his own about reforming the Law of Real Property, who has been the scourge of Mr Idle's existence ever since the fatal day when he fell into the mistake of attempting to study the law. Before that time his friends were all sociable idlers like himself. Since that time the burden of bearing with a hard-working young man has become part of his lot in life. Go where he will now, he can never feel certain that the raw-boned pupil is not affectionately waiting for him round a corner, to tell him a little more about the Law of Real Property. Suffer as he may under the infliction, he can never complain, for he must always remember, with unavailing regret, that he has his own thoughtless industry to thank for first exposing him to the great social calamity of knowing a bore.

These events of his past life, with the significant results that they brought about, pass drowsily through Thomas Idle's memory, while he lies alone on the sofa at Allonby and elsewhere, dreaming away the time which his fellow-apprentice gets through so actively out of doors. Remembering the lesson of laziness which his past disasters teach, and bearing in mind also the fact that he is crippled in one leg because he exerted himself to go up a mountain, when he ought to have known that his proper course of conduct was to stop at the bottom of it, he holds now, and will for the future firmly continue to hold, by his new resolution never to be industrious again, on any pretence whatever, for the rest of his life. The physical results of his accident have been related in a previous chapter. The moral results now stand on record; and, with the enumeration of these, that part of the present narrative which is occupied by the Episode of The Sprained Ankle may now perhaps be considered, in all its aspects, as finished and complete.

'How do you propose that we get through this present afternoon and evening?' demanded Thomas Idle, after two or three hours of the foregoing reflection at Allonby.

Mr Goodchild faltered, looked out of window, looked in again, and said, as he had so often said before, 'There is the sea, and here are the shrimps; – let us eat 'em!'

But, the wise donkey was at that moment in the act of bolting: not with the irresolution of his previous efforts which had been wanting in sustained force of character, but with real vigor of purpose: shaking the dust off his mane and hind-feet at Allonby, and tearing away from it, as if he had nobly made up his mind that he never would be taken alive. At sight of this inspiring spectacle, which was visible from his sofa, Thomas Idle stretched his neck and dwelt upon it rapturously.

'Francis Goodchild,' he then said, turning to his companion with a solemn air, 'this is a delightful little Inn, excellently kept by the most comfortable of landladies and the most attentive of landlords, but – the donkey's right!'

The words, 'There is the sea, and here are the—,' again trembled on the lips of Goodchild, unaccompanied however by any sound.

'Let us instantly pack the portmanteaus,' said Thomas Idle, 'pay the bill, and order a fly out, with instructions to the driver to follow the donkey!'

Mr Goodchild, who had only wanted encouragement to disclose the real state of his feelings, and who had been pining beneath his weary secret, now burst into tears, and confessed that he thought another day in the place would be the death of him.

So, the two idle apprentices followed the donkey until the night was far advanced. Whether he was recaptured by the town-council, or is bolting at this hour through the United Kingdom, they know not. They hope he may be still bolting; if so, their best wishes are with him.

It entered Mr Idle's head, on the borders of Cumberland, that there could be no idler place to stay at, except by snatches of a few minutes each, than a railway station. 'An intermediate station on a line – a junction – anything of that sort,' Thomas suggested. Mr Goodchild approved of the idea as eccentric, and they journeyed on and on, until they came to such a station where there was an Inn.

'Here,' said Thomas, 'we may be luxuriously lazy; other people will travel for us, as it were, and we shall laugh at their folly.'

It was a Junction-Station, where the wooden razors before mentioned shaved the air very often, and where the sharp electric-telegraph bell was in a very restless condition. All manner of cross-lines of rails came zig-zaging into it, like a Congress of iron vipers; and, a little way out of it, a pointsman in an elevated signal-box was constantly going through the motions of drawing immense quantities of beer at a public-house bar. In one direction, confused perspectives of embankments and arches were to be seen from the platform; in the other, the rails soon disentangled themselves into two tracks, and shot away under a bridge, and curved round a corner. Sidings were there, in which empty luggage-vans and cattle-boxes often butted against each other as if they couldn't agree; and warehouses were there, in which great quantities of goods seemed to have taken the veil (of the consistency of tarpaulin), and to have retired from the world without any hope of getting back to it. Refreshment-rooms were there; one, for the hungry and thirsty Iron Locomotives where their coke and water were ready, and of good quality, for they were dangerous to play tricks with; the other, for the hungry and thirsty human Locomotives, who might take what they could get, and whose chief consolation was provided in the form of three terrific urns or vases of white metal, containing nothing, each forming a breast-work for a defiant and apparently much-injured woman.

Established at this Station, Mr Thomas Idle and Mr Francis Goodchild resolved to enjoy it. But, its contrasts were very violent, and there was also an infection in it.

First, as to its contrasts. They were only two, but they were Lethargy and Madness. The Station was either totally unconscious, or wildly raving. By day, in its unconscious state, it looked as if no life could come to it – as if it were all rust, dust, and ashes – as if the last train for ever, had gone without issuing any Return-Tickets – as if the last Engine had uttered its last shriek and burst. One awkward shave of the air from the wooden razor, and everything changed. Tight office-doors flew open, panels yielded, books, newspapers travelling-caps and wrappers broke out of brick walls, money chinked, conveyances oppressed by nightmares of luggage came careering into the yard, porters started up from secret places, ditto the much-injured women, the shining bell, who lived in a little tray on stilts by himself, flew into a man's hand and clamoured violently. The pointsman aloft in the signal-box made the motions of drawing, with some difficulty, hogsheads of beer. Down Train! More beer. Up Train! More beer. Cross Junction Train! More beer. Cattle Train! More beer. Goods Train! Simmering, whistling, trembling, rumbling, thundering. Trains on the whole confusion of intersecting rails, crossing one another, bumping one another, hissing one another, backing to go forward, tearing into distance to come close. People frantic. Exiles seeking restoration to their native carriages, and banished to remoter climes. More beer and more bell. Then, in a minute, the Station relapsed, into stupor as the stoker of the Cattle Train, the last to depart, went gliding out of it, wiping the long nose of his oil-can with a dirty pocket-handkerchief.

By night, in its unconscious state, the station was not so much as visible. Something in the air, like an enterprising chemist's established in business on one of the boughs of Jack's beanstalk, was all that could be discerned of it under the stars. In a moment it would break out, a constellation of gas. In another moment, twenty rival chemists, on twenty rival beanstalks, came into existence. Then, the Furies would be seen, waving their lurid torches up and down the confused perspectives of embankments and arches – would be heard, too, wailing and shrieking. Then, the Station would be full of palpitating trains, as in the day; with the heightening difference that they were not so clearly seen as in the day, whereas the station walls, starting forward under the gas, like a hippopotamus's eyes, dazzled the human locomotives with the sauce-bottle, the cheap music, the bedstead, the distorted range of buildings where the patent safes are made, the gentleman in the rain with the registered umbrella, the lady returning from the ball with the registered respirator, and all their other embellishments. And now, the human locomotives, creased as to their countenances and purblind as to their eyes, would swarm forth in a heap, addressing themselves to the mysterious urns and the much-injured women; while the iron locomotives, dripping fire and water, shed their steam about plentifully, making the dull oxen in their cages, with heads depressed, and foam hanging from their mouths as their red looks glanced fearfully at the surrounding terrors, seem as though they had been drinking at half-frozen waters and were hung with icicles. Through the same steam would be caught glimpses of their fellow-travellers, the sheep, getting their white kid faces together, away from the bars, and stuffing the interstices with trembling wool. Also, down among the wheels of the man with the sledge-hammer, ringing the axles of the fast night-train; against whom the oxen have a misgiving that he is the man with the pole-axe who is to come by-and-bye, and so the nearest of them try to back, and get a purchase for a thrust at him through the bars. Suddenly, the bell would ring, the steam would stop with one hiss and a yell, the chemists on the beanstalks would be busy, the avenging Furies would bestir themselves, the fast night-train would melt from eye and ear, the other trains going their ways more slowly would be heard faintly rattling in the distance like old-fashioned watches running down, the sauce-bottle and cheap music retired from view, even the bedstead went to bed, and there was no such visible thing at the Station to vex the cool wind in its blowing, or perhaps the autumn lightning, as it found out the iron rails.

The infection of the Station was this: – When it was in its raving state, the Apprentices found it impossible to be there, without labouring under the delusion that they were in a hurry. To Mr Goodchild, whose ideas of idleness were so imperfect, this was no unpleasant hallucination, and accordingly that gentleman went through great exertions in yielding

to it, and running up and down the platform, jostling
everybody, under the impression that he had a highly important mission somewhere, and had not a moment to lose. But,
to Thomas Idle, this contagion was so very unacceptable as
incident of the situation, that he struck on the fourth day, and
requested to be moved.

'This place fills me with a dreadful sensation,' said Thomas,
'of having something to do. Remove me, Francis.'

'Where would you like to go next?' was the question of the
ever-engaging Goodchild.

'I have heard there is a good old Inn at Lancaster, established
in a fine old house: an Inn where they give you bride-cake
every day after dinner,' said Thomas Idle. 'Let us eat bride-
cake without the trouble of being married, or of knowing
anybody in that ridiculous dilemma.'

Mr Goodchild, with a lover's sigh, assented. They departed
from the Station in a violent hurry (for which, it is unnecessary to observe, there was not the least occasion), and were
delivered at the fine old house at Lancaster, on the same night.

It is Mr Goodchild's opinion, that if a visitor on his arrival at
Lancaster could be accommodated with a pole which would
push the opposite side of the street some yards farther off, it
would be better for all parties. Protesting against being
required to live in a trench, and obliged to speculate all day
upon what the people can possibly be doing within a mysterious opposite window, which is a shop-window to look at, but
not a shop-window in respect of its offering nothing for sale
and declining to give any account whatever of itself, Mr
Goodchild concedes Lancaster to be a pleasant place. A place
dropped in the midst of a charming landscape, a place with a
fine ancient fragment of castle, a place of lovely walks, a place
possessing staid old houses richly fitted with old Honduras
mahogany, which has grown so dark with time that it seems
to have got something of a retrospective mirror-quality into
itself, and to show the visitor, in the depths of its grain,
through all its polish, the hue of the wretched slaves who
groaned long ago under old Lancaster merchants. And Mr
Goodchild adds that the stones of Lancaster do sometimes
whisper, even yet, of rich men passed away – upon whose
great prosperity some of these old doorways frowned sullen in

the brightest weather – that their slave-gain turned to curses, as the Arabian Wizard's money turned to leaves, and that no good ever came of it, even unto the third and fourth gener- ations, until it was wasted and gone.

It was a gallant sight to behold, the Sunday procession of the Lancaster elders to Church – all in black, and looking fearfully like a funeral without the Body – under the escort of Three Beadles.

'Think,' said Francis, as he stood at the Inn window, admiring, 'of being taken to the sacred edifice by three Beadles! I have in my early time, been taken out of it by one Beadle; but, to be taken into it by three, O Thomas, is a distinction I shall never enjoy!'

Chapter IV

When Mr Goodchild had looked out of the Lancaster Inn- window for two hours on end, with great perseverance, he began to entertain a misgiving that he was growing indus- trious. He therefore set himself next, to explore the country from the tops of all the steep hills in the neighbourhood.

He came back at dinner-time, red and glowing, to tell Thomas Idle what he had seen. Thomas, on his back reading, listened with great composure, and asked him whether he really had gone up those hills, and bothered himself with those views, and walked all those miles?

'Because I want to know,' added Thomas, 'what you would say of it, if you were obliged to do it?'

'It would be different, then,' said Francis. 'It would be work, then; now, it's play.'

'Play!' repeated Thomas Idle, utterly repudiating the reply. 'Play! Here is a man goes systematically tearing himself to pieces, and putting himself through an incessant course of training, as if he were always under articles to fight a match for the champion's belt, and he calls it Play! Play!' exclaimed Thomas Idle, scornfully contemplating his one boot in the air. 'You *can't* play. You don't know what it is. You make work of everything.'

The bright Goodchild amiably smiled.

'So you do,' said Thomas. 'I mean it. To me you are an absolutely terrible fellow. You do nothing like another man. Where another fellow would fall into a footbath of action or emotion, you fall into a mine. Where any other fellow would be a painted butterfly, you are a fiery dragon. Where another man would stake a sixpence, you stake your existence. If you were to go up in a balloon, you would make for Heaven; and if you were to dive into the depths of the earth, nothing short of the other place would content you. What a fellow you are, Francis!'

The cheerful Goodchild laughed.

'It's all very well to laugh, but I wonder you don't feel it to be serious,' said Idle. 'A man who can do nothing by halves appears to me to be a fearful man.'

'Tom, Tom,' repeated Goodchild, 'if I can do nothing by halves, and be nothing by halves, it's pretty clear that you must take me as a whole, and make the best of me.'

With this philosophical rejoinder, the airy Goodchild clapped Mr Idle on the shoulder in a final manner, and they sat down to dinner.

'By the bye,' said Goodchild, 'I have been over a lunatic asylum too, since I have been out.'

'He has been,' exclaimed Thomas Idle, casting up his eyes, 'over a lunatic asylum! Not content with being as great an Ass as Captain Barclay in the pedestrian way, he makes a Lunacy Commissioner of himself – for nothing!'

'An immense place,' said Goodchild, 'admirable offices, very good arrangements, very good attendants; altogether a remarkable place.'

'And what did you see there?' asked Mr Idle, adapting Hamlet's advice to the occasion, and assuming the virtue of interest, though he had it not.

'The usual thing,' said Francis Goodchild, with a sigh. 'Long groves of blighted men-and-women-trees; interminable avenues of hopeless faces; numbers, without the slightest power of really combining for any earthly purpose; a society of human creatures who have nothing in common but that they have all lost the power of being humanly social with one another.'

'Take a glass of wine with me,' said Thomas Idle, 'and let *us* be social.'

'In one gallery, Tom,' pursued Francis Goodchild, 'which looked to me about the length of the Long Walk at Windsor, more or less—'

'Probably less,' observed Thomas Idle.

'In one gallery, which was otherwise quite clear of patients (for they were all out), there was a poor little dark-chinned, meagre man, with a perplexed brow and a pensive face, stooping low over the matting on the floor, and picking out with his thumb and forefinger the course of its fibres. The afternoon sun was slanting in at the large end-window, and there were cross patches of light and shade all down the vista, made by the unseen windows and the open doors of the little sleeping cells on either side. In about the centre of the perspective, under an arch, regardless of the pleasant weather, regardless of the solitude, regardless of approaching footsteps, was the poor little dark-chinned, meagre man, poring over the matting. "What are you doing there?" said my conductor, when we came to him. He looked up, and pointed to the matting. "I wouldn't do that, I think," said my conductor, kindly; "If I were you, I would go and read, or I would lie down if I felt tired; but I wouldn't do that." The patient considered a moment, and vacantly answered, "No, sir, I won't; I'll – I'll go and read," and so he lamely shuffled away into one of the little rooms. I turned my head before we had gone many paces. He had already come out again, and was again poring over the matting, and tracking out its fibres with his thumb and fore-finger. I stopped to look at him, and it came into my mind, that probably the course of those fibres as they plaited in and out, over and under, was the only course of things in the whole wide world that it was left to him to understand – that his darkening intellect had narrowed down to the small cleft of a light which showed him, "This piece was twisted this way, went in here, passed under, came out there, was carried on away here to the right where I now put my finger on it, and in this progress of events, the thing was made and came to be here." Then, I wondered whether he looked into the matting, next, to see if it could show him anything of the process through which *he* came to be there, so strangely poring over it. Then, I thought how all of us, GOD help us! in our different ways are poring over our bits of matting, blindly enough, and what confusions and mysteries we make in the pattern. I had a sadder fellow-feeling with the little dark-chinned, meagre man, by that time, and I came away.'

Mr Idle diverting the conversation to grouse, custards, and bride-cake, Mr Goodchild followed in the same direction. The bride-cake was as bilious and indigestible as if a real bride had cut it, and the dinner it completed was an admirable performance.

The house was a genuine old house of a very quaint description, teeming with old carvings, and beams, and panels, and having an excellent old staircase, with a gallery or upper staircase, cut off from it by a curious fencework of old oak, or of the old Honduras Mahogany wood. It was, and is, and will be, for many a long year to come, a remarkably picturesque house; and a certain grave mystery lurking in the depth of the old mahogany panels, as if they were so many deep pools of dark water – such, indeed, as they had been much among when they were trees – gave it a very mysterious character after nightfall.

When Mr Goodchild and Mr Idle had first alighted at the door, and stepped into the sombre handsome old hall, they had been received by half-a-dozen noiseless old men in black, all dressed exactly alike, who glided up the stairs with the obliging landlord and waiter – but without appearing to get into their way, or to mind whether they did or no – and who had filed off to the right and left on the old staircase, as the guests entered their sitting-room. It was then broad, bright day. But, Mr Goodchild had said, when their door was shut, 'Who on earth are those old men!' And afterwards, both on going out and coming in, he had noticed that there were no old men to be seen.

Neither, had the old men, or any one of the old men, reappeared since. The two friends had passed a night in the house, but had seen nothing more of the old men. Mr Goodchild, in rambling about it, had looked along passages, and glanced in at doorways, but had encountered no old men; neither did it appear that any old men were, by any member of the establishment, missed or expected.

Another odd circumstance impressed itself on their attention. It was, that the door of their sitting-room was never left untouched for a quarter of an hour. It was opened with hesitation, opened with confidence, opened a little way, opened a good way – always clapped-to again without a word of explanation. They were reading, they were writing, they were eating, they were drinking, they were talking, they were dozing; the door was always opened at an unexpected moment, and they looked towards it, and it was clapped-to again, and nobody was to be seen. When this had happened fifty times or so, Mr Goodchild had said to his companion, jestingly: 'I begin to think, Tom, there was something wrong about those six old men.'

Night had come again, and they had been writing for two or three hours: writing, in short, a portion of the lazy notes from which these lazy sheets are taken. They had left off writing, and glasses were on the table between them. The house was closed and quiet, and the town was quiet. Around the head of Thomas Idle, as he lay upon his sofa, hovered light; wreaths of fragrant smoke. The temples of Francis Goodchild, as he leaned back in his chair, with his two hands clasped behind his head, and his legs crossed, were similarly decorated.

They had been discussing several idle subjects of speculation, not omitting the strange old men, and were still so occupied, when Mr Goodchild abruptly changed his attitude to wind up his watch. They were just becoming drowsy enough to be stopped in the talk by any such slight check. Thomas Idle, who was speaking at the moment, paused and said, 'How goes it?'

'One,' said Goodchild.

As if he had ordered One old man, and the order were promptly executed (truly, all orders were so, in that excellent hotel), the door opened, and One old man stood there.

He did not come in, but stood with the door in his hand.

'One of the six, Tom, at last!' said Mr Goodchild, in a surprised whisper. – 'Sir, your pleasure?'

'Sir, *your* pleasure?' said the One old man.

'I didn't ring.'

'The Bell did,' said the One old man.

He said BELL, in a deep strong way, that would have expressed the church Bell.

'I had the pleasure, I believe, of seeing you, yesterday?' said Goodchild.

'I cannot undertake to say for certain,' was the grim reply of the One old man.

'I think you saw me? Did you not?'

'Saw *you*?' said the old man. 'O yes, I saw *you*. But, I see many who never see me.'

A chilled, slow, earthy, fixed old man. A cadaverous old man of measured speech. An old man who seemed as unable to wink, as if his eyelids had been nailed to his forehead. An old man whose eyes – two spots of fire – had no more motion that if they had been connected with the back of his skull by screws driven through it, and rivetted and bolted outside, among his grey hair.

The night had turned so cold, to Mr Goodchild's sensations, that he shivered. He remarked lightly, and half apologetically, 'I think somebody is walking over my grave.'

'No,' said the weird old man, 'there is no one there.'

Mr Goodchild looked at Idle, but Idle lay with his head enwreathed in smoke.

'No one there!' said Goodchild.

'There is no one at your grave, I assure you,' said the old man.

He had come in and shut the door, and he now sat down. He did not bend himself to sit, as other people do, but seemed to sink bolt upright, as if in water, until the chair stopped him.

'My friend, Mr Idle,' said Goodchild, extremely anxious to introduce a third person into the conversation.

'I am,' said the old man, without looking at him,' at Mr Idle's service.'

'If you are an old inhabitant of this place,' Francis Goodchild resumed:

'Yes.'

—'Perhaps you can decide a point my friend and I were in doubt upon, this morning. They hang condemned criminals at the Castle, I believe?'

'*I* believe so,' said the old man.

'Are their faces turned towards that noble prospect?'

'Your face is turned,' replied the old man, 'to the Castle wall. When you are tied up, you see its stones expanding and contracting violently, and a similar expansion and contraction seem to take place in your own head and breast. Then, there is a rush of fire and an earthquake, and the Castle springs into the air, and you tumble down a precipice.'

His cravat appeared to trouble him. He put his hand to his throat, and moved his neck from side to side. He was an old man of a swollen character of face, and his nose was immovably hitched up on one side, as if by a little hook inserted in that nostril. Mr Goodchild felt exceedingly uncomfortable, and began to think the night was hot, and not cold.'

'A strong description, sir,' he observed.

'A strong sensation,' the old man rejoined.

Again, Mr Goodchild looked to Mr Thomas Idle; but, Thomas lay on his back with his face attentively turned towards the One old man, and made no sign. At this time Mr Goodchild believed that he saw two threads of fire stretch from the old man's eyes to his own, and there attach themselves. (Mr Goodchild writes the present account of his experience, and, with the utmost solemnity, protests that he had the strongest sensation upon him of being forced to look at the old man along those two fiery films, from that moment.)

'I must tell it to you,' said the old man, with a ghastly and a stony stare.

'What?' asked Francis Goodchild.

'You know where it took place. Yonder!'

Whether he pointed to the room above, or to the room below, or to any room in that old house, or to a room in some other old house in that old town, Mr Goodchild was not, nor is, nor ever can be, sure. He was confused by the circumstances that the right fore-finger of the One old man seemed to dip itself in one of the threads of fire, light itself, and make a fiery start in the air, as it pointed somewhere. Having pointed somewhere, it went out.

'You know she was a Bride,' said the old man.

'I know they still send up Bride-cake,' Mr Goodchild faltered. 'This is a very oppressive air.'

'She was a Bride,' said the old man. 'She was a fair, flaxen-haired, large-eyed girl, who had no character, no purpose. A weak, credulous, incapable, helpless nothing. Not like her mother. No, no. It was her father whose character she reflected.

'Her mother had taken care to secure everything to herself, for her own life, when the father of this girl (a child at that time) died – of sheer helplessness; no other disorder – and then He renewed the acquaintance that had once subsisted between the mother and Him. He had been put aside for the flaxen-haired, large-eyed man (or non-entity) with Money. He wanted compensation in Money.

'So, he returned to the side of that woman the mother, made love to her again, danced attendance on her, and submitted himself to her whims. She wreaked upon him every whim she had, or could invent. He bore it. And the more he bore, the more he wanted compensation in Money, and the more he was resolved to have it.

'But, lo! Before he got it, she cheated him. In one of her imperious states, she froze, and never thawed again. She put her hands to her head one night, uttered a cry, stiffened, lay in that attitude certain hours, and died. And he had got no compensation from her in Money, yet. Blight and Murrain on her! Not a penny.

'He had hated her throughout that second pursuit, and had longed for retaliation on her. He now counterfeited her signature to an instrument, leaving all she had to leave, to her daughter – ten years old then – to whom the property passed absolutely, and appointing himself the daughter's Guardian. When He slid it under the pillow of the bed on which she lay, He bent down in the deaf ear of Death, and whispered: "Mistress Pride, I have determined a long time that, dead or alive, you must make me compensation in Money."

'So, now there were only two left. Which two were, He, and the fair flaxen-haired, large-eyed foolish daughter, who afterwards became the Bride.

'He put her to school. In a secret, dark oppressive, ancient house, he put her to school with a watchful and unscrupulous woman. "My worthy lady," he said, "here is a mind to be formed; will you help me to form it?" She accepted the trust. For which she, too, wanted compensation in Money, and had it.

'The girl was formed in the fear of him, and in the conviction, that there was no escape from him. She was taught, from the first, to regard him as her future husband –

the man who must marry her – the destiny that overshadowed her – the appointed certainty that could never be evaded. The poor fool was soft white wax in their hands, and took the impression that they put upon her. It hardened with time. It became a part of herself. Inseparable from herself, and only to be torn away from her, by tearing life away from her.

'Eleven years she lived in the dark house and its gloomy garden. He was jealous of the very light and air getting to her, and they kept her close. He stopped the wide chimneys, shaded the little windows, left the strong-stemmed ivy to wander where it would over the house-front, the moss to accumulate on the untrimmed fruit-trees in the red-walled garden, the weeds to over-run its green and yellow walks. He surrounded her with images of sorrow and desolation. He caused her to be filled with fears of the place and of the stories that were told of it, and then on pretext of correcting them, to be left in it in solitude, or made to shrink about it in the dark. When her mind was most depressed and fullest of terrors, then, he would come out of one of the hiding-places from which he overlooked her, and present himself as her sole resource.

'Thus, by being from her childhood the one embodiment her life presented to her of power to coerce and power to relieve, power to bind and power to loose, the ascendency over her weakness was secured. She was twenty-one years and twenty-one days old, when he brought her home to the gloomy house, his half-witted, frightened, and submissive Bride of three weeks.

'He had dismissed the governess by that time – what he had left to do, he could best do alone – and they came back, upon a rainy night, to the scene of her long preparation. She turned to him upon the threshold, as the rain was dripping from the porch, and said:

'"O sir, it is the Death-watch ticking for me!"

'"Well!" he answered. "And if it were?"

'"O sir!" she returned to him, "look kindly on me, and be merciful to me! I beg your pardon. I will do anything you wish, if you will only forgive me!"

'That had become the poor fool's constant song: "I beg your pardon," and "Forgive me!"

'She was not worth hating; he felt nothing but contempt for her. But, she had long been in the way, and he had long been weary, and the work was near its end, and had to be worked out.

'"You fool," he said. "Go up the stairs!"

'She obeyed very quickly, murmuring, "I will do anything you wish!" When he came into the Bride's Chamber, having been a little retarded by the heavy fastenings of the great door (for they were alone in the house, and he had arranged that the people who attended on them should come and go in the day), he found her withdrawn to the furthest corner, and there standing pressed against the paneling as if she would have shrunk through it: her flaxen hair all wild about her face, and her large eyes staring at him in vague terror.

'"What are you afraid of? Come and sit down by me."

'"I will do anything you wish. I beg your pardon, sir. Forgive me!" Her monotonous tune as usual.

'"Ellen, here is a writing that you must write out to-morrow, in your own hand. You may as well be seen by others, busily engaged upon it. When you have written it all fairly, and corrected all mistakes, call in any two people there may be about the house, and sign your name to it before them. Then, put it in your bosom to keep it safe, and when I sit here again to-morrow night, give it to me."

'"I will do it all, with the greatest care. I will do anything you wish."

'"Don't shake and tremble, then."

'"I will try my utmost not to do it – if you will only forgive me!"

'Next day, she sat down at her desk, and did as she had been told. He often passed in and out of the room, to observe her, and always saw her slowly and laboriously writing: repeating to herself the words she copied, in appearance quite mechanically, and without caring or endeavouring to comprehend them, so that she did her task. He saw her follow the directions she had received, in all particulars; and at night, when they were alone again in the same Bride's Chamber, and he drew his chair to the hearth, she timidly approached him from her distant seat, took the paper from her bosom, and gave it into his hand.

'It secured all her possessions to him, in the event of her death. He put her before him, face to face, that he might look at her steadily; and he asked her, in so many plain words, neither fewer nor more, did she know that?

'There were spots of ink upon the bosom of her white dress, and they made her face look whiter and her eyes look larger as she nodded her head. There were spots of ink upon the hand with which she stood before him, nervously plaiting and folding her white skirts.

'He took her by the arm, and looked her, yet more closely and steadily, in the face. "Now, die! I have done with you."

'She shrunk, and uttered a low, suppressed cry.

'"I am not going to kill you. I will not endanger my life for yours. Die!"

'He sat before her in the gloomy Bride's Chamber, day after day, night after night, looking the word at her when he did not utter it. As often as her large unmeaning eyes were raised from the hands in which she rocked her head, to the stern figure, sitting with crossed arms and knitted forehead, in the chair, they read in it, "Die!" When she dropped asleep in exhaustion, she was called back to shuddering consciousness, by the whisper, "Die!" When she fell upon her old entreaty to be pardoned, she was answered, "Die!" When she had out-watched and out-suffered the long night, and the rising sun flamed into the sombre room, she heard it hailed with, "Another day and not dead? – Die!"

'Shut up in the deserted mansion, aloof from all mankind, and engaged alone in such a struggle without any respite, it came to this – that either he must die, or she. He knew it very well, and concentrated his strength against her feebleness. Hours upon hours he held her by the arm when her arm was black where he held it, and bade her Die!

'It was done, upon a windy morning, before sunrise. He computed the time to be half-past four; but, his forgotten watch had run down, and he could not be sure. She had broken away from him in the night, with loud and sudden cries – the first of that kind to which she had given vent – and he had had to put his hands over her mouth. Since then, she had been quiet in the corner of the paneling where she had sunk down; and he had left her, and had gone back with his folded arms and his knitted forehead to his chair.

'Paler in the pale light, more colourless than ever in the leaden dawn, he saw her coming, trailing herself along the floor towards him – a white wreck of hair, and dress, and wild eyes, pushing itself on by an irresolute and bending head.

'"O, forgive me! I will do anything. O, sir, pray tell me I may live!'

'"Die!"

'"Are you so resolved? Is there no hope for me?"

'"Die!"

'Her large eyes strained themselves with wonder and fear; wonder and fear changed to reproach; reproach to blank nothing. It was done. He was not at first so sure it was done, but that the morning sun was hanging jewels in her hair – he saw the diamond, emerald, and ruby, glittering among it in little points, as he stood looking down at her – when he lifted her and laid her on her bed.

'She was soon laid in the ground. And now they were all gone, and he had compensated himself well.

'He had a mind to travel. Not that he meant to waste his Money, for he was a pinching man and liked his Money dearly (liked nothing else, indeed), but, that he had grown tired of the desolate house and wished to turn his back upon it and have done with it. But, the house was worth Money, and Money must not be thrown away. He determined to sell it before he went. That it might look the less wretched and bring a better price, he hired some labourers to work in the overgrown garden; to cut out the dead wood, trim the ivy that drooped in heavy masses over the windows and gables, and clear the walks in which the weeds were growing mid-leg high.

'He worked, himself, along with them. He worked later than they did, and, one evening at dusk, was left working alone, with his bill-hook in his hand. One autumn evening, when the Bride was five weeks dead.

'"It grows too dark to work longer," he said to himself, "I must give over for the night."

'He detested the house, and was loath to enter it. He looked at the dark porch waiting for him like a tomb, and felt that it was an accursed house. Near to the porch, and near to where he stood, was a tree whose branches waved before the old bay-window of the Bride's Chamber, where it had been done. The tree swung suddenly, and made him start. It swung again, although the night was still. Looking up into it, he saw a figure among the branches.

'It was the figure of a young man. The face looked down, as his looked up; the branches cracked and swayed; the figure rapidly descended, and slid upon its feet before him. A slender youth of about her age, with long light brown hair.

'"What thief are you?' he said, seizing the youth by the collar.

'The young man, in shaking himself free, swung him a blow with his arm across the face and throat. They closed, but the young man got from him and stepped back, crying, with great eagerness and horror, "Don't touch me! I would as lieve be touched by the Devil!"

'He stood still with his bill-hook in his hand, looking at the young man. For, the young man's look was the counterpart of her last look, and he had not expected ever to see that again.

'"I am no thief. Even if I were, I would not have a coin of your wealth, if it would buy me the Indies. You murderer!"

'"What!"

'"I climbed it," said the young man, pointing up into the tree, "for the first time, nigh four years ago. I climbed it, to look at her. I saw her. I spoke to her. I have climbed it, many a time, to watch and listen for her. I was a boy, hidden among the leaves, when from that bay-window she gave me this!"

'He showed a tress of flaxen hair, tied with a mourning ribbon.

'"Her life," said the young man, "was a life of mourning. She gave me this, as a token of it, and a sign that she was dead to every one but you. If I had been older, if I had seen her sooner, I might have saved her from you. But, she was fast in the web when I first climbed the tree, and what could I do then to break it!"

'In saying those words, he burst into a fit of sobbing and crying: weakly at first, then passionately.

'"Murderer! I climbed the tree on the night when you brought her back. I heard her, from the tree, speak of the Death-watch at the door. I was three times in the tree while you were shut up with her, slowly killing her. I saw her, from the tree, lie dead upon her bed. I have watched you, from the tree, for proofs and traces of your guilt. The manner of it, is a mystery to me yet, but I will pursue you until you have rendered up your life to the hangman. You shall never, until then, be rid of me. I loved her! I can know no relenting towards you. Murderer, I loved her!"

"The youth was bare-headed, his hat having fluttered away in his descent from the tree. He moved towards the gate. He had to pass – Him – to get to it. There was breadth for two old-fashioned carriages abreast; and the youth's abhorrence, openly expressed in every feature of his face and limb of his body, and very hard to bear, had verge enough to keep itself at a distance in. He (by which I mean the other) had not stirred hand or foot, since he had stood still to look at the boy. He faced round, now, to follow him with his eyes. As the back of the bare light-brown head was turned to him, he saw a red curve stretch from his hand to it. He knew, before he threw the bill-hook, where it had alighted; for, to his clear perception the thing was down before he did it. It cleft the head, and it remained there, and the boy lay on his face.

'He buried the body in the night, at the foot of the tree. As soon as it was light in the morning, he worked at turning up all the ground near the tree, and hacking and hewing at the neighbouring bushes and undergrowth. When the labourers came, there was nothing suspicious, and nothing was suspected.

'But he had, in a moment, defeated all his precautions, and destroyed the triumph of the scheme he had so long concerted, and so successfully worked out. He had got rid of the Bride, and had acquired her fortune without endangering his life; but, now, for a death by which he had gained nothing, he had evermore to live with a rope around his neck.

'Beyond this, he was chained to the house of gloom and horror, which he could not endure. Being afraid to sell it or to quit it, lest discovery should be made, he was forced to live in it. He hired two old people, man and wife, for his servants; and dwelt in it, and dreaded it. His great difficulty, for a long time, was the garden. Whether he should keep it trim, whether he should suffer it to fall into its former state of neglect, what would be the least likely way of attracting attention to it?

'He took the middle course of gardening, himself, in his evening leisure, and of then calling the old serving-man to help him; but, of never letting him work there alone. And he made himself an arbour over against the tree, where he could sit and see that it was safe.

'As the seasons changed, and the tree changed, his mind perceived dangers that were always changing. In the leafy time, he perceived that the upper boughs were growing into the form of the young man – that they made the shape of him exactly, sitting in a forked branch swinging in the wind. In the time of the falling leaves, he perceived that they came down from the tree, forming tell-tale letters on the path, or that they had a tendency to heap themselves into a church-yard-mound above the grave. In the winter, when the tree was bare, he perceived that the boughs swung at him the ghost of the blow the young man had given, and that they threatened him openly. In the spring, when the sap was mounting in the trunk, he asked himself, were the dried-up particles of blood mounting with it: to make out more obviously this year than last, the leaf-screened figure of the young man, swinging in the wind?

'However, he turned his Money over and over, and still over. He was in the dark trade, the gold-dust trade, and most secret trades that yielded great returns. In ten years, he had turned his Money over, so many times, that the traders and shippers who had dealings with him, absolutely did not lie – for once – when they declared that he had increased his fortune, Twelve Hundred Per Cent.

'He possessed his riches one hundred years ago, when people could be lost easily. He had heard who the youth was, from hearing of the search that was made for him; but, it died away, and the youth was forgotten.

'The annual round of changes in the tree had been repeated ten times since the night of the burial at its foot, when there was a great thunder-strom over this place. It broke at mid-night, and raged until morning. The first intelligence he heard from his old serving-man that morning, was, that the tree had been struck by Lightning.

'It had been riven down the stem, in a very surprising manner, and the stem lay in two blighted shafts: one resting against the house, and one against a portion of the old red garden-wall in which its fall had made a gap. The fissure went down the tree to a little above the earth, and there stopped. There was great curiosity to see the tree, and, with most of his former fears revived, he sat in his arbour – grown quite an old man – watching the people who came to see it.

'They quickly began to come, in such dangerous numbers, that he closed his garden-gate and refused to admit any more. But, there were certain men of science who travelled from a distance to examine the tree, and, in an evil hour, he let them in – Blight and Murrain on them, let them in!

'They wanted to dig up the ruin by the roots, and closely examine it, and the earth about it. Never, while he lived! They offered money for it. They! Men of science, whom he could have bought by the gross, with a scratch of his pen! He showed them the garden-gate again, and locked and barred it.

'But, they were bent on doing what they wanted to do, and they bribed the old serving-man – a thankless wretch who regularly complained when he received his wages, of being underpaid – and they stole into the garden by night with their lanterns, picks, and shovels, and fell to at the tree. He was lying in a turret-room on the other side of the house (the Bride's Chamber had been unoccupied ever since), but he soon dreamed of picks and shovels, and got up.

'He came to an upper window on that side, whence he could see their lanterns, and them, and the loose earth in a heap, which he had himself disturbed and put back, when it was last turned to the air. It was found! They had that minute lighted on it. They were all bending over it. One of them said, "The skull is fractured;" and another, "See here the bones;" and another, "See here the clothes;" and then the first struck in again, and said, "A rusty bill-hook!"

'He became sensible, next day, that he was already put under a strict watch, and that he could go nowhere without being followed. Before a week was out, he was taken and laid in hold. The circumstances were gradually pieced together against him, with a desperate malignity, and an appalling ingenuity. But, see the justice of men, and how it was extended to him! He was further accused of having poisoned that girl in the Bride's Chamber. He, who had carefully and expressly avoided imperilling a hair of his head for her, and who had seen her die of her own incapacity!

'There was doubt for which of the two murders he should be first tried; but, the real one was chosen, and he was found Guilty, and cast for Death. Bloodthirsty wretches! They would have made him Guilty of anything, so set they were upon having his life.

'His money could do nothing to save him, and he was hanged. *I* am He, and I was hanged at Lancaster Castle with my face to the wall, a hundred years ago!'

At this terrific announcement, Mr Goodchild tried to rise and cry out. But, the two fiery lines extending from the old man's eyes to his own, kept him down, and he could not utter a sound. His sense of hearing, however, was acute, and he could hear the clock strike Two. No sooner had he heard the clock strike Two, than he saw before him Two old men!

Two.

The eyes of each, connected with his eyes by two films of fire: each, exactly like the other: each, addressing him at precisely one and the same instant: each, gnashing the same teeth in the same head, with the same twitched nostril above them, and the same suffused expression around it. Two old men. Differing in nothing, equally distinct to the sight, the copy no fainter than the original, the second as real as the first.

'At what time,' said the Two old men, 'did you arrive at the door below?'

'At Six.'

'And there were Six old men upon the stairs!'

Mr Goodchild having wiped the perspiration from his brow, or tried to do it, the Two old men proceeded in one voice, and in the singular number: 'I had been anatomised, but had not yet had my skeleton put together and re-hung on an iron hook, when it began to be whispered that the Bride's Chamber was haunted. It *was* haunted, and I was there.

'*We* were there. She and I were there. I, in the chair upon the hearth; she, a white wreck again, trailing itself towards me on the floor. But, I was the speaker no more. She was the sole speaker now, and the one word that she said to me from midnight until dawn was, "Live!"

'The youth was there, likewise. In the tree outside the window. Coming and going in the moonlight, as the tree bent and gave. He has, ever since, been there; peeping in at me in my torment; revealing to me by snatches, in the pale lights and slatey shadows where he comes and goes, bare-headed – a bill-hook, standing edgewise in his hair.

'In the Bride's Chamber, every night from midnight until dawn – one month in the year excepted, as I am going to tell you – he hides in the tree, and she comes towards me on the floor; always approaching; never coming nearer; always visible as if by moonlight, whether the moon shines or no; always saying, from midnight until dawn, her one word, "Live!"

'But in the month wherein I was forced out of this life – this present month of thirty days – the Bride's Chamber is empty and quiet. Not so my old dungeon. Not so the rooms where I was restless and afraid, ten years. Both are fitfully haunted then. At One in the morning, I am what you saw me when the clock struck that hour – One old man. At Two in the morning, I am Two old men. At Three, I am Three. By Twelve at noon, I am Twelve old men, One for every hundred per cent of old gain. Every one of the Twelve, with Twelve times my old power of suffering and agony. From that hour until Twelve at night, I, Twelve old men in anguish and fearful foreboding, wait for the coming of the executioner. At Twelve at night, I, Twelve old men turned off, swing invisible outside Lancaster Castle, with Twelve faces to the wall!

'When the Bride's Chamber was first haunted, it was known to me that this punishment would never cease, until I could make its nature, and my story, known to two living men together. I waited for the coming of two living men together into the Bride's Chamber, years upon years. It was infused into my knowledge (of the means I am ignorant) that if two living men, with their eyes open, could be in the Bride's Chamber at One in the morning, they would see me sitting in my chair.

'At length, the whispers that the room was spiritually troubled, brought two men to try the adventure. I was scarcely struck upon the hearth at midnight (I come there as if the Lightning blasted me into being), when I heard them ascending the stairs. Next, I saw them enter. One of them was a bold, gay, active man, in the prime of life, some five and forty years of age; the other, a dozen years younger. They brought provisions with them in a basket, and bottles. A young woman accompanied them, with wood and coals for the lighting of the fire. When she had lighted it, the bold, gay, active man accompanied her along the gallery outside the room, to see her safely down the staircase, and came back laughing.

'He locked the door, examined the chamber, put out the contents of the basket on the table before the fire – little recking of me, in my appointed station on the hearth, close to him – and filled the glasses, and ate and drank. His companion did the same, and was as cheerful and confident as he: though he was the leader. When they had supped, they laid pistols on the table, turned to the fire, and began to smoke their pipes of foreign make.

'They had travelled together, and had been much together, and had an abundance of subjects in common. In the midst of their talking and laughing, the younger man made a reference to the leader's being always ready for any adventure; that one, or any other. He replied in these words: "Not quite so, Dick; if I am afraid of nothing else, I am afraid of myself."

'His companion seeming to grow a little dull, asked him, in what sense? How?

'"Why, thus," he returned. "Here is a Ghost to be disproved. Well! I cannot answer for what my fancy might do if I were alone here, or what tricks my senses might play with me if they had me to themselves. But, in company with another man, and especially with you, Dick, I would consent to outface all the Ghosts that were ever told of in the universe."

'"I had not the vanity to suppose that I was of so much importance to-night," said the other.

'"Of so much," rejoined the leader, more seriously than he had spoken yet, "that I would, for the reason I have given, on no account have undertaken to pass the night here alone."

'It was within a few minutes of One. The head of the younger man had drooped when he made his last remark, and it drooped lower now.

'"Keep awake, Dick!" said the leader, gaily. "The small hours are the worst."

'He tried, but his head drooped again.

'"Dick!" urged the leader. "Keep awake!"

'"I can't," he indistinctly muttered. "I don't know what strange influence is stealing over me. I can't."

'His companion looked at him with a sudden horror, and I, in my different way, felt a new horror also; for, it was on the stroke of One, and I felt the second watcher was yielding to me, and that the curse was upon me that I must send him to sleep.

'"Get up and walk, Dick!" cried the leader. "Try!"

'It was in vain to go behind the slumberer's chair and wake him. One o'clock sounded, and I was present to the elder man, and he stood transfixed before me.

'To him alone, I was obliged to relate my story, without hope of benefit. To him alone, I was an awful phantom making a quite useless confession. I foresee it will ever be the same. The two living men together will never come to release me. When I appear, the senses of one of the two will be locked in sleep; he will neither see nor hear me; my communication will ever be made to a solitary listener, and will ever be unserviceable. Woe! Woe! Woe!'

As the Two old men, with these words, wrung their hands, it shot into Mr Goodchild's mind that he was in the terrible situation of being virtually alone with the spectre, and that Mr Idle's immovability was explained by his having been charmed asleep at One o'clock. In the terror of this sudden discovery which produced an indescribable dread, he struggled so hard to get free from the four fiery threads, that he snapped them, after he had pulled them out to a great width. Being then out of bonds, he caught up Mr Idle from the sofa and rushed down stairs with him.

'What are you about, Francis?' demanded Mr Idle. 'My bedroom is not down here. What the deuce are you carrying me at all for? I can walk with a stick now. I don't want to be carried. Put me down.'

Mr Goodchild put him down in the old hall, and looked about him wildly.

'What are you doing? Idiotically plunging at your own sex, and rescuing them or perishing in the attempt?' asked Mr Idle, in a highly petulant state.

'The One old man!' cried Mr Goodchild, distractedly, – 'and the Two old men!'

Mr Idle deigned no other reply than 'The One old woman, I think you mean,' as he began hobbling his way back up the staircase, with the assistance of its broad balustrade.

'I assure you, Tom,' began Mr Goodchild, attending at his side, 'that since you fell asleep—'

'Come, I like that!' said Thomas Idle, 'I haven't closed an eye!'

With the peculiar sensitiveness on the subject of the disgraceful action of going to sleep out of bed, which is the lot of all mankind, Mr Idle persisted in this declaration. The same peculiar sensitiveness impelled Mr Goodchild, on being taxed with the same crime, to repudiate it with honourable resentment. The settlement of the question of The One old man and The Two old men was thus presently complicated, and soon made quite impracticable. Mr Idle said it was all bride-cake, and fragments, newly arranged, of things seen and thought about in the day. Mr Goodchild said how could that be, when he hadn't been asleep, and what right could Mr Idle have to say so, who had been asleep? Mr Idle said he had never been asleep, and never did go to sleep, and that Mr Goodchild, as a general rule, was always asleep. They consequently parted for the rest of the night, at their bedroom doors, a little ruffled. Mr Goodchild's last words were, that he had had, in that real and tangible old Inn (he supposed Mr Idle denied its existence), every sensation and experience, the present record of which is now within a line or two of completion; and that he would write it out and print it every word. Mr Idle returned that he might if he liked – and he did like, and has now done it.

Chapter V

Two of the many passengers by a certain late Sunday evening train, Mr Thomas Idle and Mr Francis Goodchild, yielded up their tickets at a little rotten platform (converted into artificial touch-wood by smoke and ashes), deep in the manufacturing bosom of Yorkshire. A mysterious bosom it appeared, upon a damp, dark, Sunday night, dashed through in the train to the music of the whirling wheels, the panting of the engine, and the part-singing of hundreds of third-class excursionists, whose vocal efforts 'bobbed arayound' from sacred to profane, from hymns, to our transatlantic sisters the Yankee Gal and Mairy Anne, in a remarkable way. There seemed to have been some large vocal gathering near to every lonely station on the line. No town was visible, no village was visible, no light was visible, but, a multitude got out singing, and a multitude took up the hymns, and adopted our transatlantic sisters, and sang of their own egregious wickedness, and of their bobbing arayound, and of how the ship it was ready and the wind it was fair, and they were bayound for the sea, Mairy Anne, until they in their turn became a getting-out multitude, and were replaced by another getting-in multitude, who did the same. And at every station, the getting-in multitude, with an artistic reference to the completeness of their chorus, incessantly cried, as with one voice while scuffling into the carriages, 'We mun aa' gang toogither!'

The singing and the multitudes had trailed off as the lonely places were left and the great towns were neared, and the way had lain as silently as a train's way ever can, over the vague black streets of the great gulfs of towns, and among their branchless woods of vague black chimneys. These towns looked, in the cinderous wet, as though they had one and all been on fire and were just put out – a dreary and quenched panorama, many miles long.

Thus, Thomas and Francis got to Leeds; of which enterprising and important commercial centre it may be observed with delicacy, that you must either take it very much or not at all. Next day, the first of the Race-Week, they took train to Doncaster.

And instantly the character, both of travellers and of luggage, entirely changed, and no other business than race-business any longer existed on the face of the earth. The talk was all of horses and 'John Scott', Guards whispered behind their hands to station-masters, of horses and John Scott. Men in cut-away coats and speckled cravats fastened with peculiar pins, and with the large bones of their legs developed under tight trousers, so that they should look as much as possible like horses' legs, paced up and down by twos at junction-stations, speaking low and moodily of horses and John Scott. The young clergyman in the black strait-waistcoat, who occupied the middle seat of the carriage, expounded in his peculiar pulpit-accent to the young and lovely Reverend Mrs Crinoline, who occupied the opposite middle-seat, a few passages of rumour relative to 'Oartheth, my love, and Mithter John Eth-COTT.' A bandy vagabond, with a head like a Dutch cheese, in a fustian stable-suit, attending on a horse-box and going about the platforms with a halter hanging round his neck like a Calais burgher of the ancient period much degenerated, was courted by the best society, by reason of what he had to hint, when not engaged in eating straw, concerning 't'harses and Joon Scott.' The engine-driver himself, as he applied one eye to his large stationary double-eye-glass on the engine, seemed to keep the other open, sideways, upon horses and John Scott.

Breaks and barriers at Doncaster station to keep the crowd off; temporary wooden avenues of ingress and egress, to help the crowd on. Forty extra porters sent down for this present blessed Race-Week, and all of them making up their betting-books in the lamp-room or somewhere else, and none of them to come and touch the luggage. Travellers disgorged into an open space, a howling wilderness of idle men. All work but race-work at a stand-still; all men at a stand-still. 'Ey my word! Deant ask noon o' us to help wi' t' luggage. Bock your opinion loike a mon. Coom! Dang it, coom, t' harses and Joon Scott!' In the midst of the idle men, all the fly horses and omnibus horses of Doncaster and parts adjacent, rampant, rearing, backing, plunging, shying – apparently the result of their hearing of nothing but their own order and John Scott.

Grand Dramatic Company from London for the Race-Week. Poses Plastiques in the Grand Assembly Room up the Stable-Yard at seven and nine each evening, for the Race-Week. Grand Alliance Circus in the field beyond the bridge, for the Race-Week. Grand Exhibition of Aztec Lilliputians, important to all who want to be horrified cheap, for the Race-Week. Lodgings, grand and not grand, but all at grand prices, ranging from ten pounds to twenty, for the Grand Race-Week!

Rendered giddy enough by these things, Messieurs Idle and Goodchild repaired to the quarters they had secured beforehand, and Mr Goodchild looked down from the window into the surging street.

'By heaven, Tom!' cried he, after contemplating it, 'I am in the Lunatic Asylum again, and these are all mad people under the charge of a body of designing keepers!'

All through the Race-Week, Mr Goodchild never divested himself of this idea. Every day he looked out of window, with something of the dread of Lemuel Gulliver looking down at men after he returned home from the horse-country; and every day he saw the Lunatics, horse-mad, betting-mad, drunken-mad, vice-mad, and the designing Keepers always after them. The idea pervaded, like the second colour in shot-silk, the whole of Mr Goodchild's impressions. They were much as follows:

Monday, mid-day. Races not to begin until to-morrow, but all the mob-Lunatics out, crowding the pavements of the one main street of pretty and pleasant Doncaster, crowding the road, particularly crowding the outside of the Betting Rooms, whooping and shouting loudly after all passing vehicles. Frightened lunatic horses occasionally running away, with infinite clatter. All degrees of men, from peers to paupers, betting incessantly. Keepers very watchful, and taking all good chances. An awful family likeness among the Keepers, to Mr Palmer and Mr Thurtell. With some knowledge of expression and some acquaintance with heads (thus writes Mr Goodchild), I never have seen anywhere, so many repetitions of one class of countenance and one character of head (both evil) as in this street at this time. Cunning, covetousness, secrecy, cold calculation, hard callousness and dire insensibility, are the uniform Keeper characteristics. Mr Palmer passes me five times in five minutes, and, as I go down the street, the back of Mr Thurtell's skull is always going on before me.

Monday evening. Town lighted up; more Lunatics out than ever; a complete choke and stoppage of the thoroughfare outside the Betting Rooms. Keepers, having dined, pervade the Betting Rooms, and sharply snap at the moneyed Lunatics. Some Keepers flushed with drink, and some not, but all close and calculating A vague echoing roar of 't' harses' and 't' races' always rising in the air, until midnight, at about which period it dies away in occasional drunken songs and straggling yells. But, all night, some unmannerly drinking-house in the neighbourhood opens its mouth at intervals and spits out a man too drunk to be retained: who thereupon makes what uproarious protest may be left in him, and either falls asleep where he tumbles, or is carried off in custody.

Tuesday morning, at daybreak. A sudden rising, as it were out of the earth, of all the obscene creatures, who sell 'correct cards of the races.' They may have been coiled in corners, or sleeping on door-steps, and, having all passed the night under the same set of circumstances, may all want to circulate their blood at the same time; but, however that may be, they spring into existence all at once and together, as though a new Cadmus had sown a race-horses teeth. There is nobody up, to buy the cards; but, the cards are madly cried. There is no patronage to quarrel for; but, they madly quarrel and fight. Conspicuous among these hyaenas, as breakfast-time discloses, is a fearful creature in the general semblance of a man: shaken off his next-to-no legs by drink and devilry, bare-headed and bare-footed, with a great shock of hair like a horrible broom, and nothing on him but a ragged pair of trousers and a pink glazed-calico coat – made on him – so very tight that it is as evident that he could never take it off, as that he never does. This hideous apparition, inconceivably drunk, has a terrible power of making a gong-like imitation of the braying of an ass: which feat requires that he should lay his right jaw in his begrimed right paw, double himself up, and shake his bray out of himself, with much staggering on his next-to-no legs, and much twirling of his horrible broom, as if it were a mop. From the present minute, when he comes in sight holding up his cards to the windows, and hoarsely proposing purchase to My Lord, Your Excellency, Colonel, the Noble Captain, and Your Honourable Worship – from the present minute until the Grand Race-Week is finished, at all hours of the morning, evening, day, and night, shall the town reverberate, at capricious intervals, to the brays of this frightful animal the Gong-Donkey.

No very great racing to-day, so no very great amount of vehicles: though there is a good sprinkling, too: from farmers' carts and gigs, to carriages with post-horses and to fours-in-hand, mostly coming by the road from York, and passing on straight through the main street to the Course. A walk in the wrong direction may be a better thing for Mr Goodchild to-day than the Course, so he walks in the wrong direction. Everybody gone to the races. Only children in the street. Grand Alliance Circus deserted; not one Star-Rider left; omnibus which forms the Pay-Place, having on separate panels Pay here for the Boxes, Pay here for the Pit, Pay here for the Gallery, hove down in a corner and locked up; nobody near the tent but the man on his knees on the grass, who is making the paper balloons for the Star young gentlemen to jump through to-night. A pleasant road, pleasantly wooded. No labourers working in the fields; all gone 't'races,' who are yet left driving on the road, stare in amazement at the recluse who is not going 't'races.' Roadside inn-keeper has gone 't'races.' Turnpike-man has gone 't'races.' His thrifty wife, washing clothes at the toll-house door, is going 't'races' to-morrow. Perhaps there may be no one left to take the toll to-morrow; who knows? Though assuredly that would be neither turnpike-like, nor Yorkshire-like. The very wind and dust seem to be hurrying 't'races,' as they briskly pass the only wayfarer on the road. In the distance, the Railway Engine, waiting at the town-end, shrieks despairingly. Nothing but the difficulty of getting off the Line, restrains that Engine from going 't'races,' too, it is very clear.

At night, more Lunatics out than last night – and more Keepers. The latter very active at the Betting Rooms, the street in front of which is now impassable. Mr Palmer as before. Mr Thurtell as before. Roar and uproar as before. Gradual subsidence as before. Unmannerly drinking house expectorates as before. Drunken negro-melodists, Gong-Donkey, and correct cards, in the night.

On Wednesday morning, the morning of the great St Leger, it becomes apparent that there has been a great influx since yesterday, both of Lunatics and Keepers. The families of the tradesmen over the way are no longer within human ken; their places know them no more; ten, fifteen, and twenty guinea lodgers fill them. At the pastry-cook's second-floor window, a Keeper is brushing Mr Thurtell's hair – thinking it his own.

In the wax-chandler's attic, another Keeper is putting on Mr Palmer's braces. In the gunsmith's nursery, a Lunatic is shaving himself. In the serious stationer's best sitting-room, three Lunatics are taking a combination-breakfast, praising the (cook's) devil, and drinking neat brandy in an atmosphere of last midnight's cigars. No family sanctuary is free from our Angelic messengers – we put up at the Angel – who in the guise of extra waiters for the grand Race-Week, rattle in and out of the most secret chambers of everybody's house, with dishes and tin covers, decanters, soda-water bottles, and glasses. An hour later. Down the street and up the street, as far as eyes can see and a good deal farther, there is a dense crowd; outside the Betting Rooms it is like a great struggle at a theatre door – in the days of theatres; or at the vestibule of the Spurgeon temple – in the days of Spurgeon. An hour later. Fusing into this crowd, and somehow getting through it, are all kinds of conveyances, and all kinds of foot-passengers; carts, with brick-makers and brick-makeresses jolting up and down on planks; drags, with the needful grooms behind, crossed-armed in the needful manner, and slanting themselves backward from the soles of their boots at the needful angle; postboys, in the shining hats and smart jackets of the olden time, when stokers were not; beautiful Yorkshire horses, gallantly driven by their own breeders and masters. Under every pole, and every shaft, and every horse, and every wheel as it would seem, the Gong-Donkey – metallically braying, when not struggling for life, or whipped out of the way.

By one o'clock, all this stir has gone out of the streets, and there is no one left in them but Francis Goodchild. Francis Goodchild will not be left in them long; for, he too is on his way 't' races.'

A most beautiful sight, Francis Goodchild finds 't' races' to be, when he has left fair Doncaster behind him, and comes out on the free course, with its agreeable prospect, its quaint Red House oddly changing and turning as Francis turns, its green grass, and fresh heath. A free course and an easy one, where Francis can roll smoothly where he will, and can choose between the start, or the coming-in, or the turn behind the brow of the hill, or any out-of-the-way point where he lists to see the throbbing horses straining every nerve, and making the sympathetic earth throb as they come by. Francis much delights to be, not in the Grand Stand, but where he can see it, rising against the sky with its vast tiers of little white dots of faces, and its last high rows and corners of people, looking like pins stuck into an enormous pin-cushion – not quite so symmetrically as his orderly eye could wish, when people change or go away. When the race is nearly run out, it is as good as the race to him to see the flutter among the pins, and the change in them from dark to light, as hats are taken off and waved. Not less full of interest, the loud anticipation of the winner's name, the swelling, and the final roar; then, the quick dropping of all the pins out of their places, the revelation of the shape of the bare pin-cushion, and the closing-in of the whole host of Lunatics and Keepers, in the rear of the three horses with bright-coloured riders, who have not yet quite subdued their gallop though the contest is over.

Mr Goodchild would appear to have been by no means free from lunacy himself at 't' races,' though not of the prevalent kind. He is suspected by Mr Idle to have fallen into a dreadful state concerning a pair of little lilac gloves and a little bonnet that he saw there. Mr Idle asserts, that he did afterwards repeat at the Angel, with an appearance of being lunatically seized, some rhapsody to the following effect: 'O little lilac gloves! And O winning little bonnet, making in conjunction with her golden hair quite a Glory in the sunlight round the pretty head, why anything in the world but you and me! Why may not this day's running – of horses, to all the rest: of precious sands of life to me – be prolonged through an everlasting autumn-sunshine, without a sunset! Slave of the Lamp, or Ring, strike we yonder gallant equestrian Clerk of the Course, in the scarlet coat, motionless on the green grass for ages! Friendly Devil on Two Sticks, for ten times ten thousand years, keep Blink-Bonny jibbing at the post, and let us have no start! Arab drums, powerful of old to summon Genii in the desert, sound of yourselves and raise a troop for me in the desert of my heart, which shall so enchant this dusty barouche (with a conspicuous excise-plate, resembling the Collector's door-plate at a turnpike), that I, within it, loving the little lilac gloves, the winning little bonnet, and the dear unknown-wearer with the golden hair, may wait by her side for ever, to see a Great St Leger that shall never be run!'

Thursday morning. After a tremendous night of crowding, shouting, drinking-house expectoration, Gong-Donkey, and correct cards. Symptoms of yesterday's gains in the way of drink, and of yesterday's losses in the way of money, abundant. Money-losses very great. As usual, nobody seems to have won; but, large losses and many losers are unquestionable facts. Both Lunatics and Keepers, in general very low. Several of both kinds look in at the chemist's while Mr Goodchild is making a purchase there, to be 'picked up.' One red-eyed Lunatic, flushed, faded, and disordered, enters hurriedly and cries savagely, 'Hond us a gloss of sal volatile in wather, or soom dommed thing o' thot sart!' Faces at the Betting-Rooms very long, and a tendency to bit nails observable. Keepers likewise given this morning to standing about solitary, with their hands in their pockets, looking down at their boots as they fit them into cracks of the pavement, and then looking up whistling and walking away. Grand Alliance Circus out, in procession; buxom lady-member of Grand Alliance, in crimson riding-habit, fresher to look at, even in her paint under the day sky, than the cheeks of Lunatics or Keepers. Spanish Cavalier appears to have lost yesterday, and jingles his bossed bridle with disgust, as if he were paying. Re-action also apparent at the Guildhall opposite, whence certain pickpockets come out handcuffed together, with that peculiar walk which is never seen under any other circumstances – a walk expressive of going to jail, game, but still of jails being in bad taste and arbitrary, and how would *you* like it if it was you instead of me, as it ought to be! Mid-day. Town filled as yesterday, but not so full; and emptied as yesterday, but not so empty. In the evening, Angel ordinary where every Lunatic and Keeper has his modest daily meal of turtle, venison, and wine, not so crowded as yesterday, and not so noisy. At night, the theatre. More abstracted faces in it, than one ever sees at public assemblies; such faces wearing an expression which strongly reminds Mr Goodchild of the boys at school who were 'going up next,' with their arithmetic or mathematics. These boys are, no doubt, going up to-morrow with *their* sums and figures. Mr Palmer and Mr Thurtell in the boxes O.P. Mr Thurtell and Mr Palmer in the boxes P.S. The firm of Thurtell, Palmer, and Thurtell, in the boxes Centre. A most odious tendency observable in these distinguished gentlemen to put vile constructions on sufficiently innocent phrases in the play, and then to applaud them in a Satyr-like manner. Behind Mr Goodchild, with a party of other Lunatics and one Keeper, the express incarnation of the thing called a 'gent.' A gentleman born; a gent manufactured. A something with a scarf round its neck, and a slipshod speech issuing from behind the scarf; more depraved, more foolish, more ignorant, more unable to believe in any noble or good thing of any kind, than the stupidest Bosjesman. The thing is but a boy in years, and is addled with drink. To do its company justice, even its company is ashamed of it, as it draws its slang criticisms on the representation, and inflames Mr Goodchild with a burning ardour to fling it into the pit. Its remarks are so horrible, that Mr Goodchild, for the moment, even doubts whether that *is* a wholesome Art, which sets women apart on a high floor before such a thing as this, though as good as its own sisters, or its own mother – whom Heaven forgive for bringing it into the world! But, the consideration that a low nature must make a low world of its own to live in, whatever the real materials, or it could no more exist than any of us could without the sense of touch, brings Mr Goodchild to reason: the rather, because the thing soon drops its downy chin upon its scarf, and slobbers itself asleep.

Friday Morning. Early fights. Gong-Donkey, and correct cards. Again, a great set towards the races, though not so great a set as on Wednesday. Much packing going on too, upstairs at the gunsmith's, the wax-chandler's, and the serious stationer's; for there will be a heavy drift of Lunatics and Keepers to London by the afternoon train. The course as pretty as ever; the great pin-cushion as like a pin-cushion, but not nearly so full of pins; whole rows of pins wanting. On the great event of the day, both Lunatics and Keepers become inspired with rage; and there is a violent scuffling, and a rushing at the losing jockey, and an emergence of the said jockey from a swaying and menacing crowd, protected by friends, and looking the worse for wear; which is a rough proceeding, though animating to see from a pleasant distance. After the great event, rills begin to flow from the pin-cushion towards the railroad; the rills swell into rivers; the rivers soon unite into a lake. The lake floats Mr Goodchild into Doncaster, past the Itinerant personage in black, by the way-side telling him from the vantage ground of a legibly printed placard on a pole that for all these things the Lord will bring him to judgement. No turtle and venison ordinary this evening; that is all over. No Betting at the rooms; nothing there but the plants in pots, which have, all the week, been stood about the entry to give it an innocent appearance, and which have sorely sickened by this time.

Saturday. Mr Idle wishes to know at breakfast, what were those dreadful groanings in his bedroom doorway in the night? Mr Goodchild answers, Nightmare. Mr Idle repels the calumny, and calls the waiter. The Angel is very sorry – had intended to explain; but you see, gentlemen, there was a gentleman dined down stairs with two more, and he had lost a deal of money, and he would drink a deal of wine, and in the night he 'took the horrors,' and got up; and as his friends could do nothing with him he laid himself down, and groaned at Mr Ide's deor. 'And he DID groan there,' Mr Idle says; 'and you will please to imagine me inside, "taking the horrors" too!'

So far, the picture of Doncaster on the occasion of its great sporting anniversary, offers probably a general representation of the social condition of the town, in the past as well as in the present time. The sole local phenomenon of the current year, which may be considered as entirely unprecedented in its way, and which certainly claims, on that account, some slight share of notice, consists in the actual existence of one remarkable individual, who is sojourning in Doncaster, and who, neither directly nor indirectly, has anything at all to do, in any capacity whatever, with the racing amusements of the week. Ranging throughout the entire crowd that fills the town, and including the inhabitants as well as the visitors, nobody is to be found altogether disconnected with the business of the day, excepting this one unparalleled man. He does not bet on the races, like the sporting men. He does not assist the races, like the jockeys, starters, judges, and grooms. He does not look on at the races, like Mr Goodchild and his fellow spectators. He does not profit by the races, like the hotel-keepers and the trades-people. He does not minister to the necessities of the races, like the booth-keepers, the postilions, the waiters, and the hawkers of Lists. He does not assist the attractions of the races, like the actors at the theatre, the riders at the circus, or the posturers at the Poses Plastiques. Absolutely and literally, he is the only individual in Doncaster who stands by the brink of the full-flowing race-stream, and is not swept away by it in common with all the rest of his species. Who is the modern hermit, this recluse of the St Leger-week, this inscrutably ungregarious being, who lives apart from the amusements and activities of his fellow-creatures? Surely, there is little difficulty in guessing that clearest and easiest of all riddles. Who could he be, but Mr Thomas Idle?

Thomas had suffered himself to be taken to Doncaster, just as he would have suffered himself to be taken to any other place in the habitable globe which would guarantee him the temporary possession of a comfortable sofa to rest his ankle on. Once established at the hotel, with his leg on one cushion and his back against another, he formally declined taking the slightest interest in any circumstance whatever connected with the races, or with the people who were assembled to see them. Francis Goodchild, anxious that the hours should pass by his crippled travelling-companion as lightly as possible, suggested that his sofa should be moved to the window, and that he should amuse himself by looking out at the moving panorama of humanity, which the view from it of the principal street presented. Thomas, however, steadily declined profiting by the suggestion.

'The farther I am from the window,' he said, 'the better, Brother Francis, I shall be pleased. I have nothing in common with the one prevalent idea of all those people who are passing in the street. Why should I care to look at them?'

'I hope I have nothing in common with the prevalent idea of a great many of them, either,' answered Goodchild, thinking of the sporting gentlemen whom he had met in the course of his wanderings about Doncaster. 'But, surely, among all the people who are walking by the house, at this very moment, you may find—'

'Not one living creature,' interposed Thomas, 'who is not, in one way or another, interested in horses, and who is not, in a greater or less degree, an admirer of them. Now, I hold opinions in reference to these particular members of the quadruped creation, which may lay claim (as I believe) to the disastrous distinction of being unpartaken by any other human being, civilised or savage, over the whole surface of the earth. Taking the horse as an animal in the abstract, Francis, I cordially despise him from every point of view.'

'Thomas,' said Goodchild, 'confinement to the house has begun to effect your biliary secretions. I shall go to the chemist's and get you some physic.'

'I object,' continued Thomas, quietly possessing himself of his friend's hat, which stood on a table near him, – 'I object, first, to the personal appearance of the horse. I protest against the conventional idea of beauty, as attached to that animal. I think his nose too long, his forehead too low, and his legs (except in the case of the cart-horse) ridiculously thin by comparison with the size of his body. Again, considering how big an animal he is, I object to the contemptible delicacy of his constitution. Is he not the sickliest creature in creation? Does any child catch cold as easily as a horse? Does he not sprain his fetlock, for all his appearance of superior strength, as easily as I sprained my ankle? Furthermore, to take him from another point of view, what a helpless wretch he is! No fine lady requires more constant waiting-on than a horse. Other animals can make their own toilette: he must have a groom. You will tell me that this is because we want to make his coat artificially glossy. Glossy! Come home, with me, and see my cat – my clever cat, who can groom herself! Look at your own dog! See how the intelligent creature curry-combs himself with his own honest teeth! Then, again, what a fool the horse is, what a poor nervous fool! He will start at a piece of white paper in the road as if it was a lion. His one idea, when he hears a noise that he is not accustomed to, is to run away from it. What do you say to those two common instances of the sense and courage of this absurdly overpraised animal? I might multiply them to two hundred, if I chose to exert my mind and waste my breath, which I never do. I prefer coming at once to my last charge against the horse, which is the most serious of all, because if affects his moral character. I accuse him boldly, in his capacity of servant to man, of slyness and treachery. I brand him publicly, no matter how mild he may look about the eyes, or how sleek he may be about the coat, as a systematic betrayer, whenever he can get the chance, of the confidence reposed in him. What do you mean by laughing and shaking your head at me?'

'Oh, Thomas, Thomas!' said Goodchild. 'You had better give me my hat; you had better let me get you that physic.'

'I will let you get anything you like, including a composing draught for yourself,' said Thomas, irritably alluding to his fellow-apprentice's inexhaustible activity, 'if you will only sit quiet for five minutes longer, and hear me out. I say again the horse is a betrayer of the confidence reposed in him; and that opinion, let me add, is drawn from my own personal experience, and is not based on any fanciful theory whatever. You shall have two instances, two overwhelming instances. Let me start the first of these by asking, what is the distinguishing quality which the Shetland Pony has arrogated to himself, and is still perpetually trumpeting through the world by means of popular report and books on Natural History? I see the answer in your face: it is the quality of being Sure-Footed. He professes to have other virtues, such as hardiness and strength, which you may discover on trial; but the one thing which he insists on your believing, when you get on his back, is that he may be safely depended on not to tumble down with you. Very good. Some years ago, I was in Shetland with a party of friends. They insisted on taking me with them to the top of a precipice that overhung the sea. It was a great distance off, but they all determined to walk it except me. I was wiser then than I was with you at Carrock, and I determined to be carried to the precipice. There was no carriage road in the island, and nobody offered (in consequence, as I suppose, of the imperfectly-civilised state of the country) to bring me a sedan-chair, which is naturally what I should have liked best. A Shetland pony was produced instead. I remembered my Natural History, I recalled popular report, and I got on the little beast's back, as any other man would have done in my position, placing implicit confidence in the sureness of his feet. And how did he repay that confidence? Brother Francis, carry your mind on from morning to noon. Picture to yourself a howling wilderness of grass and bog, bounded by low stony hills. Pick out one particular spot in that imaginary scene, and sketch me in it, with outstretched arms, curved back, and heels in the air, plunging headforemost into a black patch of water and mud. Place just behind me the legs, the body, and the head of a sure-footed Shetland pony, all stretched flat on the ground, and you will have produced an accurate representation of a very lamentable fact. And the moral device, Francis, of this picture will be to testify that when gentlemen put confidence in the legs of Shetland ponies, they will find to their cost that they are leaning on nothing but broken reeds. There is my first instance – and what have you got to say to that?'

'Nothing, but that I want my hat,' answered Goodchild, starting up and walking restlessly about the room.

'You shall have it in a minute,' rejoined Thomas. 'My second instance' – (Goodchild groaned, and sat down again) – 'My second instance is more appropriate to the present time and place, for it refers to a race-horse. Two years ago an excellent friend of mine, who was desirous of prevailing on me to take regular exercise, and who was well enough acquainted with the weakness of my legs to expect no very active compliance with his wishes on their part, offered to make me a present of one of his horses. Hearing that the animal in question has started in life on the turf, I declined accepting the gift with many thanks; adding, by way of explanation, that I looked on a race horse as a kind of embodied hurricane, upon which no sane man of my character and habits could be expected to seat himself. My friend replied that, however appropriate my metaphor might be as applied to race-horses in general, it was singularly unsuitable as applied to the particular horse which he proposed to give me. From a foal upwards this remarkable animal had been the idlest and most sluggish of his race. Whatever capacities for speed he might possess he had kept so strictly to himself, that no amount of training had ever brought them out. He had been found hopelessly slow as a racer, and hopelessly lazy as a hunter, and was fit for nothing but a quiet life of it with an old gentleman or an invalid. When I heard this account of the horse, I don't mind confessing that my heart warmed to him. Visions of Thomas Idle ambling serenely on the back of a steed as lazy as himself, presenting to a restless world the soothing and composite spectacle of a kind of sluggardly

Centaur, too peaceable in his habits to alarm anybody, swam attractively before my eyes. I went to look at the horse in the stable. Nice fellow! He was fast asleep with a kitten on his back. I saw him taken out for an airing by the groom. If he had had trousers on his legs I should not have known them from my own, so deliberately were they lifted up, so gently were they put down, so slowly did they get over the ground. From that moment I gratefully accepted my friend's offer. I went home; the horse followed me – by a slow train. Oh, Francis, how devoutly I believed in that horse! How carefully I looked after all his little comforts! I had never gone the length of hiring a man-servant to wait on myself; but I went to the expense of hiring one to wait upon him. If I thought a little of myself when I bought the softest saddle that could be had for money, I thought also of my horse. When the man at the shop afterwards offered me spurs and a whip, I turned from him with horror. When I sallied out for my first ride, I went purposely unarmed with the means of hurrying my steed. He proceeded at his own pace every step of the way; and when he stopped, at last, and blew out his sides with a heavy sigh, and turned his sleepy head and looked behind him, I took him home again, as I might take home an artless child who said to me, "If you please, sir, I am tired." For a week this complete harmony between me and my horse lasted undisturbed. At the end of that time, when he had made quite sure of my friendly confidence in his laziness, when he had thoroughly acquainted himself with all the little weaknesses of my seat (and their name is Legion), the smouldering treachery and ingratitude of the equine nature blazed out in an instant. Without the slightest provocation from me, with nothing passing him at the time but a pony-chaise driven by an old lady, he started in one instant from a state of sluggish depression to a state of frantic high spirits. He kicked, he plunged, he shied, he pranced, he capered fearfully. I sat on him as long as I could, and when I could sit no longer, I fell off. No, Francis! this is not a circumstance to be laughed at, but to be wept over. What would be said of a Man who had requited my kindness in that way? Range over all the rest of the animal creation, and where will you find me an instance of treachery so black as this? The cow that kicks down the milking-pail may have some reason for it; she may think herself taxed too heavily to contribute to the dilution of human tea and the greasing of human bread. The tiger who springs out on me unawares has the excuse of being hungry at the time, to say nothing of the further justification of being a total stranger to me. The very flea who surprises me in my sleep may defend his act of assassination on the ground that I, in my turn, am always ready to murder him when I am awake. I defy the whole body of Natural Historians to move me, logically off the ground that I have taken in regard to the horse. Receive back your hat, Brother Francis, and go the the chemist's, if you please; for I have now done. Ask me to take anything you like, except an interest in the Doncaster races. Ask me to look at anything you like, except an assemblage of people all animated by feelings of a friendly and admiring nature towards the horse. You are a remarkably well-informed man, and you have heard of hermits. Look upon me as a member of that ancient fraternity, and you will sensibly add to the many obligations which Thomas Idle is proud to owe to Francis Goodchild.'

Here, fatigued by the effort of excessive talking, disputatious Thomas waved one hand languidly, laid his head back on the sofa-pillow, and calmly closed his eyes.

At a later period, Mr Goodchild assailed his traveling companion boldly from the impregnable fortress of common sense. But Thomas, though tamed in body by drastic discipline, was still as mentally unapproachable as ever on the subject of his favourite delusion.

The view from the window after Saturday's breakfast is altogether changed. The tradesmen's families have all come back again. The serious stationer's young woman of all work is shaking a duster out of the window of the combination breakfast-room; a child is playing with a doll, where Mr Thurtell's hair was brushed; a sanitary scrubbing is in progress on the spot where Mr Palmer's braces were put on. No signs of the Races are in the streets, but the tramps and the tumble-down carts and trucks laden with drinking-forms and tables and remnants of booths, that are making their way out of the town as fast as they can. The Angel, which has been cleared for action all the week, already begins restoring every neat and comfortable article of furniture to its own neat and comfortable place. The Angel's daughters (pleasanter angels Mr Idle and Mr Goodchild never saw, nor more quietly expert in their business, nor more superior to the common vice of being above it), have a little time to rest, and to air their cheerful faces among the flowers in the yard. It is market-day. The market looks unusually natural, comfortable, and wholesome; the market-people too. The town seems quite restored, when, hark! A metallic bray – The Gong-Donkey!

The wretched animal has not cleared off with the rest, but is here, under the window. How much more inconceivably drunk now, how much more begrimed of paw, how much more tight of calico hide, how much more stained and daubed and dirty and dunghilly, from his horrible broom to his tender toes, who shall say! He cannot even shake the bray out of himself now, without laying his cheek so near to the mud of the street, that he pitches over after delivering it. Now, prone in the mud, and now backing himself up against shop-windows, the owners of which come out in terror to remove him; now, in the drinking-shop, and now in the tobacconist's, where he goes to buy tobacco, and makes his way into the parlor, and where he gets a cigar, which in half-a-minute he forgets to smoke; now dancing, now dozing, now cursing, and now complimenting My Lord, the Colonel, the Noble Captain, and Your Honourable Worship, the Gong-Donkey kicks up his heels, occasionally braying, until suddenly, he beholds the dearest friend he has in the world coming down the street.

The dearest friend the Gong-Donkey has in the world, is a sort of Jackall, in a dull mangy black hide, of such small pieces that it looks as if it were made of blacking bottles turned inside out and cobbled together. The dearest friend in the world (inconceivably drunk too) advances at the Gong-Donkey, with a hand on each thigh, in a series of humorous springs and stops, wagging his head as he comes. The Gong-Donkey regarding him with the warmest affection, suddenly perceives that he is the greatest enemy he has in the world, and hits him hard in the countenance. The astonished Jackall closes with the Donkey, and they roll over and over in the mud, pummelling one another. A Police Inspector, supernaturally endowed with patience, who has long been looking on from the Guildhall-steps, says, to a myrmidon, 'Lock 'em up! Bring 'em in!'

Appropriate finish to the Grand Race Week. The Gong-Donkey, captive and last trace of it, conveyed into limbo, where they cannot do better than keep him until next Race Week. The Jackall is wanted too, and is much looked for, over the way and up and down. But, having had the good-fortune to be undermost at the time of the capture, he has vanished into air.

On Saturday afternoon, Mr Goodchild walks out and looks at the Course. It is quite deserted; heaps of broken crockery and bottles are raised to its memory; and correct cards and other fragments of paper are blowing about it, as the regulation little paper-backs, carried by the French soldiers in the breasts, were seen, soon after the battle was fought, blowing idly about the plains of Waterloo.

Where will these present idle leaves be blown by the idle winds, and where will the last of them be one day lost and forgotten? An idle question, and an idle thought; and with it Mr Idle fitly makes his bow, and Mr Goodchild his, and thus ends the Lazy Tour of Two Idle Apprentices.

HUNTED DOWN

by Charles Dickens

Chapter I

Most of us see some romances in life. In my capacity as Chief Manager of a Life Assurance Office, I think I have within the last thirty years seen more romances than the generality of men, however unpromising the opportunity may, at first sight, seem.

As I have retired, and live at my ease, I possess the means that I used to want, of considering what I have seen, at leisure. My experiences have a more remarkable aspect, so reviewed, than they had when they were in progress. I have come home from the Play now, and can recall the scenes of the Drama upon which the curtain has fallen, free from the glare, bewilderment, and bustle of the Theatre.

Let me recall one of these Romances of the real world.

There is nothing truer than physiognomy, taken in connexion with manner. The art of reading that book of which Eternal Wisdom obliges every human creature to present his or her own page with the individual character written on it, is a difficult one, perhaps and is little studied. It may require some natural aptitude, and it must require (for everything does) some patience and some pains. That these are not usually given to it – that numbers of people accept a few stock common-place expressions of the face as the whole list of characteristics, and neither seek nor know the refinements that are truest – that You, for instance, give a great deal of time and attention to the reading of music, Greek, Latin, French, Italian, Hebrew, if you please, and do not qualify yourself to read the face of the improbable. Perhaps a little self-sufficiency may be at the bottom of this; facial expression requires no study from you, you think; it comes by nature to you to know enough about it, and you are not to be taken in.

I confess, for my part, that I *have* been taken in, over and over again. I have been taken in by acquaintances, and I have been taken in (of course) by friends; far oftener by friends than by any other class of persons. How came I to be so deceived? Had I quite misread their faces?

No. Believe me, my first impression of those people, founded on face and manner alone, was invariably true. My mistake was in suffering them to come nearer to me and explain themselves away.

Chapter II

The partition which separated my own office from our general outer office in the City was of thick plate-glass. I could see through it what passed in the outer office, without hearing a word. I had it put up in place of a wall that had been there for years – ever since the house was built. It is no matter whether I did or did not make the change in order that I might derive my first impression of strangers, who came to us on business, from their faces alone, without being influenced by anything they said. Enough to mention that I turned my glass partition to that account, and that a Life Assurance Office is at all times exposed to be practised upon by the most crafty and cruel of the human race.

It was through my glass partition that I first saw the gentleman whose story I am going to tell.

He had come in without my observing it, and had put his hat and umbrella on the broad counter, and was bending over it to take some papers from one of the clerks. He was about forty or so, dark, exceedingly well dressed in black – being in mourning – and the hand he extended with a polite air, had a particularly well-fitting black-kid glove upon it. His hair, which was elaborately brushed and oiled, was parted straight up the middle; and he presented this parting to the clerk, exactly (to my thinking) as if he had said, in so many words: 'You must take me, if you please, my friend, just as I show myself. Come straight up here, follow the gravel path, keep off the grass, I allow no trespassing.'

I conceived a very great aversion to that man the moment I thus saw him.

He had asked for some of our printed forms, and the clerk was giving them to him and explaining them. An obliged and agreeable smile was on his face, and his eyes met those of the clerk with a sprightly look. (I have known a vast quantity of nonsense talked about bad men not looking you in the face. Don't trust that conventional idea. Dishonesty will stare honesty out of countenance, any day in the week, if there is anything to be got by it.)

I saw, in the corner of his eye-lash, that he became aware of my looking at him. Immediately he turned the parting in his hair toward the glass partition, as if he said to me with a sweet smile, 'Straight up here, if you please. Off the grass!'

In a few moments he had put on his hat and taken up his umbrella, and was gone.

I beckoned the clerk into my room, and asked 'Who was that?'

He had the gentleman's card in his hand. 'Mr Julius Slinkton, Middle Temple.'

'A barrister, Mr Adams?'

'I think not, sir.'

'I should have thought him a clergyman, but for his having no Reverend here,' said I.

'Probably, from his appearance,' Mr Adams replied, 'he is reading for orders.'

I should mention that he wore a dainty white cravat, and dainty linen altogether.

'What did he want, Mr Adams?'

'Merely a form of proposal, sir, and form of reference.'

'Recommended here? Did he say?'

'Yes, he said he was recommended here by a friend of yours. He noticed you, but said that as he had not the pleasure of your personal acquaintance he would not trouble you.'

'Did he know my name?'

'O yes, sir! He said, "There is Mr Sampson, I see!"'

'A well-spoken gentleman, apparently?'

'Remarkably so, sir.'

'Insinuating manners, apparently?'

'Very much so, indeed, sir.'

'Hah!' said I. 'I want nothing at present, Mr Adams.'

Within a fortnight of that day I went to dine with a friend of mine, a merchant, a man of taste, who buys pictures and books; and the first man I saw among the company was Mr Julius Slinkton. There he was, standing before the fire, with good large eyes and an open expression of face; but still (I thought) requiring everybody to come at him by the prepared way he offered, and by no other.

I noticed him ask my friend to introduce him to Mr Sampson, and my friend did so. Mr Julius Slinkton was very happy to see me. Not too happy; there was no over-doing of the matter; happy in a thoroughly well-bred, perfectly unmeaning way.

'I thought you had met,' our host observed.

'No,' said Mr Slinkton. 'I did look in at Mr Sampson's office, on your recommendation; but I really did not feel justified in troubling Mr Sampson himself, on a point in the every-day routine of an ordinary clerk.'

I said I should have been glad to show him any attention on our friend's introduction.

'I am sure of that,' said he, 'and am much obliged. At another time, perhaps, I may be less delicate. Only, however, if I have real business; for I know, Mr Sampson, how precious business time is, and what a vast number of impertinent people there are in the world.'

I acknowledged his consideration with a slight bow. 'You were thinking,' said I, 'of effecting a policy on your life.'

'O dear no! I am afraid I am not so prudent as you may pay me the compliment of supposing me to be, Mr Sampson. I merely inquired for a friend. But you know what friends are in such matters. Nothing may ever come of it. I have the greatest reluctance to trouble men of business with inquiries for friends, knowing the probabilities to be a thousand to one that the friends will never follow them up. People are so fickle, so selfish, so inconsiderate. Don't you, in your business, find them so every day, Mr Sampson?'

I was going to give a qualified answer; but he turned his smooth, white parting on me with its 'Straight up here, if you please!' and I answered 'Yes.'

'I hear, Mr Sampson,' he resumed presently, for our friend

had a new cook, and dinner was not so punctual as usual, 'that your profession has recently suffered a great loss.'

'In money?' said I.

He laughed at my ready association of loss of money, and replied, 'No, in talent and vigour.'

Not at once following out his allusion, I considered for a moment. '*Has* it sustained a loss of that kind?' said I. 'I was not aware of it.'

'Understand me, Mr Sampson. I don't imagine that you have retired. It is not so bad as that. But Mr Meltham—'

'O, to be sure!' said I. 'Yes! Mr Meltham, the young actuary of the "Inestimable."'

'Just so,' he returned in a consoling way.

'He is a great loss. He was at once the most profound, the most original, and the most energetic man I have ever known connected with Life Assurance.'

I spoke strongly; for I had a high esteem and admiration for Meltham; and my gentleman had indefinitely conveyed to me some suspicion that he wanted to sneer at him. He recalled me to my guard by presenting that trim pathway up his head, with its infernal 'Not on the grass, if you please – the gravel.'

'You knew him, Mr Slinkton.'

'Only by reputation. To have known him as an acquaintance, or as a friend, is an honour I should have sought if he had remained in society, though I might never have had the good fortune to attain it, being a man of far inferior mark. He was scarcely above thirty, I suppose?'

'About thirty.'

'Ah!' he sighed in his former consoling way. 'What creatures we are! To break up, Mr Sampson, and become incapable of business at that time of life! – Any reason assigned for the melancholy fact?'

('Humph!' thought I, as I looked at him. 'But I WON'T go up the track, and I WILL go on the grass.')

'What reason have you heard assigned, Mr Slinkton?' I asked, point-blank.

'Most likely a false one. You know what Rumour is, Mr Sampson. I never repeat what I hear; it is the only way of paring the nails and shaving the head of Rumour. But when *you* ask me what reason I have heard assigned for Mr

Meltham's passing away from among men, it is another thing. I am not gratifying idle gossip then. I was told, Mr Sampson, that Mr Meltham had relinquished all his avocations and all his prospects, because he was, in fact, broken-hearted. A disappointed attachment I heard, – though it hardly seems probable, in the case of a man so distinguished and so attractive.'

'Attractions and distinctions are no armour against death,' said I.

'O, she died? Pray pardon me. I did not hear that. That, indeed, makes it very, very sad. Poor Mr Meltham! She died? Ah, dear me! Lamentable, lamentable!'

I still thought his pity was not quite genuine, and I still suspected an unaccountable sneer under all this, until he said, as we were parted, like the other knots of talkers, by the announcement of dinner:

'Mr Sampson, you are surprised to see me so moved on behalf of a man whom I have never known. I am not so disinterested as you may suppose. I have suffered, and recently too, from death myself. I have lost one of two charming nieces, who were my constant companions. She died young —barely three-and-twenty; and even her remaining sister is far from strong. The world is a grave!'

He said this with deep feeling, and I felt reproached for the coldness of my manner. Coldness and distrust had been engendered in me, I knew, by my bad experiences; they were not natural to me; and I often thought how much I had lost in life, losing trustfulness, and how little I had gained, gaining hard caution. This state of mind being habitual with me, I troubled myself more about this conversation than I might have troubled myself about a greater matter. I listened to his talk at dinner, and observed how readily other men responded to it, and with what a graceful instinct he adapted his subjects to the knowledge and habits of those he talked with. As, in talking with me, he had easily started the subject I might be supposed to understand best, and to be the most interested in, so, in talking with others, he guided himself by the same rule. The company was of a varied character; but he was not at fault, that I could discover, with any member of it. He knew just as much of each man's pursuit as made him agreeable to that man in reference to it, and just as little as made it natural in him to seek modestly for information when the theme was broached.

As he talked and talked – but really not too much, for the rest of us seemed to force it upon him – I became quite angry with myself. I took his face to pieces in my mind, like a watch, and examined it in detail. I could not say much against any of his features separately; I could say even less against them when they were put together. 'Then is it not monstrous,' I asked myself, 'that because a man happens to part his hair straight up the middle of his head, I should permit myself to suspect, and even to detest him?'

(I may stop to remark that this was no proof of my sense. An observer of men who finds himself steadily repelled by some apparently trifling thing in a stranger is right to give it great weight. It may be the clue to the whole mystery. A hair or two will show where a lion is hidden. A very little key will open a very heavy door.)

I took my part in the conversation with him after a time, and we got on remarkably well. In the drawing-room I asked the host how long he had known Mr Slinkton. He answered, not many months; he had met him at the house of a celebrated painter then present, who had known him well when he was travelling with his nieces in Italy for their health. His plans in life being broken by the death of one of them, he was reading with the intention of going back to college as a matter of form, taking his degree, and going into orders. I could not but argue with myself that here was the true explanation of his interest in poor Meltham, and that I had been almost brutal in my distrust on that simple head.

Chapter III

On the very next day but one I was sitting behind my glass partition, as before, when he came into the outer office, as before. The moment I saw him again without hearing him, I hated him worse than ever.

It was only for a moment that I had this opportunity; for he waved his tight-fitting black glove the instant I looked at him, and came straight in.

'Mr Sampson, good day! I presume, you see, upon your kind permission to intrude upon you. I don't keep my word in being justified by business, for my business here – if I may so abuse the word – is of the slightest nature.'

I asked, was it anything I could assist him in?

'I thank you, no. I merely called to inquire outside whether my dilatory friend had been so false to himself as to be practical and sensible. But, of course, he has done nothing. I gave him your papers with my own hand, and he was hot upon the intention, but of course he has done nothing. Apart from the general human disinclination to do anything that ought to be done, I dare say there is a specialty about assuring one's life. You find it like will-making. People are so superstitious, and take it for granted they will die soon afterwards.'

'Up here, if you please; straight up here, Mr Sampson. Neither to the right nor to the left.' I almost fancied I could hear him breathe the words as he sat smiling at me, with that intolerable parting exactly opposite the bridge of my nose.

'There is such a feeling sometimes, no doubt,' I replied; 'but I don't think it obtains to any great extent.'

'Well,' said he, with a shrug and a smile, 'I wish some good angel would influence my friend in the right direction. I rashly promised his mother and sister in Norfolk to see it done, and he promised them that he would do it. But I suppose he never will.'

He spoke for a minute or two on indifferent topics, and went away.

I had scarcely unlocked the drawers of my writing-table next morning, when he reappeared. I noticed that he came straight to the door in the glass partition, and did not pause a single moment outside.

'Can you spare me two minutes, my dear Mr Sampson?'

'By all means.'

'Much obliged,' laying his hat and umbrella on the table; 'I came early, not to interrupt you. The fact is, I am taken by surprise in reference to this proposal my friend has made.'

'Has he made one?' said I.

'Ye-es,' he answered, deliberately looking at me; and then a bright idea seemed to strike him – 'or he only tells me he has. Perhaps that may be a new way of evading the matter. By Jupiter, I never thought of that!'

Mr Adams was opening the morning's letters in the outer office. 'What is the name, Mr Slinkton?' I asked.

'Beckwith.'

I looked out at the door and requested Mr Adams, if there were a proposal in that name, to bring it in. He had already laid it out of his hand on the counter. It was easily selected from the rest, and he gave it me. Alfred Beckwith. Proposal to effect a policy with us for two thousand pounds. Dated yesterday.

'From the Middle Temple, I see, Mr Slinkton.'

'Yes. He lives on the same staircase with me; his door is opposite. I never thought he would make me his reference though.'

'It seems natural enough that he should.'

'Quite so, Mr Sampson; but I never thought of it. Let me see.' He took the printed paper from his pocket. 'How am I to answer all these questions?'

'According to the truth, of course,' said I.

O, of course!' he answered, looking up from the paper with a smile: 'I meant they were so many. But you do right to be particular. It stands to reason that you must be particular. Will you allow me to use your pen and ink?'

'Certainly.'

'And your desk?'

'Certainly.'

He had been hovering about between his hat and his umbrella for a place to write on. He now sat down in my chair, at my blotting-paper and inkstand, with the long walk up his head in accurate perspective before me, as I stood with my back to the fire.

Before answering each question he ran over it aloud, and discussed it. How long had he known Mr Alfred Beckwith? That he had to calculate by years upon his fingers. What were his habits? No difficulty about them; temperate in the last degree, and took a little too much exercise, if anything. All the answers were satisfactory. When he had written them all, he looked them over, and finally signed them in a very pretty hand. He supposed he had now done with the business. I told him he was not likely to be troubled any farther. Should he leave the papers there? If he pleased. Much obliged. Good morning.

I had had one other visitor before him; not at the office, but at my own house. That visitor had come to my bed-side when it was not yet daylight, and had been seen by no one else but by my faithful confidential servant.

A second reference paper (for we required always two) was sent down into Norfolk, and was duly received back by post. This, likewise, was satisfactorily answered in every respect. Our forms were all complied with; we accepted the proposal, and the premium for one year was paid.

Chapter IV

For six or seven months I saw no more of Mr Slinkton. He called once at my house, but I was not at home; and he once asked me to dine with him in the Temple, but I was engaged. His friend's assurance was effected in March. Late in September or early in October I was down at Scarborough for a breath of sea-air, where I met him on the beach. It was a hot evening; he came toward me with his hat in his hand; and there was the walk I had felt so strongly disinclined to take in perfect order again, exactly in front of the bridge of my nose.

He was not alone, but had a young lady on his arm.

She was dressed in mourning, and I looked at her with great interest. She had the appearance of being extremely delicate, and her face was remarkably pale and melancholy; but she was very pretty. He introduced her as his niece, Miss Niner.

'Are you strolling, Mr Sampson? Is it possible you can be idle?'

It *was* possible, and I *was* strolling.

'Shall we stroll together?'

'With pleasure.'

The young lady walked between us, and we walked on the cool sea sand, in the direction of Filey.

'There have been wheels here,' said Mr Slinkton. 'And now I look again, the wheels of a hand-carriage! Margaret, my love, your shadow without doubt!'

'Miss Niner's shadow?' I repeated, looking down at it on the sand.

'Not that one,' Mr Slinkton returned, laughing. 'Margaret, my dear, tell Mr Sampson.'

'Indeed,' said the young lady, turning to me, 'there is nothing to tell – except that I constantly see the same invalid old gentleman at all times, wherever I go. I have mentioned it to my uncle, and he calls the gentleman my shadow.'

'Does he live in Scarborough?' I asked.

'He is staying here.'

'Do you live in Scarborough?'

'No, I am staying here. My uncle has placed me with a family here, for my health.'

'And your shadow?' said I, smiling.

'My shadow,' she answered, smiling too, 'is – like myself – not very robust, I fear; for I lose my shadow sometimes, as my shadow loses me at other times. We both seem liable to confinement to the house. I have not seen my shadow for days and days; but it does oddly happen, occasionally, that wherever I go, for many days together, this gentleman goes. We have come together in the most unfrequented nooks on this shore.'

'Is this he?' said I, pointing before us.

The wheels had swept down to the water's edge, and described a great loop on the sand in turning. Bringing the loop back towards us, and spinning it out as it came, was a hand-carriage, drawn by a man.

'Yes,' said Miss Niner, 'this really is my shadow, uncle.'

As the carriage approached us and we approached the carriage, I saw within it an old man, whose head was sunk on his breast, and who was enveloped in a variety of wrappers. He was drawn by a very quiet but very keen-looking man, with iron-grey hair, who was slightly lame. They had passed us, when the carriage stopped, and the old gentleman within, putting out his arm, called to me by my name. I went back, and was absent from Mr Slinkton and his niece for about five minutes.

When I rejoined them, Mr Slinkton was the first to speak. Indeed, he said to me in a raised voice before I came up with him:

'It is well you have not been longer, or my niece might have died of curiosity to know who her shadow is, Mr Sampson.'

'An old East India Director,' said I. 'An intimate friend of our friend's, at whose house I first had the pleasure of meeting you. A certain Major Banks. You have heard of him?'

'Never.'

'Very rich, Miss Niner; but very old, and very crippled. An amiable man, sensible – much interested in you. He has just been expatiating on the affection that he has observed to exist between you and your uncle.

Mr Slinkton was holding his hat again, and he passed his hand up the straight walk, as if he himself went up it serenely, after me.

'Mr Sampson,' he said, tenderly pressing his niece's arm in his, 'our affection was always a strong one, for we have had but a few near ties. We have still fewer now. We have associations to bring us together, that are not of this world, Margaret.'

'Dear uncle!' murmured the young lady, and turned her face aside to hide her tears.

'My niece and I have such remembrances and regrets in common, Mr Sampson,' he feelingly pursued, 'that it would be strange indeed if the relations between us were cold or indifferent. If I remember a conversation we once had together, you will understand the reference I make. Cheer up, dear Margaret. Don't droop, don't droop. My Margaret! I cannot bear to see you droop!'

The poor young lady was very much affected, but controlled herself. His feelings, too, were very acute. In a word, he found himself under such great need of a restorative, that he presently went away, to take a bath of sea-water, leaving the young lady and me sitting by a point of rock, and probably presuming – but that you will say was a pardonable indulgence in a luxury – that she would praise him with all her heart.

She did, poor thing! With all her confiding heart, she praised him to me, for his care of her dead sister, and for his untiring devotion in her last illness. The sister had wasted away very slowly, and wild and terrible fantasies had come over her toward the end, but he had never been impatient with her, or at a loss; had always been gentle, watchful, and self-possessed. The sister had known him, as she had known him, to be the best of men, the kindest of men, and yet a man of such admirable strength of character, as to be a very tower for the support of their weak natures while their poor lives endured.

'I shall leave him, Mr Sampson, very soon,' said the young lady; 'I know my life is drawing to an end; and when I am gone, I hope he will marry and be happy. I am sure he has lived single so long, only for my sake, and for my poor, poor sister's.'

The little hand-carriage had made another great loop on the damp sand, and was coming back again, gradually spinning out a slim figure of eight, half a mile long.

'Young lady,' said I, looking around, laying my hand upon her arm, and speaking in a low voice, 'time presses. You hear the gentle murmur of that sea?'

She looked at me with the utmost wonder and alarm, saying, 'Yes!'

'And you know what a voice is in it when the storm comes?'
'Yes!'

'You see how quiet and peaceful it lies before us, and you know what an awful sight of power without pity it might be, this very night?'

'Yes!'

'But if you had never heard or seen it, or heard of it in its cruelty, could you believe that it beats every inanimate thing in its way to pieces, without mercy, and destroys life without remorse?'

'You terrify me, sir, by these questions!'

'To save you, young lady, to save you! For God's sake, collect your strength and collect your firmness! If you were here alone, and hemmed in by the rising tide on the flow to fifty feet above your head, you could not be in greater danger than the danger you are now to be saved from.'

The figure on the sand was spun out, and straggled off into a crooked little jerk that ended at the cliff very near us.

'As I am, before Heaven and the Judge of all mankind, your friend, and your dead sister's friend, I solemnly entreat you, Miss Niner, without one moment's loss of time, to come to this gentleman with me!'

If the little carriage had been less near to us, I doubt if I could have got her away; but it was so near that we were there before she had recovered the hurry of being urged from the rock. I did not remain there with her two minutes. Certainly within five, I had the inexpressible satisfaction of seeing her – from the point we had sat on, and to which I had returned – half supported and half carried up some rude steps notched in the cliff, by the figure of an active man. With that figure beside her, I knew she was safe anywhere.

I sat alone on the rock, awaiting Mr Slinkton's return. The twilight was deepening and the shadows were heavy, when he came round the point, with his hat hanging at his button-hole, smoothing his wet hair with one of his hands, and picking out the old path with the other and a pocket-comb.

'My niece not here, Mr Sampson?' he said, looking about.

'Miss Niner seemed to feel a chill in the air after the sun was down, and has gone home.'

He looked surprised, as though she were not accustomed to do anything without him; even to originate so slight a proceeding.

'I persuaded Miss Niner,' I explained.

'Ah!' said he. 'She is easily persuaded – for her good. Thank you, Mr Sampson; she is better within doors. The bathing-place was farther than I thought, to say the truth.'

'Miss Niner is very delicate,' I observed.

He shook his head and drew a deep sigh. 'Very, very, very. You may recollect my saying so. The time that has since intervened has not strengthened her. The gloomy shadow that fell upon her sister so early in life seems, in my anxious eyes, to gather over her, ever darker, ever darker. Dear Margaret, dear Margaret! But we must hope.'

The hand-carriage was spinning away before us at a most indecorous pace for an invalid vehicle, and was making most irregular curves upon the sand. Mr Slinkton, noticing it after he had put his handkerchief to his eyes, said:

'If I may judge from appearances, your friend will be upset, Mr Sampson.'

'It looks probable, certainly,' said I.

'The servant must be drunk.'

'The servants of old gentlemen will get drunk sometimes,' said I.

'The major draws very light, Mr Sampson.'

'The major does draw light,' said I.

By this time the carriage, much to my relief, was lost in the darkness. We walked on for a little, side by side over the sand, in silence. After a short while he said, in a voice still affected by the emotion that his niece's state of health had awakened in him.

'Do you stay here long, Mr Sampson?'

'Why, no. I am going away to-night.'

'So soon? But business always holds you in request. Men like Mr Sampson are too important to others, to be spared to their own need of relaxation and enjoyment.'

'I don't know about that,' said I. 'However, I am going back.'

'To London?'

'To London.'

'I shall be there too, soon after you.'

I knew that as well as he did. But I did not tell him so. Any more than I told him what defensive weapon my right hand rested on in my pocket, as I walked by his side. Any more than I told him why I did not walk on the sea side of him with the night closing in.

We left the beach, and our ways diverged. We exchanged good night, and had parted indeed, when he said, returning, 'Mr Sampson, *may* I ask? Poor Meltham, whom we spoke of – dead yet?'

'Not when I last heard of him; but too broken a man to live long, and hopelessly lost to his old calling.'

'Dear, dear, dear!' said he, with great feeling. 'Sad, sad, sad! The world is a grave!' And so went his way.

It was not his fault if the world were not a grave; but I did not call that observation after him, any more than I had mentioned those other things just now enumerated. He went his way, and I went mine with all expedition. This happened, as I have said, either at the end of September or beginning of October. The next time I saw him, and the last time, was late in November.

Chapter V

I had a very particular engagement to breakfast in the Temple. It was a bitter north-easterly morning, and the sleet and slush lay inches deep in the streets. I could get no conveyance, and was soon wet to the knees; but I should have been true to that appointment, though I had to wade to it up to my neck in the same impediments.

The appointment took me to some chambers in the Temple. They were at the top of a lonely corner house overlooking the river. The name, MR ALFRED BECKWITH, was painted on the outer door. On the door opposite, on the same landing, the name MR JULIUS SLINKTON. The doors of both sets of chambers stood open, so that anything said aloud in one set could be heard in the other.

I had never been in those chambers before. They were dismal, close, unwholesome, and oppressive; the furniture, originally good, and not yet old, was faded and dirty – the rooms were in great disorder; there was a strong prevailing smell of opium, brandy, and tobacco; the grate and fire-irons were splashed all over with unsightly blotches of rust; and on a sofa by the fire, in the rooms where breakfast had been prepared, lay the host, Mr Beckwith, a man with all the appearances of the worst kind of drunkard, very far advanced upon his shameful way to death.

'Slinkton is not come yet,' said this creature, staggering up when I went in; 'I'll call him – Halloa! Julius Caesar! Come and drink!' As he hoarsely roared this out, he beat the poker and tongs together in a mad way, as if that were his usual manner of summoning his associate.

The voice of Mr Slinkton was heard through the clatter from the opposite side of the staircase, and he came in. He had not expected the pleasure of meeting me. I have seen several artful men brought to a stand, but I never saw a man so aghast as he was when his eyes rested on mine.

'Julius Caesar,' cried Beckwith, staggering between us, 'Mist' Sampson! Mist' Sampson, Julius Caesar! Julius, Mist' Sampson, is the friend of my soul. Julius keeps keeps me plied with liquor, morning, noon, and night. Julius is a real benefactor. Julius threw the tea and coffee out of window when I used to have any. Julius empties all the water-jugs of their contents, and fills 'em with spirits. Julius winds me up and keeps me going – Boil the brandy, Julius!'

There was a rusty and furred saucepan in the ashes – the ashes looked like the accumulation of weeks – and Beckwith, rolling and staggering between us as if he were going to plunge headlong into the fire, got the saucepan out, and tried to force it into Slinkton's hand.

'Boil the brandy, Julius Caesar! Come! Do your usual office. Boil the brandy!'

He became so fierce in his gesticulations with the saucepan, that I expected to see him lay open Slinkton's head with it. I therefore put out my hand to check him. He reeled back to the sofa, and sat there panting, shaking, and red-eyed, in his rags of dressing-gown, looking at us both. I noticed then that there was nothing to drink on the table but brandy, and nothing to eat but salted herrings, and a hot, sickly, highly-peppered stew.

'At all events, Mr Sampson,' said Slinkton, offering me the smooth gravel path for the last time, 'I thank you for interfering between me and this unfortunate man's violence. However you came here, Mr Sampson, or with whatever motive you came here, at least I thank you for that.'

'Boil the brandy,' muttered Beckwith.

Without gratifying his desire to know how I came there, I said, quietly, 'How is your niece, Mr Slinkton?'

He looked hard at me, and I looked hard at him.

'I am sorry to say, Mr Sampson, that my niece has proved treacherous and ungrateful to her best friend. She left me without a word of notice or explanation. She was misled, no doubt, by some designing rascal. Perhaps you may have heard of it?'

'I did hear that she was misled by a designing rascal. In fact, I have proof of it.'

'Are you sure of that?' said he.

'Quite.'

'Boil the brandy,' muttered Beckwith. 'Company to breakfast, Julius Caesar. Do your usual office – provide the usual breakfast, dinner, tea, and supper. Boil the brandy!'

The eyes of Slinkton looked from him to me, and he said, after a moment's consideration,

'Mr Sampson, you are a man of the world, and so am I. I will be plain with you.'

'O no, you won't,' said I, shaking my head.

'I tell you, sir, I will be plain with you.'

'And I tell you you will not,' said I. 'I know all about you. *You* plain with any one? Nonsense, nonsense!'

'I plainly tell you, Mr Sampson,' he went on, with a manner almost composed, 'that I understand your object. You want to save your funds, and escape from your liabilities; these are old tricks of trade with you Office-gentlemen. But you will not do it, sir; you will not succeed. You have not an easy adversary to play against, when you play against me. We shall have to inquire, in due time, when and how Mr Beckwith fell into his present habits. With that remark, sir, I put this poor creature, and his incoherent wanderings of speech, aside, and wish you a good morning and a better case next time.'

While he was saying this, Beckwith had filled a half-pint glass with brandy. At this moment, he threw the brandy at his face, and threw the glass after it. Slinkton put his hands up, half blinded with the spirit, and cut with the glass across the forehead. At the sound of the breakage, a fourth person came into the room, closed the door, and stood at it; he was a very quiet but very keen-looking man, with iron-grey hair, and slightly lame.

Slinkton pulled out his handkerchief, assuaged the pain in his smarting eyes, and dabbled the blood on his forehead. He was a long time about it, and I saw that in the doing of it, a tremendous change came over him, occasioned by the change in Beckwith – who ceased to pant and tremble, sat upright, and never took his eyes off him. I never in my life saw a face in which abhorrence and determination were so forcibly painted as in Beckwith's then.

'Look at me, you villain,' said Beckwith, 'and see me as I really am. I took these rooms, to make them a trap for you. I came into them as a drunkard, to bait the trap for you. You fell into the trap, and you will never leave it alive. On the morning when you last went to Mr Sampson's office, I had seen him first. Your plot has been known to both of us, all along, and you have been counterplotted all along. What? Having been cajoled into putting that prize of two thousand pounds in your power, I was to be done to death with brandy, and, brandy not proving quick enough, with something quicker? Have I never seen you, when you thought my senses gone, pouring from your little bottle into my glass? Why, you

Murderer and Forger, alone here with you in the dead of night, as I have often been, I have had my hand upon the trigger of a pistol, twenty times, to blow our brains out!'

This sudden starting up of the thing that he had supposed to be his imbecile victim into a determined man, with a settled resolution to hunt him down and be the death of him, mercilessly expressed from head to foot, was, in the first shock, too much for him. Without any figure of speech, he staggered under it. But there is no greater mistake than to suppose that a man who is a calculating criminal, is, in any phase of his guilt, otherwise than true to himself, and perfectly consistent with his whole character. Such a man commits murder, and murder is the natural culmination of his course; such a man has to outface murder, and will do it with hardihood and effrontery. It is a sort of fashion to express surprise that any notorious criminal, having such crime upon his conscience, can so brave it out. Do you think that if he had it on his conscience at all, or had a conscience to have it upon, he would ever have committed the crime?

Perfectly consistent with himself, as I believe all such monsters to be, this Slinkton recovered himself, and showed a defiance that was sufficiently cold and quiet. He was white, he was haggard, he was changed; but only as a sharper who had played for a great stake and had been outwitted and had lost the game.

'Listen to me, you villain,' said Beckwith, 'and let every word you hear me say be a stab in your wicked heart. When I took these rooms, to throw myself in your way and lead you on to the scheme that I knew my appearance and supposed character and habits would suggest to such a devil, how did I know that? Because you were no stranger to me. I knew you well. And I knew you to be the cruel wretch who, for so much money, had killed one innocent girl while she trusted him implicitly, and who was by inches killing another.'

Slinkton took out a snuff-box, took a pinch of snuff, and laughed.

'But see here,' said Beckwith, never looking away, never raising his voice, never relaxing his face, never unclenching his hand. 'See what a dull wolf you have been, after all! The infatuated drunkard who never drank a fiftieth part of the liquor you plied him with, but poured it away, here, there, everywhere – almost before your eyes; who bought over the fellow you set to watch him and to ply him, by outbidding you in his bribe, before he had been at his work three days – with whom you have observed no caution, yet who was so bent on ridding the earth of you as a wild beast, that he would have defeated you if you had been ever so prudent – that drunkard whom you have, many a time, left on the floor of this room, and who has even let you go out of it, alive and undeceived, when you have turned him over with your foot – has, almost as often, on the same night, within an hour, within a few minutes, watched you awake, had his hand at your pillow when you were asleep, turned over your papers, taken samples from your bottles and packets of powder, changed their contents, rifled every secret of your life!'

He had another pinch of snuff in his hand, but had gradually let it drop from between his fingers to the floor; where he now smoothed it out with his foot, looking down at it the while.

'That drunkard,' said Beckwith, 'who had free acess to your rooms at all times, that he might drink the strong drinks that you left in his way and be the sooner ended, holding no more terms with you than he would hold with a tiger, has had his master-key for all your locks, his test for all your poisons, his clue to your cipher-writing. He can tell you, as well as you can tell him, how long it took to complete that deed, what doses there were, what intervals, what signs of gradual decay upon mind and body; what distempered fancies were produced, what observable changes, what physical pain. He can tell you, as well as you can tell him, that all this was recorded day by day, as a lesson of experience for future service. He can tell you, better than you can tell him, where that journal is at this moment.'

Slinkton stopped the action of his foot, and looked at Beckwith.

'No,' said the latter, as if answering a question from him. 'Not in the drawer of the writing-desk that opens with a spring; it is not there, and it never will be there again.'

'Then you are a thief!' said Slinkton.

Without any change whatever in the inflexible purpose, which it was quite terrific even to me to contemplate, and from the power of which I had always felt convinced it was impossible for this wretch to escape, Beckwith returned,

'And I am your niece's shadow, too.'

With an imprecation Slinkton put his hand to his head, tore out some hair, and flung it to the ground. It was the end of the smooth walk; he destroyed it in the action, and it will soon be seen that his use for it was past.

Beckwith went on: 'Whenever you left here, I left here. Although I understood that you found it necessary to pause in the completion of that purpose, to avert suspicion, still I watched you close, with the poor confiding girl. When I had the diary, and could read it word by word – it was only about the night before your last visit to Scarborough – you remember the night? You slept with a small flat vial tied to your wrist, – I sent to Mr Sampson, who was kept out of view. This is Mr Sampson's trusty servant standing by the door. We three saved your niece among us.'

Slinkton looked at us all, took an uncertain step or two from the place where he had stood, returned to it, and glanced about him in a very curious way – as one of the meaner reptiles might, looking for a hole to hide in. I noticed at the same time, that a singular change took place in the figure of the man – as if it collapsed within his clothes, and they consequently became ill-shapen and ill-fitting.

'You shall know,' said Beckwith, 'for I hope the knowledge will be bitter and terrible to you, why you have been pursued by one man, and why, when the whole interest that Mr Sampson represents would have expended any money in hunting you down, you have been tracked to death at a single individual's charge. I hear you have had the name of Meltham on your lips sometimes?'

I saw, in addition to those other changes, a sudden stoppage come upon his breathing.

'When you sent the sweet girl whom you murdered (you know with what artfully made-out surroundings and probabilities you sent her) to Meltham's office, before taking her abroad to originate the transaction that doomed her to the grave, it fell to Meltham's lot to see her and to speak with her. It did not fall to his lot to save her, though I know he would freely give his own life to have done it. He admired her – I would say he loved her deeply, if I thought it possible that you could understand the word. When she was sacrificed, he was thoroughly assured of your guilt. Having lost her, he had but one object left in life, and that was to avenge her and destroy you.'

I saw the villain's nostrils rise and fall convulsively; but I saw no moving at his mouth.

'That man Meltham,' Beckwith steadily pursued, 'was as absolutely certain that you could never elude him in this world, if he devoted himself to your destruction with his utmost fidelity and earnestness, and if he divided the sacred duty with no other duty in life, as he was certain that in achieving it he would be a poor instrument in the hands of Providence, and would do well before Heaven in striking you out from among living men. I am that man, and I thank God that I have done my work!'

If Slinkton had been running for his life from swift-footed savages, a dozen miles, he could not have shown more emphatic signs of being oppressed at heart and labouring for breath, than he showed now, when he looked at the pursuer who had so relentlessly hunted him down.

'You never saw me under my right name before; you see me under my right name now. You shall see me once again in the body, when you are tried for your life. You shall see me once again in the spirit, when the cord is round your neck, and the crowd are crying against you!'

When Meltham had spoken these last words, the miscreant suddenly turned away his face, and seemed to strike his mouth with his open hand. At the same instant, the room was filled with a new and powerful odour, and, almost at the same instant, he broke into a crooked run, leap, start – I have no name for the spasm – and fell, with a dull weight that shook the heavy old doors and windows in their frames.

That was the fitting end of him.

When we saw that he was dead, we drew away from the room, and Meltham, giving me his hand, said, with a weary air, 'I have no more work on earth, my friend. But I shall see her again elsewhere.'

It was in vain that I tried to rally him. He might have saved her, he said; he had not saved her, and he reproached himself; he had lost her, and he was broken-hearted.

'The purpose that sustained me is over, Sampson, and there is nothing now to hold me to life. I am not fit for life; I am weak and spiritless; I have no hope and no object; my day is done.'

In truth, I could hardly have believed that the broken man who then spoke to me was the man who had so strongly and so differently impressed me when his purpose was before him. I used such entreaties with him, as I could; but he still said, and always said, in a patient, undemonstrative way – nothing could avail him – he was broken-hearted.

He died early in the next spring. He was buried by the side of the poor young lady for whom he had cherished those tender and unhappy regrets; and he left all he had to her sister. She lived to be a happy wife and mother; she married my sister's son, who succeeded poor Meltham; she is living now, and her children ride about the garden on my walking-stick when I go to see her.

GEORGE SILVERMAN'S EXPLANATION

by Charles Dickens

Chapter I

It happened in this wise:

——But, sitting with my pen in my hand looking at those words again, without descrying any hint in them of the words that should follow, it comes into my mind that they have an abrupt appearance. They may serve, however, if I let them remain, to suggest how very difficult I find it to begin to explain my Explanation. An uncouth phrase: and yet I do not see my way to a better.

Chapter II

It happened in *this* wise:

——But, looking at those words, and comparing them with my former opening, I find they are the self-same words repeated. This is the more surprising to me, because I employ them in quite a new connexion. For indeed I declare that my intention was to discard the commencement I first had in my thoughts, and to give the preference to another of an entirely different nature, dating my explanation from an anterior period of my life. I will make a third trial, without erasing this second failure, protesting that it is not my design to conceal any of my infirmities, whether they be of head or heart.

Chapter III

Not as yet directly aiming at how it came to pass, I will come upon it by degrees. The natural manner after all, for GOD knows that is how it came upon me!

251

My parents were in a miserable condition of life, and my infant home was a cellar in Preston. I recollect the sound of Father's Lancashire clogs on the street pavement above, as being different in my young hearing from the sound of all other clogs; and I recollect that when Mother came down the cellar-steps, I used tremblingly to speculate on her feet having a good or an ill tempered look – on her knees – on her waist – until finally her face came into view and settled the question. From this it will be seen that I was timid, and that the cellar-steps were steep, and that the doorway was very low.

Mother had the gripe and clutch of Poverty upon her face, upon her figure, and not least of all upon her voice. Her sharp and high-pitched words were squeezed out of her, as by the compression of bony fingers on a leathern bag, and she had a way of rolling her eyes about and about the cellar, as she scolded, that was gaunt and hungry. Father, with his shoulders rounded, would sit quiet on a three-legged stool, looking at the empty grate, until she would pluck the stool from under him, and bid him go bring some money home. Then he would dismally ascend the steps, and I, holding my ragged shirt and trousers together with a hand (my only braces), would feint and dodge from Mother's pursuing grasp at my hair.

A worldly little devil was Mother's usual name for me. Whether I cried for that I was in the dark, or for that it was cold, or for that I was hungry, or whether I squeezed myself into a warm corner when there was a fire, or ate voraciously when there was food, she would still say: 'O you worldly little devil!' And the sting of it was, that I quite well knew myself to be a worldly little devil. Wordly as to wanting to be housed and warmed, worldly as to wanting to be fed, worldly as to the greed with which I inwardly compared how much I got of those good things with how much Father and Mother got, when, rarely, those good things were going.

Sometimes they both went away seeking work, and then I would be locked up in the cellar for a day or two at a time. I was at my worldliest then. Left alone, I yielded myself up to a worldly yearning for enough of anything (except misery), and for both the death of Mother's father, who was a machine-maker at Birmingham, and on whose decease I had heard

Mother say she would come into a whole court-full of houses 'if she had her rights'. Worldly little devil, I would stand about, musingly fitting my cold bare feet into cracked bricks and crevices of the damp cellar-floor – walking over my grand-father's body, so to speak, into the court-full of houses, and selling them for meat and drink and clothes to wear.

At last a change came down into our cellar. The universal change came down even as low as that – so will it amount to any height on which a human creature can perch – and brought other changes with it.

We had a heap of I don't know what foul litter in the darkest corner, which we called 'the bed.' For three days Mother lay upon it without getting up, and then began at times to laugh. If I had ever heard her laugh before, it had been so seldom that the strange sound frightened me. It frightened Father, too, and we took it by turns to give her water. Then she began to move her head from side to side, and sing. After that, she getting no better, Father fell a-laughing and a-singing, and then there was only I to give them both water, and they both died.

Chapter IV

When I was lifted out of the cellar by two men, of whom one came peeping down alone first, and ran away and brought the other, I could hardly bear the light of the street, I was sitting in the roadway, blinking at it, and at a ring of people collected around me, but not close to me, when, true to my character of worldly little devil, I broke silence by saying, 'I am hungry and thirsty!'

'Does he know they are dead?' asked one of another.

'Do you know your father and mother are both dead of fever?' asked a third of me, severely.

'I don't know what it is to be dead. I supposed it meant that, when the cup rattled against their teeth and the water spilt over them. I am hungry and thirsty.' That was all I had to say about it.

The ring of people widened outward from the inner side as I looked around me; and I smelt vinegar, and what I now know to be camphor, thrown in towards where I sat. Presently some one put a great vessel of smoking vinegar on the ground near me, and then they all looked at me in silent horror as I ate and drank of what was brought for me. I knew at the time they had a horror of me, but I couldn't help it.

I was still eating and drinking, and a murmur of discussion had begun to arise respecting what was to be done with me next, when I heard a cracked voice somewhere in the ring say: 'My name is Hawkyard, Mr Verity Hawkyard, of West Bromwich.' Then the ring split in one place, and a yellow-faced peak-nosed gentleman, clad all in iron-grey to his gaiters, pressed forward with a policeman and another official of some sort. He came forward close to the vessel of smoking vinegar; from which he sprinkled himself carefully, and me copiously.

'He had a grandfather at Birmingham, this young boy: who is just dead, too,' said Mr Hawkyard.

I turned my eyes upon the speaker, and said in a ravening manner: 'Where's his houses?'

'Hah! Horrible worldliness on the edge of the grave,' said Mr Hawkyard, casting more of the vinegar over me, as if to get my devil out of me. 'I have undertaken a slight – a very slight – trust in behalf of this boy; quite a voluntary trust; a matter of mere honour, if not of mere sentiment; still I have taken it upon myself, and it shall be (O yes, it shall be!) discharged.'

The bystanders seemed to form an opinion of this gentleman, much more favourable than their opinion of me.

'He shall be taught,' said Mr Hawkyard (O yes, he shall be taught!); but what is to be done with him for the present? He may be infected. He may disseminate infection.' The ring widened considerably. 'What is to be done with him?'

He held some talk with the two officials. I could distinguish no word save 'Farm-house.' There was another sound several times repeated, which was wholly meaningless to my ears then, but which I knew soon afterwards to be 'Hoghton Towers.'

'Yes,' said Mr Hawkyard, 'I think that sounds promising. I think that sounds hopeful. And he can be put by himself in a Ward, for a night or two, you say?'

It seemed to be the police-officer who had said so, for it was he who replied Yes. It was he, too, who finally took me by the arm and walked me before him through the streets, into a whitewashed room in a bare building, where I had a chair to sit in, a table to sit at, an iron bedstead and good matters to lie upon, and a rug and blanket to cover me. Where I had enough to eat, too, and was shown how to clean the tin porringer in which it was conveyed to me, until it was as good as a looking-glass. Here, likewise, I was put in a bath, and had new clothes brought to me, and my old rags were burnt, and I was camphored and vinegared, and disinfected in a variety of ways.

When all this was done – I don't know in how many days or how few, but it matters not – Mr Hawkyard stepped in at the door, remaining close to it, and said:

'Go and stand against the opposite wall, George Silverman. As far off as you can. That'll do. How do you feel?'

I told him that I didn't feel cold, and didn't feel hungry, and didn't feel thirsty. That was the whole round of human feelings, as far as I knew, except the pain of being beaten.

'Well,' said he, 'you are going, George, to a healthy farm-house to be purified. Keep in the air there, as much as you can. Live an out-of-door life there, until you are fetched away. You had better not say much – in fact, you had better be very careful not to say anything – about what your parents died of, or they might not like to take you in. Behave well, and I'll put you to school (O yes, I'll put you to school!), though I am not obligated to do it. I am a servant of the Lord, George, and I have been a good servant to him (I have!) these five-and-thirty years. The Lord has had a good servant in me, and he knows it.'

What I then supposed him to mean by this, I cannot imagine. As little do I know when I began to comprehend that he was a prominent member of some obscure denomination or congregation, every member of which held forth to the rest when so inclined, and among whom he was called Brother Hawkyard. It was enough for me to know, on that day in the Ward, that the farmer's cart was waiting for me at the street corner. I was not slow to get into it, for it was the first ride I ever had in my life.

It made me sleepy, and I slept. First, I stared at Preston streets as long as they lasted, and, meanwhile, I may have had some small dumb wondering within me whereabouts our cellar was. But I doubt it. Such a worldly little devil was I, that

I took no thought who would bury Father and Mother, or where they would be buried, or when. The question whether the eating and drinking by day, and the covering by night, would be as good at the farm-house as at the Ward, superseded those questions.

The jolting of the cart on a loose stony road awoke me, and I found that we were mounting a steep hill, where the road was a rutty by-road through a field. And so, by fragments of an ancient terrace, and by some rugged outbuildings that had once been fortified, and passing under a ruined gateway, we came to the old farm-house in the thick stone wall outside the old quadrangle of Hoghton Towers. Which I looked at, like a stupid savage; seeing no speciality in; seeing no antiquity in; assuming all farm-houses to resemble it; assigning the decay I noticed, to the one potent cause of all ruin that I knew – Poverty; eyeing the pigeons in their flights, the cattle in their stalls, the ducks in the pond, and the fowls pecking about the yard, with a hungry hope that plenty of them might be killed for dinner while I stayed there; wondering whether the scrubbed dairy vessels drying in the sunlight could be the goodly porringers out of which the master ate his belly-filling food, and which he polished when he had done, according to my Ward experience; shrinkingly doubtful whether the shadows passing over that airy height on the bright spring day were not something in the nature of frowns; sordid, afraid, unadmiring, a small Brute to shudder at.

To that time I had never had the faintest impression of beauty. I had had no knowledge whatever that there was anything lovely in this life. When I had occasionally slunk up the cellar-steps into the street and glared in at shop-windows, I had done so with no higher feelings than we may suppose to animate a mangey young dog or wolf-cub. It is equally the fact that I had never been alone, in the sense of holding unselfish converse with myself. I had been solitary often enough, but nothing better.

Such was my condition when I sat down to my dinner, that day, in the kitchen of the old farm-house. Such was my condition when I lay on my bed in the old farm-house that night, stretched out opposite the narrow mullioned window, in the cold light of the moon, like a young Vampire.

Chapter V

What do I know, now, of Hoghton Towers? Very little, for I have been gratefully unwilling to disturb my first impressions. A house, centuries old, on high ground a mile or so removed from the road between Preston and Blackburn, where the first James of England in his hurry to make money by making Baronets, perhaps, made some of those remunerative dignitaries. A house, centuries old, deserted and falling to pieces, its woods and gardens long since grass land or ploughed up, the rivers Ribble and Darwen glancing below it, and a vague haze of smoke against which not even the supernatural prescience of the first Stuart could foresee a Counterblast, hinting at Steam Power, powerful in two distances.

What did I know, then, of Hoghton Towers? When I first peeped in at the gate of the lifeless quadrangle, and started from the mouldering statue becoming visible to me like its Guardian Ghost; when I stole round by the back of the farm-house and got in among the ancient rooms, many of them with their floors and ceilings falling, the beams and rafters hanging dangerously down, the plaster dropping as I trod, the oaken panels stripped away, the windows half walled up, half broken; when I discovered a gallery commanding the old kitchen, and looked down between balustrades upon a massive old table and benches, fearing to see I know not what dead-alive creatures come in and seat themselves and look up with I know not what dreadful eyes, or lack of eyes, at me; when all over the house I was awed by gaps and chinks where the sky stared sorrowfully at me, where the birds passed, and the ivy rustled, and the stains of winter weather blotched the rotten floors; when down at the bottom of dark pits of staircase into which the stairs had sunk, green leaves trembled, butterflies fluttered, and bees hummed in and out through the broken doorways; when encircling the whole ruin were sweet scents and sights of fresh green growth and ever-renewing life, that I had never dreamed of—I say, when I passed into such clouded perception of these things as my dark soul could compass, what did I know then of Hoghton Towers?

I have written that the sky stared sorrowfully at me. Therein have I anticipated the answer. I knew that all these things looked sorrowfully at me. That they seemed to sigh or whisper, not without pity for me: 'Alas! poor worldly little devil!'

There were two or three rats at the bottom of one of the smaller pits of broken staircase when I craned over and looked in. They were scuffling for some prey that was there. And when they started and hid themselves, close together in the dark, I thought of the old life (it had grown old already) in the cellar.

How not to be this worldly little devil? How not to have a repugnance towards myself as I had towards the rats? I hid in a corner of one of the smaller chambers, frightened at myself and crying (it was the first time I had ever cried for any cause not purely physical), and I tried to think about it. One of the farm-house-ploughs came into my range of view just then, and it seemed to help me as it went on with its two horses up and down the field so peacefully and quietly.

There was a girl of about my own age in the farm-house family, and she sat opposite to me at the narrow table at meal-times. It had come into my mind at our first dinner, that she might take the fever from me. The thought had not disquieted me then; I had only speculated how she would look under the altered circumstances, and whether she would die. But it came into my mind now, that I might try to prevent her taking the fever, by keeping away from her. I knew I should have but scrambling board, if I did; so much the less worldly and less devilish the deed would be, I thought.

From that hour I withdrew myself at early morning into secret corners of the ruined house, and remained hidden there until she went to bed. At first, when meals were ready, I used to hear them calling me; and then my resolution weakened. But I strengthened it again, by going further off into the ruin and getting out of hearing. I often watched for her at the dim windows; and, when I saw that she was fresh and rosy, felt much happier.

Out of this holding her in my thoughts, to the humanising of myself, I suppose some childish love arose within me. I felt in some sort dignified by the pride of protecting her, by the pride of making the sacrifice for her. As my heart swelled with that new feeling, it insensibly softened about Mother and Father. It seemed to have been frozen before, and now to be thawed. The old ruin and all the lovely things that haunted it were not sorrowful for me only, but sorrowful for Mother and Father as well. Therefore did I cry again, and often too.

The farm-house family conceived me to be of a morose temper, and were very short with me: though they never stinted me in such broken fare as was to be got, out of regular hours. One night when I lifted the kitchen latch at my usual time, Sylvia (that was her pretty name) had but just gone out of the room. Seeing her ascending the opposite stairs, I stood still at the door. She had heard the clink of the latch, and looked round.

'George,' she called to me, in a pleased voice, 'to-morrow is my birthday, and we are to have a fiddler, and there's a party of boys and girls coming in a cart, and we shall dance. I invite you. Be sociable for once, George.'

'I am very sorry, miss,' I answered, 'but I – but no; I can't come.'

'You are a disagreeable, ill-humoured lad,' she returned, disdainfully, 'and I ought not to have asked you. I shall never speak to you again.'

As I stood with my eyes fixed on the fire after she was gone, I felt that the farmer bent his brows upon me.

'Eh, lad,' said he, 'Sylvy's right. You're as moody and broody a lad as never I set eyes on yet!'

I tried to assure him that I meant no harm; but he only said, coldly: 'Maybe not, maybe not. There! Get thy supper, get thy supper, and then thou canst sulk to thy heart's content again.'

Ah! If they could have seen me next day in the ruin, watching for the arrival of the cart full of merry young guests; if they could have seen me at night, gliding out from behind the ghostly statue, listening to the music and the fall of dancing feet, and watching the lighted farm-house windows from the quadrangle when all the ruin was dark; if they could have read my heart as I crept up to bed by the back way, comforting myself with the reflection, 'They will take no hurt from me;' they would not have thought mine a morose or an unsocial nature!

It was in these ways that I began to form a shy disposition; to be of a timidly silent character under misconstruction; to have an inexpressible, perhaps a morbid, dread of ever being sordid or worldly. It was in these ways that my nature came to shape itself to such a mould, even before it was affected by the influences of the studious and retired life of a poor scholar.

Chapter VI

Brother Hawkyard (as he insisted on my calling him) put me to school, and told me to work my way. 'You are all right, George,' he said. 'I have been the best servant the Lord has had in his service, for this five-and-thirty year (O, I have!), and he knows the value of such a servant as I have been to him (O yes he does!), and he'll prosper your schooling as a part of my reward. That's what *he'll* do, Geogre. He'll do it for me.'

From the first I could not like this familiar knowledge of the ways of the sublime inscrutable Almighty, on Brother Hawk-yard's part. As I grew a little wiser and still a little wiser, I liked it less and less. His manner, too, of confirming himself in a parenthesis: as if, knowing himself, he doubted his own word: I found distasteful. I cannot tell how much these dislikes cost me, for I had a dread that they were worldly.

As time went on, I became a Foundation Boy on a good Foundation, and I cost Brother Hawkyard nothing. When I had worked my way so far, I worked yet harder, in the hope of ultimately getting a presentation to College, and a Fellow-ship. My health has never been strong (some vapour from the Preston cellar cleaves to me I think), and what with much work and some weakness, I came again to be regarded – that is, by my fellow students – as unsocial.

All through my time as a Foundation Boy, I was within a few miles of Brother Hawkyard's congregation, and when ever I was what we called a Leave-Boy on a Sunday, I went over there at his desire. Before the knowledge became forced upon me that outside their place of meeting these Brothers and Sisters were no better than the rest of the human family, but on the whole were, to put the case mildly, as bad as most, in respect of giving short weight in their shops, and not speaking the truth: I say, before this knowledge became forced upon me, their prolix addresses, their inordinate conceit, their daring ignorance, their investment of the Supreme Ruler of Heaven and Earth with their own miserable meannesses and littlenesses, greatly shocked me. Still, as their term for the frame of mind that could not perceive them to be in an exalted state of Grace, was the 'worldly' state, I did for a time suffer tortures under my inquiries of myself whether that young worldly-devilish spirit of mine could secretly be lingering at the bottom of my non-appreciation.

Brother Hawkyard was the popular expounder in this assembly, and generally occupied a platform (there was a little platform with a table on it, in lieu of a pulpit), first, on a Sunday afternoon. He was by trade a drysalter. Brother Gimblet, an elderly man with a crabbed face, a large dog's-eared shirt collar, and a spotted blue neckerchief reaching up behind to the crown of his head, was also a drysalter, and an expounder. Brother Gimblet professed the greatest admiration for Brother Hawkyard; but (I had thought more than once) bore him a jealous grudge.

Let whosoever may peruse these lines kindly take the pains here to read twice, my solemn pledge that what I write of the language and customs of the congregation in question, I write scrupulously, literally, exactly, from the life and the truth.

On the first Sunday after I had won what I had so long tried for, and when it was certain that I was going up to College, Brother Hawkyard concluded a long exhortation thus:

'Well my friends and fellow-sinners, now I told you when I began, that I didn't know a word of what I was going to say to you (and No, I did not!) but that it was all one to me, because I knew the Lord would put into my mouth the words I wanted.'

('That's it!' From Brother Gimblet.)

'And he did put into my mouth the words I wanted.'

('So he did!' From Brother Gimblet.)

'And why?'

('Ah! Let's have that!' from Brother Gimblet.)

'Because I have been his faithful servant for five-and-thirty years, and because he knows it. For five-and-thirty years! And he knows it, mind you! I got those words that I wanted, on account of my wages. I got 'em from the Lord, my fellow-sinners. Down. I said "Here's a heap of wages due; let us have something down on account." And I got it down, and I paid it over to you, and you won't wrap it up in a napkin, nor yet in a towel, not yet in a pockethankercher, but you'll put it out at good interest. Very well. Now my brothers and sisters and fellow-sinners, I am going to conclude with a question, and I'll make it so plain (with the help of the Lord, after five-and-thirty years, I should rather hope!) as that the Devil shall not be able to confuse it in your heads. Which he would be overjoyed to do.'

('Just his way. Crafty old blackguard!' from Brother Gimblet.)

'And the question is this. Are the Angels learned?'

('Not they. Not a bit on it.' From Brother Gimblet, with the greatest confidence.)

'Not they. And where's the proof? Sent ready-made by the hand of the Lord. Why, there's one among us here now, that has got all the Learning that can be crammed into him. *I* got him all the Learning that could be crammed into him. His grandfather' (this I had never heard before) 'was a Brother of ours. He was Brother Parksop. That's what he was. Parksop. Brother Parksop. His worldly name was Parksop, and he was a Brother of this Brotherhood. Then wasn't he Brother Parksop?'

('Must be. Couldn't help hisself.' From Brother Gimblet.)

'Well. He left that one now here present among us, to the care of a Brother-Sinner of his (and that Brother-Sinner, mind you, was a sinner of a bigger size in his time than any of you, Praise the Lord!), Brother Hawkyard. Me. *I* got him, without fee or reward – without a morsel of myrrh, or frankincense, nor yet amber, letting alone the honeycomb – all the Learning that could be crammed into him. Has is brought him into our Temple, in the spirit? No. Have we had any ignorant Brothers and Sisters that didn't know round O from crooked S, come in among us meanwhile? Many. Then the Angels are *not* learned. Then they don't so much as know their alphabet. And now, my friends and fellow-sinners, having brought it to that, perhaps some Brother present – perhaps you, Brother Gimblet – will pray a bit for us?'

Brother Gimblet undertook the sacred function, after having drawn his sleeve across his mouth, and muttered:

'Well! I don't know as I see my way to hitting any of you quite in the right place neither.' He said this with a dark smile, and then began to bellow. What we were specially to be preserved from, according to his solicitations, was despoilment of the orphan, suppression of the testamentary intentions on the part of a Father or (say) Grandfather, appropriation of the orphan's house-property, feigning to give in charity to the wronged one from whom we withheld his due; and that class of sins. He ended with the petition, 'Give us peace!' Which, speaking for myself, was very much needed after twenty minutes of his bellowing.

Even though I had not seen him when he rose from his knees, steaming with perspiration, glance at Brother Hawkyard; and even though I had not heard Brother Hawkyard's tone of congratulating him on the vigour with which he had roared; I should have detected a malicious application in this prayer. Unformed suspicions to a similar effect had sometimes passed through my mind in my earlier school-days, and had always caused me great distress, for they were worldly in their nature, and wide, very wide, of the spirit that had drawn me from Sylvia. They were sordid suspicions, without a shadow of proof. They were worthy to have originated in the unwholesome cellar. They were not only without proof, but against proof. For, was I not myself a living proof of what Brother Hawkyard had done? And without him, how should I ever have seen the sky look sorrowfully down upon that wretched boy at Hoghton Towers?

Although the dread of a relapse into a state of savage selfishness was less strong upon me as I approached manhood, and could act in increased degree for myself, yet I was always on my guard against any tendency to such relapse. After getting these suspicions under my feet, I had been troubled by not being able to like Brother Hawkyard's manner, or his professed religion. So it came about, that as it would be an act of reparation for any such injury my struggling thoughts had unwillingly done him, if I wrote, and placed in his hands before going to College, a full acknowledgement of his goodness to me, and an ample tribute of thanks. It might serve as an implied vindication of him against and dark scandal from a rival Brother, and Expounder, or from any other quarter.

Accordingly, I wrote the document with much care. I may add with much feeling, too, for it affected me as I went on. Having no set studies to pursue, in the brief interval between leaving the Foundation and going to Cambridge, I determined to walk out to his place of business and give it into his own hands.

It was a winter afternoon when I tapped at the door of his little counting-house, which was at the further end of his long low shop. As I did so (having entered by the back yard, where casks and boxes were taken in, and where there was the inscription 'Private Way to the Counting-House'), a shopman called to me from the counter that he was engaged.

'Brother Gimblet,' said the shopman (who was one of the Brotherhood), 'is with him.'

I thought this all the better for my purpose, and made bold to tap again. They were talking in a low tone, and money was passing, for I heard it being counted out.

'Who is it?' asked Brother Hawkyard, sharply.

'George Silverman,' I answered, holding the door open. 'May I come in?'

Both Brothers seemed so astounded to see me, that I felt shyer than usual. But they looked quite cadaverous in the early gaslight, and perhaps that accidental circumstance exaggerated the expression of their faces.

'What is the matter?' asked Brother Hawkyard.

'Aye! What is the matter?' asked Brother Gimblet.

'Nothing at all,' I said, diffidently producing my document. 'I am only the bearer of a letter from myself.'

'From yourself, George?' cried Brother Hawkyard.

'And to you,' said I.

'And to me, George?'

He turned paler, and opened it hurriedly; but looking over it, and seeing generally what it was, became less hurried, recovered his colour, and said: 'Praise the Lord!'

'That's it!' cried Brother Gimblet. 'Well put! Amen.'

Brother Hawkyard then said, in a livelier strain: 'You must know, George, that Brother Gimblet and I are going to make our two businesses, one. We are going into partnership. We are settling it now. Brother Gimblet is to take one clear half of the profits. (O yes! And he shall have it, he shall have it to the last farthing!)'

'D.V!' said Brother Gimblet, with his right fist firmly clenched on his right leg.

'There is no objection,' pursued Brother Hawkyard, 'to my reading this aloud, George?'

As it was what I expressly desired should be done, after yesterday's prayer, I more than readily begged him to read it aloud. He did so, and Brother Gimblet listened with a crabbed smile.

'It was in a good hour that I came here,' he said, wrinkling up his eyes. 'It was in a good hour likewise, that I was moved yesterday to depict for the terror of evil-doers, a character the direct opposite of Brother Hawkyard's. But it was the Lord that done it. I felt him at it, while I was perspiring.'

After that, it was proposed by both of them that I should attend the congregation once more, before my final departure. What my shy reserve would undergo from being expressly preached at and prayed at, I knew beforehand. But I reflected that it would be for the last time, and that it might add to the weight of my letter. It was well known to the Brothers and Sisters that there was no place taken for me in *their* Paradise, and if I showed this last token of deference to Brother Hawkyard, notoriously in despite of my own sinful inclinations, it might go some little way in aid of my statement that he had been good to me, and that I was grateful to him. Merely stipulating, therefore, that no express endeavour should be made for my conversion – which would involve the rolling of several Brothers and Sisters on the floor, declaring that they felt all their sins in a heap on their left side, weighing so many pounds avoirdupois – as I knew from what I had seen of those repulsive mysteries – I promised.

Since the reading of my letter, Brother Gimblet had been at intervals wiping one eye with an end of his spotted blue neckerchief, and grinning to himself. It was, however, a habit that Brother had, to grin in an ugly manner even while expounding. I call to mind a delighted snarl with which he used to detail from the platform, the torments reserved for the wicked (meaning all human creation, except the Brotherhood), as being remarkably hideous.

I left the two to settle their articles of partnership, and count money; and I never saw them again but on the following

Sunday. Brother Hawkyard died within two or three years, leaving all he possessed to Brother Gimblet, in virtue of a will dated (as I have been told) that very day.

Now, I was so far at rest with myself when Sunday came, knowing that I had conquered my own mistrust, and righted Brother Hawkyard in the jaundiced vision of a rival, that I went, even to that coarse chapel, in a less sensitive state than usual. How could I foresee that the delicate, perhaps the diseased, corner of mind, where I winced and shrunk when it was touched or was even approached, would be handled as the theme of the whole proceedings?

On this occasion, it was assigned to Brother Hawkyard to pray, and to Brother Gimblet to preach. The prayer was to open the ceremonies; the discourse was to come next. Brothers Hawkyard and Gimblet were both on the platform: Brother Hawkyard on his knees at the table, unmusically ready to pray: Brother Gimblet sitting against the wall, grinningly ready to preach.

'Let us offer up the sacrifice of prayer, my brothers and sisters and fellow-sinners.' Yes. But it was I who was the sacrifice. It was our poor sinful worldly-minded Brother here present, who was wrestled for. The now-opening career of this our unawakened Brother might lead to his becoming a minister of what was called The Church. That was what *he* looked to. The Church. Not the chapel, Lord. The Church. No rectors, no vicars, no archdeacons, no bishops, no arch-bishops, in the chapel; but, O Lord, many such in the Church! Protect our sinful Brother from his love of lucre. Cleanse from our unawakened Brother's breast, his sin of worldly-mindedness. The prayer said infinitely more in words, but nothing more to any intelligible effect.

Then Brother Gimblet came forward, and took (as I knew he would) the text, My kingdom is not of this world. Ah! But whose was, my fellow-sinners? Whose? Why, our Brother's here present was. The only kingdom he had an idea of, was of this world. ('That's it!' from several of the congregation.) What did the woman do, when she lost the piece of money? Went and looked for it. What should our brother do when he lost his way? ('Go and look for it,' from a Sister.) Go and look for it. True. But must he look for it in the right direction, or in the wrong? ('In the right,' from a Brother.) There spake the prophets! He must look for it in the right direction, or he couldn't find it. But he had turned his back upon the right direction, and he wouldn't find it. Now, my fellow-sinners, to show you the difference betwixt worldly-mindedness and unworldly-mindedness, betwixt kingdoms not of this world and kingdoms *of* this world, here was a letter wrote by even our worldly-minded Brother unto Brother Hawkyard. Judge, from hearing of it read, whether Brother Hawkyard was the faithful steward that the Lord had in his mind only t'other day, when, in this very place, he drew you the picter of the unfaithful one. For it was him that done it, not me. Don't doubt that!

Brother Gimblet then grinned and bellowed his way through my composition, and subsequently through an hour. The service closed with a hymn, in which the Brothers unanimously roared, and the Sisters unanimously shrieked, at me, that I by wiles of worldly gain was mock'd, and they on waters of sweet love were rock'd; that I with Mammon struggled in the dark, while they were floating in a second Ark.

I went out from all this, with an aching heart and a weary spirit; not because I was quite so weak as to consider these narrow creatures, interpreters of the Divine majesty and wisdom; but because I was weak enough to feel as though it were my hard fortune to be misrepresented and mis-understood, when I most tried to subdue any risings of mere worldliness within me, and when I most hoped that, by dint of trying earnestly, I had succeeded.

Chapter VII

My timidity and my obscurity occasioned me to live a secluded life at College, and to be little known. No relative ever came to visit me, for I had no relative. No intimate friends broke in upon my studies, for I made no intimate friends. I supported myself on my scholarship, and read much. My College time was otherwise not so very different from my time at Hoghton Towers.

Knowing myself to be unfit for the noisier stir of social existence, but believing myself qualified to do my duty in a moderate though earnest way if I could obtain some small preferment in the Church, I applied my mind to the clerical profession. In due sequence I took orders, was ordained, and began to look about me for employment. I must observe that I had taken a good degree, that I had succeeded in winning a good fellowship, and that my means were ample for my retired way of life. By this time I had read with several young men, and the occupation increased my income, while it was highly interesting to me. I once accidentally overheard our greatest Don say, to my boundless joy: 'That he heard it reported of Silverman that his gift of quiet explanation, his patience, his amiable temper, and his conscientiousness, made him the best of Coaches.' May my 'gift of quiet explanation' come more seasonably and powerfully to my aid in this present explanation than I think it will!

It may be, in a certain degree, owing to the situation of my College rooms (in a corner where the daylight was sobered), but it is in a much larger degree referable to the state of my own mind, that I seem to myself, on looking back to this time of my life, to have been always in the peaceful shade. I can see others in the sunlight; I can see our boats' crews and our athletic young men, on the glistening water, or speckled with the moving lights of sunlit leaves; but I myself am always in the shadow looking on. Not unsympathetically – GOD forbid! – but looking on, alone, much as I looked at Sylvia from the shadows of the ruined house, or looked at the red gleam shining through the farmer's windows, and listened to the fall of dancing feet, when all the ruin was dark, that night in the quadrangle.

I now come to the reason of my quoting that laudation of myself above given. Without such reason: to repeat it would have been mere boastfulness.

Among those who had read with me, was Mr Fareway, second son of Lady Fareway, widow of Sir Gaston Fareway, Baronet. This young gentleman's abilities were much above the average, but he came of a rich family, and was idle and luxurious. He presented himself to me too late, and afterwards came to me too irregularly, to admit of my being of much service to him. In the end I considered it my duty to dissuade him from going up for an examination which he could never pass, and he left College without taking a degree. After his departure, Lady Fareway wrote to me representing the justice of my returning half my fee, as I had been of so little use to her son. Within my knowledge a similar demand had not been made in any other case, and I most freely admit that the justice of it had not occurred to me until it was pointed out. But I at once perceived it, yielded to it, and returned the money.

Mr Fareway had been gone two years or more and I had forgotten him, when he one day walked into my rooms as I was sitting at my books.

Said he, after the usual salutations had passed: 'Mr Silverman, my mother is in town here, at the hotel, and wishes me to present you to her.'

I was not comfortable with strangers, and I dare say I betrayed that I was a little nervous or unwilling. For said he, without my having spoken:

'I think the interview may tend to the advancement of your prospects.

It put me to the blush to think that I should be tempted by a worldly reason, and I rose immediately.

Said Mr Fareway, as we went along: 'Are you a good hand at business?'

'I think not,' said I.

Said Mr Fareway then: 'My Mother is.'

'Truly?' said I.

'Yes. My mother is what is usually called a managing woman. Doesn't make a bad thing, for instance, even out of the spendthrift habits of my eldest brother abroad. In short, a managing woman. This is in confidence.'

He had never spoken to me in confidence, and I was surprised by his doing so. I said I should respect his confidence, of course, and said no more on the delicate subject. We had but a little way to walk, and I was soon in his mother's company. He presented me, shook hands with me, and left us two (as he said) to business.

I saw in my Lady Fareway, a handsome well-preserved lady of somewhat large stature, with a steady glare in her great round dark eyes that embarrassed me.

Said my Lady: 'I have heard from my son, Mr Silverman, that you would be glad of some preferment in the Church?'

I gave my Lady to understand that was so.

'I don't know whether you are aware,' my Lady proceeded, 'that we have a presentation to a Living? I say *we* have, but in point of fact *I* have.'

I gave my Lady to understand that I had not been aware of this.

Said my Lady: 'So it is. Indeed, I have two presentations; one, to two hundred a year; one, to six. Both livings are in our county: North Devonshire, as you probably know. The first is vacant. Would you like it?'

What with my Lady's eyes, and what with the suddenness of this proposed gift, I was much confused.

'I am sorry it is not the larger presentation,' said my Lady, rather coldly, 'though I will not, Mr Silverman, pay you the bad compliment of supposing that *you* are, because tht would be mercenary. And mercenary I am persuaded you are not.'

Said I, with my utmost earnestness: 'Thank you, Lady Fareway, thank you, thank you! I should be deeply hurt if I thought I bore the character.'

'Naturally,' said my Lady. 'Always detestable, but particularly in a clergyman. You have not said whether you would like the Living?'

With apologies for my remissness or indistinctness, I assured my Lady that I accepted it most readily and gratefully. I added that I hoped she would not estimate my appreciation of the generosity of her choice by my flow of words, for I was not a ready man in that respect when taken by surprise, or touched at heart.

'The affair is concluded,' said my Lady. 'Concluded. You will find the duties very light, Mr Silverman. Charming house; charming little garden, orchard, and all that. You will be able to take pupils. By the bye! – No. I will return to the word afterwards. What was I going to mention, when it put me out?'

My Lady stared at me, as if I knew. And I didn't know. And that perplexed me afresh.

Said my Lady, after some consideration: 'Oh! Of course. How very dull of me! The last incumbent – least mercenary man I ever saw – in consideration of the duties being so light and the house so delicious, couldn't rest, he said, unless I permitted him to help me with my correspondence, accounts, and various little things of that kind; nothing in themselves, but which it worries a lady to cope with. Would Mr Silverman also, like to—? Or shall I—?'

I hastened to say that my poor help would be always at her ladyship's service.

'I am absolutely blessed,' said my Lady, casting up her eyes (and so taking them off of me for one moment), 'in having to do with gentlemen who cannot endure an approach to the idea of being mercenary!' She shivered at the word. 'And now as to the pupil.'

'The—?' I was quite at a loss.

'Mr Silverman, you have no idea what she is. She is,' said my Lady, laying her touch upon my coat sleeve, 'I do verily believe, the most extraordinary girl in this world. Already knows more Greek and Latin than Lady Jane Grey. And taught herself! Has not yet, remember, derived a moment's advantage from Mr Silverman's classical acquirements. To say nothing of mathematics, which she is bent upon becoming versed in, and in which (as I hear from my son and others) Mr Silverman's reputation is so deservedly high!'

Under my Lady's eyes, I must have lost the clue, I felt persuaded; and yet I did not know where I could have dropped it.

'Adelina,' said my Lady, 'is my only daughter. If I did not feel quite convinced that I am not blinded by a mother's partiality; unless I was absolutely sure that when you know her, Mr Silverman, you will esteem it a high and unusual privilege to direct her studies; I should introduce a mercenary element into this conversation, and ask you on what terms—'

I entreated my Lady to go no further. My Lady saw that I was troubled, and did me the honour to comply with my request.

Chapter VIII

Everything in mental acquisition that her brother might have been, if he would; and everything in all gracious charms and admirable qualities that no one but herself could be; this was Adelina.

I will not expatiate upon her beauty. I will not expatiate upon her intelligence, her quickness of perception, her powers of memory, her sweet consideration from the first moment for the slow-paced tutor who ministered to her wonderful gifts. I was thirty then; I am over sixty now; she is ever present to me in these hours as she was in those, bright and beautiful and young, wise and fanciful and good.

When I discovered that I loved her, how can I say. In the first day? In the first week? In the first month? Impossible to trace. If I be (as I am) unable to represent to myself any previous period of my life as quite separable from her attracting power, how can I answer for this one detail!

Whensoever I made the discovery, it laid a heavy burden on me. And yet, comparing it with the far heavier burden that I afterwards took up, it does not seem to me, now, to have been very hard to bear. In the knowledge that I did love her, and that I should love her while my life lasted, and that I was ever to hide my secret deep in my own breast, and she was never to find it, there was a kind of sustaining joy, or pride, or comfort, mingled with my pain.

But later on – say a year later on – when I made another discovery, then indeed my suffering and my struggle were strong. That other discovery was—?

These words will never see the light, if ever, until my heart is dust; until her bright spirit has returned to the regions of which, when imprisoned here, it surely retained some unusual glimpse of remembrance; until all the pulses that ever beat around us shall have long been quiet; until all the fruits of all the tiny victories and defeats achieved in our little breasts shall have withered away. That discovery was, that she loved me.

She may have enhanced my knowledge, and loved me for that; she may have overvalued my discharge of duty to her, and loved me for that; she may have refined upon a playful compassion which she would sometimes show for what she called my want of wisdom according to the light of the world's dark lanterns, and loved me for that; she may – she must – have confused the borrowed light of what I had only learned, with its brightness in its pure original rays; but she loved me at that time, and she made me know it.

Pride of family and pride of wealth put me as far off from her in my Lady's eyes as if I had been some domesticated creature of another kind. But they could not put me further from her than I put myself when I set my merits against hers. More than that. They could not put me, by millions of fathoms, half so low beneath her as I put myself when in imagination I took advantage of her noble trustfulness, took the fortune that I knew she must possess in her own right, and left her to find herself in the zenith of her beauty and genius, bound to poor rusty plodding Me.

No. Worldliness should not enter here, at any cost. If I had tried to keep it out of other ground, how much harder was I bound to try to keep it from this sacred place.

But there was something daring in her broad generous character that demanded at so delicate a crisis to be delicately and patiently addressed. After many and many a bitter night (O I found I could cry, for reasons not purely physical, at this pass of my life!) I took my course.

My Lady had in our first interview unconsciously over-stated the accommodation of my pretty house. There was room in it for only one pupil. He was a young gentleman near coming of age, very well connected, but what is called a poor relation. His parents were dead. The charges of his living and reading with me were defrayed by an uncle, and he and I were to do our utmost together for three years towards qualifying him to make his way. At this time he had entered into his second year with me. He was well-looking, clever, energetic, enthusiastic, bold; in the best sense of the term, a thorough young Anglo-Saxon.

I resolved to bring these two together.

Chapter IX

Said I, one night, when I had conquered myself: 'Mr Granville:' Mr Granville Wharton his name was: 'I doubt if you have ever yet so much as seen Miss Fareway.'

'Well, sir,' returned he, laughing, 'you see her so much yourself, that you hardly leave another fellow a chance of seeing her.'

'I am her tutor, you know,' said I.

And there the subject dropped for that time. But I so contrived, as that they should come together shortly afterwards. I had previously so contrived as to keep them asunder, for while I loved her – I mean before I had determined on my sacrifice – a lurking jealousy of Mr Granville lay within my unworthy breast.

It was quite an ordinary interview in the Fareway Park; but they talked easily together for some time; like takes to like, and they had many points of resemblance. Said Mr Granville to me, when he and I ate at our supper that night: 'Miss Fareway is remarkably beautiful, sir, and remarkably engaging. Don't you think so?' – 'I think so,' said I. And I stole a glance at him, and saw that he had reddened and was thoughtful. I remember it most vividly, because the mixed feeling of grave pleasure and acute pain that the slight circumstance caused me, was the first of a long, long series of such mixed impressions under which my hair turned slowly grey.

I had not much need to feign to be subdued, but I counterfeited to be older than I was, in all respects (Heaven knows, my heart being all too young the while!), and feigned to be more of a recluse and bookworm than I had really become, and gradually set up more and more of a fatherly manner towards Adelina. Likewise, I made my tuition less imaginative than before; separated myself from my poets and philosophers; was careful to present them in their own light, and me, their lowly servant, in my own shade. Moreover, in the matter of apparel I was equally mindful. Not that I had ever been dapper that way, but that I was slovenly now.

As I depressed myself with one hand, so did I labour to raise Mr Granville with the other; directing his attention to such subjects as I too well knew most interested her, and fashioning him (do not deride or misconstrue the expression, unknown reader of this writing, for I have suffered!) into a greater resemblance to myself in my solitary one strong aspect. And gradually, gradually, as I saw him take more and more to these thrown-out lures of mine, then did I come to know better and better that love was drawing him on, and was drawing Her from me.

So passed more than another year; every day a year in its number of my mixed impresions of grave pleasure and acute pain; and then, these two being of age and free to act legally for themselves, came before me, hand in hand (my hair being now quite white), and entreated me that I would unite them together. 'And indeed, dear Tutor,' said Adelina, 'it is but consistent in you that you should do this thing for us, seeing that we should never have spoken together that first time but for you, and that but for you we could never have met so often afterwards.' The whole of which was literally true, for I had availed myself of my many business attendances on, and conferences with, my Lady, to take Mr Granville to the house, and leave him in the outer room with Adelina.

I knew that my Lady would object to such a marriage for her daughter, or to any marriage that was other than an exchange of her for stipulated lands, good, and moneys. But, looking on the two, and seeing with full eyes that they were both young and beautiful; and knowing that they were alike in the tastes and acquirements that will outlive youth and beauty; and considering that Adelina had a fortune now, in her own keeping; and considering further that Mr Granville, though for the present poor, was of a good family that had never lived in a cellar in Preston; and believing that their love would endure, neither having any great discrepancy to find out in the other; I told them of my readiness to do this thing which Adelina asked of her dear Tutor, and to send them forth, Husband and Wife, into the shining world with golden gates that awaited them.

It was on a summer morning that I rose before the sun, to compose myself for the crowning of my work with this end. And my dwelling being near to the sea, I walked down to the rocks on the shore, in order that I might behold the sun rise in his majesty.

The tranquillity upon the Deep and on the firmament, the orderly withdrawal of the stars, the calm promise of coming day, the rosy suffusion of the sky and waters, the ineffable splendour that then burst forth, attuned my mind afresh after the discords of the night. Methought that all I looked on said to me, and that all I heard in the sea and in the air said to me: 'Be comforted, mortal, that thy life is so short. Our preparation for what is to follow, has endured, and shall endure, for unimaginable ages.'

I married them. I knew that my hand was cold when I placed it on their hands clasped together; but the words with which I had to accompany the action, I could say without faltering, and I was at peace.

They being well away from my house and from the place, after our simple breakfast, the time was come when I must do what I had pledged myself to them that I would do: break the intelligence to my Lady.

I went up to the house, and found my Lady in her ordinary business-room. She happened to have an unusual amount of commissions to entrust to me that day, and she had filled my hands with papers before I could originate a word.

'My Lady' – I then began, as I stood beside her table.

'Why, what's the matter?' she said, quickly, looking up.

'Not much, I would fain hope, after you shall have prepared yourself, and considered a little.'

'Prepared myself! And considered a little. You appear to have prepared *yourself* but indifferently, anyhow, Mr Silverman.' This, mighty scornfully, as I experienced my usual embarrassment under her stare.

Said I, in self-extenuation, once for all: 'Lady Fareway, I have but to say for myself that I have tried to do my duty.'

'For yourself?' repeated my Lady. 'Then there are others concerned, I see. Who are they?'

I was about to answer, when she made towards the bell with a dart that stopped me, and said: 'Why, where is Adelina!'

'Forbear. Be calm, my Lady. I married her this morning to Mr Granville Wharton.'

She set her lips, looked more intently at me than ever, raised her right hand and smote me hard upon the cheek.

'Give me back those papers, give me back those papers!' She tore them out of my hands and tossed them on her table. Then seating herself defiantly in her great chair, and folding her arms, she stabbed me to the heart with the unlooked-for reproach: 'You worldly wretch!'

'Worldly?' I cried. 'Worldly!'

'This, if you please,' she went on with supreme scorn, pointing me out as if there were some one there to see: 'this, if you please, is the disinterested scholar, with not a design beyond his books! This, if you please, is the simple creature whom any one could over-reach in a bargain! This, if you please, is Mr Silverman! Not of this world, not he! He has too much simplicity for this world's cunning. He has too much singleness of purpose to be a match for this world's double-dealing – What did he give you for it?'

'For what? And who?'

'How much,' she asked, bending forward in her great chair, and insultingly tapping the fingers of her right hand on the palm of her left: 'how much does Mr Granville Wharton pay you for getting him Adelina's money? What is the amount of your percentage upon Adelina's fortune? What were the terms of the agreement that you proposed to this boy when you, the Reverend George Silverman, licensed to marry, engaged to put him in possession of this girl? You made good terms for yourself, whatever they were. He would stand a poor chance against your keenness.'

Bewildered, horrified, stunned by this cruel perversion, I could not speak. But I trust that I looked innocent, being so.

'Listen to me, shrewd hypocrite,' said my Lady, whose anger increased as she gave it utterance. 'Attend to my words, you cunning schemer who carried this plot through with such a practised double face that I have never suspected you. I had my projects for my daughter; projects for family connexion; projects for fortune. You have thwarted them, and over-reached me; but I am not one to be thwarted and over-reached, without retaliation. Do you mean to hold this Living, another month?'

'Do you deem it possible, Lady Fareway, that I can hold it another hour, under your injurious words?'

'Is it resigned then?'

'It was mentally resigned, my Lady, some minutes ago.'

'Don't equivocate, sir. *Is* it resigned?'

'Unconditionally and entirely. And I would that I had never, never, come near it!'

'A cordial response from me to *that* wish, Mr Silverman! But take this with you, sir. If you had not resigned it, I would have had you deprived of it. And though you have resigned it, you will not get quit of me as easily as you think for. I will

pursue you with this story. I will make this nefarious conspiracy of yours, for money, known. You have made money
by it, but you have, at the same time, made an enemy by it.
You will take good care that the money sticks to you; *I* will
take good care that the enemy sticks to you.'

Then said I, finally: 'Lady Fareway, I think my heart is
broken. Until I came into this room just now, the possibility
of such mean wickedness as you have imputed to me, never
dawned upon my thoughts. Your suspicions—'

'Suspicions. Pah!' said she indignantly. 'Certainties.'

'Your certainties, my Lady, as you call them; your suspicions, as I call them; are cruel, unjust, wholly devoid of
foundation in fact. I can declare no more, except that I have
not acted for my own profit or my own pleasure. I have not in
this proceeding, considered myself. Once again, I think my
heart is broken. If I have unwittingly done any wrong with a
righteous motive, that is some penalty to pay.'

She received this with another and a more indignant 'Pah!'
and I made my way out of her room (I think I felt my way out
with my hands, although my eyes were open), almost suspecting that my voice had a repulsive sound, and that I was a
repulsive object.

There was a great stir made, the Bishop was appealed to. I
received a severe reprimand, and narrowly escaped suspen-
sion. For years a cloud hung over me, and my name was
tarnished. But my heart did not break, if a broken heart
involves death; for I lived through it.

They stood by me, Adelina and her husband, through it all.
Those who had known me at College, and even most of those
who had only known me there by reputation, stood by me
too. Little by little, the belief widened that I was not capable of
what was laid to my charge. At length, I was presented to a
College-Living in a sequestered place, and there I now pen my
Explanation. I pen it at my open window in the summer-time;
before me, lying the churchyard, equal resting-place for sound
hearts, wounded hearts, and broken hearts. I pen it for the
relief of my own mind, not foreseeing whether or no it will
ever have a reader.

SKETCHES OF YOUNG COUPLES

by Charles Dickens

The Young Couple

There is to be a wedding this morning at the corner house in
the terrace. The pastry-cook's people have been there half a
dozen times already; all day yesterday there was a great stir
and bustle, and they were up this morning as soon as it was
light. Miss Emma Fielding is going to be married to young
Mr Harvey.

Heaven alone can tell in what bright colours this marriage is
painted upon the mind of the little housemaid at number six,
who has hardly slept a wink all night with thinking of it, and
now stands on the unswept door-steps leaning upon her
broom, and looking wistfully towards the enchanted house.
Nothing short of omniscience can divine what visions of the
baker, or the greengrocer, or the smart and most insinuating
butterman, are flitting across her mind – what thoughts of
how she would dress on such an occasion, if she were a lady –
of how she would dress, if she were only a bride – of how
cook would dress, being bridesmaid, conjointly with her sister
'in place' at Fulham, and how the clergyman, deeming them
so many ladies, would be quite humbled and respectful. What
day-dreams of hope and happiness – of life being one perpetual
holiday, with no master and no mistress to grant or withhold
it – of every Sunday being a Sunday out – of pure freedom as
to curls and ringlets, and no obligation to hide fine heads of
hair in caps – what pictures of happiness, vast and immense to
her, but utterly ridiculous to us, bewilder the brain of the little
housemaid at number six, all called into existence by the
wedding at the corner!

We smile at such things, and so we should, though perhaps

for a better reason than commonly presents itself. It should be pleasant to us to know that there are notions of happiness so moderate and limited, since upon those who entertain them, happiness and lightness of heart are very easily bestowed.

But the little housemaid is awakened from her reverie, for forth from the door of the magical corner house there runs towards her, all fluttering in smart new dress and streaming ribands, her friend Jane Adams, who comes all out of breath to redeem a solemn promise of taking her in, under cover of the confusion, to see the breakfast table spread forth in state, and – sight of sights! – her young mistress ready dressed for church.

And there, in good truth, when they have stolen upstairs on tiptoe and edged themselves in at the chamber-door – there is Miss Emma 'looking like the sweetest picter,' in a white chip bonnet and orange flower, and all other elegancies becoming a bride (with the make, shape, and quality of every article of which the girl is perfectly familiar in one moment, and never forgets to her dying day) – and there is Miss Emma's mamma in tears, and Miss Emma's sister with her arms round her neck, and the other bridesmaid all smiles and tears, quieting the children, who would cry more but that they are so finely dressed, and yet sob for fear sister Emma should be taken away – and it is all so affecting, that the two servant-girls cry more than anybody; and Jane Adams, sitting down upon the stairs, when they have crept away, declares that her legs tremble so that she don't know what to do, and that she will say for Miss Emma, that she never had a hasty word from her, and that she does hope and pray she may be happy.

But Jane soon comes round again, and then surely there never was anything like the breakfast table, glittering with plate and china, and set out with flowers and sweets, and long-necked bottles, in the most sumptuous and dazzling manner. In the centre, too, is the mighty charm, the cake, glistening with frosted sugar, and garnished beautiful. They agree that there ought to be a little Cupid under one of the barley-sugar temples, or at least two hearts and an arrow; but, with this exception, there is nothing to wish for, and a table could not be handsomer. As they arrive at this conclusion, who should come in but Mr John! to whom Jane says that it's only Anne from number six; and John says *he* knows, for he's often winked his eye down the area, which causes Anne to blush and look confused. She is going away, indeed; when Mr John will have it that she must drink a glass of wine, and he says never mind it's being early in the morning, it won't hurt her: so they shut the door and pour out the wine; and Anne drinking Jane's health, and adding, 'and here's wishing you yours, Mr John,' drinks it in a great many sips – Mr John all the time making jokes appropriate to the occasion. At last Mr John, who has waxed bolder by degrees, pleads the usage at weddings, and claims the privilege of a kiss, which he obtains after a great scuffle; and footsteps being now heard on the stairs, they disperse suddenly.

By this time a carriage has driven up to convey the bride to church, and Anne of number six prolonging the process of 'cleaning her door,' has the satisfaction of beholding the bride and bridesmaids, and the papa and mamma, hurrying into the same and drive rapidly off. Nor is this all, for soon other carriages begin to arrive with a posse of company all beautifully dressed, at whom she could stand and gaze for ever; but having something else to do, is compelled to take one last long look and shut the street-door.

And now the company have gone down to breakfast, and tears have given place to smiles, for all the corks are out of the long-necked bottles, and their contents is disappearing rapidly. Miss Emma's papa is at the top of the table; Miss Emma's mamma at the bottom; and beside the latter are Miss Emma herself and her husband – admitted on all hands to be the handsomest and most interesting young couple ever known. All down both sides of the table, too, are various young ladies, beautiful to see, and various young gentlemen who seem to think so; and there, in a post of honour, is an unmarried aunt of Miss Emma's, reported to possess unheard-of riches, and to have expressed vast testamentary intentions respecting her favourite niece and new nephew. This lady has been very liberal and generous already, as the jewels worn by the bride abundantly testify, but that is nothing to what she means to do, or even to what she has done, for she put herself in close communication with the dressmaker three months ago, and prepared a wardrobe (with some articles worked by her own hands) fit for a Princess. People may call her an old maid, and so she may be, but she is neither cross nor ugly for all that; on the contrary, she is very cheerful and pleasant-looking, and very kind and tender-hearted: which is no matter of surprise except to those who yield to popular prejudices without thinking why, and will never grow wiser and never know better.

Of all the company though, none are more pleasant to behold or better pleased with themselves than two young children, who, in honour of the day, have seats among the guests. Of these, one is a little fellow of six or eight years old, brother to the bride, – and the other a girl of the same age, or something younger, whom he calls 'his wife.' The real bride and bridegroom are not more devoted than they: he all love and attention, and she all blushes and fondness, toying with a little bouquet which he gave her this morning, and placing the scattered rose-leaves in her bosom with nature's own coquettishness. They have dreamt of each other in their quiet dreams, these children, and their little hearts have been dispraised in jest. When will there come in after-life a passion so earnest, generous, and true as theirs; what, even in its gentlest realities, can have the grace and charm that hover round such fairy lovers!

By this time the merriment and happiness of the feast have gained their height; certain ominous looks begin to be exchanged between the bridesmaids, and somehow it gets whispered about that the carriage which is to take the young couple into the country has arrived. Such members of the party as are most disposed to prolong its enjoyments, affect to consider this a false alarm, but it turns out too true, being speedily confirmed, first by the retirement of the bride and a select file of intimates who are to prepare her for the journey, and secondly by the withdrawal of the ladies generally. To this there ensues a particularly awkward pause, in which everybody essays to be facetious, and nobody succeeds; at length the bridegroom makes a mysterious disappearance in obedience to some equally mysterious signal; and the table is deserted.

Now, for at least six weeks last past it has been solemnly devised and settled that the young couple should go away in secret; but they no sooner appear without the door than the drawing-room windows are blocked up with ladies waving their handkerchiefs and kissing their hands, and the dining-room panes with gentlemen's faces beaming farewell in every queer variety of its expression. The hall and steps are crowded with servants in white favours, mixed up with particular friends and relations who have darted out to say goodbye; and foremost in the group are the tiny lovers arm in arm, thinking, with fluttering hearts, what happiness it would be to dash away together in that gallant coach, and never part again.

The bride has barely time for one hurried glance at her old home, when the steps rattle, the door slams, the horses clatter on the pavement, and they have left it far away.

A knot of women servants still remain clustered in the hall, whispering among themselves, and there of course is Anne from number six, who has made another escape on some plea or other, and been an admiring witness of the departure. There are two points on which Anne expatiates over and over again, without the smallest appearance of fatigue or intending to leave off; one is, that she 'never see in all her life such a – oh such a angel of a gentleman as Mr Harvey' – and the other, that she 'can't tell how it is, but, it don't seem a bit like a work-a-day, or a Sunday neither – it's all so unsettled and unregular.'

The Formal Couple

The formal couple are the most prim cold, immovable, and unsatisfactory people on the face of the earth. Their faces, voices, dress, house, furniture, walk, and manner, are all the essence of formality, unrelieved by one redeeming touch of frankness, heartiness, or nature.

Everything with the formal couple resolves itself into a matter of form. They don't call upon you on your account, but their own; not to see how you are, but to show how they are: it is not a ceremony to do honour to you, but to themselves – not due to your position, but to theirs. If one of a friend's children die, the formal couple are as sure and punctual in sending to the house as the undertaker; if a friend's family be increased, the monthly nurse is not more attentive than they. The formal couple, in fact, joyfully sieze all occasions of testifying their good-breeding and precise observance of the little usages of society; and for you, who are the means to this end, they care as much as a man does for the tailor who has enabled him to cut a figure, or a woman for the milliner who has assisted her to a conquest.

Having an extensive connexion among that kind of people who make acquaintances and eschew friends, the formal gentleman attends from time to time a great many funerals, to which he is formally invited, and to which he formally goes, as returning a call for the last time. Here his deportment is of the most faultless description; he knows the exact pitch of voice it is proper to assume, the sombre look he ought to wear, the melancholy tread which should be his gait for the day. He is perfectly acquainted with all the dreary courtesies to be observed in a mourning-coach; knows when to sigh, and when to hide his nose in the white handkerchief; and looks into the grave and shakes his head when the ceremony is concluded, with the sad formality of a mute.

'What kind of funeral was it?' says the formal lady, when he returns home. 'Oh!' replies the formal gentleman, 'there never was such a gross and disgusting impropriety; there were no feathers.' 'No feathers!' cries the lady, as if on wings of black feathers dead people fly to Heaven, and, lacking them, they must of necessity go elsewhere. Her husband shakes his head; and further adds, that they had seed-cake instead of plum-cake, and that it was all white wine. 'All white wine!' exclaims his wife. 'Nothing but sherry and madeira,' says the husband. 'What! No port?' 'Not a drop.' No port, no plums, and no feathers! 'You will recollect, my dear,' says the formal lady, in a voice of stately reproof, 'that when we first met this poor man who is now dead and gone, and he took that very strange course of addressing me at dinner without being previously introduced, I ventured to express my opinion that the family were quite ignorant of etiquette, and very imperfectly acquainted with the decencies of life. You have now had a good opportunity of judging for yourself, and all I have to say is, that I trust you will never go to a funeral *there* again.' 'My dear,' replies the formal gentleman, 'I never will.' So the informal deceased is cut in his grave; and the formal couple, when they tell the story of the funeral, shake their heads, and wonder what some people's feelings *are* made of, and what their notions of propriety *can* be!

If the formal couple have a family (which they sometimes have), they are not children, but little, pale, sour, sharp-nosed men and women; and so exquisitely brought up, that they might be very old dwarfs for anything that appeareth to the contrary. Indeed, they are so acquainted with forms and conventionalities, and conduct themselves with such strict decorum, that to see the little girl break a looking-glass in some wild outbreak, or the little boy kick his parents, would be to any visitor an unspeakable relief and consolation.

The formal couple are always sticklers for what is rigidly proper, and have a great readiness in detecting hidden impropriety of speech or thought, which by less scrupulous people would be wholly unsuspected. Thus, if they pay a visit to the theatre, they sit all night in a perfect agony lest anything improper or immoral should proceed from the stage; and if anything should happen to be said which admits of a double construction, they never fail to take it up directly, and to express by their looks the great outrage which their feelings have sustained. Perhaps this is their chief reason for absenting themselves almost entirely from places of public amusement. They go sometimes to the Exhibition of the Royal Academy; – but that is often more shocking than the stage itself, and the formal lady thinks that it really is high time Mr Etty was prosecuted and made a public example of.

We made one at a christening party not long since, where there were amongst the guests a formal couple, who suffered the acutest torture from certain jokes, incidental to such an occasion, cut – and very likely dried also – by one of the godfathers; a red-faced elderly gentleman, who, being highly popular with the rest of the company, had it all his own way, and was in great spirits. It was at supper-time that this gentleman came out in full force. We – being of a grave and quiet demeanour – had been chosen to escort the formal lady downstairs, and, sitting beside her, had a favourable opportunity of observing her emotions.

We have a shrewd suspicion that, in the very beginning, and in the first blush – literally the first blush – of the matter, the formal lady had not felt quite certain whether the being present at such a ceremony, and encouraging, as it were, the public exhibition of a baby, was not an act involving some degree of indelicacy and impropriety; but certain we are, that when the baby's health was drunk, and allusions were made, by a grey-headed gentleman proposing it, to the time when he had dandled in his arms the young Christian's mother – certain we are that then the formal lady took the alarm, and recoiled from the old gentleman as from a hoary profligate. Still she bore it; she fanned herself with an indignant air, but still she bore it. A comic song was sung, involving a confession from some imaginary gentleman that he had kissed a female, and yet the formal lady bore it. But when at last, the health of the godfather before-mentioned being drunk, the godfather rose to return thanks, and in the course of his observations darkly hinted at babies yet unborn, and even contemplated the possibility of the subject of that festival having brothers and sisters, the formal lady could endure no more, but, bowing slightly round, and sweeping haughtily past the offender, left the room in tears, under the protection of the formal gentleman.

The Loving Couple

There cannot be a better practical illustration of the wise saw and ancient instance, that there may be too much of a good thing, than is presented by a loving couple. Undoubtedly it is meet and proper that two persons joined together in holy matrimony should be loving, and unquestionably it is pleasant to know and see that they are so; but there is a time for all things, and the couple who happen to be always in a loving state before company, are well-nigh intolerable.

And in taking up this position we would have it distinctly understood that we do not seek alone the sympathy of bachelors, in whose objection to loving couples we recognise interested motives and personal considerations. We grant that to that unfortunate class of society there may be something very irritating, tantalising, and provoking, in being compelled to witness those gentle endearments and chaste interchanges which to loving couples are quite the ordinary business of life. But while we recognise the natural character of the prejudice to which these unhappy men are subject, we can neither receive their biased evidence, nor address ourself to their inflamed and angered minds. Dispassionate experience is our only guide; and in these moral essays we seek no less to reform hymeneal offenders than to hold out a timely warning to all rising couples, and even to those who have not yet set forth upon their pilgrimage towards the matrimonial altar.

Let all couples, present or to come, therefore profit by the example of Mr and Mrs Leaver, themselves a loving couple in the first degree.

Mr and Mrs Leaver are pronounced by Mrs Starling, a widow lady who lost her husband when she was young, and lost herself about the same time – for by her own count she has never since grown five years older – to be a perfect model of wedded felicity. 'You would suppose,' says the romantic lady, 'that they were lovers only just now engaged. Never was such happiness! They are so tender, so affectionate, so attached to each other, so enamoured, that positively nothing can be more charming!'

'Augusta, my soul,' says Mr Leaver. 'Augustus, my life,' replies Mrs Leaver. 'Sing some little ballad, darling' quoth Mr Leaver. 'I couldn't, indeed, dearest,' returns Mrs Leaver. 'Do, my dove,' says Mr Leaver. 'I couldn't possibly, my love,' replies Mrs Leaver; 'and it's very naughty of you to ask me.' 'Naughty, darling!' cries Mr Leaver. 'Yes, very naughty, and very cruel,' returns Mrs Leaver, 'for you know I have a sore throat, and that to sing would give me great pain. You're a monster, and I hate you. Go away!' Mrs Leaver has said 'go away,' because Mr Leaver has tapped her under the chin: Mr Leaver not doing as he is bid, but on the contrary, sitting down beside her, Mrs Leaver slaps Mr Leaver; and Mr Leaver in return slaps Mrs Leaver, and it being now time for all persons present to look the other way, they look the other way, and hear a still small sound as of kissing, at which Mrs Starling is thoroughly enraptured, and whispers her neighbour that if all married couples were like that, what a heaven this earth would be!

The loving couple are at home when this occurs, and maybe only three or four friends are present, but, unaccustomed to reserve upon this interesting point, they are pretty much the same abroad. Indeed upon some occasions, such as a pic-nic or a water-party, their lovingness is even more developed, as we had an opportunity last summer of observing in person.

There was a great water-party made up to go to Twickenham and dine, and afterwards dance in an empty villa by the river-side, hired expressly for the purpose. Mr and Mrs Leaver were of the company; and it was our fortune to have a seat in the same boat, which was an eight-oared galley, manned by amateurs, with a blue striped awning of the same pattern as their Guernsey shirts, and a dingy red flag of the same shade as the whiskers of the stroke oar. A coxswain being appointed, and all other matters adjusted, the eight gentlemen threw themselves into strong paroxysms, and pulled up with the tide, stimulated by the compassionate remarks of the ladies, who one and all exclaimed, that it seemed an immense exertion – as indeed it did. At first we raced the other boat, which came alongside in gallant style; but this being found an unpleasant amusement, as giving rise to a great quantity of splashing, and rendering the cold pies and other viands very moist, it was unanimously voted down, and we were suffered to shoot a-head, while the second boat followed ingloriously in our wake.

It was at this time that we first recognised Mr Leaver. There were two firemen-watermen in the boat, lying by until somebody was exhausted; and one of them, who had taken upon himself the direction of affairs, was heard to cry in a gruff voice, 'Pull away, number two – give it her, number two – take a longer reach, number two – now, number two, sir, think you're winning a boat.' The greater part of the company had no doubt begun to wonder which of the striped Guernseys it might be that stood in need of such encouragement, when a stifled shriek from Mrs Leaver confirmed the doubtful and informed the ignorant; and Mr Leaver, still further disguised in a straw hat and no neckcloth, was observed to be in a fearful perspiration, and failing visibly. Nor was the general consternation diminished at this instant by the same gentleman (in the performance of an accidental acquatic feat, termed 'catching a crab') plunging suddenly backward, and displaying nothing of himself to the company, but two violently struggling legs. Mrs Leaver shrieked again several times, and cried piteously – 'Is he dead? Tell me the worst. Is he dead?'

Now, a moment's reflection might have convinced the loving wife, that unless her husband were endowed with some most surprising powers of muscular action, he never could be dead while he kicked so hard; but still Mrs Leaver cried, 'Is he dead? Is he dead?' and still everybody else cried – 'No, no, no,' until such time as Mr Leaver was replaced in a sitting posture, and his oar (which had been going through all kinds of wrong-headed performances on its own account) was once more put in his hand, by the exertions of the two firemen-watermen. Mrs Leaver then exclaimed, 'Augustus, my child, come to me'; and Mr Leaver said, 'Augusta, my love, compose yourself, I am not injured.' But Mrs Leaver cried again more piteously than before, 'Augustus, my child, come to me'; and now the company generally, who seemed to be apprehensive that if Mr Leaver remained where he was, he might contribute more than his proper share towards the drowning of the party, disinterestedly took part with Mrs Leaver, and said he really ought to go, and that he was not strong enough for such violent exercise, and ought never to have undertaken it. Reluctantly, Mr Leaver went, and laid himself down at Mrs Leaver's feet, and Mrs Leaver stooping over him said, 'Oh, Augustus, how could you terrify me so?' and Mr Leaver said, 'Augusta, my sweet, I never meant to terrify you'; and Mrs Leaver said, 'You are faint, my dear'; and Mr Leaver said, 'I am rather so, my love'; and they were very loving indeed under Mrs Leaver's veil, until at length Mr Leaver came forth again, and pleasantly asked if he had not heard something said about bottled stout and sandwiches.

Mrs Starling, who was one of the party, was perfectly delighted with this scene, and frequently murmured half-aside, 'What a loving couple you are!' or 'How delightful it is to see man and wife so happy together!' To us she was quite poetical (for we are a kind of cousins), observing that hearts beating in unison like that made life a paradise of sweets; and that when kindred creatures were drawn together by sympathies so fine and delicate, what more than mortal happiness did not our souls partake! To all this we answered 'Certainly,' or

'Very true,' or merely sighed, as the case might be. At every new act of the loving couple, the widow's admiration broke out afresh; and when Mrs Leaver would not permit Mr Leaver to keep his hat off, lest the sun should strike to his head, and give hime a brain fever, Mrs Starling actually shed tears, and said it reminded her of Adam and Eve.

The loving couple were thus loving all the way to Twickenham, but when we arrived there (by which time the amateur crew looked very thirsty and vicious) they were more playful than ever, for Mrs Leaver threw stones at Mr Leaver, and Mr Leaver ran after Mrs Leaver on the grass, in a most innocent and enchanting manner. At dinner, too, Mr Leaver *would* steal Mrs Leaver's tongue, and Mrs Leaver *would* retaliate upon Mr Leaver's fowl; and when Mrs Leaver was going to take some lobster salad, Mr Leaver wouldn't let her have any, saying that it made her ill, and she was always sorry for it afterwards, which afforded Mrs Leaver an opportunity of pretending to be cross, and showing many other prettinesses. But this was merely the smiling surface of their loves, not the mighty depths of the stream, down to which the company, to say the truth, dived rather unexpectedly, from the following accident. It chanced that Mr Leaver took upon himself to propose the bachelors who had first originated the notion of that entertainment, in doing which, he affected to regret that he was no longer of their body himself, and pretended grievously to lament his fallen state. This Mrs Leaver's feelings could not brook, even in jest, and consequently, exclaiming aloud, 'He loves me not, he loves me not!' she fell in a very pitiable state into the arms of Mrs Starling, and, directly becoming insensible, was conveyed by that lady and her husband into another room. Presently Mr Leaver came running back to know if there was a medical gentleman in company, and as there was (in what company is there not?) both Mr Leaver and the medical gentleman hurried away together.

The medical gentleman was the first who returned, and among his intimate friends he was observed to laugh and wink, and look as unmedical as might be; but when Mr Leaver came back he was very solemn, and in answer to all inquiries, shook his head, and remarked that Augusta was far too sensitive to be trifled with – an opinion which the widow subsequently confirmed. Finding that she was in no imminent peril, however, the rest of the party betook themselves to dancing on the green, and very merry and happy they were, and a vast quantity of flirtation there was; the last circumstance being no doubt attributable, partly to the fineness of the weather, and partly to the locality, which is well known to be favourable to all harmless recreations.

In the bustle of the scene, Mr and Mrs Leaver stole down to the boat, and disposed themselves under the awning, Mrs Leaver reclining her head upon Mr Leaver's shoulder, and Mr Leaver grasping her hand with great fervour, and looking in her face from time to time with a melancholy and sympathetic aspect. The widow sat apart, feigning to be occupied with a book, but stealthily observing them from behind her fan; and the two firemen-watermen, smoking their pipes on the bank hard by, nudged each other, and grinned in enjoyment of the joke. Very few of the party missed the loving couple; and the few who did, heartily congratulated each other on their disappearance.

The Contradictory Couple

One would suppose that two people who are to pass their whole lives together, and must necessarily be very often alone with each other, could find little pleasure in mutual contradiction; and yet what is more common than a contradictory couple?

The contradictory couple agree in nothing but contradiction. They return home from Mrs Bluebottle's dinner-party, each in an opposite corner of the coach, and do not exchange a syllable until they have been seated for at least twenty minutes by the fireside at home, when the gentleman, raising his eyes from the stove, all at once breaks silence:

'What a very extraordinary thing it is,' says he, 'that you *will* contradict, Charlotte!' '*I* contradict!' cries the lady, 'but that's just like you.' 'What's like me?' says the gentleman sharply. 'Saying that I contradict you,' replies the lady. 'Do you mean to say that you do *not* contradict me?' retorts the gentleman; 'do you mean to say that you have not been contradicting me the whole of this day? Do you mean to tell me now, that you have not?' 'I mean to tell you nothing of the kind,' replies the lady quietly; 'when you are wrong, of course I shall contradict you.'

During this dialogue the gentleman has been taking his brandy-and-water on one side of the fire, and the lady, with her dressing-case on the table, has been curling her hair on the other. She now lets down her back hair, and proceeds to brush it; preserving at the same time an air of conscious rectitude and suffering virtue, which is intended to exasperate the gentleman – and does so.

'I do believe,' he says, taking the spoon out of his glass, and tossing it on the table, 'that of all the obstinate, positive, wrong-headed creatures that were ever born, you are the most so, Charlotte.' 'Certainly, certainly, have it your own way, pray. You see how much *I* contradict you,' rejoins the lady. 'Of course, you didn't contradict me at dinner-time – oh no, not you!' says the gentleman. 'Yes, I did,' says the lady. 'Oh, you did,' cries the gentleman; 'you admit that?' 'If you call that contradiction, I do,' the lady answers; 'and I say again, Edward, that when I know you are wrong, I will contradict you. I am not your slave.' 'Not my slave!' repeats the gentleman bitterly; 'and you still mean to say that in the Blackburns' new house there are not more than fourteen-doors, including the door of the wine-cellar!' 'I mean to say,' retorts the lady, beating time with her hair-brush on the palm of her hand, 'that in that house there are fourteen doors and no more.' 'Well then—' cries the gentleman, rising in despair, and pacing the room with rapid strides. 'By G—, this is enough to destroy a man's intellect, and drive him mad!'

By and by the gentleman comes-to a little, and passing his hand gloomily across his forehead, reseats himself in his former chair. There is a long silence, and this time the lady begins. 'I appealed to Mr Jenkins, who sat next to me on the sofa in the drawing-room during tea—' 'Morgan, you mean,' interrupts the gentleman. 'I do not mean anything of the kind,' answers the lady. 'Now, by all that is aggravating and impossible to bear,' cries the gentleman, clenching his hands and looking upwards in agony, 'she is going to insist upon it that Morgan is Jenkins!' 'Do you take me for a perfect fool?'

exclaimes the lady; 'do you suppose I don't know the one from the other? Do you suppose I don't know that the man in the blue coat was Mr Jenkins?' 'Jenkins in a blue coat!' cries the gentleman with a groan; 'Jenkins in a blue coat! A man who would suffer death rather than wear anything but brown!' 'Do you dare to charge me with telling an untruth?' demands the lady, bursting into tears. 'I charge you, ma'am,' retorts the gentleman, starting up, 'with being a monster of contradiction, a monster of aggravation, a-a-a-Jenkins in a blue coat! What have I done that I should be doomed to hear such statements!'

Expressing himself with great scorn and anguish, the gentleman takes up his candle and stalks off to bed, where feigning to be fast asleep when the lady comes upstairs drowned in tears, murmuring lamentations over her hard fate and indistinct intentions of consulting her brothers, he undergoes the secret torture of hearing her exclaim between whiles, 'I know there are only fourteen doors in the house, I know it was Mr Jenkins, I know he had a blue coat on, and I would say it as positively as I do now, if they were the last words I had to speak!'

If the contradictory couple are blessed with children, they are not the less contradictory on that account. Master James and Miss Charlotte present themselves after dinner, and being in perfect good humour, and finding their parents in the same amiable state, augur from these appearances half a glass of wine a-piece and other extraordinary indulgences. But unfortunately Master James, growing talkative upon such prospects, asks his mamma how tall Mrs Parsons is, and whether she is not six feet high; to which his mamma replies, 'Yes, she should think she was, for Mrs Parsons is a very tall lady indeed; quite a giantess.' 'For Heaven's sake, Charlotte,' cries her husband, 'do not tell the child such preposterous nonsense. Six feet high!' 'Well,' replies the lady, 'surely I may be permitted to have an opinion; my opinion is, that she is six feet high – at least six feet.' 'Now you know, Charlotte,' retorts the gentleman sternly, 'that that is *not* your opinion – that you have no such idea – and that you only say this for the sake of contradiction.' 'You are exceedingly polite,' his wife replies; 'to be wrong about such a paltry question as anybody's height, would be no great crime; but I say again, that I believe Mrs Parsons to be six feet – more than six feet; nay, I believe you know her to be full six feet, and only say she is not, because I say she is.' This taunt disposes the gentleman to become violent, but he checks himself, and is content to mutter in a haughty tone, 'Six feet – ha! ha! Mrs Parsons six feet!' and the lady answers, 'Yes, six feet. I am sure I am glad you are amused, and I'll say it again – six feet.' Thus the subject gradually drops off, and the contradiction begins to be forgotten, when Master James, with some undefined notion of making himself agreeable, and putting things to rights again, unfortunately asks his mamma what the moon's made of; which gives her occasion to say that he had better not ask her, for she is always wrong and never can be right; that he only exposes her to contradiction by asking any question of her; and that he had better ask his papa, who is infallible, and never can be wrong. Papa, smarting under this attack, gives a terrible pull at the bell, and says, that if the conversation is to proceed in this way, the children had better be removed. Removed they are, after a few tears and many struggles; and Pa having looked at Ma sideways for a minute or two, with a baleful eye, draws his pocket-handkerchief over his face, and composes himself for his after-dinner nap.

The friends of the contradictory couple often deplore their frequent disputes, though they rather make light of them at the same time: observing, that there is no doubt they are very much attached to each other, and that they never quarrel except about trifles. But neither the friends of the contradictory couple, nor the contradictory couple themselves, reflect that as the most stupendous objects in nature are but vast collections of minute particles, so the slightest and least considered trifles make up the sum of human happiness or misery.

The Doting Couple
(The couple who dote upon their children)

The couple who dote upon their children have usually a great many of them: six or eight at least. The children are either the

healthiest in all the world, or the most unfortunate in existence. In either case, they are equally the theme of their doting
parents, and equally a source of mental anguish and irritation
to their doting parents' friends.

The couple who dote upon their children recognise no dates
but those connected with their births, accidents, illnesses, or
remarkable deeds. They keep a mental almanack with a vast
number of Innocents'-days, all in red letters. They recollect
the last coronation, because on that day little Tom fell down
the kitchen stairs; the anniversary of the Gunpowder Plot,
because it was on the fifth of November that Ned asked
whether wooden legs were made in heaven and cocked hats
grew in gardens. Mrs Whiffler will never cease to recollect the
last day of the old year as long as she lives, for it was on that
day that the baby had the four red spots on its nose which they
took for measles: nor Christmas-day, for twenty-one days
after Christmas-day the twins were born; nor Good Friday,
for it was on a Good Friday that she was frightened by the
donkey-cart when she was in the family way with Georgina.
The movable feasts have no motion for Mr and Mrs Whiffler,
but remain pinned down tight and fast to the shoulders of
some small child, from whom they can never be separated any
more. Time was made, according to their creed, not for slaves
but for girls and boys; the restless sands in his glass are but
little children at play.

As we have already intimated, the children of this couple
can know no medium. They are either prodigies of good
health or prodigies of bad health; whatever they are, they must
be prodigies. Mr Whiffler must have to describe at his office
such excruciating agonies constantly undergone by his eldest
boy, as nobody else's eldest boy ever underwent; or he must
be able to declare that there never was a child endowed with
such amazing health, such an indomitable constitution, and
such a cast-iron frame, as his child. His children must be, in
some respect or other, above and beyond the children of all
other people. To such an extent is this feeling pushed, that we
were once slightly acquainted with a lady and gentleman who
carried their heads so high and became so proud after their
youngest child fell out of a two-pair-of-stairs window without
hurting himself much, that the greater part of their friends

were obliged to forego their acquaintance. But perhaps this may be an extreme case, and one not justly entitled to be considered as a precedent of general application.

If a friend happen to dine in a friendly way with one of these couples who dote upon their children, it is nearly impossible for him to divert the conversation from their favourite topic. Everything reminds Mr Whiffler of Ned, or Mrs Whiffler of Mary Anne, or of the time before Ned was born, or the time before Mary Anne was thought of. The slightest remark, however harmless in itself, with awaken slumbering recollections of the twins. It is impossible to steer clear of them. They will come uppermost, let the poor man do what he may. Ned has been known to be lost sight of for half an hour, Dick has been forgotten, the name of Mary Anne has not been mentioned, but the twins will out. Nothing can keep down the twins.

'It's a very extraordinary thing, Saunders,' says Mr Whiffler to the visitor, 'but – you have seen our little babies, the – the – twins?' The friend's heart sinks within him as he answers, 'Oh, yes – often.' 'Your talking of the Pyramids,' says Mr Whiffler, quite as a matter of course, 'reminds me of the twins. It's a very extraordinary thing about those babies – what colour should you say their eyes were?' 'Upon my word,' the friend stammers, 'I hardly know how to answer' – the fact being, that except as the friend does not remember to have heard of any departure from the ordinary course of nature in the instance of these twins, they might have no eyes at all for aught he has observed to the contrary. 'You wouldn't say they were red, I suppose?' says Mr Whiffler. The friend hesitates, and rather thinks they are; but inferring from the expression of Mr Whiffler's face that red is not the colour, smiles with some confidence, and says, 'No, no! Very different from that.' 'What should you say to blue?' says Mr Whiffler. The friend glances at him, and observing a different expression in his face, ventures to say, 'I should say they *were* blue – a decided blue.' 'To be sure!' cries Mr Whiffler, triumphantly, 'I knew you would! But what should you say if I was to tell you that the boy's eyes are blue and the girl's hazel, eh?' 'Impossible!' exclaims the friend, not at all knowing why it should be impossible. 'A fact, notwithstanding,' cries Mr Whiffler; 'and let me tell you, Saunders, *that's* not a common thing in twins, or a circumstance that'll happen every day.'

In this dialogue Mrs Whiffler, as being deeply responsible for the twins, their charms and singularities, has taken no share; but she now relates, in broken English, a witticism of little Dick's bearing upon the subject just discussed, which delights Mr Whiffler beyond measure, and causes him to declare that he would have sworn that was Dick's if he had heard it anywhere. Then he requests that Mrs Whiffler will tell Saunders what Tom said about mad bulls; and Mrs Whiffler relating the anecdote, a discussion ensues upon the different character of Tom's wit and Dick's wit, from which it appears that Dick's humour is of a lively turn, while Tom's style is the dry and caustic. This discussion, being enlivened by various illustrations, lasts a long time, and is only stopped by Mrs Whiffler instructing the footman to ring the nursery bell, as the children were promised that they should come down and taste the pudding.

The friend turns pale when this order is given, and paler still when it is followed up by a great pattering on the staircase, (not unlike the sound of rain upon a skylight,) a violent bursting open of the dining-room door, and the tumultuous appearance of six small children, closely succeeded by a strong nursery-maid with a twin in each arm. As the whole eight are screaming, shouting, or kicking – some influenced by a ravenous appetite, some by a horror of the stranger, and some by a conflict of the two feelings – a pretty long space elapses before all their heads can be ranged round the table and anything like order restored; in bringing about which happy state of things both the nurse and footman are severely scratched. At length Mrs Whiffler is heard to say, 'Mr Saunders, shall I give you some pudding?' A breathless silence ensues, and sixteen small eyes are fixed upon the guest in expectation of his reply. A wild shout of joy proclaims that he has said 'No, thank you.' Spoons are waved in the air, legs appear above the table-cloth in uncontrollable ecstasy, and eighty short fingers dabble in damson syrup.

While the pudding is being disposed of, Mr and Mrs Whiffler look on with beaming countenances, and Mr Whiffler nudging his friend Saunders, begs him to take notice of Tom's eyes, or Dick's chin, or Ned's nose, or Mary Anne's hair, or Emily's figure, or little Bob's calves, or Fanny's mouth, or Carry's head, as the case may be. Whatever the attention of Mr Saunders is called to, Mr Saunders admires of course; though he is rather confused about the sex of the youngest branches and looks at the wrong children, turning to a girl when Mr Whiffler directs his attention to a boy, and falling into raptures with a boy when he ought to be enchanged with a girl. Then the dessert comes, and there is a vast deal of scrambling after fruit, and sudden spiriting forth of juice out of tight oranges into infant eyes, and much screeching and wailing in consequence. At length it becomes time for Mrs Whiffler to retire, and all the children are by force of arms compelled to kiss and love Mr Saunders before going upstairs, except Tom, who, lying on his back in the hall, proclaims that Mr Saunders 'is a naughty beast'; and Dick, who having drunk his father's wine when he was looking another way, is found to be intoxicated and is carried out, very limp and helpless.

Mr Whiffler and his friend are left alone together, but Mr Whiffler's thoughts are still with his family, if his family are not with him. 'Saunders' says he, after a short silence, 'if you please, we'll drink Mrs Whiffler and the children.' Mr Saunders feels this to be a reproach against himself for not proposing the same sentiment, and drinks it in some confusion. 'Ah!' Mr Whiffler sighs, 'these children, Saunders, make one quite an old man.' Mr Saunders things that if they were his, they would make him a very old man; but he says nothing. 'And yet,' pursues Mr Whiffler, 'what can equal domestic happiness? What can equal the engaging ways of children! Saunders, why don't *you* get married?' Now, this is an embarrassing question, because Mr Saunders has been thinking that if he had at any time entertained matrimonial designs, the revelation of that day would surely have routed them for ever. 'I am glad, however,' says Mr Whiffler, 'that you *are* a bachelor – glad on one account, Saunders; a selfish one, I admit. Will you do Mrs Whiffler and myself a favour?' Mr Saunders is surprised – evidently surprised; but he replies, 'with the greatest pleasure.' 'Then, will you, Saunders,' says Mr Whiffler, in an impressive manner, 'will you cement and consolidate our friendship by coming into the family (so to speak) as a godfather?' 'I shall be proud and delighted,' replies Mr Saunders: 'which of the children is it? Really, I thought they were all christened; or—' 'Saunders,' Mr Whiffler interposes, 'they *are* all christened; you are right. The fact is, that Mrs Whiffler is – in short, we expect another.' 'Not a ninth!' cries the friend, all aghast at the idea. 'Yes, Saunders,' rejoins Mr Whiffler, solemnly, 'a ninth. Did we drink Mrs Whiffler's health? Let us drink it again, Saunders, and wish her well over it!'

Doctor Johnson used to tell a story of a man who had but one idea, which was a wrong one. The couple who dote upon their children are in the same predicament: at home or abroad, at all times, and in all places, their thoughts are bound up in this one subject, and have no sphere beyond. They relate the clever things their offspring say or do, and weary every company with their prolixity and absurdity. Mr Whiffler takes a friend by the button at a street corner on a windy day to tell him a *bon mot* of his youngest boy's; and Mrs Whiffler, calling to see a sick acquaintance, entertains her with a cheerful account of all her own past sufferings and present expectations. In such cases the sins of the fathers indeed descend upon the children; for people soon come to regard them as predestined little bores. The couple who dote upon their children cannot be said to be actuated by a general love for these engaging little people (which would be a great excuse); for they are apt to underrate and entertain a jealousy of any children but their own. If they examined their own hearts, they would, perhaps, find at the bottom of all this, more self-love and egotism than they think of. Self-love and egotism are bad qualities, of which the unrestrained exhibition, though it may be sometimes amusing, never fails to be wearisome and unpleasant. Couples who dote upon their children, therefore, are best avoided.

The Cool Couple

There is an old-fashioned weather-glass representing a house with two doorways, in one of which is the figure of a gentleman, in the other the figure of a lady. When the weather is to be fine the lady comes out and the gentleman goes in; when wet, the gentleman comes out and the lady goes in. They never seek each other's society, and never elevated and depressed by the same cause, and have nothing in common. They are the model of a cool couple, except that there is something of politeness and consideration about the behaviour of the gentleman in the weather-glass, in which, neither of the cool couple can be said to participate.

The cool couple are seldom alone together, and when they are, nothing can exceed their apathy and dullness: the gentleman being for the most part drowsy, and the lady silent. If they enter into conversation, it is usually of an ironical or recriminatory nature. Thus, when the gentleman has indulged in a very long yawn and settled himself more snugly in his easy-chair, the lady will perhaps remark, 'Well, I am sure, Charles! I hope you're comfortable.' To which the gentleman replies, 'Oh yes, he's quite comfortable – quite.' 'There are not many married men, I hope,' returns the lady, 'who seek comfort in such selfish gratifications as you do.' 'Nor many wives who seek comfort in such selfish gratifications as *you* do, I hope,' retorts the gentleman. 'Whose fault is that?' demands the lady. The gentleman, becoming more sleepy, returns no answer. 'Whose fault is that?' the lady repeats. The gentleman still returning no answer, she goes on to say that she believes there never was in all this world anybody so attached to her home, so thoroughly domestic, so unwilling to seek a moment's gratification or pleasure beyond her own fireside as she. God knows that before she was married she never thought or dreamt of such a thing; and she remembers that her poor papa used to say again and again, almost every day of his life, 'Oh, my dear Louisa, if you only marry a man who understands you, and takes the trouble to consider your happiness and accommodate himself a very little to your disposition, what a treasure he will find in you!' She supposes her papa knew what her disposition was – he had known her long enough – he ought to have been acquainted with it, but what can she do? If her home is always dull and lonely, and her husband is always absent and finds no pleasure in her society, she is naturally sometimes driven (seldom enough, she is sure) to seek a little recreation elsewhere; she is not expected to pine and mope to death, she hopes. 'Then come, Louisa,' says the gentleman, waking up as suddenly as he fell asleep, 'stop at home this evening, and so will I.' 'I shoud be sorry to suppose, Charles, that you took a pleasure in aggravating me,' replies the lady; 'but you know as well as I do that I am particularly engaged to Mrs Mortimer, and that it would be an act of the grossest rudeness and ill-breeding, after accepting a seat in her box and preventing her from inviting anybody else, not to go.' 'Ah! there it is!' says the gentleman, shrugging his shoulders, 'I knew that perfectly well. I knew you couldn't devote an evening to your own home. Now all I have to say, Louisa, is this – recollect that *I* was quite willing to stay at home, and that it's no fault of *mine* we are not oftener together.'

With that the gentleman goes away to keep an old appointment at his club, and the lady hurries off to dress for Mrs Mortimer's; and neither thinks of the other until by some odd chance they find themselves alone again.

But it must not be supposed that the cool couple are habitually a quarrelsome one. Quite the contrary. These differences are only occasions for a little self-excuse, – nothing more. In general, they are as easy and careless, and dispute as seldom, as any common acquaintances may; for it is neither worth their while to put each other out of the way, nor to ruffle themselves.

When they meet in society, the cool couple are the best-bred people in existence. The lady is seated in a corner among a little knot of lady friends, one of whom exclaims, 'Why, I vow and declare there is your husband, my dear!' 'Whose? – mine?' she says, carelessly. 'Ay, yours, and coming this way too.' 'How very odd!' says the lady, in a languid tone, 'I thought he had been at Dover.' The gentleman coming up, and speaking to all the other ladies and nodding slightly to his wife, it turns out that he has been at Dover, and has just now returned. 'What a strange creature you are!' cries his wife; 'and what on earth brought you here, I wonder?' 'I came to look after you, *of course,*' rejoins her husband. This is so pleasant a jest that the lady is mightily amused, as are all the other ladies similarly situated who are within hearing; and while they are enjoying it to the full, the gentleman nods again, turns upon his heel, and saunters away.

There are times, however, when his company is not so agreeable, though equally unexpected; such as when the lady has invited one or two particular friends to tea and scandal, and he happens to come home in the very midst of their diversion. It is a hundred chances to one that he remains in the house half an hour, but the lady is rather disturbed by the intrusion, notwithstanding, and reasons within herself – 'I am sure I never interfere with him, and why should he interfere with me? It can scarcely be accidental; it never happens that I have a particular reason for not wishing him to come home, but he always comes. It's very provoking and tiresome; and I am sure when he leaves me so much alone for his own pleasure, the least he could do would be to do as much for mine.' Observing what passes in her mind, the gentleman, who has come home for his own accommodation, makes a merit of it with himself; arrives at the conclusion that it is the very last place in which he can hope to be comfortable; and determines, as he takes up his hat and cane, never to be so virtuous again.

Thus a great many cool couples go on until they are cold couples, and the grave has closed over their folly and indifference. Loss of name, station, character, life itself, has ensued from causes as slight as these, before now; and when gossips tell such tales, and aggravate their deformities, they elevate their hands and eyebrows, and call each other to witness what a cool couple Mr and Mrs So-and-So always were, even in the best of times.

The Plausible Couple

The plausible couple have many titles. They are 'a delightful couple,' an 'affectionate couple,' 'a most agreeable couple,' 'a good-hearted couple,' and 'the best-natured couple in existence.' The truth is, that the plausible couple are people of the world; and either the way of pleasing the world has grown much easier than it was in the days of the old man and his ass, or the old man was but a bad hand at it, and knew very little of the trade.

'But is it really possible to please the world?' says some doubting reader. It is indeed. Nay, it is not only very possible, but very easy. The ways are crooked, and sometimes foul and low. What then? A man need but crawl upon his hands and knees, know when to close his eyes and when his ears, when to stoop and when to stand upright; and if by the world is meant that atom of it in which he moves himself, he shall please it, never fear.

Now, it will be readily seen, that if a plausible man or woman have an easy means of pleasing the world by an adaptation of self to all its twistings and twinings, a plausible man *and* woman, or, in other words, a plausible couple, playing into each other's hands, and acting in concert, have a manifest advantage. Hence it is that plausible couples scarcely ever fail of success on a pretty large scale; and hence it is that if the reader, laying down this unwieldy volume at the next full stop, will have the goodness to review his or her circle of acquaintance, and to search particularly for some man and wife with a large connexion and a good name, not easily referable to their abilities or their wealth, he or she (that is, the male or female reader) will certainly find that gentleman or lady, on a very short reflection, to be a plausible couple.

The plausible couple are the most ecstatic people living: the most sensitive people – to merit – on the face of the earth. Nothing clever or virtuous escapes them. They have microscopic eyes for such endowments, and can find them anywhere. The plausible couple never fawn – oh no! They don't even scruple to tell their friends of their faults. One is too generous, another too candid; a third has a tendency to think all people like himself, and to regard mankind as a company of angels; a fourth is kindhearted to a fault. 'We never flatter, my dear Mrs Jackson,' say the plausible couple; 'we speak our minds. Neither you nor Mr Jackson have faults enough. It may sound strangely, but it is true. You have not faults enough. You know our way – we must speak out, and always do. Quarrel with us for saying so, if you will; but we repeat it – you have not faults enough!'

The plausible couple are no less plausible to each other than to third parties. They are always loving and harmonious. The plausible gentleman calls his wife 'darling,' and the plausible lady addresses him as 'dearest.' If it be Mr and Mrs Bobtail Widger, Mrs Widger is 'Lavinia, darling,' and Mr Widger is

'Bobtail, dearest.' Speaking of each other, they observe the same tender form. Mrs Widger relates what 'Bobtail' said, and Mr Widger recounts what 'darling' thought and did.

If you sit next to the plausible lady at a dinner-table, she takes the earliest opportunity of expressing her belief that you are acquainted with the Clickits; she is sure she has heard the Clickits speak of you – she must not tell you in what terms, or you will take her for a flatterer. You admit a knowledge of the Clickits; the plausible lady immediately launches out in their praise. She quite loves the Clickits. Were there ever such true-hearted, hospitable, excellent people – such a gentle, interesting little woman as Mrs Clickit, or such a frank, unaffected creature as Mr Clickit? Were there ever two people, in short, so little spoiled by the world as they are? 'As who, darling?' cries Mr Widger, from the opposite side of the table. 'The Clickits, dearest,' replies Mrs Widger. 'Indeed you are right, darling,' Mr Widger rejoins; 'the Clickits are a very high-minded, worthy, estimable couple.' Mrs Widger remarking that Bobtail always grows quite eloquent upon this subject, Mr Widger admits that he feels very strongly whenever such people as the Clickits and some other friends of his (here he glances at the host and hostess) are mentioned; for they are an honour to human nature, and do one good to think of. '*You* know the Clickits, Mrs Jackson?' he says, addressing the lady of the house. 'No, indeed; we have not that pleasure,' she replies. 'You astonish me!' exclaims Mr Widger: 'not know the Clickits! Why, you are the very people of all others who ought to be their bosom friends. You are kindred beings; you are one and the same thing: – not know the Clickits! Now *will* you know the Clickits? Will you make a point of knowing them? Will you meet them in a friendly way at our house one evening, and be acquainted with them?' Mrs Jackson will be quite delighted; nothing would give her more pleasure. 'Then, Lavinia, my darling,' says Mr Widger, 'mind you don't lose sight of that; now, pray take care that Mr and Mrs Jackson know the Clickits without loss of time. Such people ought not to be strangers to each other.' Mrs Widger books both families as the centre of attraction for her next party; and Mr Widger, going on to expatiate upon the virtues of the Clickits, adds to their other moral qualities, that they keep one of the neatest phaetons in town, and have two thousand a year.

As the plausible couple never laud the merits of any absent person, without dexterously contriving that their praises shall reflect upon somebody who is present, so they never depreciate anything or anybody, without turning their depreciation to the same account. Their friend, Mr Slummery, say they, is unquestionably a clever painter, and would no doubt be very popular, and sell his pictures at a very high price, if that cruel Mr Fithers had not forestalled him in his department of art, and made it thoroughly and completely his own – Fithers, it is to be observed, being present and within hearing, and Slummery elsewhere. Is Mrs Tabblewick really as beautiful as people say? Why, there indeed you ask them a very puzzling question, because there is no doubt that she is a very charming woman, and they have long known her intimately. She is no doubt beautiful, very beautiful; they once thought her the most beautiful woman ever seen; still if you press them for an honest answer, they are bound to say that this was before they had ever seen our lovely friend on the sofa (the sofa is hard by, and our lovely friend can't help hearing the whispers in which this is said); since that time, perhaps, they have been hardly fair judges; Mrs Tabblewick is no doubt extremely handsome, – very like our friend, in fact, in the form of the features, – but in point of expression, and soul, and figure, and air altogether – oh dear!

But while the plausible couple depreciate, they are still careful to preserve their character for amiability and kind feeling; indeed the depreciation itself is often made to grow out of their excessive sympathy and good will. The plausible lady calls on a lady who dotes upon her children, and is sitting with a little girl upon her knee, enraptured by her artless replies, and protesting that there is nothing she delights in so much as conversing with these fairies; when the other lady inquires if she has seen young Mrs Finching lately, and whether the baby has turned out a finer one than it promised to be. 'Oh dear!' cries the plausible lady, 'you can-not think how often Bobtail and I have talked about poor Mrs Finching – she is such a dear soul, and was so anxious that the baby should be a fine child – and very naturally, because she was very much here at one time, and there is, you know, a natural emulation among mothers – that it is impossible to tell you how much we have felt for her.' 'Is it weak or plain, or what?' inquires the other. 'Weak or plain, my love,' returns the plausible lady, 'it's a fright – a perfect little fright; you never saw such a miserable creature in all your days. Positively you must not let her see one of these beautiful dears again, or you'll break her heart, you will indeed – Heavens bless this child, see how she is looking in my face! Can you conceive anything prettier than that? If poor Mrs Finching could only hope – but that's impossible – and the gifts of Providence, you know – What *did* I do with my pocket-handkerchief!'

What prompts the mother, who dotes upon her children, to comment to her lord that evening on the plausible lady's engaging qualities and feeling heart, and what is it that procures Mr and Mrs Bobtail Widger an immediate invitation to dinner?'

The Nice Little Couple

A custom once prevailed in old-fashioned circles, that when a lady or gentleman was unable to sing a song, he or she should enliven the company with a story. As we find ourself in the predicament of not being able to describe (to our own satisfaction) nice little couples in the abstract, we purpose telling in this place a little story about a nice little couple of our acquaintance.

Mr and Mrs Chirrup are the nice little couple in question. Mr Chirrup has the smartness, and something of the brisk, quick manner of a small bird. Mrs Chirrup is the prettiest of all little women, and has the prettiest little figure conceivable. She has the neatest little foot, and the softest little voice, and the pleasantest little smile, and the tidiest little curls, and the brightest little eyes, and the quietest little manner, and is, in short, altogether one of the most engaging of all little women, dead or alive. She is a condensation of all the domestic virtues – a pocket edition of the young man's best companion – a little woman at a very high pressure, with an amazing quantity of goodness and usefulness in an exceedingly small space. Little as she is, Mrs Chirrup might furnish forth matter for the moral equipment of a score of housewives, six feet high in their stockings – if, in the presence of ladies, we may be allowed the expression – and of corresponding robustness.

Nobody knows all this better than Mr Chirrup, though he rather takes on that he doesn't. Accordingly he is very proud of his better-half, and evidently considers himself, as all other people consider him, rather fortunate in having her to wife. We say evidently, because Mr Chirrup is a warm-hearted little fellow; and if you catch his eye when he has been slyly glancing at Mrs Chirrup in company, there is a certain complacent twinkle in it, accompanied, perhaps, by a half-expressed toss of the head, which as clearly indicates what has been passing in his mind as if he had put it into words, and shouted it out through a speaking-trumpet. Moreover, Mr Chirrup has a particularly mild and bird-like manner of calling Mrs Chirrup 'my dear'; and – for he is of a jocose turn – of cutting little witticisms upon her, and making her the subject of various harmless pleasantries, which nobody enjoys more thoroughly than Mrs Chirrup herself. Mr Chirrup, too, now and then affects to deplore his bachelor-days, and to bemoan (with a marvellously contented and smirking face) the loss of his freedom, and the sorrow of his heart at having been taken captive by Mrs Chirrup – all of which circumstances combine to show the secret triumph and satisfaction of Mr Chirrup's soul.

We have already had occasion to observe that Mrs Chirrup is an incomparable housewife. In all the arts of domestic arrangement and management, in all the mysteries of confectionery-making, pickling, and preserving, never was such a thorough adept as that nice little body. She is, besides, a cunning worker in muslin and fine linen, and a special hand at marketing to the very best advantage. But if there be one branch of housekeeping in which she excels to an utterly unparalleled and unprecedented extent, it is in the important one of carving. A roast goose is universally allowed to be the great stumbling-block in the way of young aspirants to perfection in this department of science; many promising carvers, beginning with legs of mutton, and preserving a good reputation through fillets of veal, sirloin of beef, quarters of lamb, fowls, and even ducks, have sunk before a roast goose, and lost caste and character for ever. To Mrs Chirrup the

resolving a goose into its smallest component parts is a
pleasant pastime – a practical joke – a thing to be done in a
minute or so, without the smallest interruption to the conversation of the time. No handing the dish over to an unfortunate
man upon her right or left, no wild sharpening of the knife, no
hacking and sawing at an unruly joint, no noise, no splash, no
heat, no leaving off in despair; all is confidence and cheerfulness. The dish is set upon the table, the cover is removed; for
an instant, and only an instant, you observe that Mrs
Chirrup's attention is distracted; she smiles, but heareth not.
You proceed with your story; meanwhile the glittering knife
is slowly upraised, both Mrs Chirrup's wrists are slightly but
not ungracefully agitated, she compresses her lips for an
instant, then breaks into a smile, and all is over. The legs of the
bird slide gently down into a pool of gravy, the wings seem to
melt from the body, the breast separates into a row of juicy
slices, the smaller and more complicated parts of his anatomy
are perfectly developed, a cavern of stuffing is revealed, and
the goose is gone!

To dine with Mr and Mrs Chirrup is one of the pleasantest
things in the world. Mr Chirrup has a bachelor friend, who
lived with him in his own days of single blessedness, and to
whom he is mightily attached. Contrary to the usual custom,
this bachelor friend is no less a friend of Mrs Chirrup's, and
consequently, whenever you dine with Mr and Mrs Chirrup,
you meet the bachelor friend. It would put any reasonably-
conditioned mortal into good-humour to observe the entire
unanimity which subsists between these three; but there is a
quiet welcome dimpling in Mrs Chirrup's face, a bustling
hospitality oozing as it were out of the waistcoat-pockets of
Mr Chirrup, and a patronising enjoyment of their cordiality
and satisfaction on the part of the bachelor friend, which is
quite delightful. On these occasions Mr Chirrup usually takes
an opportunity of rallying the friend on being single, and the
friend retorts on Mr Chirrup for being married, at which
moments some single young ladies present are like to die of
laughter; and we have more than once observed them bestow
looks upon the friend, which convinces us that his position is
by no means a safe one, as, indeed, we hold no bachelor's to be
who visits married friends and cracks jokes on wedlock, for

certain it is that such men walk among traps and nets and pitfalls innumerable, and often find themselves down upon their knees at the altar rails, taking M or N for their wedded wives, before they know anything about the matter.

However, this is no business of Mr Chirrup's, who talks, and laughs, and drinks his wine, and laughs again, and talks more, until it is time to repair to the drawing-room, where, coffee served and over, Mrs Chirrup prepares for a round game, by sorting the nicest possible little fish into the nicest possible little pools, and calling Mr Chirrup to assist her, which Mr Chirrup does. As they stand side by side, you find that Mr Chirrup is the least possible shadow of a shade taller than Mrs Chirrup, and that they are the neatest and best-matched little couple that can be, which the chances are ten to one against your observing with such effect at any other time, unless you see them in the street arm-in-arm, or meet them some rainy day trotting along under a very small umbrella. The round game (at which Mr Chirrup is the merriest of the party) being done and over, in course of time a nice little tray appears, on which is a nice little supper; and when that is finished likewise, and you have said 'Good night,' you find yourself repeating a dozen times, as you ride home, that there never was such a nice little couple as Mr and Mrs Chirrup.

Whether it is that pleasant qualities, being packed more closely in small bodies than in large, come more readily to hand than when they are diffused over a wider space, and have to be gathered together for use, we don't know, but as a general rule – strengthened like all other rules by its exceptions – we hold that little people are sprightly and good-natured. The more sprightly and good-natured people we have, the better; therefore, let us wish well to all nice little couples, and hope that they may increase and multiply.

The Egotistical Couple

Egotism in couples is of two kinds. It is our purpose to show this by two examples.

The egotistical couple may be young, old, middle-aged, well to do, or ill to do; they may have a small family, a large family, or no family at all. There is no outward sign by which an egotistical couple may be known and avoided. They come upon you unawares; there is no guarding against them. No man can of himself be forewarned or forearmed against an egotistical couple.

The egotistical couple have undergone every calamity, and experienced every pleasurable and painful sensation of which our nature is susceptible. You cannot by possibility tell the egotistical couple anything they don't know, or describe to them anything they have not felt. They have been everything but dead. Sometimes we are tempted to wish they had been even that, but only in our uncharitable moments, which are few and far between.

We happened the other day, in the course of a morning call, to encounter an egotistical couple, nor were we suffered to remain long in ignorance of the fact, for our very first inquiry of the lady of the house brought them into active and vigorous operation. The inquiry was of course touching the lady's health, and the answer happened to be, that she had not been very well. 'Oh my dear!' said the egotistical lady, 'don't talk of not being well. We have been in *such* a state since we saw you last!' – The lady of the house happening to remark that her lord had not been well either, the egotistical gentleman struck in: 'Never let Briggs complain of not being well – never let Briggs complain, my dear Mrs Briggs, after what I have undergone within these six weeks. He doesn't know what it is to be ill, he hasn't the least idea of it; not the faintest conception.' – 'My dear,' interposed his wife smiling, 'you talk as if it were almost a crime in Mr Briggs not to have been as ill as we have been, instead of feeling thankful to Providence that both he and our dear Mrs Briggs are in such blissful ignorance of real suffering.' – 'My love,' returned the egotistical gentleman, in a low and pious voice, 'you mistake me; – I feel grateful – very grateful. I trust our friends may never purchase their experience as dearly as we have bought ours; I hope they never may!'

Having put down Mrs Briggs upon this theme, and settled the question thus, the egotistical gentleman turned to us, and, after a few preliminary remarks, all tending towards and leading up to the point he had in his mind, inquired if we happened to be acquainted with the Dowager Lady Snorflerer. On our replying in the negative, he presumed we had often met Lord Slang, or beyond all doubt, that we were on intimate terms with Sir Chipkins Glogwog. Finding that we were equally unable to lay claim to either of these distinctions, he expressed great astonishment, and turning to his wife with a retrospective smile, inquired who it was that had told that capital story about the mashed potatoes. 'Who, my dear?' returned the egotistical lady, 'why Sir Chipkins, of course; how can you ask! Don't you remember his applying it to our cook, and saying that you and I were so like the Prince and Princess, that he could almost have sworn we were they?' 'To be sure, I remember that,' said the egotistical gentleman; 'but are you quite certain that didn't apply to the other anecdote about the Emperor of Austria and the pump?' 'Upon my word then, I think it did,' replied his wife. 'To be sure it did,' said the egotistical gentleman, 'it was Slang's story, I remember now, perfectly.' However, it turned out, a few seconds afterwards, that the egotistical gentleman's memory was rather treacherous, as he began to have a misgiving that the story had been told by the Dowager Lady Snorflerer the very last time they dined there; but there appearing, on further consideration, strong circumstantial evidence tending to show that this couldn't be, inasmuch as the Dowager Lady Snorflerer had been, on the occasion in question, wholly engrossed by the egotistical lady, the egotistical gentleman recanted this opinion; and after laying the story at the doors of a great many great people, happily left it at last with the Duke of Scuttlewig: – observing that it was not extraordinary he had forgotten his Grace hitherto, as it often happened that the names of those with whom we were upon the most familiar footing were the very last to present themselves to our thoughts.

It not only appeared that the egotistical couple knew everybody, but that scarcely any event of importance or notoriety had occurred for many years with which they had not been in some way or other connected. Thus we learned that when the well-known attempt upon the life of George the Third was made by Hatfield in Drury Lane theatre, the egotistical gentleman's grandfather sat upon his right hand and was the first man who collared him; and that the egotistical lady's aunt, sitting within a few boxes of the royal party, was the only person in the audience who heard his Majesty exclaim, 'Charlotte, Charlotte, don't be frightened, don't be frightened; they're letting off squibs, they're letting off squibs.' When the fire broke out, which ended in the destruction of the two houses of parliament, the egotistical couple, being at the time at a drawing-room window on Blackheath, then and there simultaneously exclaimed, to the astonishment of a whole party – 'It's the House of Lords!' Nor was this a solitary instance of their peculiar discernment, for chancing to be (as by a comparison of dates and circumstances they afterwards found) in the same omnibus with Mr Greenacre, when he carried his victim's head about town in a blue bag, they both remarked a singular twitching in the muscles of his countenance; and walking down Fish Street Hill, a few weeks since, the egotistical gentleman said to his lady – slightly casting his eyes to the top of the Monument – 'There's a boy up there, my dear, reading a Bible. It's very strange. I don't like it. – In five seconds, afterwards, Sir,' says the egotistical gentleman, bringing his hand together with one violent clap – 'the lad was over!'

Diversifying these topics by the introduction of many others of the same kind, and entertaining us between whiles with a minute account of what weather and diet agreed with them, and what weather and diet disagreed with them, and at what time they usually got up, and at what time went to bed, with many other particulars of their domestic economy too numerous to mention; the egotistical couple at length took their leave, and afforded us an opportunity of doing the same.

Mr and Mrs Sliverstone are an egotistical couple of another class, for all the lady's egotism is about her husband, and all the gentleman's about his wife. For example: – Mr Sliverstone is a clerical gentleman, and occasionally writes sermons, as clerical gentlemen do. If you happen to obtain admission at the street-door while he is so engaged, Mrs Sliverstone appears on tip-toe, and speaking in a solemn whisper, as if there were at least three or four particular friends upstairs, all upon the point of death, implores you to be very silent, for Mr Sliverstone is composing, and she need not say how very important it is that

he should not be disturbed. Unwilling to interrupt anything
so serious, you hasten to withdraw, with many apologies; but
this Mrs Sliverstone will by no means allow, observing, that
she knows you would like to see him, as it is very natural you
should, and that she is determined to make a trial for you, as
you are a great favourite. So you are led upstairs – still on
tip-toe – to the door of a little back room, in which, as the lady
informs you in a whisper, Mr Sliverstone always writes. No
answer being returned to a couple of soft taps, the lady opens
the door, and there, sure enough, is Mr Sliverstone, with
dishevelled hair, powdering away with pen, ink, and paper, at
a rate which, if he has any power of sustaining it, would settle
the longest sermon in no time. At first he is too much
absorbed to be roused by this intrusion; but presently looking
up, says faintly, 'Ah!' and pointing to his desk with a weary
and languid smile, extends his hand, and hopes you'll forgive
him. Then Mrs Sliverstone sits down beside him, and taking
his hand in hers, tells you how that Mr Sliverstone has been
shut up there ever since nine o'clock in the morning (it is by
this time twelve at noon,) and how she knows it cannot be
good for his health, and is very uneasy about it. Unto this Mr
Sliverstone replies firmly, that 'It must be done'; which
agonises Mrs Sliverstone still more, and she goes on to tell you
that such were Mr Sliverstone's labours last week – what with
the buryings, marryings, churchings, christenings, and all
together – that when he was going up the pulpit stairs on
Sunday evening, he was obliged to hold on by the rails, or he
would certainly have fallen over into his own pew. Mr
Sliverstone, who has been listening and smiling meekly, says,
'Not quite so bad as that, not quite so bad!' he admits though,
on cross-examination, that he *was* very near falling upon the
verger who was following him up to bolt the door; but adds,
that it was his duty as a Christian to fall upon him, if need
were, and that he, Mr Sliverstone (and possibly the verger
too), ought to glory in it.

This sentiment communicates new impulse to Mrs Sliverstone, who launches into new praises of Mr Sliverstone's
worth and excellence, to which he listens in the same meek
silence, save when he puts in a word of self-denial relative to
some question of face, as – 'Not seventy-two christenings that

week, my dear. Only seventy-one, only seventy-one.' At length his lady has quite concluded, and then he says, Why should he repine, why should he give way, why should he suffer his heart to sink within him? Is it he who toils and suffers? What has she gone through, he should like to know? What does she go through every day for him and for society?

With such an exordium Mr Sliverstone launches out into glowing praises of the conduct of Mrs Sliverstone in the production of eight young children, and the subsequent rearing and fostering of the same; and thus the husband magnifies the wife, and the wife the husband.

This would be well enough if Mr and Mrs Sliverstone kept it to themselves, or even to themselves and a friend or two; but they do not. The more hearers they have, the more egotistical the couple become, and the more anxious they are to make believers in their merits. Perhaps this is the worst kind of egotism. It has not even the poor excuse of being spontaneous, but is the result of a deliberate system and malice aforethought. Mere empty-headed conceit excites our pity, but ostentatious hypocrisy awakens our disgust.

The Couple Who Coddle Themselves

Mrs Merrywinkle's maiden name was Chopper. She was the only child of Mr and Mrs Chopper. Her father died when she was, as the play-books express it, 'yet an infant'; and so old Mrs Chopper, when her daughter married, made the house of her son-in-law her home from that time henceforth, and set up her staff of rest with Mr and Mrs Merrywinkle.

Mr and Mrs Merrywinkle are a couple who coddle themselves; and the venerable Mrs Chopper is an aider and abettor in the same.

Mr Merrywinkle is a rather lean and long-necked gentleman, middle-aged and middle-sized, and usually troubled with a cold in the head. Mrs Merrywinkle is a delicate-looking lady, with very light hair, and is exceedingly subject to the same unpleasant disorder. The venerable Mrs Chopper – who is strictly entitled to the appellation, her daughter not being very young, otherwise than by courtesy, at the time of her marriage, which was some years ago – is a mysterious old lady who lurks behind a pair of spectacles, and is afflicted with a chronic disease, respecting which she has taken a vast deal of medical advice, and referred to a vast number of medical books, without meeting any definition of symptoms that at all suits her, or enables her to say, 'That's my complaint.' Indeed, the absence of authentic information upon the subject of this complaint would seem to be Mrs Chopper's greatest ill, as in all other respects she is an uncommonly hale and hearty gentlewoman.

Both Mr and Mrs Merrywinkle wear an extraordinary quantity of flannel, and have a habit of putting their feet in hot water to an unnatural extent. They likewise indulge in chamomile tea and such-like compounds, and rub themselves on the slightest provocation with camphorated spirits and other lotions applicable to mumps, sore-throat, rheumatism, or lumbago.

Mr Merrywinkle's leaving home to go to business on a damp or wet morning is a very elaborate affair. He puts on wash-leather socks over his stockings, and India-rubber shoes above his boots, and wears under his waistcoat a cuirass of hare-skin. Besides these precautions, he winds a thick shawl round his throat, and blocks up his mouth with a large silk handkerchief. Thus accoutred, and furnished besides with a great-coat and umbrella, he braves the dangers of the streets; travelling in severe weather at a gentle trot, the better to preserve the circulation, and bringing his mouth to the surface to take breath, but very seldom, and with the utmost caution. His office-door opened, he shoots past his clerk at the same pace, and diving into his own private room, closes the door, examines the window-fastenings, and gradually unrobes himself: hanging his pocket-handkerchief on the fender to air, and determining to write to the newspapers about the fog, which, he says, 'has really got to that pitch that it is quite unbearable.'

In this last opinion Mrs Merrywinkle and her respected mother fully concur; for though not present, their thoughts and tongues are occupied with the same subject, which is their constant theme all day. If anybody happens to call, Mrs Merrywinkle opines that they must assuredly be mad, and her first salutation is, 'Why, what in the name of goodness can bring you out in such weather? You know you *must* catch your death.' This assurance is corroborated by Mrs Chopper, who adds, in further confirmation, a dismal legend concerning an individual of her acquaintance who, making a call under precisely parallel circumstances, and being then in the best health and spirits, expired in forty-eight hours afterwards, of a complication of inflammatory disorders. The visitor, rendered not altogether comfortable perhaps by this and other pre-cedents, inquires very affectionately after Mr Merrywinkle, but by so doing brings about no change of the subject; for Mr Merrywinkle's name is inseparably connected with his complaints, and his complaints are inseparably connected with Mrs Merrywinkle's; and when these are done with, Mrs Chopper, who has been biding her time, cuts in with the chronic disorder – a subject upon which the amiable old lady never leaves off speaking until she is left alone, and very often not then.

But Mr Merrywinkle comes home to dinner. He is received by Mrs Merrywinkle and Mrs Chopper, who, on his remarking that he thinks his feet are damp, turn pale as ashes and drag him upstairs, imploring him to have them rubbed directly with a dry coarse towel. Rubbed they are, one by Mrs Merrywinkle and one by Mrs Chopper, until the friction causes Mr Merrywinkle to make horrible faces, and look as if he had been smelling very powerful onions; when they desist, and the patient, provided for his better security with thick worsted stockings and list slippers, is borne downstairs to dinner. Now, the dinner is always a good one, the appetites of the diners being delicate, and requiring a little of what Mrs Merrywinkle calls 'tittivation'; the secret of which is under-stood to lie in good cookery and tasteful spices, and which process is so successfully performed in the present instance, that both Mr and Mrs Merrywinkle eat a remarkably good dinner, and even the afflicted Mrs Chopper wields her knife and fork with much of the spirit and elasticity of youth. But Mr Merrywinkle, in his desire to gratify his appetite, is not unmindful of his health, for he has a bottle of carbonate of soda with which to qualify his porter, and a little pair of scales in which to weigh it out. Neither in his anxiety to take care of his body is he unmindful of the welfare of his immortal part, as he always prays that for what he is going to receive he may be made truly thankful; and in order that he may be as thankful as possible, eats and drinks to the utmost.

Either from eating and drinking so much, or from being the victim of this constitutional infirmity, among others, Mr Merrywinkle, after two or three glasses of wine, falls fast asleep; and he has scarcely closed his eyes, when Mrs Merrywinkle and Mrs Chopper fall asleep likewise. It is on awakening at tea-time that their most alarming symptoms prevail; for then Mr Merrywinkle feels as if his temples were tightly bound round with the chain of the street-door, and Mrs Merrywinkle as if she had made a hearty dinner of half-hundredweights, and Mrs Chopper as if cold water were running down her back, and oyster-knives with sharp points were plunging of their own accord into her ribs. Symptoms like these are enough to make people peevish, and no wonder that they remain so until supper-time, doing little more than doze and complain, unless Mr Merrywinkle calls out very loudly to a servant 'to keep that draught out,' or rushes into the passage to flourish his fist in the countenance of the twopenny-postman, for daring to give such a knock as he had just performed at the door of a private gentleman with nerves.

Supper, coming after dinner, should consist of some gentle provocative; and therefore the tittivating art is again in requisition, and again done honour to by Mr and Mrs Merrywinkle, still comforted and abetted by Mrs Chopper. After supper, it is ten to one but the last-named old lady becomes worse, and is led off to bed with the chronic complaint in full vigour. Mr and Mrs Merrywinkle, having administered to her a warm cordial, which is something of the strongest, then repair to their own room, where Mr Merrywinkle, with his legs and feet in hot water, superintends the mulling of some wine which he is to drink at the very moment he plunges into bed, while Mrs Merrywinkle, in garments whose nature is unknown to and unimagined by all but unmarried men, takes four small pills with a spasmodic look between each, and finally comes to something hot and fragrant out of another little saucepan, which serves as her composing-draught for the night.

There is another kind of couple who coddle themselves, and who do so at a cheaper rate and on more spare diet, because they are niggardly and parsimonious; for which reason they are kind enough to coddle their visitors too. It is unnecessary to describe them, for our readers may rest assured of the accuracy of these general principles: – that all couples who coddle themselves are selfish and slothful – that they charge upon every wind that blows, every rain that falls, and every vapour that hangs in the air, the evils which arise from their own imprudence or the gloom which is engendered in their own tempers – and that all men and women, in couples or otherwise, who fall into exclusive habits of self-indulgence, and forget their natural sympathy and close connexion with everybody and everything in the world around them, not only neglect the first duty of life, but, by a happy retributive justice, deprive themselves of its truest and best enjoyment.

The Old Couple

They are grandfather and grandmother to a dozen grown people and have great-grandchildren besides; their bodies are bent, their hair is grey, their step tottering and infirm. Is this the lightsome pair whose wedding was so merry, and have the young couple indeed grown old so soon!

It seems but yesterday – and yet what a host of cares and griefs are crowded into the intervening time which, reckoned by them, lengthens out into a century! How many new associations have wreathed themselves about their hearts since then! The old time is gone, and a new time has come for others – not for them. They are but the rusting link that feebly joins the two, and is silently loosening its hold and dropping asunder.

It seems but yesterday – and yet three of their children have sunk into the grave, and the tree that shades it has grown quite old. One was an infant – they wept for him; the next a girl, a slight young thing too delicate for earth – her loss was hard indeed to bear. The third, a man. That was the worst of all, but even that grief is softened now.

It seems but yesterday – and yet how the gay and laughing faces of that bright morning have changed and vanished from above ground! Faint likenesses of some remain about them yet, but they are only seen in dreams, and even they are unlike what they were, in eyes so old and dim.

One or two dresses from the bridal wardrobe are yet preserved. They are of a quaint and antique fashion, and seldom seen except in pictures. White has turned yellow, and brighter hues have faded. Do you wonder, child? The wrinkled face was once as smooth as yours, the eyes as bright, the shrivelled skin as fair and delicate. It is the work of hands that have been dust these many years.

Where are the fairy lovers of that happy day whose annual return comes upon the old man and his wife, like the echo of some village bell which has long been silent? Let yonder peevish bachelor, racked by rheumatic pains, and quarrelling with the world, let him answer to the question. He recollects something of a favourite playmate; her name was Lucy – so they tell him. He is not sure whether she was married, or went abroad, or died. It is a long while ago, and he don't remember.

Is nothing as it used to be; does no one feel, or think, or act, as in days of yore? Yes. There is an aged woman who once lived servant with the old lady's father, and is sheltered in an alms-house not far off. She is still attached to the family, and loves them all; she nursed the children in her lap, and tended in their sickness those who are no more. Her old mistress has still something of youth in her eyes; the young ladies are like what she was but not quite so handsome, nor are the gentlemen as stately as Mr Harvey used to be. She has seen a great deal of trouble; her husband and her son died long ago; but she has got over that, and is happy now – quite happy.

If ever her attachment to her old protectors were disturbed by fresher cares and hopes, it has long since resumed its former current. It has filled the void in the poor creature's heart, and replaced the love of kindred. Death has not left her alone, and this, with a roof above her head, and a warm hearth to sit by, makes her cheerful and contented. Does she remember the marriage of great-grandmamma? Ay, that she does, as well – as if it was only yesterday. You wouldn't think it to look at her now, and perhaps she ought not to say so of herself, but she was as smart a young girl then as you'd wish to see. She recollects she took a friend of hers upstairs to see Miss Emma dressed for church; her name was – ah! she forgets the name, but she remembers that she was a very pretty girl, and that she married not long afterwards, and lived – it has quite passed out of her mind where she lived – but she knows she had a bad husband who used her ill, and that she died in Lambeth workhouse. Dear, dear, in Lambeth workhouse!

And the old couple – have they no comfort or enjoyment of existence? See them among their grandchildren and great-grandchildren; how garrulous they are, how they compare one with another, and insist on likenesses which no one else can see; how gently the old lady lectures the girls on points of breeding and decorum, and points the moral by anecdotes of herself in her young days – how the old gentleman chuckles over boyish feats and roguish tricks, and tells long stories of a 'barring-out' achieved at the school he went to: which was very wrong, he tells the boys, and never to be imitated of course, but which he cannot help letting them know was very pleasant too – especially when he kissed the master's niece. This last, however, is a point on which the old lady is very tender, for she considers it a shocking and indelicate thing to talk about, and always says so whenever it is mentioned, never failing to observe that he ought to be very penitent for having been to sinful. So the old gentleman gets no further, and what the schoolmaster's niece said afterwards (which he is always going to tell) is lost to posterity.

The old gentleman is eighty years old, to-day – 'Eighty years old, Crofts, and never had a headache,' he tells the barber who shaves him (the barber being a young fellow, and very subject to that complaint). 'That's a great age, Croft,' says the old gentleman. 'I don't think it's sich a wery great age, Sir,' replies the barber. 'Crofts,' rejoins the old gentleman, 'you're talking nonsense to me. Eighty not a great age?' 'It's a wery great age, Sir, for a gentleman to be as healthy and active as you are,' returns the barber; 'but my grandfather, Sir, he was ninety-four.' 'You don't mean that, Crofts?' says the old gentleman. 'I do indeed, Sir,' retorts the barber, 'and as wiggerous as Julius Caesar, my grandfather was.' The old gentleman muses a little time, and then says, 'What did he die of, Crofts?' 'He died accidentally, Sir,' returns the barber; 'he didn't mean to do it. He always would go a running about the streets – walking never satisfied *his* spirit – and he run against a post and died of a hurt in his chest.' The old gentleman says no more until the shaving is concluded, and then he gives Crofts half-a-crown to drink his health. He is a little doubtful of the barber's veracity afterwards, and telling the anecdote to the old lady, affects to make very light of it – though to be sure (he adds) there was old Parr, and in some parts of England, ninety-five or so is a common age, quite a common age.

This morning the old couple are cheerful but serious, recalling old times as well as they can remember them, and dwelling upon many passages in their past lives which the day brings to mind. The old lady reads aloud, in a tremulous voice, out of a great Bible, and the old gentleman with his hand to his ear, listens with profound respect. When the book is closed, they sit silent for a short space, and afterwards resume their conversation, with a reference perhaps to their dead children, as a subject not unsuited to that they have just left. By degrees they are led to consider which of those who survive are the most like those dearly-remembered objects, and so they fall into a less solemn strain, and become cheerful again.

How many people in all, grandchildren, great-grand-children, and one or two intimate friends of the family, dine together to-day at the eldest son's to congratulate the old couple, and wish them many happy returns, is a calculation beyond our powers; but this we know, that the old couple no sooner present themselves, very sprucely and carefully attired, than there is a violent shouting and rushing forward of the younger branches with all manner of presents, such as pocket-books, pencil-cases, pen-wipers, watch-papers, pin-cushions, sleeve-buckles, worked-slippers, watch-guards, and even a nutmeg-grater: the latter article being presented by a very chubby and very little boy, who exhibits it in great triumph as an extraordinary variety. The old couple's emotion at these tokens of remembrance occasions quite a pathetic scene, of which the chief ingredients are a vast quantity of kissing and hugging, and repeated wipings of small eyes and noses with small square pocket-handkerchiefs, which don't come at all easily out of small pockets. Even the peevish bachelor is moved, and he says, as he presents the old gentleman with a queer sort of antique ring from his own finger, that he'll be de'ed if he doesn't think he looks younger than he did ten years ago.

But the great time, is after dinner, when the dessert and wine are on the table, which is pushed back to make plenty of room, and they are all gathered in a large circle round the fire, for it is then – the glasses being filled, and everybody ready to drink the toast – that two great-grandchildren rush out at a given signal, and presently return, dragging in old Jane Adams leaning upon her crutched stick, and trembling with age and pleasure. Who so popular as poor old Jane, nurse and story-teller in ordinary to two generations; and who so happy as she, striving to bend her stiff limbs into a curtsey, while tears of pleasure steal down her withered cheeks!

The old couple sit side by side, and the old time seems like yesterday indeed. Looking back upon the path they have travelled, its dust and ashes disappear; the flowers that withered long ago, show brightly again upon its borders, and they grow young once more in the youth of those about them.

Conclusion

We have taken for the subjects of the foregoing moral essays, twelve samples of married couples, carefully selected from a large stock on hand, open to the inspection of all comers. These samples are intended for the benefit of the rising generation of both sexes, and, for their more easy and pleasant information, have been separately ticketed and labelled in the manner they have seen.

We have purposely excluded from consideration the couple in which the lady reigns paramount and supreme, holding such cases to be of a very unnatural kind, and like hideous births and other monstrous deformities, only to be discreetly and sparingly exhibited.

And here our self-imposed task would have ended, but that to these young ladies and gentlemen who are yet revolving singly round the church, awaiting the advent of that time when the mysterious laws of attraction shall draw them towards it in couples, we are desirous of addressing a few last words.

Before marriage and afterwards, let them learn to centre all their hopes of real and lasting happiness in their own fireside; let them cherish the faith that in home, and all the English virtues which the love of home engenders, lies the only true source of domestic felicity; let them believe that round the household gods, contentment and tranquillity cluster in their gentlest and most graceful forms; and that many weary hunters of happiness through the noisy world, have learnt this truth too late, and found a cheerful spirit and a quiet mind only at home at last.

How much may depend on the education of daughters and the conduct of mothers; how much of the brightest part of our old national character may be perpetuated by their wisdom or frittered away by their folly – how much of it may have been lost already, and how much more in danger of vanishing every day – are questions too weighty for discussion here, but well deserving a little serious consideration from all young couples nevertheless.

To that one young couple on whose bright destiny the thoughts of nations are fixed, may the youth of England look, and not in vain, for an example. From that one young couple, blessed and favoured as they are, may they learn that even the glare and glitter of a court, the splendour of a palace, and the pomp and glory of a throne, yield in their power of conferring happiness, to domestic worth and virtue. From that one young couple may they learn that the crown of a great empire, costly and jewelled though it be, gives place in the estimation of a Queen to the plain gold ring that links her woman's nature to that of tens of thousands of her humble subjects, and guards in her woman's heart one secret store of tenderness, whose proudest boast shall be that it knows no Royalty save Nature's own, and no pride of birth but being the child of heaven!

So shall the highest young couple in the land for once hear the truth, when men throw up their caps, and cry with loving shouts——

GOD BLESS THEM

THE BLOOMSBURY CHRISTENING

by Charles Dickens

Mr Nicodemus Dumps, or, as his acquaintance called him, 'long Dumps,' was a bachelor, six feet high, and fifty years old: cross, cadaverous, odd, and ill-natured. He was never happy but when he was miserable; and always miserable when he had the best reason to be happy. The only real comfort of his existence was to make everybody about him wretched – then he might be truly said to enjoy life. He was afflicted with a situation in the Bank worth five hundred a year, and he rented a 'first-floor furnished,' at Pentonville, which he originally took because it commanded a dismal prospect of an adjacent churchyard. He was familiar with the face of every tombstone, and the burial service seemed to excite his strongest sympathy. His friends said he was surly – he insisted he was nervous; they thought him a lucky dog, but he protested that he was 'the most unfortunate man in the world.' Cold as he was, and wretched as he declared himself to be, he was not wholly susceptible of attachments. He revered the memory of Hoyle, as he was himself an admirable and imperturbable whist-player, and he chuckled with delight at a fretful and impatient adversary. He adored King Herod for his massacre of the innocents; and if he hated one thing more than another, it was a child. However, he could hardly be said to hate anything in particular, because he disliked everything in general; but perhaps his greatest antipathies were cabs, old women, doors that would not shut, musical amateurs, and omnibus cads. He subscribed to the 'Society for the Suppression of Vice' for the pleasure of putting a stop to any harmless amusements; and he contributed largely towards the support of two itinerant Methodist parsons, in the amiable hope that if circumstances rendered any people happy in this world, they might perchance be rendered miserable by fears for the next.

Mr Dumps had a nephew who had been married about a year, and who was somewhat of a favourite with his uncle, because he was an admirable subject to exercise his misery-creating powers upon. Mr Charles Kitterbell was a small, sharp, spare man, with a very large head, and a broad, good-humoured countenance. He looked like a faded giant, with the head and face partially restored; and he had a cast in his eye which rendered it quite impossible for any one with whom he conversed to know where he was looking. His eyes appeared fixed on the wall, and he was staring you out of countenance; in short, there was no catching his eye, and perhaps it is a merciful dispensation of Providence that such eyes are not catching. In addition to these characteristics, it may be added that Mr Charles Kitterbell was one of the most credulous and matter-of-fact little personages that ever took *to* himself a wife, and *for* himself a house in Great Russell Street, Bedford Square. (Uncle Dumps always dropped the 'Bedford Square,' and inserted in lieu thereof the dreadful words 'Tottenham-court Road.')

'No, but, uncle, 'pon my life you must – you must promise to be godfather,' said Mr Kitterbell, as he sat in conversation with his respected relative one morning.

'I cannot, indeed I cannot,' returned Dumps.

'Well, but why not? Jemima will think it very unkind. It's very little trouble.'

'As to the trouble,' rejoined the most unhappy man in existence. 'I don't mind that; but my nerves are in that state – I cannot go through the ceremony. You know I don't like going out. For God's sake, Charles, don't fidget with that stool so; you'll drive me mad.' Mr Kitterbell, quite regardless of his uncle's nerves, had occupied himself for some ten minutes in describing a circle on the floor with one leg of the office-stool on which he was seated, keeping the other three up in the air, and holding fast on by the desk.

'I beg your pardon, uncle,' said Kitterbell, quite abashed, suddenly releasing his hold of the desk, and bringing the three wandering legs back to the floor, with a force sufficient to drive them through it.

'But come, don't refuse. If it's a boy, you know, we must have two godfathers.'

'*If* it's a boy!' said Dumps; 'why can't you say at once whether it *is* a boy or not?'

'I should be very happy to tell you, but it's impossible I can undertake to say whether it's a girl or a boy, if the child isn't born yet.'

'Not born yet!' echoed Dumps, with a gleam of hope lighting up his lugubrious visage. 'Oh, well, it *may* be a girl, and then you won't want me; or if it is a boy, it *may* die before it is christened.'

'I hope not,' said the father that expected to be, looking very grave.

'I hope not,' acquiesced Dumps, evidently pleased with the subject. He was beginning to get happy. '*I* hope not, but distressing cases frequently occur during the first two or three days of a child's life; fits, I am told, are exceedingly common, and alarming convulsions are almost matters of course.'

'Lord, uncle!' ejaculated little Kitterbell, gasping for breath.

'Yes; my landlady was confined – let me see – last Tuesday: an uncommonly fine boy. On the Thursday night the nurse was sitting with him upon her knee before the fire, and he was as well as possible. Suddenly he became black in the face, and alarmingly spasmodic. The medical man was instantly sent for, and every remedy was tried, but—'

'How frightful!' interrupted the horror-stricken Kitterbell.

'The child died, of course. However, your child *may* not die; and if it should be a boy, and should *live* to be christened, why I suppose I must be one of the sponsors.' Dumps was evidently good-natured on the faith of his anticipations.

'Thank you, uncle,' said his agitated nephew, grasping his hand as warmly as if he had done him some essential service. 'Perhaps I had better not tell Mrs K what you have mentioned.'

'Why, if she's low-spirited, perhaps you had better not mention the melancholy case to her,' returned Dumps, who of course had invented the whole story; 'though perhaps it would be but doing your duty as a husband to prepare her for the *worst*.'

A day or two afterwards, as Dumps was perusing a morning paper at the chop-house which he regularly frequented, the following paragraph met his eye:

Births. – On Saturday, the 18th inst., in Great Russell Street, the lady of Charles Kitterbell, Esq., of a son.

'It *is* a boy!' he exclaimed, dashing down the paper, to the astonishment of the waiters. 'It *is* a boy!' But he speedily regained his composure as his eye rested on a paragraph quoting the number of infant deaths from the bills of mortality.

Six weeks passed away, and as no communication had been received from the Kitterbells, Dumps was beginning to flatter himself that the child was dead, when the following note painfully resolved his doubts:

> Great Russell Street,
> *Monday Morning.*

Dear Uncle. You will be delighted to hear that my dear Jemima has left her room, and that your future godson is getting on capitally. He was very thin at first, but he is getting much larger, and nurse says he is filling out every day. He cries a good deal, and is a very singular colour, which made Jemima and me rather uncomfortable; but as nurse says it's natural, and as of course we know nothing about these things yet, we are quite satisfied with what nurse says. We think he will be a sharp child; and nurse says she's sure he will, because he never goes to sleep. You will readily believe that we are all very happy, only we're a little worn out for want of rest, as he keeps us awake all night; but this we must expect, nurse says, for the first six or eight months. He has been vaccinated, but in consequence of the operation being rather awkwardly performed, some small particles of glass were introduced into the arm with the matter. Perhaps this may in some degree account for his being rather fractious; at least, so nurse says. We propose to have him christened at twelve o'clock on Friday, at Saint George's Church, in Hart Street, by the name of Frederick Charles William. Pray don't be later than a quarter before twelve. We shall have a very few friends in the evening, when of course we shall see you. I am sorry to say that the dear boy appears rather restless and uneasy to-day: the cause, I fear, is fever.

Believe me, dear Uncle,
Yours affectionately,
CHARLES KITTERBELL.

PS. I open this note to say that we have just discovered the cause of little Frederick's restlessness. It is not fever, as I apprehended, but a small pin, which nurse accidentally stuck in his leg yesterday evening. We have taken it out, and he appears more composed, though he still sobs a good deal.

It is almost unnecessary to say that the perusal of the above interesting statement was no great relief to the mind of the hypochondriacal Dumps. It was impossible to recede, however, and so he put the best face – that is to say, an uncommonly miserable one – upon the matter; and purchased a handsome silver mug for the infant Kitterbell, upon which he ordered the initials 'F.C.W.K.,' with the customary untrained grape-vine-looking flourishes, and a large full stop, to be engraved forthwith.

Monday was a fine day, Tuesday was delightful, Wednesday was equal to either, and Thursday was finer than ever; four successive fine days in London! Hackney-coachmen became revolutionary, and crossing-sweepers began to doubt the existence of a First Cause. The *Morning Herald* informed its readers that an old woman in Camden Town had been heard to say that the fineness of the season was 'unprecedented in the memory of the oldest inhabitant'; and Islington clerks, with large families and small salaries, left off their black gaiters, disdained to carry their once green cotton umbrellas, and walked to town in the conscious pride of white stockings and cleanly brushed Bluchers. Dumps beheld all this with an eye of supreme contempt – his triumph was at hand. He knew that if it had been fine for four weeks instead of four days, it would rain when he went out; he was lugubriously happy in the conviction that Friday would be a wretched day – and so it was. 'I knew how it would be,' said Dumps, as he turned round opposite the Mansion House at half-past eleven o'clock on the Friday morning. 'I knew how it would be. *I* am concerned, and that's enough' – and certainly the appearance of the day was sufficient to depress the spirits of a much more buoyant-hearted individual than himself. It had rained, without a moment's cessation, since eight o'clock; everybody that passed up Cheapside, and down Cheapside, looked wet, cold, and dirty. All sorts of forgotten and long-concealed umbrellas had been put into requisition. Cabs whisked about, with the 'fare' as carefully boxed up behind two glazed calico curtains as any mysterious picture in any one of Mrs Radcliffe's castles; omnibus horses smoked like steam-engines; nobody thought of 'standing up' under doorways or arches; they were painfully convinced it was a hopeless case; and so everybody went hastily along, jumbling and jostling, and swearing and perspiring, and slipping about, like amateur skaters behind wooden chairs on the Serpentine on a frosty Sunday.

Dumps paused; he could not think of walking, being rather smart for the christening. If he took a cab he was sure to be spilt, and a hackney-coach was too expensive for his economical ideas. An omnibus was waiting at the opposite corner – it was a desperate case – he had never heard of an omnibus upsetting or running away, and if the cad did knock him down, he could 'pull him up' in return.

'Now, sir!' cried the young gentleman who officiated as 'cad' to the 'Lads of the Village,' which was the name of the machine just noticed. Dumps crossed.

'This vay, sir!' shouted the driver of the 'Hark-away,' pulling up his vehicle immediately across the door of the opposition – 'This vay, sir – he's full.' Dumps hesitated, whereupon the 'Lads of the Village' commenced pouring out a torrent of abuse against the 'Hark-away'; but the conductor of the 'Admiral Napier' settled the contest in a most satisfactory manner, for all parties, by seizing Dumps round the waist, and thrusting him into the middle of his vehicle which had just come up and only wanted the sixteenth inside.

'All right,' said the 'Admiral,' and off the thing thundered, like a fire-engine at full gallop, with the kidnapped customer inside, standing in the position of a half doubled-up bootjack, and falling about with every jerk of the machine, first on the one side, and then on the other, like a 'Jack-in-the-green,' on May Day, setting to the lady with a brass ladle.

'For Heaven's sake, where am I to sit?' inquired the miserable man of an old gentleman, into whose stomach he had just fallen for the fourth time.'

'Anywhere but on my *chest*, sir,' replied the old gentleman in a surely tone.

'Perhaps the *box* would suit the gentleman better,' suggested a very damp laywer's clerk, in a pink shirt, and a smirking countenance.

After a great deal of struggling and falling about, Dumps at last managed to squeeze himself into a seat, which, in addition to the slight disadvantage of being between a window that would not shut, and a door that must be open, placed him in close contact with a passenger, who had been walking about all the morning without an umbrella, and who looked as if he had spent the day in a full water-butt – only wetter.

'Don't bang the door so,' said Dumps to the conductor, as he shut it after letting out four of the passengers; 'I am very nervous – it destroys me.'

'Did any gen'l'm'n say anthink?' replied the cad, thrusting in his head, and trying to look as if he didn't understand the request.

'I told you not to bang the door so!' repeated Dumps, with an expression of countenance like the knave of clubs, in convulsions.

'Oh! vy, it's rather a sing'ler circumstance about this here door, in that it von't shut without banging,' replied the conductor; and he opened the door very wide, and shut it again with a terrific bang, in proof of the assertion.

'I beg your pardon, sir,' said a little prim, wheezing old gentleman, sitting opposite Dumps, 'I beg your pardon; but have you ever observed, when you have been in an omnibus on a wet day, that four people out of five always come in with large cotton umbrellas, without a handle at the top, or the brass spike at the bottom?'

'Why, sir,' returned Dumps, as he heard the clock strike twelve, 'it never struck me before; but now you mention it, I— Hollo! Hollo!' shouted the persecuted individual, as the omnibus dashed past Drury Lane, where he had directed to be set down. 'Where is the cad?'

'I think he's on the box, sir,' said the young gentleman

before noticed in the pink shirt, which looked like a white one ruled with red ink.

'I want to be set down!' said Dumps in a faint voice, overcome by his previous efforts.

'I think these cads want to be *set down*,' returned the attorney's clerk, chuckling at his sally.

'Hollo!' cried Dumps again.

'Hollo!' echoed the passengers. The omnibus passed Saint Giles Church.

'Hold hard!' said the conductor; 'I'm blowed if we ha'n't forgot the gen'l'm'n as vas to be set down at Doory Lane. Now, sir, make haste, if you please,' he added, opening the door, and assisting Dumps out with as much coolness as if it was 'all right.' Dumps's indignation was for once getting the better of his cynical equanimity. 'Drury Lane!' he gasped, with the voice of a boy in a cold bath for the first time.

'Doory Lane, sir? – Yes, sir – third turning on the right-hand side, sir.'

Dumps's passion was paramount: he clutched his umbrella, and was striding off with the firm determination of not paying the fare. The cad by a remarkable coincidence, happened to entertain a directly contrary opinion, and Heaven knows how far the altercation would have proceeded, if it had not been most ably and satisfactorily brought to a close by the driver.

'Hollo!' said that respectable person, standing up on the box, and leaning with one hand on the roof of the omnibus. 'Hollo, Tom! Tell the gentleman if so be as he feels aggrieved, we will take him up to the Edge-er (Edgware) Road for nothing, and set him down at Doory Lane when we comes back. He can't reject that, anyhow.'

The argument was irresistible: Dumps paid the disputed sixpence, and in a quarter of an hour was on the staircase of No. 14, Great Russell Street.

Everything indicated that preparations were making for the reception of 'a few friends' in the evening. Two dozen extra tumblers, and four ditto wine-glasses – looking anything but transparent, with little bits of straw in them – were on the slab in the passage, just arrived. There was a great smell of nutmeg, port wine, and almonds, on the staircase; the covers were taken off the stair-carpet, and the figure of Venus on the first landing looked as if she were ashamed of the composition-candle in her right hand, which contrasted beautifully with the lamp-blacked drapery of the goddess of love. The female servant (who looked very warm and bustling) ushered Dumps into a front drawing-room, very prettily furnished, with a plentiful sprinkling of little baskets, paper table-mats, china watchmen, pink and gold albums, and rainbow-bound little books on the different tables.

'Ah, uncle!' said Mr Kitterbell, 'how d'ye do? Allow me – Jemima, my dear – my uncle. I think you've seen Jemima before, sir?'

'Have had the *pleasure*,' returned Dumps, his tone and look making it doubtful whether in his life he had ever experienced the sensation.

'I'm sure,' said Mrs Kitterbell, with a languid smile, and a slight cough. 'I'm sure – hem – any friend – of Charles's – hem – much less a relation, is—'

'I knew you'd say so, my love,' said little Kitterbell, who, while he appeared to be gazing on the opposite houses, was looking at his wife with a most affectionate air: 'Bless you!' The last two words were accompanied with a simper, and a squeeze of the hand, which stirred up all Uncle Dumps's bile.

'Jane, tell nurse to bring down baby,' said Mrs Kitterbell, addressing the servant. Mrs Kitterbell was a tall, thin young lady, with very light hair, and a particularly white face – one of those young women who almost invariably, though one hardly knows why, recall to one's mind the idea of a cold fillet of veal. Out went the servant, and in came the nurse, with a remarkably small parcel in her arms, packed up in a blue mantle trimmed with white fur. This was the baby.

'Now, uncle,' said Mr Kitterbell, lifting up that part of the mantle which covered the infant's face, with an air of great triumph, '*Who* do you think he's like?'

'He! He! Yes, who?' said Mrs K, putting her arm through her husband's, and looking up into Dumps's face with an expression of as much interest as she was capable of displaying.

'Good God, how small he is!' cried the amiable uncle, starting back with well-feigned surprise; '*remarkably* small indeed.'

. 'Do you think so?' inquired poor little Kitterbell, rather alarmed. 'He's a monster to what he was – ain't he, nurse?'

'He's a dear,' said the nurse, squeezing the child, and evading the question – not because she scrupled to disguise the fact, but because she couldn't afford to throw away the chance of Dumps's half-crown.

'Well, but who is he like?' inquired little Kitterbell.

Dumps looked at the little pink heap before him, and only thought at the moment of the best mode of mortifying the youthful parents.

'I really don't know *who* he's. like,' he answered, very well knowing the reply expected of him.

'Don't you think he's like *me*?' inquired his nephew with a knowing air.

'Oh, *decidedly* not!' returned Dumps, with an emphasis not to be misunderstood. 'Decidedly not like you. Oh, certainly not.'

'Like Jemima?' asked Kitterbell, faintly.

'Oh, dear no; not in the least. I'm no judge, of course, in such cases; but I really think he's more like one of those little carved representations on a tombstone!' The nurse stooped down over the child, and with great difficulty prevented an explosion of mirth. Pa and ma looked almost as miserable as their amiable uncle.

'Well!' said the disappointed little father, 'you'll be better able to tell what he's like by and by. You shall see him this evening with his mantle off.'

'Thank you,' said Dumps, feeling particularly grateful.

'Now, my love,' said Kitterbell to his wife, 'it's time we were off. We're to meet the other godfather and the god-mother at the church, uncle – Mr and Mrs Wilson from over the way – uncommonly nice people. My love, are you well wrapped up?'

'Yes, dear.'

'Are you sure you won't have another shawl?' inquired the anxious husband.

'No, sweet,' returned the charming mother, accepting Dumps's proffered arm; and the little party entered the hackney-coach that was to take them to the church; Dumps amusing Mrs Kitterbell by expatiating largely on the danger of measles, thrush, teeth-cutting, and other interesting diseases to which children are subject.

The ceremony (which occupied about five minutes) passed off without anything particular occurring. The clergyman had to dine some distance from town, and had two churchings, three christenings, and a funeral to perform in something less than an hour. The godfathers and godmother, therefore, promised to renounce the devil and all his works – 'and all that sort of thing' – as little Kitterbell said – 'in less than no time'; and with the exception of Dumps nearly letting the child fall into the font when he handed it to the clergyman, the whole affair went off in the usual business-like and matter-of-course manner, and Dumps re-entered the Bank-gates at two o'clock with a heavy heart, and the painful conviction that he was regularly booked for an evening party.

Evening came – and so did Dumps's pumps, black silk stockings, and white cravat which he had ordered to be forwarded, per boy, from Pentonville. The depressed godfa- ther dressed himself at a friend's counting-house, from whence, with his spirits fifty degrees below proof, he sallied forth – as the weather had cleared up, and the evening was tolerably fine – to walk to Great Russell Street. Slowly, he paced up Cheapside, Newgate Street, down Snow Hill, and up Holborn ditto, looking as grim as the figure-head of a man-of-war, and finding out fresh causes of misery at every step. As he was crossing the corner of Hatton Garden, a man apparently intoxicated, rushed against him, and would have knocked him down, had he not been providentially caught by a very genteel young man, who happened to be close to him at the time. The shock so disarranged Dumps's nerves, as well as his dress, that he could hardly stand. The gentleman took his arm, and in the kindest manner walked with him as far as Furnival's Inn. Dumps, for about the first time in his life; felt grateful and polite; and he and the gentlemanly-looking young man parted with mutual expressions of good-will.

'There are at least some well-disposed men in the world,' ruminated the misanthropical Dumps, as he proceeded towards his destination.

Rat – tat – ta-ra-ra-ra-ra-rat – knocked a hackney-coachman at Kitterbell's door, in imitation of a gentleman's servant, just as Dumps reached it; and out came an old lady in a large toque, and an old gentleman in a blue coat, and three female copies of the old lady in pink dresses, and shoes to match.

'It's a large party,' sighed the unhappy godfather, wiping the perspiration from his forehead, and leaning against the area-railings. It was some time before the miserable man could muster up courage to knock at the door, and when he did, the smart appearance of a neighbouring greengrocer (who had been hired to wait for seven-and-sixpence, and whose calves alone were worth double the money), the lamp in the passage and the Venus on the landing, added to the hum of many voices, and the sound of a harp and two violins, painfully convinced him that his surmises were but too well founded.

'How are you?' said little Kitterbell, in a greater bustle than ever, bolting out of the little back-parlour with a corkscrew in his hand, and various particles of sawdust, looking like so many inverted commas, on his inexpressibles.

'Good God!' said Dumps, turning into the aforesaid parlour to put his shoes on, which he had brought in his coat-pocket, and still more appalled by the sight of seven fresh-drawn corks, and a corresponding number of decanters. 'How many people are there upstairs?'

'Oh, not above thirty-five. We've had the carpet taken up in the back drawing-room, and the piano and the card-tables are in the front. Jemima thought we'd better have a regular sit-down supper in the front-parlour, because of the speechifying, and all that. But, Lord! uncle, what's the matter?' continued the excited little man, as Dumps stood with one shoe on, rummaging his pockets with the most frightful distortion of visage. 'What have you lost? Your pocket-book?'

'No,' returned Dumps, diving first into one pocket and then into the other, and speaking in a voice like Desdemona with the pillow over her mouth.

'Your card-case? Snuff-box? The key of your lodgings?' continued Kitterbell, pouring question on question with the rapidity of lightning.

'No! No!' ejaculated Dumps, still diving eagerly into his empty pockets.

'Not – not – the *mug* you spoke of this morning?'

'Yes, the *mug*!' replied Dumps, sinking into a chair.

'How *could* you have done it?' inquired Kitterbell. 'Are you sure you brought it out?'

'Yes! Yes! I see it all!' said Dumps, starting up as the idea flashed across his mind; 'miserable dog that I am – I was born to suffer. I see it all: it was the gentlemanly-looking young man!'

'Mr Dumps!' shouted the greengrocer in a stentorian voice, as he ushered the somewhat recovered godfather into the drawing-room half an hour after the above declaration. 'Mr Dumps!' – everybody looked at the door, and in came Dumps, feeling about as much out of place as a salmon might be supposed to be on a gravel-walk.

'Happy to see you again,' said Mrs Kitterbell, quite unconscious of the unfortunate man's confusion and misery; 'you must allow me to introduce you to a few of our friends: – my mamma, Mr Dumps – my papa and sisters.' Dumps seized the hand of the mother as warmly as if she was his own parent, bowed *to* the young ladies, and *against* a gentleman behind him, and took no notice whatever of the father, who had been bowing incessantly for three minutes and a quarter.

'Uncle,' said little Kitterbell, after Dumps had been introduced to a select dozen or two, 'you must let me lead you to the other end of the room, to introduce you to my friend Danton. Such a splendid fellow! – I'm sure you'll like him – this way,' – Dumps followed as tractably as a tame bear.

Mr Danton was a young man of about five-and-twenty, with a considerable stock of impudence, and a very small share of ideas: he was a great favourite, especially with young ladies of from sixteen to twenty-six years of age, both inclusive. He could imitate the French-horn to admiration, sang comic songs most inimitably, and had the most insinuating way of saying impertinent nothings to his doting female admirers. He had acquired, somehow or other, the reputation of being a great wit, and, accordingly, whenever he opened his mouth, everybody who knew him laughed very heartily.

The introduction took place in due form. Mr Danton bowed, and twirled a lady's handkerchief, which he held in his hand, in a most comic way. Everybody smiled.

'Very warm,' said Dumps, feeling it necessary to say something.

'Yes. It was warmer yesterday,' returned the brilliant Mr Danton – A general laugh.

'I have great pleasure in congratulating you on your first appearance in the character of a father, sir,' he continued, addressing Dumps – 'godfather, I mean.' – The young ladies were convulsed, and the gentlemen in ecstasies.

A general hum of admiration interrupted the conversation, and announced the entrance of nurse with the baby. A universal rush of the young ladies immediately took place. (Girls are always *so* fond of babies in company.)

'Oh, you dear!' said one.

'How sweet!' cried another, in a low tone of the most enthusiastic admiration.

'Heavenly!' added a third.

'Oh! What dear little arms!' said a fourth, holding up an arm and fist about the size and shape of the leg of a fowl cleanly picked.

'Did you ever?' – said a little coquette with a large bustle, who looked like a French lithograph, appealing to a gentleman in three waistcoats – 'Did you ever?'

'Never in my life,' returned her admirer, pulling up his collar.

'Oh! *do* let me take it, nurse,' cried another young lady. 'The love!'

'Can it open its eyes, nurse?' inquired another, affecting the utmost innocence. Suffice it to say, that the single ladies unanimously voted him an angel, and that the married ones, *nem. con.*, agreed that he was decidely the finest baby they had ever beheld – except their own.

The quadrilles were resumed with great spirit. Mr Danton was universally admitted to be beyond himself; several young ladies enchanted the company and gained admirers by singing 'We met' – 'I saw her at the Fancy Fair' – and other equally sentimental and interesting ballads. 'The young men,' as Mrs Kitterbell said, 'made themselves very agreeable'; the girls did not lose their opportunity; and the evening promised to go off excellently. Dumps didn't mind it: he had devised a plan for himself – a little bit of fun in his own way – and he was almost happy! He played a rubber and lost every point. Mr Danton said he could not have lost every point, because he made a point of losing: everybody laughed tremendously. Dumps retorted with a better joke, and nobody smiled, with the exception of the host, who seemed to consider it his duty to laugh till he was black in the face, at everything. There was only one drawback – the musicians did not play with quite as much spirit as could have been wished. The cause, however, was satisfactorily explained; for it appeared, on the testimony of a gentleman who had come up from Gravesend in the afternoon, that they had been engaged on board a steamer all day, and had played almost without cessation all the way to Gravesend, and all the way back again.

The 'sit-down supper' was excellent; there were four barley-sugar temples on the table, which would have looked beautiful if they had not melted away when the supper began; and a water-mill, whose only fault was that instead of going round, it ran over the table-cloth. Then there were fowls, and tongue, and trifle, and sweets, and lobster salad, and potted beef – and everything. And little Kitterbell kept calling out for clean plates, and the clean plates did not come; and then the gentlemen who wanted the plates said they didn't mind, they'd take a lady's; and then Mrs Kitterbell applauded their gallantry, and the greengrocer ran about till he thought his seven-and-sixpence was very hardly earned; and the young ladies didn't eat much for fear it shouldn't look romantic, and the married ladies ate as much as possible, for fear they shouldn't have enough; and a great deal of wine was drunk, and everybody talked and laughed considerably.

'Hush! Hush!' said Mr Kitterbell, rising and looking very important. 'My love (this was addressed to his wife at the other end of the table), take care of Mrs Maxwell, and your mamma, and the rest of the married ladies; the gentlemen will persuade the young ladies to fill their glasses, I am sure.'

'Ladies and gentlemen,' said long Dumps, in a very sepulchral voice and rueful accent, rising from his chair like the ghost of Don Juan, 'will you have the kindness to charge your glasses? I am desirous of proposing a toast.'

A dead silence ensued, and the glasses were filled – everybody looked serious.

'Ladies and gentlemen,' slowly continued the ominous Dumps, 'I' – (here Mr Danton imitated two notes from the

French-horn, in a very loud key, which electrified the nervous toast-proposer, and convulsed his audience).

'Order! Order!' said little Kitterbell, endeavouring to suppress his laughter.

'Order!' said the gentlemen.

'Danton, be quiet,' said a particular friend on the opposite side of the table.

'Ladies and gentlemen,' resumed Dumps, somewhat recovered, and not much disconcerted, for he was always a pretty good hand at a speech – 'In accordance with what is, I believe, the established usage on these occasions, I, as one of the godfathers of Master Frederick Charles William Kitterbell' – (here the speaker's voice faltered, for he remembered the mug) – 'venture to rise to propose a toast. I need hardly say that it is the health and prosperity of that young gentleman, the particular event of whose early life we are here met to celebrate' – (applause). 'Ladies and gentlemen, it is impossible to suppose that our friends here, whose sincere well-wishers we all are, can pass through life without some trials, considerable suffering, severe affliction, and heavy losses!' – Here the arch-traitor paused, and slowly drew forth a long, white pocket-handkerchief – his example was followed by several ladies. 'That these trials may be long spared them is my most earnest prayer, my most fervent wish' (a distinct sob from the grandmother). 'I hope and trust, ladies and gentlemen, that the infant whose christening we have this evening met to celebrate, may not be removed from the arms of his parents by premature decay' (several cambrics were in requisition): 'that his young and now *apparently* healthy form, may not be wasted by lingering disease.' (Here Dumps cast a sardonic glance around, for a great sensation was manifest among the married ladies.) 'You, I am sure, will concur with me in wishing that he may live to be a comfort and a blessing to his parents.' ('Hear, hear!' and an audible sob from Mr Kitterbell.) 'But should he not be what we could wish – should he forget in after-times the duty which he owes to them – should they unhappily experience that distracting truth, "how sharper than a serpent's tooth it is to have a thankless child"' – Here Mrs Kitterbell, with her handkerchief to her eyes, and accompanied by several ladies, rushed from the room, and went into violent hysterics in the passage, leaving her better-half in almost as bad a condition, and a general impression in Dumps's favour; for people like sentiment, after all.

It need hardly be added, that this occurrence quite put a stop to the harmony of the evening. Vinegar, hartshorn, and cold water, were now as much in request as negus, rout-cakes, and *bon-bons* had been a short time before. Mrs Kitterbell was immediately conveyed to her apartment, the musicians were silenced, flirting ceased, and the company slowly departed. Dumps left the house at the commencement of the bustle, and walked home with a light step, and (for him) a cheerful heart. His landlady, who slept in the next room, has offered to make oath that she heard him laugh, in his peculiar manner, after he had locked his door. The assertion, however, is so improbable, and bears on the face of it such strong evidence of untruth, that it has never obtained credence to this hour.

The family of Mr Kitterbell has considerably increased since the period to which we have referred: he has now two sons and a daughter; and as he expects, at no distant period, to have another addition to his blooming progeny, he is anxious to secure an eligible godfather for the occasion. He is determined, however, to impose upon him two conditions. He must bind himself, by a solemn obligation, not to make any speech after supper; and it is indispensable that he should be in no way connected with 'the most miserable man in the world'.